Stone Creek Series

Chocolate Covered Mistletoe

Candy Coated Promises

Pumpkin Spiced Possibilites

CHOCOLATE COVERED MISTLETOE

Samantha Baca

Cover Design: Richard Baca
Image(s): Canva

One

Brooke

"What in Sam Hill is that?!" I exclaimed as I shook my head and wiped my hands on the towel before tossing it to the counter, storming out of the bakery into the brisk winter air. A shiver ran through me as I marched across the gravel parking lot and stood below the workers who were hanging a new sign above what used to be the local flower shop. It had been across from my shop for years. I held my hand up, shielding my eyes from the sun that was beating down behind where they stood on their ladders, taking in the large, oversized sign.

"What do ya'll think you're doing? What is this?" I pointed to the sign as the two teenage boys looked dumbly at me as if they really needed to explain to me what a damn sign was. I rolled my eyes, reminding myself that I would need to explain to their mother, Sheila, that I'm not that stupid after they run home and tell her all about it. Sheila and I have been best friends since we were in diapers but that didn't mean that her teenage boys didn't gossip as easily as teenage girls at a slumber party.

"It's a sign, Ms. Hansen," Oliver shouted down to me, not realizing that he didn't have to yell that loud. I could hear him just fine from where I was.

"I can see that Ollie, but why are you putting it up?" I looked around, trying to find someone who had more information as to what was going on. My shop, *Sweet as Sugar*, was one of five in the little strip mall on Main Street and all of the shop owners had come to know each other over the years. If something was happening, we all knew about it. "Who told you to hang it up?" I asked as they pulled it up higher before mounting it to the wall. It was a black banner with gold fancy writing that said *Delectable Delicacies.*

"I did," a deep voice said behind me, startling me as I spun around to come face to face with the one and only person that I never wanted to see again in my life. Ryder Jones. I tilted my head up to see him, his brown hair showing natural highlights from the sun as his hazel eyes quickly traveled over the length of my body before meeting my eyes.

I forced myself to take a deep breath as I clenched and unclenched my fists that were balled up at my sides. I hadn't seen Ryder since he left Stone Creek, Tennessee ten years ago when he ventured off to Nashville to be with the so-called love of his life who was pursuing a singing career.

"What are you doing back?" I asked dryly.

"I came back because my father died," he said sadly, shoving his hands into his jean pockets as he rocked back on his heels.

"Yes, I am aware that he died. But you darted out of town faster than lightning after his funeral. None of us thought we would ever see you again after that."

"I had business to attend to in Nashville. But, now I'm back in Stone Creek. For good." He smiled his stupid, crooked smile, the dimples on both sides as prominent as I remembered.

"What's with the sign?" I nodded to where the boys had finished hanging the banner and were climbing down from their ladders to look at it.

"It's for my business. People might be confused if I keep the old sign up and don't sell any actual flowers," he arched an eyebrow and watched for my reaction.

"You're closing your dad's flower shop?" I asked as my mouth hung open in shock. "How could you do that?"

"It's simple really, I don't know a damn thing about flowers so I would be a terrible shop owner. My mom and I talked about it and decided it was best to let his legacy pass on with him," he explained casually, looking past me to see the sign. "Besides, I had a very successful business in Nashville that I think would do just as well here, so I'm using the space my dad left me and starting my own business."

"*Delectable Delicacies*? What exactly is your business?" I asked, knowing full well what he was going to say before he said it.

"It's a specialty shop with the finest sweets you've ever tasted. From cakes to truffles, I have something for everyone. I'll have to modify things a little bit but overall it will be the luxurious feel of a big city shop mixed in with the comfort of small-town living. A little slice of heaven, if you will."

"You cannot be serious," I snapped, shaking my head as the anger started to rise inside of me.

"Oh, I'm dead serious."

"You're going to open a bakery right across from mine? Are you out of your mind?" I shrieked, throwing my hands up in the air. "Don't you see how rude that is?!"

"It's business, Brooke, it's not like I planned to turn my life upside down and move back to Stone Creek just so I could make your life a living hell. I didn't ask to come back. I had a great life in Nashville with a business that was booming. I came back to take care of my mom because she's all that I have left, and I'm all that she has left. It was the right thing to do, which meant that I had to make sacrifices to what was best for all of us." He sucked in a deep breath and drug a hand through his hair as he looked away. "I'm sorry that my father died and left me his flower shop and that I have no desire to try to keep flowers alive. I'm not a bad person, Brooke. I'm just trying to make the best out of what I've been given. This isn't personal, it's simply business."

I worked my jaw back and forth as I glared at him and shook my head one last time before walking back to my shop. My momma always said that if I didn't have anything nice to say, I shouldn't say anything at all. Even though she stole it from *Bambi*, it still had been a valuable life lesson. Needless to say, I didn't plan on talking to Ryder anytime soon.

Two

Ryder

"Can you get all of that packed up and shipped over to the new location by this weekend?" I asked, making a note of when the last of my supplies would arrive on the pad in front of me. My best friend and former business partner had agreed to finish packing up everything that I wasn't able to bring with me before I moved back. It was a rush to get things closed down and finalized but luckily Parker was there to finish everything that I had to leave behind.

We had been business partners for ten years and had started the bakery in Nashville shortly after I moved there. He handled the business side of things while I handled the food side of things. I was scared shitless to start over again, this time on my own, but fate hadn't left me many options. If I wanted this business to continue to do well, I had better get my head out of my ass and learn from Parker while he was still willing to teach me. I wrapped up my phone call and scribbled down another date on the notepad before drawing circles around it several times.

My goal was to have a grand opening of the new bakery a few weeks before Christmas but that was already proving to be too tight of a schedule. The last few things from the other shop were scheduled to arrive by December 15th. That was a tentative date – and only three days away – not something I was willing to risk my reputation on. Instead, I decided to go with December 21st and prayed that I wouldn't be too late with people getting orders in for holiday parties and whatnot.

I glanced around the empty building, remembering days from my childhood when I would come to visit my dad and help out every now and then when he needed it. I wasn't much help other than when someone needed to pay for their bouquets but I still liked to pretend I was a valuable employee. I would stand in the middle of the room, looking around as I pictured myself being the owner someday and making my dad proud. I chuckled as I realized I was standing in the same spot, looking around, the proud new owner. Hopefully, my dad was smiling down on me from heaven and not cringing as he saw what I was trying to do.

The room was already filled with a handful of tables and chairs, the new tile floor already installed, and the display cases set up toward the back. Everything was starting to come together, slowly but surely. I still needed to paint the walls and hang up the wall decorations I had brought from the other store, but my mind was too busy to focus on any of that.

Instead, it was wrapped around thoughts of the fiery woman

with icy blue eyes and chestnut brown hair that swayed across her back as her curvy little figure stalked off, giving me the coldest welcome home I had received so far. Granted, I probably deserved it after the way I had left things with Brooke before I went to Nashville but surely she couldn't still be holding a grudge against me this long… Could she?

My mom hadn't mentioned anything about Brooke's reaction to seeing me when I came back for the funeral but with how quickly her Alzheimer's was taking over, it was hard to know for sure. Very few people in town knew about it, my dad had constantly worked to keep it that way. The people of Stone Creek loved my mother and many had grown up with her, however, small-town gossip spreads quicker than a wildfire and my dad desperately wanted to spare my mom from taking the brunt of it.

Despite the rumors of me running off to the big city and abandoning my parents, I had kept in very close contact with them over the years. We started with weekly phone calls when I first moved to Nashville but as time went on, weeks turned into months and so on. My dad and I tried to talk as often as we could, especially once I knew my mom wasn't doing well. Nothing could have prepared me for my father having a massive heart attack but I was thankful that at least I had been given the opportunity to talk with him about what kind of care my mom was needing these days.

I glanced up at the clock, the only thing I had gotten around to hanging since I started moving stuff in yesterday. It was after two and I knew that the schools would be letting out soon, meaning that the majority of the kids would pass through the Sky View shopping center on their way. I wanted to get back into the swing of small-town living which meant that I needed to start making friends with those who mattered most. The kids.

My goal was to whip up a quick batch of cake pops that I could hand out as they walked by. It would be a nice treat for them on their way home and no doubt would create some buzz and excitement as they told their parents about them. The best business comes from word of mouth, and in this case—from kids who love sweets. I walked into the back kitchen area and let my shoulders fall when I saw the piles of supplies that still needed to be unpacked. There were a thousand things on my to-do list but right now I only cared about one. The cake pops.

After ten minutes of sorting through boxes and unpacking bags, I had the ingredients and utensils I needed except for the flour. I looked down at my watch and groaned when I saw that it was already getting late and I was surely going to miss my window if I didn't get started. The closest store in town that would have flour was at least fifteen minutes away, which would eat up thirty minutes just getting there and back. I let out a heavy sigh as I grabbed a measuring cup and slid my phone into my pocket, heading to the one place that I knew would have flour.

A bell chimed over my head as I opened the door to *Sweet As Sugar*. It was adorable inside with a welcoming vibe. There were a handful of booths scattered around the small room with a counter and display case in the back. The walls were lined with pictures of children eating sweets, which I had no doubt were the locals. Everything about the bakery screamed small-town and made me feel right at home.

A few seconds later a woman with blue hair piled in a messy knot on her head came around the corner and stopped in her tracks when she saw me. Her fair skin turned the slightest shade of pink as her mouth slightly parted open in surprise. I turned my head to the side for a second to suppress the chuckle as I watched her look over me like I was a giant piece of meat and she hadn't eaten in days.

"Hi, how can I help you?" she asked, her voice soft and overly flirty.

"Is Brooke here?" I returned the smile that she was still wearing as she glanced down and noticed the measuring cup in my hand. The flirty look she had been wearing was gone in a second as her eyes narrowed and her hands flew to her hips.

"You're that guy, aren't you? The hotshot, big city prick who is opening a bakery right across from us?" she sneered as she studied me. I could hear movement in the kitchen and hoped that Brooke would hear us talking and come out to save me.

I blew out a breath and let my shoulders relax as I offered her the cutest smile that I had, hoping she would put her fangs away.

"Hi, I'm Ryder Jones," I said, stepping closer and offering her my hand as I shifted the measuring cup to the other. She looked down at my hand then back up at me as she arched a pierced eyebrow.

"Oh, I know who you are. I've heard all about you and your fancy little chocolate shop over there. Whatever you're here for—we aren't interested." She glanced over her shoulder as the kitchen door swung open and Brooke walked out. She paused for a moment to look between us, trying to figure out what was going on. As quickly as she saw me, the look on her face turned into the anger I had seen on it not that long ago.

"What do you want?" she snapped, standing next to the blue-haired demon.

"Now is that really the southern way to greet a customer?" I teased, taking a step closer to her.

"Customer?" she asked as her eyebrows shot up high onto her forehead. "What exactly are you here to buy? Forgiveness?"

Ouch. Now that fucking hurt. I looked away, embarrassed, trying not to let her see the sting of what she said. I shook my head and decided this was a terrible idea. Why I had thought that Brooke would be anything like the girl I had left behind ten years ago was completely beyond me.

"You know what, never mind. Let's just forget that I came by." I pulled my mouth into a tight smile and bowed my head once at them before I turned to walk out.

"What did you come over for?" Her voice was suddenly gentler.

"Forget about it, it was nothing."

"Ryder…" she warned.

"I came to see if I could borrow flour. I wanted to make some quick cake pops to hand out to the kids as they walked home from school, but it's getting late and it's not that important anyway. Sorry for bothering you."

I lowered my head and turned to walk out, ignoring whatever it was she said before the door closed and drowned her out.

Three

Brooke

"I know we are supposed to hate the enemy, but damn is the enemy fine!" Autumn shrieked as we watched Ryder walk out and leave while I was in the middle of a sentence. I turned to look at her, giving her my best motherly look I had, given that I didn't have any kids.

"Really Autumn?" I tilted my head to the side and looked at her, annoyance filling every fiber of my being. The problem was that I wasn't actually annoyed with her, she was right—he was fine. I don't remember the last time I saw a man who looked as good as Ryder. But I didn't need her standing beside me, ogling over the way his jeans wrapped around his tight ass and how she was sure he could crack a walnut on his ripped abs. She was overly dramatic, to say the least, but now that she mentioned it, I wondered just how defined he was; his fitted t-shirt showing off his muscles he most like achieved effortlessly.

Life was just that way. Some of us had to work our asses off and were given average bodies with problem areas like thick thighs and an ass that consistently knocked over the bag of flour every time they turned around. I wasn't fat, but Lord knows that I was far from skinny. My mom always told me to embrace my curvy figure and that someday I would find a guy who would be anxious to take this body for a drive. The thought of it still made me blush to this day when I would think about her advice but she was never one to be shy about what she thought.

My mind had been circling back to the disappointment on Ryder's face when he said he was coming over to borrow some flour to make cake pops for the kids. It had warmed my heart that he would think to do something nice for the kids. When I first opened my bakery, I used to make sweet treats for the kids as well but as time went on and I got busier, it sort of just fell to the wayside and I stopped making time to do it. I glanced at the clock on the wall as I scooped a few cups of flour into a large bowl and walked over to Ryder's shop.

It didn't look like the door was locked, but I still didn't want to just barge on in. I knocked on the metal frame of the door and stepped back, looking around while I waited for him to come up front to answer it. A few minutes later there was still no sign of him. I knocked louder this time and stepped back when I saw him come out of the kitchen to answer the door. A faint smile crossed his face before it quickly disappeared.

"What's up?" he asked as if he had no idea why I was there. I lifted the bowl of flour and held it to him as if I was offering a baby Simba to him. He arched an eyebrow and looked down into the bowl, spying the contents before looking back at me with confusion on his face.

"You needed flour," I explained, nodding to the bowl. "So, I brought you some."

"Thank you, you didn't have to do that," he said, his tone almost curt.

"I know I didn't *have to*. I wanted to."

"Why?" He leaned against the door frame and tilted his head.

"I don't know?" I shrugged my shoulders, suddenly irritated with the conversation. "Can't somebody do something nice for you?"

"Nice? You want to talk about being nice?" His eyes widened with anger. "You have no idea what nice is if you think you're being nice. I appreciate the flour, really, but aside from that, you've been anything but nice."

I swallowed hard, having a flashback of a similar conversation not that long ago. One that shattered my heart into a million pieces and destroyed the friendship I thought we had. I lowered my head and thought about what to say, fighting the urge to hash out the problems that we never resolved when he left ten years ago.

"I'm sorry," I whispered, unable to say anything more. He nodded and clenched his jaw. I extended my hand closer to him, offering the bowl of flour as he reached out and took it. I turned and walked away, trying to force the toxic emotions from rising to the surface.

14

Four

Ryder

"Hey, ma, would you like mashed potatoes or baked potatoes with dinner tonight?" I called from the kitchen, hoping she could hear me over Wheel of Fortune. I waited a few more seconds then turned down the heat on the stove and tossed the spatula in the sink before walking around the corner to check on her.

She was sitting in my dad's old recliner, feet propped up as she curled under a heavy blanket that she had knitted when I was little. It was worn out and had been heavily used over the years, but I knew none of us would ever part with that blanket. She looked completely at peace as she stared at the tv, completely unaware that I was there. I quietly walked over to her and squatted down beside her, placing my hand gently on top of hers. She turned to look at me, her face lighting up the way it did every time she saw me since I'd been back.

"Oh, Walter, I didn't see you there," she said softly and patted my hand.

"Mom, it's me, Ryder" I whispered loud enough for her to hear as I tried to force the tears from my eyes. She looked at me with confusion etched on her face as she tried to make sense of what I was saying. I waited patiently for her to remember. Sometimes she did, sometimes she didn't and I would just go about, pretending to be my dad Walter if that's what she needed me to be.

"Yes, son, that is you," she said with a smile as she reached up and patted my cheek. I smiled beneath the fragile hands that were trembling with her touch.

"What kind of potatoes would you like for dinner tonight? I'm making fried chicken," I said, hoping she would stay with me long enough to decide.

"Whatever you want, dear, whatever you want." She smiled as she turned her attention back to the tv and I knew that I had lost her again. I walked back to the kitchen and filled a pot with hot water before setting it on the stove to boil. As I waited for the temperature to heat, I stood in front of the counter and planted my hands on the surface as I lowered my head and cried. Coming back hadn't been something that I would have ever expected to happen but now that I was here and really in the thick of things, I couldn't imagine how hard it must have been for my dad to have had to handle all of this on a daily basis. He had no help and on top of it, he kept my mom's illness a secret. My heart ached for the loss of my dad. I also had a great amount of guilt eating away at me for not coming back sooner to help him and spend time with my mom while she could still remember it. The tears ran down my face, leaving a hot trail behind them as I waited for the water to boil.

The nights were always the same and wrapped up early after dinner. I set a plate out for Ruby, my mom's childhood best friend, knowing that she would be by any minute. Ruby was a recent widow, having lost her husband a few months before my dad died. I had been told before I came back that she was one of the few people in town who knew about my mom and she had offered to come help me care for her after my dad died. She usually joined us for the dinners I made but tonight she had called to let me know that she was running late.

After dinner, she would help my mom into the shower and get her ready for bed. Even with the heart-shattering moments I had endured with my mom since I had been back, my favorite parts of the day were the evenings when Ruby would come over and they would sit and talk, reminiscing about old times and laughing at fond memories. My mom didn't always remember things from the past, but she still had a strong connection to Ruby and would find herself laughing at the stories as if it was the first time she heard it.

It was close to eight when Ruby came down the hall and plopped down on the couch across from me. I reached over and turned the tv down so we could talk.

"How was she tonight?" I asked.

"It seems like she's having a rough day today but I told her some of her favorite stories and she still laughed, so I'll take it as a win. She seems like she's wearing down some…" her voice trailed off and I swallowed hard as I looked away and focused on the infomercial on the tv.

"I'm sorry honey, I know you were hoping that it was better news," she said quietly, pulling my attention back to her. I nodded as I tried to force the emotions to simmer down.

"I miss her," I whispered, still unable to look at her for fear of her seeing the breakdown that was about to happen. "I should have come back sooner."

"We all have moments in life where we feel like we should have done something different, but you can't dwell on something that you can't change. What's done is done and all you can do is try harder with the opportunities you have left."

I forced a smile, knowing she was right.

"I heard a sweet man was handing out cake pops to the kids after school today," she said with a smile. I turned and looked at her, the pride in her face beaming through her smile. "That was awfully kind of you. Everyone is talking about it because the kids won't stop talking about it." She laughed and pointed a finger at me as if she knew that was my plan all along.

"Hey, I just wanted to do something nice for the kids. If it happened to get people talking about my new business, so be it," I shrugged and laughed when she tossed a throw pillow at me.

"Are you going to set up a booth for the Winter Fair in a few weeks?" she asked curiously.

"I don't think so," I said dismissively, as if I hadn't been thinking about it every time I saw a flyer slapped onto something all over town.

"Why not? It's the biggest event in Stone Creek. You know that" she chided. "You should set up a booth and let everyone get a taste of the delicious treats you make."

"I'm pretty sure Brooke will have her booth set up so there will be plenty of sweets already." I was making up excuses but the problem was that I didn't want to keep stepping on Brooke's toes since that's what she seemed to think I was doing since I had been back.

"Oh, Brooke…" she sighed and gave me a knowing look.

"What?" I threw my hands up and laughed, shaking my head as I tried to ignore the conversation that was about to happen.

"I've heard all about the heat flying around between the two of you since you've been back."

"Heat? More like I'm trying to walk through the fire she's breathing out the second she even sees me."

"I heard you gave her plenty of heat yourself if you know what I'm saying." She raised her eyebrows and wiggled them.

"Oh please, I seriously doubt that. She has not moved on from the past and is determined to make me pay for something that happened ten years ago. I was twenty-five and thought I was in love—can't we just agree that I was stupid and move on?"

"You were in *love* with her *best friend*. The only person that she had ever confided in that she had feelings for *you*. When she tried to talk to you, to tell you not to go, you blew her off and ignored her. Called her jealous when in reality, she was just trying to warn you that Lauren was cheating on you and had told Brooke about it. So yes, you were stupid," she laughed, "But you still owe her an apology for what you did."

I ran a hand down my face, feeling the prickly stubble that I needed to go shave. Yet another thing on my never-ending to-do list.

"Yeah, I know," I sighed and leaned back against the couch. "But how am I supposed to apologize when she shoots daggers at me the second she sees me?"

"Where there's a will, there's a way." She smiled and stood up, leaving me alone with too much to think about.

<u>Five</u>

Brooke

A few days had passed since I had talked to Ryder, things still feeling as awkward and uncomfortable as ever the few times we had seen each other. It felt strange having him back in town and running into him everywhere I went, even when I tried to avoid him. I knew that the market on Main Street was always busy on the weekends and that he would likely go by there to stock up on things for work, like flour, so I purposely avoided going until Monday morning when I knew he would be at the shop.

I couldn't shake the image of the kids flocking over to see him when they realized that he had cake pops for them, their smiling faces beaming from across the parking lot. It wasn't necessarily that I was surprised to see the kids that happy—you could give them a sticker and they would be just as excited. I was really touched by how happy Ryder had looked. He smiled down at them with the warmest look on his face as he passed the tray around for them to each take one. Butterflies had fluttered about in my stomach as I remembered the last time I had seen him that happy.

The market was relatively empty as I pushed my cart through the aisles, grabbing the few things that I needed for the week while looking at the stuff that I definitely didn't need. Like wine. Bottles and bottles of wine that lined the shelves and would look beautiful next to a warm fire with blankets spread out in front of it while Ryder and I made passionate love all night long. I felt my cheeks flush as I quickly sped past the display and tried to get the thoughts out of my head. As I turned the corner, I felt a jolt as my shopping cart collided with another.

My eyes slowly traveled up, finding the most beautiful hazel eyes staring back at me as our carts bounced off each other. If Ryder was as shocked to run into me as I was to run into him, he certainly didn't act like it. A tight smile pulled across his face as his knuckles turned white from gripping the handle of the cart while he watched me. I felt my heart racing in my chest, desperate to avoid him like I had been trying to do. I offered a quick smile before looking away and pulling my cart back so I could squeeze past him to get down the aisle.

As I started to push my cart past his, his hand reached over and grabbed onto mine, stopping it. I looked up at him, trying to figure out what the look in his eyes meant. It wasn't one I had seen before and it made me uneasy the longer he stayed silent and said nothing while holding onto the cart.

"I'm sorry, I didn't see you there," I said quietly, ready to take off the first chance I got.

"It's no big deal," he replied as his hand stayed firmly wrapped around the top of my cart.

"Well then, I better get going." I raised my eyebrows and nodded behind him, just in case he was confused about what I was trying to do.

"Actually, I was hoping to talk to you real quick." He let go of the cart and stepped to the side to let another customer pass by us, waiting until they had grabbed their bottle of wine and were on their way before he started talking again. "I wanted to say sorry," he said quietly.

I let out the breath I had been holding and waited for him to go on. It was nice of him to apologize but I had no idea why he was apologizing to me. When he stayed quiet for too long, I raised my eyebrows again and held my hand in the air as I shrugged my shoulders.

"If it's about us running into each other, I'm sorry too. Now can I go?" I asked with a sudden irritation in my voice.

He shook his head and drug a hand through his hair before locking eyes with me.

"I'm sorry for what happened when I left ten years ago, Brooke. I was young and stupid, and I should have listened to you when you tried to warn me about Lauren."

I felt the blood rush from my head, suddenly feeling dizzy as I never saw that one coming. Even though it had been a long time ago, it still hurt as if it had just happened yesterday. I could still remember the night that I bared my soul to him, begging him not to leave and trying to make him believe me that my so-called best friend wasn't the person who he thought she was. Growing up, I had two best-friends- Sheila and Lauren. We did everything together and were always inseparable. After high school, we stayed friends but each of us took a different path that ended up having an impact on our friendship. Sheila was the first to get married and start having babies at eighteen, while Lauren and I were nowhere ready for any sort of commitment.

When I found out that Ryder was in love with Lauren, it broke my heart. I had spent so many nights crying against her shoulder as I tried to figure out why he never saw me as more than a friend. In reality, it was that he was in love with someone else. Lauren had promised me that she would never allow anything to happen with Ryder because she was my sister and it was somewhere in the girl code that you don't get with a guy that one of your sisters likes.

Fast forward to a year later and I was standing outside, in the pouring rain, telling Ryder how much I loved him, as I broke his heart by telling him how unfaithful Lauren had been. They hadn't been dating long but if she said to jump, he would ask how high. It drove me crazy that he was willing to pack up his entire life and move to Nashville, not realizing that Lauren only wanted to go there because of another man. The guy that she had been having an affair with promised her a chance at the music career she had always wanted. Everyone in town laughed and looked the other way when she started telling them her plan. They all knew she couldn't sing for shit.

"Are you okay over there?" Ryder asked as he waved a hand in front of my face, pulling me out of the trance I was in. I nodded as I pulled in my bottom lip and chewed it, trying to force the recurring emotions to the side before I exploded in anger. Again.

"Yeah, I'm fine. But that was ten years ago so it doesn't matter at this point," I snapped as I grabbed onto the handle of the shopping cart and tried to push it forward before he reached out and stopped me again.

"It does matter because I can see that you're still upset about it," he said softly.

"If you didn't care about me being upset back then, why do you care now?" I turned and narrowed my eyes at him. His face softened as he flinched at the words.

"Because I made a lot of mistakes in the past few years and I'm trying to fix them. It may not be important to you but it's important to me. I want to try and fix things between us so we can move on and live in the same town without you constantly trying to hide from me."

I swallowed hard. How did he know that's what I had been doing?

"Fine, apology accepted," I said bitterly. "Now can I go?" I tilted my head to the side, trying to keep up the rough exterior so he wouldn't see how vulnerable I was feeling.

"You're the most stubborn person I know, you know that?"

"Yeah, well, I guess it's an upgrade from the jealous girl you left behind ten years ago." I arched an eyebrow as I watched his face fall before he let go of my cart and I pushed it past him.

I wrapped up the rest of my shopping and rushed out of the store into the blistering cold. I walked quickly, forcing a fake smile at the group of carolers who were huddled together by the entrance singing Silent Night. Christmas was less than ten days away and I had never been further from being in the holiday spirit.

<u>Six</u>

Ryder

Well, that didn't go as well as I had planned, I thought as I stood in front of the cashier, watching the handful of sugary items slide down the conveyor belt as she rang them up. A few minutes later, she had tossed the last bag of powdered sugar into the brown paper bag that was nearly bursting at the seams. She turned back to the register and tapped her long fingernail on the screen a couple of times before turning to me and giving me the total. I nodded in agreement and handed her my credit card.

"Someone has quite the sweet tooth," she said in a flirty tone as she handed the card back to me and waited for the transaction to finish processing. She was a pretty girl, probably late teens or early twenties if that. Her blonde hair was pulled up into a ponytail with side-swept bangs that hung right above her chocolate-colored eyes. I glanced at the bags that were lined up and waiting for me, bags of sugar and chocolate peeking out of the tops of each one. I chuckled as I imagined how it must look to those who didn't know me yet and didn't know what I did for a living.

"I'm a chocolatier," I explained politely. Her brows pulled together in confusion as she thought about it.

"Is that like a three musketeer or something?" She pushed her lips out and crinkled her nose as if the thought of it grossed her out.

"No," I laughed at how young and let's be honest, ditzy, she was. "A chocolatier is someone who makes chocolates. I have a shop, just down the road, *Delectable Delicacies*." I smiled, hoping she had at least seen the new sign for it. She shrugged and shook her head as she waited for the receipt to finish printing before ripping it off and handing it to me.

"Haven't seen it but I'm sure someday you'll be just as popular as that Hershey guy," she said enthusiastically as she blew a bubble with the wad of gum in her mouth.

"Hershey guy?" I arched an eyebrow as I reached across and started loading the bags into the shopping cart to take out to my car. It was too cold to try to carry all four bags at once and honestly, I didn't trust them not to break given how full she had packed them.

"You know, the guy who makes kisses," she squealed before puckering her lips into a kiss.

I laughed and nodded my head as I grabbed the last bag and set it down in front of me.

"Hopefully someday I'll be just as popular," I teased as I smiled and walked away.

Ten minutes later I had pulled into the parking lot, the gravel crunching beneath my tires. It surprised me that they still had never gotten around to paving this damned parking lot after all of these years. I understood that Stone Creek was a small town but lord knows we weren't still living in the 1800s. I climbed out of my car and grabbed two bags, setting one on each hip as I carried them to the door and set them down. I went back and grabbed the other two, setting them down before unlocking and opening the door.

The warmth from inside greeted me as I pushed the door open and held it with my foot, reaching down to grab the first two bags. As I was bent over I heard a loud whistle over my shoulder as footsteps came up behind me. I stood up and turned around, making sure to keep the bags steady so I didn't drop them.

"Well aren't you a fine looking piece of ass in those tight jeans," Parker teased as he reached down and grabbed the other two bags for me. I laughed as we went inside and he helped me take them to the kitchen in the back. We set them down on the long metal island in the center and looked at each other.

"Did you come all the way down from Nashville just to check out my ass?" I asked as I wiggled my eyebrows suggestively at him.

"You know it," he chuckled. "Nashville is completely dried up with a real ass shortage since you left."

I had been unloading the bags when I suddenly stopped and looked at him, a hurt expression on my face.

"Wait—are you saying I have a fine ass, or that I was an ass?" I leaned forward and glared at him.

"You already know the answer to that one," he joked before ducking as I tossed the clean towel that was on the counter at his head. I finished unloading the bags and worked on getting the refrigerated items put away before they went bad.

"So, what are you really doing down here?" I asked, crossing my arms over my chest as I leaned against the counter behind me.

"What? Can't a business partner come down and check to make sure the other partner isn't fucking things up?"

I stayed silent, giving him a look, before he sighed, slumped his shoulders and leaned against the opposite counter, mimicking my stance.

"Alright, so maybe I thought you could use a friend down here while you try to get everything up and running. There's a lot going on with getting the new shop open, as well as you taking care of your mom. It's also the first Christmas without your dad so I just thought maybe you could use some support right now." He smiled warmly as his body relaxed.

"Thank you," I said, suddenly overwhelmed with emotion. "I really appreciate that." I tried to choke back the tears that were threatening to spill over. I wasn't the type of person that cried easily but after my dad died, everything in my world felt like it had fallen apart and tears seemed to be my new norm. I sucked in a deep breath and pushed off the counter, ready to change the subject.

"So, why don't I show you around and give you the official tour?" I said enthusiastically.

"There's more to this?" he teased, his eyes nearly bugging out of his head as he followed me.

He was right though, there wasn't much more to show him that he hadn't already seen. We'd spent a few minutes obsessing over the kitchen and how there was so much more space than we'd had in the shop in Nashville. Granted, there was quite a bit of construction that I had to do as soon as I decided to convert this place into a bakery instead of a flower shop. Overall I was happy with the new kitchen that we had created from the back storage area that my dad had used to store the flowers that weren't out on display.

By noon, we were getting ready to head out for lunch when I heard the sound of a big truck outside as they released the parking brake. We glanced out the door and I felt immediate relief when I saw that they were finally here to deliver the rest of the stuff that I had been waiting for from Nashville. Parker clapped me on the back and smiled as he said, "I told you it would get here in time," and walked outside to greet the driver.

I had been overly stressed, wondering when everything else would get here and if it would be in time for the grand opening this Saturday. They had originally promised to have it here by December 16th and I was thankful that they had delivered. Literally and figuratively. That left five days to get things cleaned, set up, and tested before I had to get busy prepping everything for the big day. An hour later, we waved as the driver pulled out of the parking lot and went on his way. I was feeling on top of the world with having Parker in town as well as having the supplies I needed. As we were heading out the door for lunch, I grabbed the stack of flyers that I had printed for the grand opening and took them with us.

"Where do you want to eat?" I asked as I pulled the door shut and locked it behind me. Parker was looking around, checking out the few other shops around us. There were five shops in the tiny strip mall, all lined up to form a half-circle. My shop was on the corner, directly across from Brooke's, which sat squarely in the middle of everything else.. My eyes quickly wandered over to the sight of Brooke, bending over as she wrote an updated special on the sandwich board right outside the entrance to *Sweet As Sugar*. Last I had heard, she was only offering the typical bakery items- cakes, cookies, brownies, and a killer peach cobbler. But on her sign, she was advertising a new lunch special: grilled bacon and gouda cheese panini.

"That looks good," he said as he nodded in the general direction of Brooke's ass as she reached down to pick up the piece of chalk that she had dropped. Two perfectly round globes greeted us as she crouched lower, trying to catch the rolling piece of chalk that slid under a bistro table.

"It's a bakery," I deadpanned, trying to sound as uninterested as possible. "There are other places we can go eat." Which honestly, there weren't but I wasn't about to tell him that the other five options weren't nearly as good as what I imagined that panini would taste like. My mouth watered just thinking about it. I suddenly remembered seeing a large block of gouda cheese and a massive amount of bread in her cart this morning when I ran into her, which made sense now as to why she waited to go shopping until Monday morning. And here I thought it was just because she was avoiding me.

"It says they have a bacon and gouda panini, sounds like lunch food to me." He eyed me suspiciously.

"Fine," I sighed as I shoved my keys into my pocket. "If that's what you really want," I mumbled, as we started walking across the parking lot. Brooke grabbed the chalk before she stood up and turned around, surprise on her face when she saw us behind her. Her hand flew to her chest, forcing her to drop the chalk once again. I let out a soft laugh as I bent down and picked it up, handing it to her as I watched her look over Parker.

"Brooke, this is my friend, Parker. Parker, this is Brooke." I looked between the two of them as I introduced them.

"Nice to officially meet you, Brooke," he said as he extended his hand and side-eyed me. "I've heard a lot about you."

I rolled my eyes as I looked away, praying that he wasn't about to tell her about the drunken night that I had rambled on and on about her for hours after I had just moved to Nashville.

"Nice to meet you too," she smiled as she shook his hand. "I would say that I've heard a lot about you as well, but that would be a lie. Ryder didn't keep in touch with any of us little people after he left for the big city." She tilted her head to the side and smirked at me as I clenched my jaw in response. This woman sure had a way of getting my blood to boil despite the cold temperature as the snow started to fall again. It looked like we were going to have a white Christmas after all if it kept coming down the way the local weatherman had predicted.

"Well, Ryder definitely didn't lie when he said you were a fireball," Parker shot back at her playfully. I watched as a blush flashed across her face before she glanced at me from the corner of her eye.

"So, what can I do for you?" she asked, turning her attention from Parker to me as she crossed her arms over her chest and shivered. My eyes were suddenly drawn to the sight of her cleavage under the knit sweater as she pushed her arms together to keep warm.

"We came for the lunch special," I said, nodding to the board beside us. She quickly looked down as if she had forgotten that she had one.

"Right!," she said excitedly. "Come on in and I'll get some going for you guys." She stepped to the side and pulled the door open, waiting for us to go inside. The smell that wafted out was an incredible mixture of spiced apples mixed with fresh bread and I wondered if she was baking the apple bread that she used to make when we were growing up. It sure smelled like it. We stepped inside as she followed us before making her way behind the counter.

"Did you both want the panini special?" she asked as she pulled out the notepad and pen from beside the register.

"That sounds good to me," Parker said with a smile.

"Same," I added in.

"Okay, I'll get those started. Do you want pasta salad or chips?"

"Chips?" I asked.

She puckered her lips and squinched up her nose before

responding.

"It's a bag of kettle chips from the store. But the pasta salad is fresh, I just made it this morning," she said hurriedly as if she was embarrassed to offer us pre-packaged chips from the store.

"I'll do the pasta salad," Parker and I both said at once before laughing and walking over to take a seat at the booth by the window. I glanced back to the counter as Brooke wrote something down before going to the back to start our order.

"So, that's Brooke?" Parker said, pulling my attention away.

"That is Brooke," I sighed and looked out the window.

"How has it been with her since you've been back?"

"Fine, I guess," I shrugged and continued to avoid looking at him.

"Just fine?" He raised an eyebrow.

"Alright, it's been awful. She's still pissed about what happened when I left and has been shitty with me since I got back. I ran into her this morning and tried to apologize but she didn't seem to care, she just disregarded it and went on with her day."

He nodded and looked out the window which made me relieved that he wasn't going to keep pushing. We stayed quiet for a while, neither of us saying anything as we watched the snow fall peacefully outside. My head turned as I heard the kitchen door swing open, Brooke carrying a tray with our food on it. She carefully reached in front of us, setting our plates down before pulling her hand away.

"I'll bring you some water unless you want something else?" She looked between us as we eagerly shoved the hot sandwiches into our mouths, the aroma too good to wait. I held my hand up and shook my head to decline anything other than water as Parker did the same. She smiled as she watched us eat before she darted off to the back then came back with two glasses of ice water.

"This is delicious," Parker said as he covered his mouth with his hand while he finished chewing his bite. I nodded in agreement as I finished my bite.

"It really is, you've outdone yourself," I added before she whipped her head around to look at me. "Sorry, I mean, I haven't been around to know whether you've outdone yourself but this is probably the best panini I've ever eaten," I explained as I saw her face relax.

"Thank you, I'm glad you're both enjoying it," she said before she turned to walk away.

"Are you coming to our grand opening on Saturday?" Parker asked, stopping her in her tracks before she turned around. She looked between us, confused.

"I'm sorry, I don't know what you're talking about," she said with her eyes narrowed.

"*Delectable Delicacies* is having their official grand opening on Saturday and we would love for you to be there." Parker leaned back against the booth and smiled. I glared at him for a quick second before I felt Brooke's eyes shift to me as she turned to face me.

"I don't think I'll be able to make it, but thank you for the invite."

She looked between us, her lips pulled into a thin line before she turned and walked away. I tossed my napkin on the table and looked out of the window, too frustrated to look at Parker without reaching across the table and strangling him.

Seven

Brooke

"Howdy, howdy, who's ready to get rowdy?" Sheila yelled as she walked in, the bell above the door ringing behind her. I rolled my eyes and laughed, knowing that she was already up to something before she even made her way back to the kitchen. It didn't matter that there was a big sign plastered to the door that said: "employees only". As far as she was concerned, she was an employee. Or at least that's what she kept telling me. I finished icing the top of the cake I was working on when I heard her voice get louder as she greeted Autumn before swinging the door open and barging in.

"Well isn't that the cutest little Christmas cake I've ever seen?" she said as she walked over and bent down, taking in the details of the fondant I had spent all afternoon working on after Ryder and his friend left.

"Thanks," I sighed, taking a step back to look at it. It was all coming together just how I had pictured when I first agreed to do it. My back was starting to ache and my feet were killing me but according to the clock I only had forty-five minutes before Mrs. Crosby would be by to pick it up. "I just have a few more details to go and then I'll be done."

"Is this for Neil's retirement party tonight?" She turned to set her purse down on the empty counter behind me before hopping up to sit on it.

"Yeah, Mrs. Crosby will be by soon so I need to finish this before she gets here. Why are you all chipper, and what not?" I asked as I leaned forward and added another fondant leaf to the corner of the cake.

"I was about to head out to do some Christmas shopping and thought maybe my best friend in the WHOLE WIDE WORLD would want to go with me. We can drink hot chocolate and link our arms together as we go skipping from store to store singing Christmas carols." Her blue eyes lit up as she said it, immediately giving it away that she was up to something. I arched an eyebrow and waited. She blew out a breath and pulled the beanie off her head, letting her fiery red hair cascade down her back.

"Fine, I have to shop for the asshole and I don't want to be tempted to buy him laxatives for Christmas so I thought maybe you could go with me and we could find something together. You know, like a '*Merry Christmas you fucking piece of shit that knocked me up four times before you abandoned your family to chase your dreams of being a wannabe rock star*' kind of gift."

I laughed so hard that I snorted and had to turn away from the cake to avoid any unfortunate incidents. As dramatic as she was being, she wasn't that far off. Her ex-husband was a complete and total douchebag but she also should have learned that after he knocked her up the first time. In her defense, things had been good between them at the beginning but then they kept having kids one after another. Once they had four under four, he decided this wasn't the life he wanted.

She was a great mother and things were definitely easier for her now that the kids were in their teens but she definitely had a hell of a time raising them on her own when he first left. If it was me, I would bake him a cake filled with laxatives and watch the rat bastard suffer while shitting his brains out all day on Christmas. Maybe she was just a better person than I was.

"While I love your plan—and I do love it—I don't think it's going to work out that well."

She sighed and slouched her shoulders.

"Alright, what's wrong with it? Am I being too harsh? Should I be considering something nicer, or more Christmas-y, like pajamas?"

"No, it's not that at all," I assured her as I went back to work on the cake. "You just have some flawed expectations if you think that we can sing and skip while drinking hot chocolate. I've seen how clumsy you are—you'll fall and take me down with you and then I'll have to break up with you as my best friend because you made me spill my hot chocolate."

"And no one messes with your hot chocolate," she said before I could say it. We both laughed as I added the final touch to the cake and stepped back to look at it.

"What do you think?" I asked, knowing that it didn't matter if she didn't like it. After four hours, I was ready to call this cake what it was. Done.

She scooted forward and slid off the counter, coming to stand next to me as she admired it.

"It's really beautiful, you did a great job." She wrapped her arms around my shoulders and gave me a quick squeeze.

"Thanks," I said as I smiled at her and glanced at the clock hanging on the wall behind her. Ten minutes left but if I knew Mrs. Crosby, she would be here in five.

"Awesome, I'm going to run to the little girl's room while you get that packed up, then we can get out of here and do some shopping." She turned to walk into the employee bathroom in the back when she heard me groan at the idea of shopping. "You can't be a grinch forever. Maybe I'll find some mistletoe and attach it to a hat that you can wear around town until someone slips a present in your stocking if you know what I mean?" She winked dramatically as she said it.

"You're disgusting," I replied as I shook my head and turned my attention back to getting the cake boxed up. I heard the bathroom door close and was relieved that I had a few minutes to spare before I heard the bell ring up front as Mrs. Crosby came in. I closed the lid on the cake and taped the sides to make sure everything stayed secure before I picked it up and carried it out to the front.

Autumn smiled and squealed when she saw it, completely different from when she had seen it a few hours ago after I had just started to work on it. She went to the register and began to ring Mrs. Crosby up for me while they continued to talk about how beautiful the cake was. Her husband, Neil, was retiring after thirty years as the school crossing guard. I could still remember seeing him every day, helping the children cross the street as we went to and from school. Stone Creek wasn't very big and everyone in town was well aware of how to act in a school zone, or just being close to a school for that matter. But still, Mr. Crosby had taken the job and did it with pride every single day. I remembered him taking my small hand and helping me cross the street plenty of times when I was a little girl.

I was still lost in thought as I watched her walk out the door with the cake, excitement on her face. She carefully loaded it into the passenger side of her car before she hurried around to the other side to get in. The door from the kitchen swung open and Sheila came walking out with her purse already on one arm with mine hanging off the other.

"You ready to go?" she asked cheerfully?

I looked down at my flour and frosting covered apron then at her. She was wearing tight fitted jeans that wrapped perfectly around her petite frame and a white cashmere turtleneck sweater that hugged her perky, yet overly plump, breasts. A beautiful silver locket hung down between her cleavage, adding to the overall outfit that she had probably spent two minutes throwing together. She was naturally beautiful without trying, which always surprised me as to why she was still single. Not that the men in town hadn't tried. Sheila had been saying that she wasn't interested in a relationship ever since Rodney left her twelve years ago.

"I'm kind of a mess, I should at least go home and change first," I said, hoping she would change her mind about wanting to go.

"No need, I already stopped by your place and grabbed you something to change into. It's on your desk in the back, so go, get moving before the stores start to close and we don't get any shopping done." She nodded to the back and eyed me like I was one of her children until I gave in and walked back to find she had laid out a pair of jeans, my favorite sweater, and a pair of over the knee boots I had been wanting but refused to buy. I ran my hand along the soft leather and closed my eyes for a second to keep from crying. We had been out shopping together months ago when I had seen these and fell in love with them but couldn't afford them.

We had been out for a girls' weekend while her parents took her kids on a camping trip and decided to do some shopping in Clarksville which was an hour drive from Stone Creek and the stores were way more expensive than anything in our small town. The nice thing about shopping in a bigger city was that we could find things that we couldn't find at our teeny-tiny shops, and it was more of a treat to splurge on the finer things every now and then.

"We don't have all day, just put those sexy boots on your tired feet and let's get going," Sheila called from up front. I sighed and shook my head before slipping into the bathroom to change. I tossed my dirty clothes onto my desk and headed up front.

"I've got everything here, go and have fun," Autumn said as if sensing my reservations about leaving.

"You sure?" I raised an eyebrow.

"Yes, *mom*, I'm sure. I've already cleaned up and plan to close by five if we don't have anyone coming in to place any holiday orders. After that, I'll stick around to work on the supply list before I go."

"Okay, I'll have my phone on if you need me. See you in the morning." I smiled and walked out, knowing that Autumn was fully capable of handling everything on her own. I felt Sheila's arm slide into mine and laughed as we linked arms and started walking. I figured she wanted to check out the other stores in the shopping center first since they were the most popular but when she started to pull me in the opposite direction, I started to panic.

"Where are you going?" I asked as I tried to slow her down as she pulled harder.

"There is this new chocolate place that I HAVE TO TRY! Come on, I want to see if it's open yet," she squealed as we walked toward Ryder's shop. I stopped in my tracks and glared at her.

"You know damn well whose shop that is," I said, letting her arm drop as my hand planted itself on my hip.

"Yeah, and?"

"I've had enough of Ryder, I don't feel like going into his shop. If you want to go, you have to go by yourself. Besides, I think they said the grand opening is Saturday so I doubt that it's even open yet." I walked over and sat on the edge of the cement planter box that lined the edge of where the sidewalk bordered the parking lot. Her eyes widened as she listened to what I said.

"Oh really? And when did you talk to Ryder to find out about a grand opening?" she asked as she stepped closer and stood in front of me. Then suddenly it clicked and her eyes went even bigger. "Who are *they*?"

I blew out a frustrated breath and glanced over my shoulder at the shop.

"Ryder and his friend came by my shop today for lunch. His friend, Parker, asked if I was coming to the grand opening on Saturday."

"Who is this guy Parker? Is he single? Cute?" she scrunched her nose up and wrinkled her brows.

"I thought you weren't interested in dating anyone?" I teased and tried to change the subject.

"That was before I realized that WE are about to turn 35 and WE need to find men in our lives." She sat down next to me and nudged me with her shoulder.

"Why do WE have to do everything together? Can't your 35-year-old self go man-hunting on your own?"

"I could, but it would be more fun if we did it together. Then we can skip and drink wine while we compare horror stories of dates gone wrong while we wait for our Prince Charming to come along and rescue us," she said in a sing-song tone.

"Why are we always drinking and skipping? It seems like such a bad idea," I groaned. "Almost as bad as us dating."

She laughed and grabbed my arm, pulling me up as she dragged me with her to *Delectable Delicacies*.

Eight

Ryder

The afternoon had been quiet with Parker working on paperwork while I started unpacking everything that had come in this morning. Finally, an hour ago, it felt like the shop was set up and ready to go. I decided to get a head start on making some of my favorite holiday chocolates, to not only ensure that I really did have everything I needed but more importantly, that everything was working properly before Saturday's grand opening. This wasn't my first grand opening but even though I knew more than half of the people who would be there, I had never been this nervous or anxious starting my own shop in my life. Maybe it was all of the pressure I was putting on myself to take over my dad's shop and turn it into something he would be proud of.

I gently wiped the sides of the tray of chocolate-covered cashews and set them next to the trays of chocolate-covered peanuts and almonds. Everything was coming together smoothly and before I knew it, I had a display case full of chocolate-covered treats. I stepped back to admire my work when I heard the bell chime as the front door opened. I wasn't technically open yet, however, I also knew better than to turn anyone away in a small town. Plus it wouldn't hurt to sell some of the chocolates I had made while they were fresh.

My eyes narrowed as I tried to see who was coming in as the sun reflected off of the glass of the door, nearly blinding me. I needed to make a note to have that fixed as soon as possible. A few seconds later, I held my breath as I looked at the two women standing at the entrance. Brooke looked around nervously as she tugged on the sleeve of her sweater, obviously wishing she was anywhere but here right now. The sun caught her brown hair and cast a beautiful warm glow on it, reminding me just how gorgeous she was. My eyes slowly traveled over her body, admiring the way her jeans hugged every curve while taking note of the sexy boots she was wearing with them. I silently wished she would turn around so I could check out her plump ass in something other than the loose pants she's worn the past few times I've seen her.

It made sense not to wear tight or restrictive clothes when you were rushing around a kitchen like a mad man but now that I saw her in this, I never wanted her to wear her work clothes ever again. Maybe I could somehow convince her that it's a new trend to bake in jeans and a tight t-shirt, or maybe even nothing at all? I shook my head to try to get rid of the image before I embarrassed myself. That was something that I could save for later. A better time, a better place.

I had been so caught up checking Brooke out that I had spaced that there was someone else who had come in with her. I glanced up and saw Sheila walking over to me, a huge smile on her face. I returned her smile, genuinely happy to see her. She came running the last few steps and leaped into my arms as I wrapped her in a big hug and gently squeezed her.

"It's so good to have you back," she whispered as she pulled back and cupped my cheeks in her hands. "I'm so sorry about your dad, we all miss him so much."

I lifted my hands and gently squeezed hers while she still held onto my face.

"Thank you, it's good to be back. And I miss him too."

She smiled a sad smile as we slowly let go of each other's hands and stepped to the side. Brooke had finally walked over and was standing next to Sheila, glancing behind us toward the display case.

"Hey," I said as I nodded at Brooke, hoping things would be a little easier between us than they were earlier. I was still feeling frustrated with how things had been going but it seemed every time I made any effort with her, it was quickly rejected and ended up being all for nothing.

"Hi." Her eyes quickly met mine before she pulled away and stepped to the side to look at the chocolates in the case.

"You've been busy," she said as she bent forward and studied each piece.

"I had a little time on my hands this afternoon and wanted to make sure everything was up and running before the grand opening on Saturday," I explained as I saw Parker come out from the kitchen. He stopped in his tracks when he saw there were customers and was about to turn around and go back to the kitchen when he spotted Brooke. His eyes widened as he wiggled his eyebrows before noticing Sheila. As if having Brooke here wasn't enough of a reason for him to stay and make my life hell, he now found a new target and headed over.

"Is there anything that you don't cover in chocolate?" Brooke mumbled more as a statement than an actual question.

"I'm sure he's willing to experiment with body parts if the right woman came along," Parker teased as he walked over, forcing Brooke's head to whip up as she started to blush. I worked my jaw back and forth as I glared at him before turning my attention to Brooke. Her expression was priceless and no matter how much she tried to hide it, she looked like she was considering what he just said.

"I wouldn't know anything about that," Brooke said curtly before looking away from Parker and at me. She gave me the same look she had in her eyes the night everything between us changed after she had admitted that she was falling in love with me. Feeling bolder than usual and tired of the bullshit from the past, I decided to push back.

"I still have a few extra hours that I could spare if you're interested." I looked her dead in the eye and held her gaze as I raised my eyebrows and rocked back on my heels. I expected her to blush and look away like she always did but instead, she surprised me.

"I have better things to do than to mess with little boys who still play with their food." She tilted her head as she challenged me to respond, instead, I rolled my eyes and looked away. "Did you get what you came in here for?" She asked as she turned to Sheila and glared at her. I really got under her skin, that was apparent. Suddenly I had the urge to get even further beneath it, just to see how feisty she was these days.

"Actually, I needed to see about placing a holiday order for Christmas Eve. My ex-in-laws are coming to town and I promised the kids that we would have something nice for them."

I watched as she nervously looked at Parker who was still standing off to the side watching everything in silence. He was watching her intently and I was surprised when I didn't see him flinch when she mentioned former in-laws or kids. Maybe since he was older than me and turning forty this year, it didn't bother or surprise him to hear that a woman had been married and had kids.

"Yeah, we can get an order placed for you," I said as I noticed Brooke walking off toward the door to go outside. "Parker here will get you started." I clapped him on the back and smirked as I took off to the front after Brooke. I could hear his jaw drop to the floor when he realized that I had left him alone with a beautiful woman and he had no fucking idea what to do with placing an order for her. Maybe now he would understand that karma could bite you in the ass pretty quickly and he would stay out of things with Brooke.

I reached forward and grabbed the door before it could close and slid outside as Brooke was walking over to the bench that sat in front of the gift shop, separating our stores. She turned around and sat down, shivering against the cold chill, before she looked up and spotted me. She shook her head and scowled as she looked the other way. I turned around and sat down next to her, leaning forward to rest my elbows on my thighs as I looked out into the nearly empty parking lot.

"Why do you hate me so much?" I asked as I kept staring straight ahead. I felt her shift, scooting slightly away from me as she crossed her leg in the opposite direction.

"I don't hate you," she said softly, her arms crossed over her chest as her purse rested on her thigh.

"You sure seem like you do. There's a lot of anger whenever I try to talk to you." I slightly turned to look at her over my shoulder.

"Maybe I never really got over what happened." She shrugged.

"I can see that," I joked, immediately regretting it when her head turned and she glared at me. "I don't blame you though, I would have been angry too. And in all honesty, I should have listened to you."

"But you didn't."

"But I didn't," I sighed as I leaned back and rested against the cold wood of the bench. I had played that night over and over in my head so many times that I could recite each word that was said verbatim. It was one of those things that felt like they happened in slow motion and you knew that there was going to be a terrible outcome but yet there wasn't anything you could do to stop it other than watch in agony.

"I knew that Lauren was cheating on me," I admitted,

embarrassed. I felt the bench shift as she shifted and turned to look at me, a puzzled look on her face when we locked eyes.

"Then why didn't you tell me? Why did you let me go on and on, embarrassing myself as I begged you to stay?" The hurt in her voice felt like a knife plunging through to my chest. "Why did you still go with her?"

"Because," I took a deep breath, unsure of whether I was ready to say this out loud for the first time to anyone. "It was easier to move away with someone who didn't love me than it was to stay here and admit that I was falling in love with you."

I heard her gasp as she brought her hand to her chest and stared at me.

"What?" she whispered.

"I was falling in love with you, Brooke, but I didn't feel like I was allowed to. You were like my little sister when we were growing up, then you were one of my best friends. I didn't know how to handle it and I kept fighting what I was feeling. I wasn't going to move to Nashville with Lauren but then you said you were falling in love with me and I got scared… So I went so that I could keep from hurting you." I tried to swallow down the emotion that was bubbling up, forcing myself not to lose it in front of her.

"You hurt me even more with what you did. You left *AFTER* I told you I had feelings for you, and you left with my best friend who was cheating on you." She shook her head and turned to the side, her fingers trembling as she wiped a tear away as it slid down her cheek.

"I know and I'm so sorry. I will never stop apologizing for what I did." I turned to look at her, reaching over to gently touch her chin as I tried to get her to look at me. Her eyes were filled with tears as her lip trembled. "I was young and stupid, nothing will ever change that. But I knew the moment I left that I had made a *HUGE* mistake. The only reason that I didn't come back to fix it was because I thought you deserved someone better than that. Someone who would know better than to hurt you like that in the first place."

Her head tilted forward as she began to cry. Shaky sobs escaped her throat as I wrapped my arm around to hold her. For once, she didn't try to fight me.

Nine

Brooke

"What are you going to wear to the Winter Fair?" Sheila called from the living room while I worked on getting changed in my bedroom.

"I have no idea, why?" I answered as I shimmied out of my flour crusted work pants and sat down to put on sweats. It was a Friday night with a busy day ahead of me tomorrow so I was feeling relieved to stay in and do nothing. Today had kicked my butt with getting everything ready for the Winter Fair tomorrow. Even with Sheila and Autumn's help, it still felt like there was a lot left to get done. I grabbed a hair tie and threw my hair up into a wild mess of a bun and walked down the hallway to the living room.

I smiled when I saw that Sheila had already turned on the Christmas tree and started a fire while I was changing. This time of year was always hard for her because her custody agreement required that her ex-husband have the kids the week before Christmas, including Christmas Eve, and she got them again starting Christmas day. The loser didn't want them any other time of the year but had made sure to request the week before Christmas just to spite her, knowing that she loved doing Christmas stuff with them each night leading up to Christmas.

A lot of happy memories were made when they were little and thankfully he didn't ask for this ridiculous agreement until a few years ago, when they were old enough that he didn't have to do much to take care of them. Sheila had ten years of creating Christmas traditions with them before he robbed her of that. I grabbed the bottle of wine from the fridge and swiped two glasses from the wine rack before plopping down next to her on the couch. I pulled the cork out, relieved that it still had a satisfying popping sound when I opened it.

I filled two glasses and handed her one as I leaned back against the couch and pulled my feet up under me. We were due for another storm soon and the temperature was dropping quickly in anticipation of it. My toes felt like ice as I dug them down under the couch cushion.

"Did you finish your shopping for the kids yet?" I asked, hoping to change the subject from the Winter Fair.

"Almost," she sighed and took a sip of wine. "The older they get, the harder they are to shop for. I wish I could just buy them Legos and be done with it compared to what they actually want these days."

I laughed and lowered my glass to the coffee table knowing that she wasn't being dramatic when she said they were hard to shop for these days. I still needed to get their gifts and had no idea what to get them. It used to be that I could get them all similar gifts since they were so close in age and they would all share. But now that her oldest was sixteen and her youngest was twelve, those days were long gone.

"Well, Oliver thinks that he should get a car because he's sixteen and all of his friends have cars. I reminded him that he only has 2 friends and they drive the same car their daddy drove when I was in high school so it's nothing to brag about. Thomas wants everything Oliver wants so I had to explain that a fourteen-year-old was definitely not getting a car. We settled on a new video game. Megan wants to get her belly button pierced and Sally wants a boyfriend."

I laughed so hard as she ran down the list that I snorted, which got her laughing with me. She rolled her eyes and looked toward the fire, lost in thought.

"Sally is only twelve—she better not get a boyfriend before I do," I warned playfully, hoping to lighten the mood.

"Seriously, that's the same thing I told her. If mama can't date, neither can she." She winked and raised her wine glass to clink with mine that I had picked up from the table.

"Well, in all fairness, it's not that you *can't* date," I teased. "It's that you've been refusing to date since Rodney left."

Her face fell a little as sadness flashed across it.

"Sorry," I whispered. Her eyes looked up and met mine as she smiled.

"Don't be, it's okay. But I'll stay on this no-dating streak as long as I have to if that means she stops asking for a boyfriend. Maybe Santa can bring me a special friend this year, one that lasts a while and takes batteries." She giggled and lifted the glass to her lips before the blush could fully reach her cheeks.

"There's always Ryder's friend, he seemed pretty interested the other day when he couldn't take his eyes off you." I wiggled my eyebrows and waited for her reaction. As much as I had hated being there, I enjoyed watching as Sheila and Parker subtly checked each other out. It felt like being in middle school again when you were still terrified of someone finding out that you liked them. Okay, so maybe that wasn't limited to middle school.

"No way!" she shrieked as if I just proposed something ridiculous. She swatted her hand in the air as she finished her glass of wine and looked at me. "He was not looking at me, and there's no way that a guy like him would be interested in a girl like me."

"What's that supposed to mean?" I tilted my head slightly and gave her my full attention.

"It means that no one is looking to start something with a single mom of four rowdy kids and baby daddy drama."

"Sheila, you are beautiful, and caring, and one of the most giving people that I have ever met. ANY man would be lucky to have you, and I mean that. Rodney was a dumbass but he gave you four incredible blessings. Don't ever think any less of yourself because one person wasn't worthy of who you really are."

Her eyes filled with tears which forced mine to tear up as well. I grabbed the bottle of wine from the coffee table and refilled our glasses.

"So, are you going to let Megan pierce her belly button?" I asked, laughing at the expression she made in response.

"Over my dead body," she snorted.

"We had piercings at her age…" I smiled and shrugged my shoulders.

"Yeah, and I was pregnant a few years later, waddling down the aisle to collect my diploma before my water broke."

"Ah, those were the good days," I joked.

"Yeah, I miss those days sometimes. The late-night bonfires and drinking cheap wine while the guys ran around and acted a fool. We had some of the best nights together before everything fell apart."

I pressed my lips into a thin line, knowing where she was going with the conversation.

"Yeah, and some of the worst nights too."

"I saw you and Ryder talking on the bench after you walked out." Her tone changed, more sympathetic as I nodded in agreement.

"Then I saw him hold you as you cried."

I glanced up at her, the tears threatening to make a return if I started talking about it again.

"I've been wanting to ask you about it since then but I decided to be a grown-up and give you some space. More importantly, I was hoping that you would come to me, wanting to talk about it." She paused for a second and looked at me. "But, since that doesn't seem to be the case, I'm just going to keep pushing until you tell me what happened."

I blew out a deep breath and thought about what to say. The truth was that I had been wanting to talk to her about it since it happened but I could barely get my head around it myself.

"Ryder and I talked about the night that he left." I stared at the wall, watching as the embers of the fire danced wildly around the wood as it burned.

"And…"

"And he said that he knew he was stupid for leaving but he did it to protect me."

"Protect you? From what?" She pulled her brows together.

"From hurting me. He thought I deserved better than to fall for someone who was too afraid to admit that they had fallen in love with me. He said that he had been feeling it but when I confessed my feelings to him, it scared him and that's what forced him to leave with Lauren. Apparently, if I wouldn't have told him that I was falling in love with him, he never would have left with her."

I turned my attention back to her, chuckling when I saw her staring at me with her wine glass suspended in the air.

"What?!"

I nodded my head and let her have a few minutes to try to process it. Hell, it was days later and I was still trying to process it myself.

"That's so crazy!" she exhaled before taking a drink. "So, does he still have feelings for you?"

"I have no idea, but I doubt it. It's been ten years and a lot has changed since then. We've changed since then. I can't imagine that someone would just stay secretly in love with someone for that long and not move on."

"But you did," she said quietly, her words going straight to my heart.

CHOCOLATE COVERED MISTLETOE

Ten

Ryder

"You ready to do this?" Parker asked as he walked excitedly to the front door and turned the closed sign to open before unlocking the door. It was barely ten in the morning and I felt like I was on my eighth cup of coffee as my nerves shot through the roof in anticipation of the grand opening. With it being both four days until Christmas and also the Winter Fair, things around town were starting to feel busy, let alone trying to squeeze in the grand opening of a new sweet shop.

Ruby had been talking to everyone she could, letting them know about the grand opening and asking them to check it out before the Winter Fair started that afternoon. Parker and I had decided it was best to hype this up as a quick, three-hour event and then call it quits so we didn't have to compete with the fair. Besides, Ruby quickly reminded me that it had been awhile since I had been in town during the holidays and suggested that I plan to attend the fair to get back into the holiday spirit that I used to love when I was growing up. A lot of things in my life had changed since then but she was right. It was time for me to slow down and remember why I used to cherish this time of year.

I heard the bell chime above the door as I nodded yes, the anxiety quickly replaced by excitement. The door opened and I held my breath as people started floating in, spreading out and filling the room with the sound of holiday cheer as they started to browse. I had brought in a few extra tables and spaced them out with enough room to let people move freely through the shop, making the display counter and register the final stop on their path. Each table was covered with a beautiful deep red tablecloth and had a gold platter filled with samples as the centerpiece. Alongside each platter were small gift boxes filled with different chocolates that included a gift tag attached to the sheer, glittery wrapping paper Ruby had found at the last minute after I came up with the idea to offer gift sets last night.

Ruby and Parker had stayed up with me until two in the morning, packaging the chocolates as I made them. Ruby even had the brilliant idea to create kid-friendly boxes complete with chocolate-covered cherries decorated as mice. A few hours in and we were covered in chocolate when my mom came into the kitchen and found us, a huge smile on her face. Never in a million years would I have imagined that I would be laughing and joking with my mom in the kitchen that I grew up in, just like when I was little. She had a wonderful night and I woke up feeling hopeful that maybe she would have more good days now that I was back home. I shook my head to clear the thought as the first customer walked up to the counter with a handful of gift boxes in their arms and a smudge of chocolate in the corner of their mouth.

The first two and a half hours had flown by and I was busier than I could have ever imagined. It seemed that not only had all of the town locals come by but people from nearby towns came to check out the hottest new sweet shop in Stone Creek as well. The gift boxes had sold out completely within the first hour of us being open which was not something that I had expected. Before I could freak out about not having time to make more, Ruby came waltzing in with my mom, arms linked together with huge smiles on their faces. I was worried at first about having my mom out in public since no one knew about her recent dementia diagnosis. Seeing how happy she was with Ruby, I decided to embrace the holiday buzz around me, excited to see my mom out enjoying herself. The two of them quickly shuffled to the kitchen to help Parker as he tried to throw together more gift boxes with some of the chocolates we had for the display case.

It was almost time for the grand opening to be over, which I was thankful for because we had officially run out of chocolates aside from the few samples that were left on the empty tables. I leaned back against the counter and rolled my neck, trying to alleviate some of the tension that had been building all morning. I smiled and waved at Ruby as she and my mom left, the door chiming as it opened. I closed my eyes for a second, taking in the sound of pure silence. The sound of muffled whispers forced my eyes open to find Brooke and Sheila walking toward me, arms linked together as Sheila looked like she was trying to skip. Brooke shot her a quick look, causing Sheila's face to fall into a childish pout before she turned and smiled at me.

"Sorry we're so late, did we miss the big grand opening?" Sheila asked as she looked around. As her eyes wandered around the room I couldn't help but notice that she didn't seem to be looking for chocolate. I chuckled and shook my head as I leaned forward and rested my arms on the top of the display case.

"Parker is in the kitchen," I said with a wink as I nodded behind me. Her face was redder than the tablecloths covering the empty tables as she tucked her chin and looked down.

"Why would I care where he is?" Her voice was quiet as she mumbled the words, still refusing to make eye contact with me.

"I don't know, maybe because he hasn't stopped watching the front door all morning, waiting to see when you were going to come in." I glanced at Brooke and the loving smile on her face as she watched Sheila's head whip up with a beaming grin.

"Really?" she squealed excitedly before looking at Brooke as if she just found out that Santa was real. They exchanged a look that made me wonder what exactly they had been talking about when Sheila raised her eyebrows and subtly nodded in my direction. Now it was Brooke's turn to blush.

"Are you ready for the Winter Fair?" I asked Brooke, hoping to pull her attention to me. It had only been a few days since I had seen her but I was dying to talk to her after my confession. I had been so busy trying to get everything set up for the grand opening that I hadn't had a chance to go talk to her. I wanted to see how she was feeling after finding out that I was in love with her before I left for Nashville. I had played the conversation over and over again in my head the past few nights as I struggled to fall asleep, trying to dissect every tiny piece of it to see if there was any possible chance that she still felt the same way about me. Ten years might have passed but I still loved her as much today as I did the day I walked out and broke her heart.

"I think so," she sighed. "But it's too late at this point if not. Autumn is working on getting the last few things set up before we get over there, but we wanted to stop by and say congratulations on your grand opening." She smiled but it didn't fully reach her eyes.

"I'm sure you'll be just fine," I tried to assure her, not knowing what she was really worried about. The Winter Fair had always been a fun event, from what I remembered, and people were just excited to be out with each other, celebrating the holidays while they finished any last-minute holiday shopping.

"I wasn't planning for all of the extra traffic, but it seems a certain grand opening brought a swarm of people in from out of town so I'm worried that I won't have enough for the fair." She scrunched her face up in the cutest frown I had ever seen as she tucked a stray strand of hair behind her ear. I was thankful to see her wearing jeans and a cream-colored sweater instead of the loose clothes she wears in the kitchen. She looked like the kind of woman you would see in one of those cheesy Christmas movies, right before she finds the love of her life and they live happily ever after.

"Well, I'm about done here. I can help whip some stuff up for you if you want me to." I smiled and prayed that she would take me up on the offer so I could have a chance to spend some time with her today. Slowly, she looked around and raised an eyebrow at me as her gaze landed on the mistletoe

Ruby had insisted on hanging at the end of the display case for decoration.

"I don't think you have anything left," she giggled, "Unless you're going to dip that mistletoe in chocolate, I think you're out of luck my friend."

I looked up and pretended to consider it, getting a laugh out of her in return. Her smile was finally a genuine one that lit up her face and had me smiling along with her. I felt her gaze land on mine as we shared this blissful moment before the kitchen door swung open and Parker walked out.

"You ready to get go—" he paused mid-sentence as his eyes landed on Sheila. I watched as she blushed and turned slightly to the side, pretending to look at the empty platter on the table beside her. "Hi, I didn't know anyone was here." He walked over and stood next to her as they quietly started their own conversation.

"So, back to what I was saying," I said gently as she turned around to look at me. "I'm happy to come over to your shop and help you if you think you might need more—what did you decide to make for this one?" I knew that every year Brooke created a new recipe for the Winter Fair and it was exclusive to that event. The people around town would anxiously wait for the fair, knowing that she wouldn't tell anyone what it was going to be before then. They would line up at her booth, making sure they grabbed a slice of whatever it was that she had decided to grace them with.

"You know I don't tell anyone what my secret item is before the fair," she warned playfully.

"Well, I'm not just anyone. I'm the king of chocolates that just sold over 300 gift boxes and cleared out an entire display case, as well as racked up over twenty custom orders before Christmas Eve. So yeah, I'm kind of special," I winked. "And if you tell me then I can help you and you can be the queen of the fair tonight."

"I'm the queen of the fair every year, nothing's going to change that." She smiled playfully and licked her lips. The action alone sent a chill through me as I imagined what it would be like to feel that tongue caress my body.

"Alright, *Queen*, but when you're panicking because you're running low and people are mad because they don't get some of whatever it is you decided to make- don't blame me," I smirked and shrugged my shoulders as I leaned against the counter behind me.

She glanced at Sheila before looking up at the clock hanging above me and sighed.

"Fine," she exhaled dramatically. "I'm making White Chocolate Cranberry Fudge. If you really want to help you can meet me in my kitchen in thirty minutes. I need to go make sure Autumn is ready to go, then I'll be back."

"I'll be there," I smiled and winked. She smiled and started to walk off before she paused and turned to look at me.

"Thank you, you really don't have to do this but I do appreciate the help."

I nodded and watched as she walked over to Sheila and wrapped her arm in hers as she whispered something in her ear. A few minutes later they waved and walked out the door.

"What was that all about?" Parker asked as he walked over and stood next to me, looking at the door.

"Making amends for the mistakes I've made along the way." I avoided looking at him as I started to think through my plan.

"So you're going to go spend your day making fudge as a way to say sorry for walking away and breaking her heart ten years ago?"

"No, I'm going to spend my day trying to make her see that I have never stopped loving her. I'll spend the rest of my *life* trying to make it up to her."

He smiled as he patted me on the back before walking back to the kitchen to clean up, leaving me alone with my thoughts.

Eleven

Brooke

I shifted my weight as I tried to balance the grocery bags on my hip and opened the door, letting it swing open and hit the wall as the bell chimed overhead. My fingers dug into the bottom of one of the bags, struggling to keep my grip on it as Ryder came up behind me, startling me.

"Need some help?" he asked as I jumped and let the bag go. His hand darted out and grabbed the bag before it could hit the ground. I blew out the breath I had been holding and looked up at him as he reached over and grabbed one of the other bags from me, lightening my load.

"You scared the shit out of me," I said as I walked inside and made my way to the kitchen, propping the door open with my hip as he followed behind me.

"You said thirty minutes," he answered with his brows pulled together.

"Huh?" I set the bags on the island that separated us in the middle of the kitchen and placed my palms down on the cool metal top as I looked at him, confused.

"You said to meet you in thirty minutes. It's been thirty minutes and here I am, meeting you." He shrugged his shoulders as if it should all make sense now. "I didn't mean to scare you, I thought you had heard me walking up behind you."

My heart was still racing as I tried to calm myself. Things were hectic when I went to check on Autumn. She had started early because a line of out-of-towners had already formed, anxious to see what *Sweet As Sugar* had in store for the fair this year. I did a quick inventory check while I was there and started to worry about how quickly we were going to run out of fudge before I ran over to the store for more supplies, knowing that I didn't have enough at the shop to make what we would need. What should have been thirty minutes felt like the longest hour of my life with everything being so rushed and stressful.

"I'm sorry, I'm just a little out of sorts right now," I tried to explain without getting into too many details. I forced a smile and turned my attention to gathering the things we would need so we could get started.

"Don't be sorry, I'm happy to help. Just tell me what you need me to do." He gave me the happiest smile that I had seen from him in I don't even know how long. When was the

last time I had seen him happy? Like really, really happy? He cracked his knuckles and waited for my instructions.

"Okay," I sighed heavily and looked around for where to start so we weren't in each other's way. "Here are the bags of white chocolate," I said as I unloaded them from the bag and set them between us. "And here are the cans of sweetened condensed milk. I have the recipe written down on that paper by the measuring cups but once you have it all mixed you can just pop it into the microwave and we'll go from there."

He arched an eyebrow at me as he stepped back and folded his arms across his chest.

"You brought me over here to help you make *microwaved* fudge? That's a sin against all things sweet and you know it," he teased playfully.

I rolled my eyes and laughed.

"Trust me, I wanted to do something way better than *microwave fudge*," I said sarcastically, "but there wasn't enough time to try to pull something together with the extra work I've been doing with adding in a lunch menu around here. Trust me, I'm ashamed that I'm cheating too, but when you see it- it'll be beautiful. And what's even better is that it tastes *delicious,* so no one will even know." I smiled smugly and narrowed my eyes at him as he continued to raise his eyebrow at the situation.

"They will if I tell them…"

My eyes went wide as my hand flew to my hip, shaking my head as he watched with humor in his eyes.

"You wouldn't."

"Oh, I would…" He stepped forward and leaned against the island, bringing him close enough that I could smell the faint smell of his cologne. "But, I could be bribed… if the price is right."

"Oh so now you're blackmailing me?" I feigned shock as I grabbed a bag of chocolate chips and dumped them into the bowl before mixing in the can of milk and popping it into the microwave.

"You bet your sweet ass I am. I know what this secret is worth." He licked his lips as the grin spread further across his face.

"Okay, fine," I shrugged my shoulders. "What do you want?"

"Have dinner with me." There was a slight change in his voice as if it was hard for him to ask the question, his face hardening as he waited for my answer.

"Dinner?"

"Yeah, it's usually the meal that comes after lunch for those of us who stop long enough to actually eat," he said as he nodded behind me to the empty Snickers wrapper laying on the counter.

"Just dinner?" I asked cautiously, unsure of what he was asking. I heard the microwave ding, thankful for the distraction. I grabbed the bowl and pulled it out, setting it on the island as I stirred the chocolate and condensed milk together. I quickly added in the vanilla and dried cranberries, mixing thoroughly before I got too sidetracked.

"Did you have something else in mind that you were wanting to do in addition?" His face lit up with amusement as mine turned a dark shade of red. I stood, paralyzed, trying to force my mind to think of something intelligent to say back to him but it was completely blank. Taking full advantage of the situation and my stunned silence, he kept going. "Were you wanting to take me up on the offer to experiment with chocolate?" He slowly walked around the island, heading straight toward me as he slowly ran his fingers along the top of the island.

He stood in front of me, just inches away, studying me as my breathing started to get heavier. His eyes stayed fixed on mine as he reached over and slid the bowl over to him. Everything felt like it was happening in slow motion as he reached inside the bowl and ran his finger along the top of it, covering it in melted chocolate. He brought his finger to his mouth, his lips wet as they parted before he licked the chocolate off. I swallowed hard as I tried to look away, completely mesmerized by how seductive he made it look. Without thinking, I pulled my bottom lip in between my teeth as a soft moan escaped my throat. His eyes danced wildly as he watched my reaction, my chest rising and falling heavily.

I sucked in a deep breath and pulled my shoulders back, trying to force myself out of this fog.

"We better get moving before this sets, or *no one* will get any of my delicious *microwave fudge*," I said as steadily as I could. "And you better wash that finger before you touch anything else in my kitchen," I scolded as I shook my finger at him and turned my attention back to the fudge. I tried to look away before I saw the sexy, mischievous smile on his face as he chuckled and muttered *yes ma'am* before walking over to the sink and washing his hands.

Two hours later, the kitchen was packed with boxes of fudge that had already cooled and were packaged as well as the pans that covered the island from the last ten batches we had made. Never in my life had I ever made this much fudge. My feet hurt and my back was aching but I was relieved that we had plenty to get us through the rest of the fair, maybe a little bit extra left over. Ruby and Parker had come by earlier with Ryder's mom, Arlene, to help deliver some of the fudge that was ready to take to Autumn.

"Well, I think you are officially out of everything you need to make fudge. Are you good or do you need me to run to the store and get more?" Ryder asked as he leaned back against the counter and looked around the room.

"I think we're good, this should be plenty." I let out a heavy, tired sigh and rubbed the back of my neck with my hand, hoping to get some relief from the headache that was starting to build.

"Alright, well let me know what you want to do with the rest of these and I'll help you finish packing them up. Are some of these for samples or are you doing more gift boxes?"

"I would love to make as many gift boxes as possible. Lord knows that I need this to be a successful day," I muttered, not realizing what I had said until I felt his gaze on me.

"Why is that?" he asked as he started working on cutting the fudge into neat squares to be boxed up.

"Oh, it's nothing. I was just rambling on." I waved my hand dismissively, hoping he would drop the subject.

"I know you better than that, Brooke. Even after ten years, I still know when you're lying. So spill it, what's going on?" He looked up at me with a look of concern on his face. I rolled my shoulders and looked at him, frustrated that he still knew me so well.

"Mr. Rey, the guy who owns the strip mall, recently decided that he needed to raise the rent for those of us who still pay rent. Since three out of five of the shops own their space, he is only able to raise the rent for two of us and it's going to be a little steep. I'm trying to figure out how to bring in extra money to afford the increase that he's proposing. It won't go into effect until February but that's not that far away so I've been trying to save up what I can now. I don't want to be blindsided by it when he finally decides what he's doing."

"Mr. Rey? The old man that was tormenting people before I left? He's still around?" He frowned as he kept working on cutting the rest of the fudge.

"Yeah, he's still around. And still tormenting people."

"My dad never mentioned anything about him, I guess I just figured he died," he said with a fake scared face which made me laugh.

"That's probably because your dad didn't have to deal with him anymore. He bought his shop a few years ago after the original owner of the strip mall decided to sell it. Everyone had the option to buy their shops and those of us who didn't got stuck with Mr. Rey. I wanted to buy mine outright but I didn't have the cash saved up for it." I smiled when I remembered sitting down and talking about my options with Ryder's dad before he passed. "You know, your dad offered to buy my shop for me. Offered me a loan that I could pay back over however long I needed. Anything to keep me from having to be indebted to Mr. Rey."

"Sounds like my dad," he smiled.

"Your dad was a good man, he really cared about this town and the people in it."

He nodded his head and looked away, sadness taking over the playful smile I had seen not that long ago.

"I'm sorry for bringing him up, I didn't mean to upset you," I said quietly as I worked on placing the cut fudge into the gift boxes.

"Don't be, it's nice to hear people talk about him. I just wish I would have come back sooner." He set the knife down on the counter and wiped his hands on the apron he was wearing. "And I'm sorry, I didn't know about the stuff with Mr. Rey. I feel like shit for opening a shop across from you when you're already busting your ass to find a way to stay afloat with the new rent increase. I should have looked into things more before I came barreling in and making a bigger mess of everything."

My shoulders slumped when I heard how remorseful he was. I never wanted him to feel bad about taking over his dad's shop. It wasn't like he was the reason I was working sixty hours a week and dreaming of burnt paninis when I actually got to sleep. I couldn't let him take the blame for the problems I had, they would have been there regardless of what he chose to do with the shop that his dad left him.

"Ryder, please don't feel bad. This has nothing to do with you.

This is because I didn't buy the shop when I had the chance. It was a choice that I made, not anyone else."

"Yeah, but now we have competing businesses and I have a shop that is paid for. I don't have the same stress or worries that you do and that's pretty shitty."

"Your dad wanted to leave that shop for you. He was so proud of you and used to tell everyone about the incredible stuff you were doing in Nashville. He would have wanted you to take that shop and turn it into something that you were passionate about. And you did. Don't feel bad about that, feel good that you're doing what he would have wanted you to do."

He nodded his head as he closed the lid on the last box of fudge and slapped a sticker on it. He pushed it to the side and laid his palms flat on the island as he looked at me.

"Well, at least now I know why you had daggers coming out of your eyes the first time you saw me when they were hanging up the sign at my shop," he laughed.

I rolled my eyes and laughed with him.

"There were other reasons too, but that was literally the worst timing ever. I had just finished meeting with Mr. Rey a few minutes before I saw the sign going up. It felt like such a punch to the gut when I just learned that not only was my rent going up but now I had direct competition not even fifty feet away. It was a bad day, to say the least, and I'm sorry I wasn't more welcoming."

We stood there, lost in the moment for a few seconds before I heard the bell chime up front as the door opened. I wasn't expecting anyone and the confused look on his face as he shrugged told me that he wasn't either. I grabbed my phone off of the counter behind me and tucked it into my pocket as I made my way up front with Ryder right behind me. As I swung the door open and walked into the room, I froze in my tracks.

"Hey, Ryder, they told me I would find you here…" A wicked smile crossed her face as she looked from me to Ryder.

"Lauren?" he asked as shocked as I was to see her. Everything became a blur after that as the pounding in my ears grew louder, blocking out the bullshit words that came spewing out of her mouth.

Twelve

Ryder

"What are you doing here, Lauren?" I asked sternly as I watched Brooke stare at her in disbelief. Lauren smiled smugly at her but thankfully I don't think Brooke had noticed it. I wasn't sure if she even realized that we were still here, she looked that dazed and out of it. Suddenly, she snapped out of it and looked at me, ignoring Lauren.

"I need to get these over to Autumn, can you lock up for me when you're done?" she asked without waiting for my answer. A few seconds later, she was gone, loading up the last of the gift boxes in the kitchen. I worked my jaw back and forth as I stared at Lauren, waiting for her to tell me why the hell she was there. She hadn't changed any since the last time I saw her. Her hair was a little bit longer with fresh highlights that contrasted against the dark sandy brown color of her hair.

"I came to see you, to be with you, silly," she said as she reached over and ran a hand up my arm before I pulled away. Her brown eyes went wide as she flinched at my reaction.

"That's bullshit and you know it," I scoffed as I looked over my shoulder to see Brooke coming out with a box filled to the top with gift boxes. "Let me help you with that," I offered, turning my attention away from Lauren.

"I'm fine. Thank you," she snapped coldly as she pushed past me and walked out the door. I closed my eyes, hating that everything had been going so well between us today, only to be ruined by this.

"There wasn't a life insurance policy, Lauren. If you came for money, I don't have any. Why don't you go back to Nashville and look for a new soul to steal?"

She brought a freshly manicured hand to her chest and stared at me as a single, perfectly timed tear slid down her cheek.

"I can't believe that you would honestly think so little of me." She sniffled, pulling out all of the stops.

"Really? What else am I supposed to think? You cheated on me for years, told me how I would never amount to anything and then sent me emails with the details of your fuck fests with whatever his name was."

Her face fell as she lowered her eyes and wrapped her arms around herself.

"I'm sorry, I was a terrible person back then. I was immature and needed to grow up. I didn't realize what a good man I had until I lost you. But I know it now, and I want another chance." She reached out to touch my arm again. "Please."

"Look, I don't have time for this. And honestly, I'm not interested in starting anything up with you. That was a mistake in the past and I'm not looking to make it again. If you don't mind, I need to go so I can help Brooke." I nodded toward the door, hoping she would get my not so subtle hint.

"It's always been her, hasn't it?" She tilted her head to the side and waited as she crossed her arms over her chest.

"Yeah, it has. And it always will be. Now, I need to-"

Suddenly the door flew open as Ruby rushed in, looking frantic.

"She's gone, I can't find her anywhere!"

"Who's gone?" I asked as I rushed over to where she was.

"Your mom, she's gone. I took my eyes off of her for two seconds to talk to the pastor and she must have started to wander. I'm so sorry, Ryder, I'm so sorry." Her lip trembled as I pulled her in for a quick hug.

"It's okay, we'll find her. But we better get going before it gets dark."

She nodded her head yes as I gently walked her outside, Lauren right behind us. I patted my pocket to make sure I still had the keys to the shop that Brooke had dropped earlier when she was trying to get the door open with her arms full. Relieved when I found them, I pushed past Lauren, pulled the door shut and locked it.

"I can help you guys look for her, what does she look like?" Lauren said cheerfully with a smile.

"If you don't remember what this boy's mama looks like, you're not here for the right reason little girl," Ruby snorted as she started walking toward Main Street with my arm wrapped around her. I let out a laugh as I gently squeezed her and forgot all about Lauren as we started making our way through the crowd that was already filling the street for the fair. I tried to keep myself calm so I could focus as I desperately searched for my mom.

Thirteen

Brooke

"Thank you so much, have a Merry Christmas," I said with a smile as I handed the Crosbys the stack of gift boxes they had just purchased. They were one of the cutest couples in Stone Creek and married the longest. I watched as they stuffed the boxes into the tote bag that was hanging on the side of his walker and got situated before she wrapped her arm in his and they walked off together.

"They are just the cutest," Autumn said as she looked to where I was looking.

"Yeah, they are," I smiled, envious of the love they had. I had been desperately trying to forget about Ryder and Lauren from the second I left the shop, but it seemed every couple at the Winter Fair wanted to wait until I was back before they stopped by my booth. Love was all around me and I was fighting the urge to vomit.

I looked off to the side, watching as the crowd of people moved around each other, laughter and voices filling the air. This was my favorite time of the year and I absolutely loved the Winter Fair. It never felt like Christmas until the fair, then the next few days felt magical leading up to Christmas. I was lost in thought when I heard Autumn talking to a customer, her voice calm and soft like it was when she was speaking to someone older.

"I'm sorry, who are you looking for?" Autumn asked as she leaned forward to try to hear the woman better.

"Walter, I need to find my Walter."

"Your walker?" Autumn pulled her brows together and gave her a few minutes to try to get her thoughts together.

"No, my WALTER. Where is he? I need Walter!" The rising panic in her voice immediately grabbed my attention as I looked over and saw Ryder's mom. It had been a while since I had seen her. Hell, it had been a while since anyone in town had seen her. She looked the same as I had remembered, only now she looked panicked and out of sorts.

"Arlene?" I asked gently, loud enough for her to hear me over the buzz of the voices around us. She turned to look at me, not recognizing me as she stared blankly at me.

"Do you know where my Walter is?" Her eyes started rapidly scanning the crowd behind her as I made my way out of the booth and walked over to her.

"Hey, why don't you come sit down and I'll see if I can help you?" I gently reached out and helped her turn around, walking her into the booth and helping her sit down on the folding metal chair behind the table. I bent down and squatted in front of her so I could make sure that I was at eye level before talking to her.

"Arlene, do you remember me? My name is Brooke. I own the bakery across the street from Walter's flower shop." I wasn't sure what was going on but she seemed very confused and I was worried that she was having a panic attack, looking for her dead husband.

"Yes," she said slowly as she started to smile. Her hands reached for mine and I scooted a little closer so she could hold them. "I remember you, dear. My Walter always says such nice things about you. He really likes your banana bread." She giggled and her eyes lit up. I felt the tears well up inside as I thought back to the last time I had made the banana bread she was talking about. It was probably at least two or three years ago, around the time Walter started to act more stressed and everyone stopped seeing Arlene around town.

"That's right," I said cheerfully.

"Do you know where he is?" she asked sadly, gripping my hands a little tighter.

I felt a lump in my throat as I struggled with what to say. I needed to find Ryder and let him know that his mom was here but I also couldn't leave her right now. I had no idea what to do so I did the only thing I could think of, I lied.

"I don't know where he is but I'm going to ask my friend, Autumn, to go find him," I assured her as I slowly stood up and leaned in closer to Autumn. "Go find Ryder and tell him that his mom is at our booth and hurry," I whispered to her. She nodded and grabbed her phone, shoving it in her pocket before she took off jogging through the crowd.

I sat in the empty seat next to Arlene and tried to keep her calm while I waited for Ryder.

"Would you like some fudge?" I asked as I reached over and grabbed one of the gift boxes. "It's white chocolate cranberry." I smiled big as I held the box out to her, feeling elated when she took it. She reminded me of a little girl on Christmas the way she carefully undid the red ribbon that was wrapped around it before opening the lid and picking up a piece. Her eyes lit up as she held it in the air, the sugar sprinkles glistening in the lights that were strung throughout the booth.

"This looks too good to eat," she joked as she took a bite and closed her eyes. "But, I'm going to eat it anyway. My Walter is really going to love this."

I smiled and looked away, relieved when a couple from out of town came up and started asking questions about the fair. It felt like Autumn was gone forever but it was only twenty minutes before she came running back, breathless, with Ryder right behind her. Not too far off in the distance was Ruby. I watched as Ryder's eyes darted around, looking for his mother before the couple in front of the booth walked away and he spotted her handing me the money. He walked up to the booth and looked down at his mother who had a huge smile on her face.

"What's going on, mom?" he asked with a smile that matched hers.

"I'm selling fudge!"

"You are?" His eyebrows shot up high on his forehead as he turned to look at me. I shook my head and shrugged, letting him know that it was nothing.

"She's done a great job, I might have to hire her full time," I joked.

"I take my eyes off of you for a few seconds and you go find the prettiest girl at the fair with the best treats?" Ruby teased as she came around the back and gave me a quick hug before leaning down to hug Arlene.

"Did anyone find Walter?" Arlene asked, looking between all of us.

"Why don't we get you home and we'll talk about it on the way?" Ruby said softly, reaching down to help her up.

"Okay, I am getting tired." Arlene stood up and steadied herself against Ruby before turning to me. "Thank you for keeping me company, sometimes I get so lonely and I feel a little lost."

"It was my pleasure," I replied as steadily as I could. "Don't forget your fudge." I nodded toward the box, happy to see her smiling again as she picked it up.

"I can get her home if you want to stay at the fair," Ryder said to Ruby before she swatted his hand away as he tried to help Arlene walk.

"You go have fun, I'm tired too so I'll get her home and we'll talk later." She leaned in and planted a kiss on Ryder's

cheek before turning to smile at me. "Have a good night, dear, and thank you for taking care of Arlene."

"It wasn't a problem at all, have a good night too, Ruby."

We stayed in awkward silence for a few minutes until Ruby and Arlene were out of sight and on their way to Ruby's car.

"Thank you for taking care of her, I'm sorry if she was any trouble." Ryder stepped to the side to let a customer get to the booth where Autumn was waiting. I walked around and followed him off to the side of the street to talk in private.

"It wasn't a big deal at all, I promise. She seemed really confused though, is she okay?" I didn't want to pry or stick my nose in his business but I was genuinely concerned about her.

"She has Alzheimer's and it's gotten worse since my dad passed. Ruby tries to help me as much as possible but my dad didn't want everyone in town to know about it. He was afraid that people would start talking about her and treating her differently so we all agreed to keep it a secret. That's why no one sees her around town anymore." He lowered his head and ran a hand along the back of his neck.

"I'm so sorry, that has to be really tough. Has she had it for a long time?"

"A couple of years. My dad was handling it on his own and then when he passed, I knew that I needed to come down here so I could help out. I wasn't planning to come back but then everything happened so quickly and I feel like I haven't been able to catch my breath since."

His eyes met mine and I could see the pain and grief behind them. I felt terrible for the way I had treated him when he first got back, especially now that I knew everything he had been dealing with on his own that no one knew about. He selflessly gave up the life he had created for himself in Nashville to come back and take care of his mom. My heart tightened at the thought of how much he'd been through and how much he was still going through after seeing Arlene tonight. I wondered if he had to remind her daily that her husband had died?

"If there is ever anything that I can do to help, please let me know." I tilted my head to the side, hoping he would look at me and feel the emotion I felt for his situation.

"Thank you, I appreciate it."

Suddenly I saw Ryder's expression change as his face hardened and goosebumps tickled my skin. I didn't have to turn around to know who was behind me.

"Hey, I heard they found your mom. Looks like we can pick up where we left off," Lauren said as she grabbed his hand and started to pull him away. I chewed the inside of my cheek as I looked away.

"Yeah, I better get going," I said, giving a tight smile to both of them as I turned to walk away.

"Brooke…" he called as I kept walking without looking back.

Fourteen

Ryder

Sunday used to be my favorite day of the week because it was
the only day that I took off and tried to get the stuff done that
I needed to throughout the week. But today—today was by
far my least favorite day—ever. I had spent the night awake,
restless, trying to figure out how to get Brooke to talk to me so
I could make things right but every time I tried, Lauren got in
the way.

I had tried to talk to her a few times at the fair before
everything closed down. I even tried to help her pack up
and take everything back to her shop before I was quickly
dismissed. I tried calling her, thanks to Sheila who had taken
pity on me and given me her number, but she refused my calls.
And my voicemails. Even my text messages. I was two steps
away from walking over to her house and banging

on her door until she let me in before Parker talked me out of it and told me what a crazed lunatic I would look like.

So instead, I'd spent my night pacing around the kitchen until I came up with the brilliant plan to bake her an "I'm sorry" loaf of banana bread. Okay, so technically I made fifteen, but there was an entire bunch of bananas that were about to go bad and needed to be used. Around four this morning, I finally sat down in my dad's recliner and closed my eyes, hoping that there would be some sort of magic in the old thing and he would tell me what to do.

Two hours later, I was woken up by the sound of a frying pan clattering around in the kitchen when I found my mom attempting to fry some eggs for breakfast. I rushed in and pulled her away from the stove before she could burn herself and offered her a slice of banana bread to hold her over while I cooked breakfast. I felt bad that we were suddenly out of eggs—oops, but she seemed to forget all about them when she smelled the bacon cooking.

I yawned as I slid the bacon onto her plate and grabbed the toast that had just popped up in the toaster. I walked into the living room and smiled when I saw her curled up under a blanket in my dad's chair, watching tv. She looked so calm and relaxed that it started to make me feel the same way. I set our plates down on the coffee table and sat down on the couch beside her, thankful for a peaceful moment with her.

"Breakfast is ready, mom," I said, pulling her attention away from the tv.

"Thank you, son," she smiled warmly and reached over to pat

my hand. It took me a minute before I realized that for the first time since I had been back, she knew who I was. She wasn't confused, thinking that I was my dad.

"You know who I am?" I asked gently, turning to look at her. Her eyes were a dark green this morning and looked full of life.

"Yes, dear, I know who you are. Your dad told me that you were coming home soon, I've been expecting you." Her voice was cheerful and my heart sank when I realized that she wasn't as clear-headed as I had hoped.

"Dad's not here anymore, mom." I tried to force a smile on my face for her sake, but my body refused to do it.

"I know dear, he told me that too."

"What do you mean that he told you? When did you talk to dad?" I asked against my better judgment as I studied her.

"In my dream last night. Your dad comes to talk to me often or at least it feels like he does. I don't know how many times exactly. But he talks to me and keeps me company until he's ready to come back for me." She let out a heavy sigh before she turned to look at me. I tried to look away, to blink away the tears before she saw them but I was too late. She reached over and ran her thumb across my cheek, wiping the lone tear that had managed to escape.

"It's okay, dear, you don't have to be sad." She smiled and pulled her hand away as she turned back to watch the tv and I knew that my moment with her was over. I had lost her again.

We ate breakfast in silence as she watched her show and laughed at the slapstick comedy. I tried to loosen up and enjoy it but my mind was too busy focusing on everything else that I needed to get done. Ruby would be here soon to spend time with my mom so I could get to the shop to work on the custom orders that I needed to get going ASAP. It was three days until Christmas which left me exactly two days to get everything ready by noon on Christmas Eve. I was feeling the pressure as I checked on my mom one last time before going to the kitchen to clean up the mess. A few minutes later, I heard the front door open as Ruby walked in and smiled at me.

"Morning, sunshine. You look like shit," she joked as she pulled her coat off and hung it on the hook by the door before pulling her scarf around her neck and hanging it up as well. "How was your night or should I not ask?"

"I didn't get more than a few hours of sleep and that was after I was up until four baking over a dozen loaves of banana bread. I woke up to mom trying to cook herself breakfast."

"Oh, Lord. Was she okay?" Ruby's face fell as concern filled her eyes.

"Yeah, I got to her just in time. She had turned on all four burners without realizing she had turned on any of them. She was seconds away from catching the sleeve of her robe on fire when I walked in."

Ruby blew out a breath and folded her arms across her chest.

"We're going to have to do something else, it's getting worse with trying to keep her safe. You can't be here to watch her 24/7," Ruby said sympathetically.

"I know, I know," I sighed. I had been thinking the same thing all morning but still had yet to come up with a way to fix it.

"I'm not trying to overstep, you know that, but I could come live here with her if you want?"

"Ruby, I couldn't ask you to do that." I shook my head knowing that she would be giving up so much to do that for us.

"Why not?" She pulled her brows together and narrowed her eyes at me.

"Because you love that house, you've lived there as long as I've been alive. You have your own life and if you move in here with us, that life will be drastically changed." I explained as I worked on loading the dirty dishes into the dishwasher.

"Ryder, I loved that house when Johnny was still alive and our kids still came to visit. Now I'm there all by myself in that big house and I'll be honest with you—it gets a little lonely there sometimes. It's not full of the warmth and happiness that it used to have. That all disappeared a long time ago and that's okay. I still have memories of the happy times but I don't need a massive, empty house to keep me happy. I would rather be close to the people who still make me happy. And I need to feel *useful*," she said dramatically as her eyes almost popped out of her head.

I stopped for a minute and thought about what she was offering. While it would be great to have her here with me all the time to help with my mom, I still felt bad for taking advantage of her generosity.

"I feel like I would be taking advantage of you," I said cautiously.

"Oh hush," she waved her hand at me and shushed me. "I wouldn't offer to do it if I didn't want to. Besides, my youngest daughter is moving back with her husband and three kids—they could use the space without me in their hair all the time. But I don't want to be in yours either, so you'll need to be honest with me on whether you think this could even work."

"I would love to have you here, and I know my mom would love the company as well," I said with a warm smile and held my arms out for a hug. She wrapped her arms around me and for a moment it felt like a huge weight had been lifted.

"I will try to stay out of the way," she whispered before she pulled away.

"You could never be in the way, Ruby. Thank you for coming to help us, it means a lot to me."

She reached up and patted my cheek, the way she always did ever since I was a little boy.

"Well, I hate to rush off but I've got a ton on my to-do list today," I apologized as I glanced back at the sink full of dishes that didn't fit in the dishwasher.

"Don't worry about any of that, I'll take care of it later. Go, get your stuff done and don't forget to stop by and make amends with Brooke." She winked playfully.

"It's not that easy, but thanks." I forced another smile, feeling that heavy weight quickly returning.

"Sure it is. You love her. She loves you. Now you just fix whatever needs fixing and then you two can make up and be together," she said happily as she walked over to the sink and gently pushed me out of the way so she could get to the dishes.

"I don't think love is involved here, in fact, I'm pretty sure she's back to hating me," I winced as I said it and waited for her to ask what I had done this time.

She studied my face for a few seconds before turning her attention back to the sink full of dishes as she pushed them out of the way to slide the stopper in before turning the hot water on to fill the sink.

"There are a lot of things that I know nothing about in this life—technology, new slang, the inability of the youth in this town to wear pants that cover their ass—but one thing that I do know is true love when I see it. And Ryder, I've seen it between you and Brooke. Now it's up to you to show her how much you've loved her all along."

"We were starting to talk, and she even agreed to go on a date with me."

Ruby arched an eyebrow in surprise as a smug smile pulled across her face.

"Okay, so maybe she wasn't fully on board with it being a date, but either way—she agreed to have dinner with me. But then Lauren showed up and every time Brooke sees her, she just shuts down and walks away. I don't know how to get her to see that there's nothing between Lauren and me. It's like the worst decision of my life from ten years ago is this constant thorn in my side, intent on fucking up every chance I get with Brooke."

"Once you deal with the thorn, the pain will go away and the true beauty of the rose will shine through," Ruby replied softly.

I ran a hand down my face and shook my head before looking at her. It was way too early in the morning to be solving riddles.

"Okay, I have no idea what that's supposed to mean so I'm going to leave you with your Beauty and The Beast riddle while I get going or I'm never going to get anything done today." I leaned forward and planted a kiss on her cheek as she chuckled before I left.

Thirty minutes later, I was standing outside Brooke's door, freezing my ass off as the snow fell around me, holding a loaf of banana bread wrapped in saran wrap with a red bow on top. I waited a solid thirty seconds before I reached forward and rang the bell again, knowing she was inside as I had just heard her talking to someone a few seconds ago. I could hear her voice drift further away and wondered if she knew it was me at the door and was purposely not answering it.

I was about to ring it again when the door swung open and Sheila smiled at me from the other side. Her hair was pulled up into a knot on her head, looking like she had just woken up. Which she probably had given that she was still wearing red and green striped Elf looking pajamas. I bit down on the inside of my cheek to keep from laughing as I took in the sight.

"Good morning," I said as I tried to push the laughter out of my voice. I pressed my lips together in an attempt to keep from smiling and giving it away that I thought she looked ridiculous.

"Morning," she said, eyeing me carefully.

"Is Brooke here?" I asked as a gust of wind blew right past me, sending a cold chill through me.

"Maybe… depends on what you want." She raised an eyebrow as she made no attempts to move from the doorway. I arched my brow back at her and tilted my head to the side.

"Fine," she sighed as she grabbed the side of the door and pulled it back, making room for me to go inside. "You can come in but you better share whatever that is that you brought with you." She pointed toward the loaf of bread before walking past me and sitting down on the couch as Brooke walked into the living room and stopped in her tracks when she saw me. I burst out in laughter when I saw that she was wearing matching elf pajamas and looked as ridiculous as Sheila. I turned my head and pretended to cough, hoping that it would look believable. As I turned back around, I found her glaring at me, hands on her hips.

"I'm sorry, I wasn't expecting you two to match," I explained as I pointed a finger between the two of them. "I brought you a loaf of banana bread." I held it out for her even though she made no attempt to move any closer to grab it.

Sheila looked nervously between the two of us before getting up and grabbing it from me before returning to her spot on the couch.

"Thanks," she said cheerfully as Brooke and I remained in our silent stare down.

"Look, I wanted to talk to you about what happened last night," I said, taking a step toward her. She held up her hand and stopped me.

"Don't bother, it's fine. I've heard everything that I needed to hear."

I felt like my heart sank and formed a knot in my stomach.

"I don't have any idea what you've heard but I would really like it if you would at least let me tell you my side of the story."

"Look, whatever you thought this was going to be between us—it's not. I'm sorry, I'm glad that you're back as a friend but I don't mess around with guys who are engaged." Brooke's tone was so harsh and full of anger that I almost missed what she said.

I pulled my head back in confusion and turned to look at Sheila, hoping she would be able to help me shed some light on what had just happened. *Engaged??* What the actual fuck was going on?

"I'm sorry—what?" I asked as I turned my attention back to Brooke and took a step closer to her. She quickly took a step back, acting like she was afraid to be that close to me. Not that I blamed her, I usually treated people who were engaged like they had the plague too but for different reasons. Before Brooke, that was something that I had hoped I would never catch—feelings.

"Lauren told us last night about the big news," Sheila said quietly from the couch. "She showed us the ring and told us about how you guys had just gotten engaged before your dad died and that you had to come back right away to get things situated while she wrapped things up in Nashville. But now she's back for good since you guys are getting married here in the spring."

Her eyes locked onto mine and I saw the desperate plea of her asking me to tell her that it was all a huge lie, one big misunderstanding. The problem was- it wasn't.

Fifteen

Brooke

"You did the right thing," Sheila assured me as she covered her slice of banana bread in butter before leaning back against the couch to eat it. Ryder had left twenty minutes ago and I was still fuming from seeing him. After Lauren cornered Sheila and me in the parking lot last night and told us all about her engagement, I hadn't stopped being livid. Livid with Ryder. With myself. With the entire situation. At first, we brushed Lauren off as telling another lie for attention but when she held her hand out and showed us the vintage wedding ring that had once belonged to Ryder's grandma, we knew that she wasn't lying.

"I don't even know what the right thing is anymore," I mumbled as I shoved the last bite of bread into my mouth, not bothering to wipe away the crumbs that had fallen onto my shirt. I glanced down at the elf pajamas I was still wearing and shook my head, embarrassed that Ryder had seen me in them.

"At least this bread is really good, I was *starving,*" Sheila said as sat forward and grabbed the knife to cut another piece. More than half the loaf was already gone as we ate as if we hadn't had a meal in days.

"I'm surprised it's not covered in chocolate," I snorted, feeling petty but not having anything else to complain about.

"I bet it would be delicious covered in chocolate," she teased while wiggling her eyebrows suggestively. I rolled my eyes and pushed the plate away from me as I leaned back on the couch and pulled my legs up underneath me.

"You want everything covered in chocolate." I reached across and poked her leg with my toes.

"What can I say? I LOVE chocolate." She let out a dreamy sigh and batted her eyes at me.

"Well, I guess you missed your chance to have Ryder cover you in chocolate now that he's engaged."

"Oh please, he never wanted to cover anyone in chocolate but you. And from the look of how he was acting this morning, I think he still wants to."

"Sheila, he's ENGAGED. Like past the point of just seeing someone—he's about to marry someone and spend the rest of his life with them. I think that offer is long gone. And it should be, I don't mess around with a guy in a relationship." I shrugged my shoulders and tried to sound as tough as I wanted to feel.

"I just don't get why he would be flirting so much with you and then ask you to dinner, if he was engaged? That doesn't make any sense," Sheila said as she turned to face me on the couch.

"Well, maybe he's just that kind of guy? He knew that Lauren was cheating on him before he left—maybe it doesn't bother him. Maybe he's just a terrible guy and we never knew it."

Sheila was quiet for a few minutes before she spoke, thinking through what she wanted to say.

"Do you really believe that?"

"What?" I asked.

"That he's a terrible guy who would cheat on his fiancé with a woman he's been in love with all of his life?"

I swallowed hard to push away the emotion that was threatening to bubble up inside. It didn't matter what I thought. It was too late. He was with someone else and the past no longer mattered.

"No, I don't think he's a terrible guy," I said sadly. "I think he's a wonderful guy who stepped up to help a friend in need yesterday and who has gone out of his way to apologize for something he did ten years ago. But I also think that this wonderful, loving guy—he doesn't belong to me. He never has and he never will."

I pulled my hand up into my sleeve and used it to wipe away the tears that ran down my face, a harsh reminder of what my reality actually was.

Sixteen

Ryder

I was working on my eighth batch of chocolate truffles when I heard a knock on the door. I set down the silicone mold I had just finished washing and dried my hands on the towel that hung by the sink before going up front to see who was showing up on a Sunday. I was supposed to be closed. As I got closer to the door, it looked like whoever had been there was already gone. I unlocked the door and opened it, checking to see if there was possibly a package left outside since my car was in the parking lot. It would be odd but not unheard of in a small town. After all, everyone knew where you were at all times, whether you wanted them to or not.

As soon as I opened the door, I saw someone pop around from the side of the wall, scaring the shit out of me. My hand flew to my chest as I took a step back and glared at Lauren. She giggled and stepped closer, the smell of her perfume floating around her. I narrowed my eyes and glared at her before stepping to the side to block her from coming in. Her smile was quickly replaced with a pouty frown as she pursed her lips and looked up at me under the thick coat of mascara she was wearing.

"What are you doing here?" I snapped angrily.

"We need to talk," she said sweetly as she reached forward to touch my arm. I jerked back and she flinched the same way she did every time she's tried it since she's been back.

"The only thing we need to talk about is why you're still wearing the ring you were supposed to send back with Parker and why the fuck you've been going around town telling everyone that we're engaged and you're moving back to be with me."

Her brown eyes darkened, turning almost black, as she looked at me with anger etched on her face.

"Did you really think that you could end our engagement through a text message? Do you think that's how you break up with a girl like me?" she shrieked, forcing the vein in her forehead to protrude.

"You know as well as I do that we were never really engaged. The whole thing was a stupid, drunken mistake that I've regretted since the moment it happened. Why don't you just give me the ring back and you can be on your way, looking for the next soul to steal from some poor, unsuspecting chump?"

"I'm not here to return the ring," she said through gritted teeth. "I'm here to talk about our future and to make plans for it."

"Lauren, we don't have a future together and you know it. Like I've already told you, there wasn't a life insurance policy—I didn't inherit any butt loads of money. I'm as broke now as I was when you walked out and left me in Nashville."

She turned her head to the side and looked out at the parking lot as she worked her jaw back and forth in frustration. Her foot started to tap anxiously on the sidewalk while she tried to figure out a new angle.

"The ring, Lauren…" I said impatiently as I held out my hand. "Now!"

The stern tone in my voice startled her as she jumped and turned to face me, fear in her eyes. I blew out a heavy breath and raised my eyebrows at her as I stared her down, getting tired and frustrated with her games. I pushed my hand toward her and nodded down at it, her eyes following mine. She shook her head and rolled her eyes as she pulled the ring off of her finger and tossed it into my hand. My hand quickly closed around it before it bounced off and fell to the floor.

"Happy?" she sneered as she smirked at me.

"Tremendously," I taunted as I gave her the fake smile that I knew she hated. "Now, why don't you do us all a favor and go back to Nashville where you belong?"

"You just made the biggest mistake of your life, you know that?"

"No, I made that mistake ten years ago when I walked away from Brooke and fell for your bullshit and followed you to Nashville."

She licked her lips and I expected her to say something, instead, she turned on her heel and walked away. I watched as she stormed off, the sound of her boots fading in the distance. I slid the ring into my pocket and went back inside to finish the custom orders that felt like they would never end.

Not even ten minutes later, I was in the middle of another order of truffles when I heard a knock on the front door again. I grunted and walked up front, expecting to see Lauren back for more. Once again, there was no one at the door when I got there, making me even more irritated than I was before. I was about to turn around and go back to the kitchen when I heard another soft knock. I whipped the door open, having had enough of Lauren's bullshit.

"What the fuck do you want now?" I bit out before looking to see who was there.

Brooke's face dropped in surprise as she stared at me in disbelief.

"I'm sorry, apparently this isn't a good time," she said quickly as she turned to walk away. "Sorry for bothering you."

"Brooke," I called out as I leaned against the open door and smiled when she stopped and turned around, shoving her hands into her coat pocket as the snow blew around her. "Do you want to come inside and get out of the cold?"

She smiled tightly and nodded before rushing over and shivering as she slid in between me and the door. There was already a light dusting of snow in her hair which started to melt once she was inside where it was warm.

"I don't want to bother you if you're busy. You seemed mad," she said as I closed the door behind her and locked it.

"I thought you were Lauren," I explained with a heavy sigh. She nodded and looked away as if the topic of Lauren made her uncomfortable.

"I am not Lauren." She chewed her bottom lip nervously before glancing out the window to avoid looking at me.

"No, you certainly are not," I assured her, feeling more relaxed now that she was here. "So, what's up?" I asked as I started walking back to the kitchen and nodded for her to follow me. I realized then that I had been in her kitchen but she hadn't been in mine yet. It was a weird thing to feel proud about but I knew that if anyone would appreciate all of the work it took to convert the flower shop into a functional kitchen, it would be Brooke.

Her eyes were wide as she looked around in amazement, her fingers lightly running across the stainless steel surface of the counters as she walked around and took everything in.

"This is an incredible kitchen," she said cheerfully as she glanced over her shoulder to smile at me. "You would never know how big it is from the outside but now that I'm in here, I can't imagine going back to my small, rickety kitchen again," she teased.

"Well, you're welcome in here anytime but I have to warn you that I may put you to work if you're in here," I winked and walked over to the island to work on the truffles. Her smile spread across her face as she looked around and saw the stuff I was working on. She pushed her lips together to try to hold the laughter in and ended up snorting instead. I laughed as she turned around to try to hide her face while the blush crept up her fair skin.

"What's so funny?" I asked as I leaned forward and rested my palms on the island.

"Nothing," she snorted, bursting into another fit of laughter. "I'm sorry, really, it's not that funny," she insisted as she tried to be serious. I arched an eyebrow and waited.

"Fine," she laughed. "I was just wondering if there's anything that you don't cover in chocolate? But then I remembered that the bread wasn't dipped in chocolate this morning, so there ya go—I have my answer." Her eyes danced wildly with amusement as she watched my reaction.

"Trust me, I know my way around chocolate and I wouldn't be so quick to judge my skills if I were you." I winked as I pulled my lower lip in through my teeth and watched her squirm.

We stayed quiet, staring at each other for what felt like minutes. I was scared to look away and lose this moment with her. Suddenly she shifted her weight as her fingers started pulling at a loose thread in the sleeve of her coat and I knew that she was back to feeling anxious and nervous around me again.

"I just wanted to come by to say that I was sorry for how I reacted this morning and to thank you for the bread. Who you're dating—or rather, engaged to, isn't any of my business and it wasn't fair for me to treat you that way. It's not like we were dating." She shrugged and tilted her head to the side as if she was trying to remember if there was more that she wanted to say.

"You're welcome for the bread and you did have a right to react the way you did. I've made it very clear that I'm interested in you and recently admitted to having feelings for you before I left. Then, I asked you to have dinner with me and I spent the day helping you make fudge. I would hope that those things would show you how much you really mean to me, Brooke. And I'm sorry that you found out about the engagement before I could tell you, I really am." I ran a hand through my hair and prayed that she would be open to listening, given that she had that scared look on her face that usually meant she was about to run away. I needed her to listen to me and hear my side of what happened.

"I just don't get why you would go through all of that effort with me if you were engaged to Lauren?" She narrowed her eyes at me.

"It's a long story but I promise, I wasn't engaged to her. She just didn't want to believe it."

"I'm going to need more than that," she said with a laugh.

"Right after my dad died, I was sitting at home one night, holding this ring in my hand that was given to me after his funeral. My aunt told me that my dad wanted me to have the ring so I could find a woman who deserved me and spend my life with someone who made me happy. I had a couple of beers and the next thing I knew, I was buzzed. Lauren had been calling since I got back but I hadn't bothered to call her. Out of nowhere, she shows up, trying to be my 'friend'. Apparently, in my drunken stupor, I asked her to marry me and move back to Stone Creek with me," I sighed.

"I don't remember proposing to her, obviously, but the next day I woke up next to her in my bed and she was wearing the ring. She insisted that I was so romantic when I proposed to her and got furious when I told her that I didn't remember it. It's been a nightmare ever since."

"Do you think that you really proposed to her while you were drunk? That maybe it brought up feelings that you still had for her?"

"No, I honestly don't. I think Lauren found the ring and took advantage of the situation. She was way too anxious to help me with settling my dad's estate so I think she's just stayed around because she expects that there was a life insurance policy or some sort of inheritance that I haven't told her about."

"Well, that sounds like Lauren," she muttered and looked away.

"Yeah, it really does."

"I ran into her on my way over here today." She looked up and watched as anger flashed across my face. I hated that Lauren always had to be vengeful and knew that she was the one who had approached Brooke, again.

"Technically, I was on my way to my shop but she felt the need to stop me and tell me that you were all mine and that I could finally have her sloppy seconds because she was through with you. I wasn't planning to come over to see you but when she kept watching me with those hateful eyes, I came over just to spite her." She laughed and shook her head. "It's stupid and petty, I know."

"Well, then I guess I owe her a thank you," I said with a crooked smile.

"Why's that?"

"Because thanks to her, it got you over here so we could talk. I was starting to run out of ideas on how to get you to let down that damn wall you keep putting up every time I come around."

"I don't put up a wall…"

"Yes, you do, and it's ice-cold and frozen." I stepped around the side of the island and walked toward her.

"Are you insinuating that I'm ice cold?"

"Mmmhmm," I whispered as I stood in front of her, lowering my head to look at her. "But don't worry, I know exactly how to heat things up and thaw that frozen heart of yours."

"Does it involve chocolate?" she asked as she rubbed her lips together. I shook my head and smiled, pretending to be insulted as I gently reached out and put my hands on her hips. I felt her body immediately tense before she slowly exhaled and looked up at me.

"It sure does," I licked my lips suggestively. "Nice, warm, chocolate."

She giggled as I lowered my head and placed my lips on hers, feeling relieved when I felt her hand wrap around my head as she kissed me back.

Seventeen

Brooke

"I'm coming," I called as I pushed the gold hoop earring through my ear and stopped to glance at myself in the mirror as butterflies fluttered around in my stomach. I ran a hand down the front of my dress, feeling nervous about wearing it out in public. Sheila had convinced me to purchase it months ago, and then it sat in my closet the entire summer because I was too scared to wear it. The dress was a vibrant fuchsia color and hit right above my knee. It was fun and flowy, hugging my curves perfectly without being too tight or provocative. It was a whopping two degrees outside and the snow was steadily falling, but I wanted to look sexy for my first official date with Ryder.

It was Christmas Eve which meant that everything would be closing down early and we wouldn't have any dinner options unless we wanted to drive to another town. I had no idea what he had up his sleeve. He just said to get dressed up and be ready by seven. I pulled on the white faux fur coat that Sheila had loaned me for the date and grabbed my purse from the counter as I swung the door open and smiled. Ryder brought a hand to his mouth as he took a step back and looked me up and down, making me both anxious and horny at the same time. When was the last time that a guy had ever looked at me like that?

His cologne drifted in with the light gust of wind that blew past him, making me feel weak in the knees. He looked incredibly sexy in his dark denim jeans and navy cashmere sweater, a different look than I had seen him in before.

"You look incredible," he said softly as he stepped inside and gave me a quick kiss on the cheek.

"Thank you," I said with a smile, feeling giddy and excited to be with him.

"Are you ready to go?" He stepped to the side and held his hand out for me to walk in front of him. I glanced down at the snow that was sticking to the ground and started to reconsider whether I should go change into something that didn't involve a six-inch heel that would definitely break in the snow.

"Maybe I should change my shoes real quick, I don't want to risk falling or freezing my butt off in these," I said warily as I looked back at him.

"We're not going far, I think you'll be okay," he assured me with a smile as we walked outside and I locked the door behind us.

A few minutes later and we were pulling into the parking lot of the strip mall. I felt a bubble of disappointment when I realized where we were.

"Don't look so sad, you have no idea what I have planned for you," he joked as he put the car in park and hopped out before running to the other side to help me out. He held my elbow as he led me over to the door of his shop and quickly worked to unlock the door. A few seconds later, we walked inside and I waited while he went over to turn the lights on. It took a few seconds for the lights to come on but when they did I found a beautiful table in the middle of the room, set up for us.

It was a round table with a white tablecloth and a slim vase with a single red rose in the center. The table was set beautifully with matching china and a bucket filled with ice off to the side with champagne inside. Everything was perfect and reminded me of being in one of those fancy 5-star restaurants that I always see on tv. I looked over my shoulder and smiled at him, still in shock over how much effort he had put into this.

"I know everyone closes early tonight, so I thought I could make you dinner instead," he whispered in my ear as he came and stood behind me, wrapping his arms around my waist as I leaned against his tight chest.

"It's beautiful, thank you. But you didn't have to go through all of this trouble for me." I looked up at him and gave him a light kiss on the lips.

"That kiss alone was worth it," he teased before walking me over to the table and pulling out a chair for me to sit. "Have a seat and I'll be back in a few minutes. And while I'm gone, here's some champagne to get this evening started." He winked and pulled the cork out, the popping sound sending a thrill of excitement through me. Slowly, he poured some into each of the glasses on the table, handing me one before he rushed off to the kitchen.

I lifted the glass to my lips and took a sip, closing my eyes as the cold bubbles made their way down my throat. A few minutes later, he returned with two bowls of salad and a basket of fresh bread. Everything was perfect and I felt like royalty the way he was pampering me. After we finished our salad and bread, we sat together for a few minutes enjoying our champagne before the timer in the kitchen dinged to let him know that dinner was ready.

The kitchen door swung open as he carried our plates in, the robust aroma floating through the air as it made my stomach growl. He set my plate down in front of me, a thick piece of steak cooked just the way I liked it with a side of roasted potatoes and steamed asparagus. My mouth watered as I waited for him to get situated before diving in.

The room was quiet and peaceful as we ate, the soft sound of Christmas music playing overhead. I worked through eating as much as I could without making myself sick and finally had to throw in the towel. Literally. His eyes lit up when he looked over and saw my plate, nearly empty, as I leaned back and wished I had worn something a little looser than this dress.

"Did you enjoy dinner?" he asked as he raised his glass to his lips and took a drink.

"Very much, thank you," I replied softly. "Though it does make me regret wearing this dress. You know, it wasn't this tight when I left." I laughed and playfully pulled at the fabric of it.

"You can always take it off," he winked and leaned back in his chair.

"As tempting as that sounds, I'm not that kind of girl." I pursed my lips and narrowed my eyes.

"Just trying to be helpful." He laughed and held his hands up in defense.

"I'm sure you are," I laughed. "Besides, it wouldn't be fair that I was the only one who was naked…"

"If that's the problem, I have the solution," he said as he stood up and started to pull his sweater over his head. He stopped midway, showing me his ripped abs before pulling it back down and laughing. My heart was racing at the thought of him taking it off.

"Tease," I joked and took another sip of champagne. His eyebrows shot up and he tilted his head to look at me.

"Did you just call me a tease?"

"Yup."

"Oh baby, you have no idea just how much of a tease I can be," he said cockily as he slowly grabbed the bottom of his sweater and pulled it up and over his head. In one swift movement, he tossed it across the room and stalked toward me. I swallowed hard as I watched him, his eyes fixated on me as he got closer. He grabbed my hand and placed it on his stomach, slowly moving it down to the top of his jeans.

"You want more?" he asked, his voice suddenly gruff. His hand held mine firmly in place as I felt his breathing increase the longer I touched him. I crossed my legs and scooted closer to him, wanting to feel the heat that was coming from his body. I stared at him, his perfectly chiseled body, and thought about running my tongue across it.

"Do you want more, Brooke?" he asked again, this time there was new desperation in his voice. I nodded my head unable to speak. He sucked a deep breath in and pulled away, rushing off to the kitchen. I sat there stunned, trying to figure out what just happened when I saw him come back with a bottle of chocolate syrup. He handed it to me and nodded for me to take it.

"You're kidding, right?" I asked in disbelief. I had always heard of people using food items in foreplay but he wasn't actually serious about covering each other in chocolate. Was he?

"Not even a little. You wanted to know if there was anything that I don't cover in chocolate- here's your answer." He stood before me the same way he was a few seconds ago as I held the cold bottle of syrup in my hands. I looked up at him, uncertain of whether he was serious when he gave me the sexiest smile I had ever seen.

Slowly, I stood up and with a shaky hand, pulling open the top of the bottle before gently squirting it onto his chest. He sucked in a deep breath as the cold chocolate touched his skin and let it out steadily as he waited for me. I leaned closer and lowered my head, looking up at him from under my eyelashes as I trailed my tongue along the chocolate that was running down his chest. I felt his body react beneath my touch, spurring me to keep going. I lazily ran my tongue across his body, closing my eyes as I imagined things going further.

I moved my head lower, sliding my tongue along his stomach until I reached the top of his jeans. I dropped to my knees and looked up at him as I unbuttoned his jeans before slowly sliding the zipper down, letting them fall to his ankles. His eyes stayed watching me while I slid my hands up his thighs and pulled down his boxer briefs, freeing the massive erection that greeted me. I kept my eyes on him as I reached for the bottle of chocolate syrup and squirted it onto his dick. His eyes closed immediately as he took in a deep breath, his fists clenched by my head.

I leaned forward and licked the syrup, spreading it along the length of his cock before pulling back and taking him in my mouth. I heard him gasp as I took him in further, pushing as deep into my throat as possible. It was making me wet to feel how his body was responding to me as I pulled back and began to work his shaft with my hand while I sucked on his head. He was big, to say the least, and at one point, I had to use both hands to fully wrap around him while I sucked him harder. His breathing quickened as his hand reached out and grabbed a fistful of my hair, turning me on even more.

"Fuck, Brooke, I'm gonna come baby," he moaned breathlessly as I grabbed onto him even tighter and quickened my pace as his body trembled in front of me, hot liquid shooting down the back of my throat.

Once I knew that he was done, I slowly pulled him out of my mouth and stood up. He was gorgeous in his jeans and fitted sweater, but he was downright sexy standing in front of me completely naked.

"That was fucking incredible," he mumbled as I leaned up to kiss him on the cheek. He turned my head toward him with his finger and kissed me deeply, wrapping his arms around me as he reached down and grabbed my ass.

"Now it's my turn to make you feel incredible," he said as he grabbed my ass and lifted me up, my legs wrapping around his waist as the sheer fabric of my panties felt the warmth of his dick. His fingers gently spread my ass cheeks apart, forcing the thin piece of my thong to ride up. He walked over and sat me down on one of the longer tables by the window and stepped back. I quickly reached down to fix my dress when his hand reached over and stopped me as he shook his head no. I glanced behind me, the cold chill from the glass window reminding me that we were at the very front of the shop and that if anyone were walking by, they would be able to see us.

"What if someone sees us?" I asked as I nodded to the window behind me.

"They can watch me fuck you as an early Christmas present," he answered as he moved closer, still fully naked as his dick started to get hard again. My eyes went wide at the thought of someone watching.

"Does that bother you? Knowing that someone might be watching as I eat you out?" He stood in front of me and gently moved my hair to the side as he reached behind me to unzip my dress. He pulled the zipper down slowly as he kept talking quietly in my ear. "What if they stop and watch as I finger you?

Maybe it's a guy who finds it so fucking hot that he whips his dick out and jacks off while he watches us. Do you want that? Do you want some other guy to come while he watches me fuck you, Brooke?"

I was panting, my chest heaving, my body desperate for him to touch me.

"Yes," I moaned as he slid the fabric of the dress down my body, letting it pool at my waist. He stepped back and looked at me while I squirmed anxiously.

"Take off your bra," he instructed as he reached down and grabbed his cock. I felt the air rush out of me as I watched, the site of it exhilarating.

I reached back and unhooked my bra, letting it fall as his eyes stayed glued to me while his hand worked himself faster.

"Lay down on the table and take your dress off."

I nodded and slowly did as he asked, making sure to keep my balance so I didn't fall. The table was long and felt sturdy enough, but I didn't want to risk anything. I was about to reach down and take my heels off when he stopped me.

"Leave them on," he whispered. "Same with your panties."

I smiled nervously and laid down, feeling on display as he walked over and bent down in front of me. He reached down and pushed my panties to the side as he kissed my pussy, catching me off guard. My head whipped up as I looked down at him. I wasn't against oral sex, not by any means, but I definitely wasn't expecting him to just dive on in. I gave him a puzzled look before he looked up above us and laughed.

"Mistletoe," he nodded at it. "It doesn't specify where I get to kiss you so I figured I would just take advantage and go for what I wanted."

"I'm surprised it's not covered in chocolate," I teased as I laid back down.

"No, but you're about to be," he murmured as he rushed over and grabbed the bottle from the table where I had left it. Within seconds I felt the cold rush as it drizzled across my body before the warmth of his tongue started to lick it up. My body was on fire as his tongue worked it's magic on me, forcing me over the edge as I screamed his name while riding my orgasm on the cold surface of the table beneath me.

I was feeling on top of the world when he made his way back up, looking completely satisfied himself with chocolate smeared on his chin and cheeks. He helped me up and I thought we were going to move somewhere else to finish. Instead, he pushed the tables apart and had me stand behind one of them as he gently spread my legs apart while I was still wearing my heels. He leaned forward and kissed the back of my neck as he plowed into me, taking me from behind in front of the window.

"I bet his dick is so hard right now, watching me fuck your tight little pussy. I bet he wishes he was in here with us. He could stand in front of you while you suck his huge cock, taking him down your throat while my dick fucks you from behind. Do you want that, Brooke?" he groaned as he pounded me even harder. Suddenly, I imagined the picture he was describing and felt like I was going to come again.

"Yes, Ryder, yes! I want that so bad," I screamed as I reached down and pinched my nipple with one hand, bracing myself against the table with the other while he fucked me with my panties still on. A few seconds later I was climaxing a second time while he came inside of me.

132

Eighteen

Ryder

Last night had been absolutely amazing with Brooke and I was still grinning about it this morning when I sat down with my mom and Ruby to open presents. The night had been exactly what I had hoped it would be- easy going and romantic, but then it took a turn and ended up being hotter than hell.

In all of my wildest fantasies, I never would have pictured Brooke being such a sexual person but I loved that about her. The way her beautiful face looked as she held me in her mouth, sucking me dry. Or the way her body responded to my touch, coming undone with the dirty words I whispered in her ear as I plowed into her. I would have bet money that she was a sweet, gentle lover but after last night I was itching to see what else she liked.

After we finished opening gifts, I wandered into the kitchen to fix a late breakfast, biding my time while I knew Brooke was at her parents' house for Christmas. She mentioned that she planned to be home around lunchtime so we could get together before her dinner plans. I was anxious to see her and felt down that I couldn't spend the entire day with her, but we had also both agreed that we would wait a little longer before we started telling anyone that we were dating.

"So I heard you had your own little Christmas party last night," Ruby said slyly as she buttered her toast before looking up at me.

"Hmm?" I pretended not to know what she was talking about as I shoved a fork full of scrambled eggs into my mouth and chewed.

"Really? Okay," she laughed and held her hands up. "I won't pry but I will say that a little birdie told me they saw you with a pretty girl going into your shop last night, and both of you looked dressed to the nines. Maybe like you were on a date?"

She wiggled her eyebrows and laughed, causing me to laugh as I tried to avoid the knowing look she was giving me.

"Okay," I said as I set my fork down on the plate and pushed it away. I wiped my mouth with a napkin then turned my attention to Ruby. "I took Brooke there last night as our first official date, and I made her dinner. That's all there is to it. Just a friendly, first date." I shrugged and leaned back against the couch and raised my cup to take a sip of coffee.

"From what I heard— it was more than just "friendly" from what you did in front of the window."

I spit coffee across the room, feeling the burn as it came out of my nose. I reached for the napkin and started to dry my face as Ruby burst into laughter next to me.

"Oh man, I was just waiting to see if I could get a rise out of you but I didn't think you'd really fall for it!" She laughed louder as she slapped her knee. My mom turned her attention from her show on tv and smiled as she watched us, not having any idea what had just happened.

I finished cleaning up the mess, too embarrassed to look at Ruby knowing that she would know there was truth to what she had said about the window. I kept my head down and cleaned the coffee table so it was cleaner than the day my dad bought it. I tossed the used napkin on my plate and got up, clearing the other plates as I shook my head and laughed.

It was finally time to go see Brooke so I said goodbye as quickly as I could and snuck out of the house before anyone could ask where I was going. As if she was just as excited to see me as I was to see her, Brooke was waiting at the door as soon as I pulled up. I grabbed her gift from the passenger seat before I got out and jogged up the few steps to her door, my spirits dropping when I saw the look on her face.

"Hey, Merry Christmas," I said as I wrapped her in a hug. I was relieved when she hugged me tightly, knowing that I wasn't the problem. "What's wrong?" I asked as I pulled back and looked at her. I could tell she had been crying, her makeup slightly smudged under her eyes. She shook her head and we walked inside as she closed the door behind us.

"Brooke, what happened? Why are you so upset? Did something happen at your parent's house?"

"No, no, nothing like that," she sighed and sat on the couch as I followed and sat next to her. She reached over and picked up an envelope off of the coffee table, handing it to me. "That was under my door when I got back from my parents."

I opened the envelope and pulled out a letter from the scumbag landlord at the strip mall. The letter had been typed up and a sloppy signature from him attached to the bottom. I quickly scanned it again, not believing what I was reading. In bold letters in the middle of the page was the confirmation that he was raising her rent by almost $500 a month, effective February 1st.

"You've got to be kidding me," I mumbled as I ran a hand down my face. "This guy has some nerve."

"You're telling me." She leaned forward and folded her hands together in her lap. "I have no idea what I'm going to do. Obviously, there's no way I'm going to be able to come up with an extra $500 in rent by February, and my only other option is to back out of the lease agreement and find another place. But that would also mean that I would have to spend money that I don't have and build something from the ground up." She looked at me and took a deep breath before leaning back and cuddling one of the throw pillows in between us.

My mind was racing, going back and forth between thoughts of how to cheer her up and how to smash someone's head in without getting caught. Suddenly, I had the perfect idea and prayed that she would jump on board.

"Move in with me," I blurted out, getting a panicked look from her in return.

"Not like- move into my house- move in, but move into my shop with me. We can combine our businesses and have a one-stop-shop where people can get a variety of sweet treats."

"You're crazy, I couldn't do that." She shook her head and eyed me as if I might be on drugs.

"Why not? There's plenty of room for both of us, you've been in the kitchen and loved it. We make similar stuff so it's not like we'll have clashing aromas. It's perfect." I smiled, hoping she would consider it.

"I don't know..."

"What else are you going to do? You said it yourself that your only other option is to back out of the lease and find something else. This can be that something else."

"Are you sure you want to be around me all the time? Can we even work together without getting in each other's way? And what would I do about Autumn?" Her questions came out in one long-winded breath that had a hint of excitement.

"We seemed to do just fine the other day when we worked on the fudge together. There's also the other half of the kitchen that's empty— I can get another counter and an extra fridge so we both have our own designated space. And I don't have anyone up front so Autumn can come on board too."

"Okay, this might actually work. What is the monthly rent?" she asked as her eyes lit up.

"Zero."

"No Ryder, I want to pay my share. Please give me a number and as long as it's lower than the one on that paper you have a deal."

"I'm not going to charge you, Brooke."

"Why not?"

"Because you don't worry about stuff like that with someone you love," I said quietly.

"Someone you love?" She raised her eyebrows as hope flashed across her face. I nodded yes and looked deep into her eyes.

"Brooke Hansen, I knew I loved you in sixth grade when you were the only girl who didn't freak out when we had to dissect the frog in science class. You shed one single tear and said your goodbye before you jumped on in. I love that you go after what you want in life, and I hope that will always be me. I love you."

"I love you too, Ryder," she whispered as she leaned over and wrapped her arms around my neck to kiss me. As she pulled away, I instantly missed the way her lips felt on mine.

"I made you something for Christmas," she said happily as she reached over and grabbed a neatly wrapped box and handed it to me. I smiled and reached for hers that I had set on the table.

"Okay, but open mine first," I insisted as I handed it to her. She smiled as she took it and slid the ribbon off before her grin spread across her face as she opened it and pulled out a piece of chocolate-covered mistletoe.
"I know how much you've been looking forward to the

chocolate covered mistletoe," I teased as I reached over and grabbed it, slowly moving it over her body like a metal detector. "But the real gift is that you get to pick where the mistletoe lands and where you want me to kiss first."

I watched as her cheeks flushed before her hand lowered the mistletoe exactly where I wanted it. I quietly mumbled *ho ho ho* in her ear before giving her the gift she *really* wanted.

Four hours later, she was scrambling to slide her shoes on as we rushed out the door to head over to Sheila's house for dinner. We were already late but after her last orgasm, neither of us was able to move as quickly as we needed to.

"Does she know I'm coming with you?" I asked as I glanced over at Brooke sitting next to me in the passenger seat.

"I didn't have a chance to tell her but it's Sheila and she loves surprises. She'll be thrilled you're there."

I felt guilty for showing up unexpectedly but once Sheila opened the door and saw me, her face lit up brighter than her giant Christmas tree in the corner as she wrapped her arms around me and pulled me in for a hug.

"I'm so happy you are joining us!" She exclaimed as we walked in and hung our coats on the rack by the door.

"Thank you for having me, I'm sorry about the last-minute surprise," I said apologetically.

"Don't worry about it, the more the merrier," she brushed me off and walked past us into the kitchen where she grabbed two glasses of wine and turned to hand them to us. "Besides, it's nice to have company this time of year," she smiled and looked past us at Parker who was sitting at the table playing a game of Uno with her kids. I wrapped my arm around Brooke's waist and pulled her close to me as I felt my heart overflowing with happiness.

Epilogue

Brooke

"Hey buddy, you're in my work space," I giggled, Ryder's hands sliding around my waist as I tried to frost the cake I was working on.

"I can't help myself, that cake looks good enough to eat but you look even better," he teased, his voice low in my ear as he planted kisses down my neck.

"Your face is cold." I shivered as a chill ran through me.

"Yeah, it started snowing again as I was leaving the store. It's supposed to come down pretty heavy the rest of the day. I'm hoping we can still make it to our reservation but if not, I'll make you a nice dinner here like I did for Christmas Eve…" His hand slid up my waist and cupped my breast, forcing me to drop the spatula in my hand before I ruined the cake. I leaned against him and enjoyed feeling his hands roam over my body.

"Christmas Eve was great, but I think New Year's Eve was even better," I said as I tilted my head up and kissed his chin, the scruff of his beard tickling my lips.

"Mmmm," he murmured against my ear as he pressed himself against me from behind. "Who knew that champagne would still be so bubbly when you licked it off someone's stomach?" he teased as he stepped back and let go of me. We both knew that if we didn't stop now, we would be naked and going at it, and this cake wouldn't be ready by two-thirty when Mrs. Forsythe came in to pick it up. I turned to look at him, smiling when I saw him pull off the black beanie that I had knitted him for Christmas. It was a last-minute gift idea and I was so nervous that he would hate it. He's proudly worn it almost every day, except for when I bug him to wash it every now and then.

I went back to working on the cake, smoothing out the sides before adding a few decorative flowers to the top of it. Once everything was finished, I added the cake topper and stepped back to look at my work. I heard the bell ding up front, knowing that Mrs. Forsythe was here for the cake. I carefully slid it into the box and closed the lid. It felt good to be working at a slower pace than I was before the holidays and for once, I wasn't slammed with orders while adding on the stress of creating a larger menu that I honestly couldn't keep up with if I tried.

I walked up front and got a big hug from Mrs. Forsythe before she rushed off with the cake for the baby shower she was hosting in a few hours. The day was quiet for the most part, though we did have a rush this morning with a few stragglers coming in to get chocolates *after* they had realized it was Valentine's Day and hadn't thought to get anything ahead of time. Everyone else had placed custom orders with Ryder for his chocolate-covered strawberries or chocolate truffles. We had spent the past few days working for hours on the custom orders, all of which had been picked up this morning.

I pushed myself up on the counter behind the register and wrapped my legs around Ryder's waist as he stood in front of me. Slowly I leaned forward and kissed him, feeling all of the stress and tension melt away as his hands stretched across my thighs. He reached forward and grabbed my ass, pulling me closer to him as we deepened the kiss. Out of nowhere, the door opened and the bell chimed as we pulled apart and looked to see who had come in.

"Ugh, you guys really need to get a room. No one needs to see that," Sheila whined as she walked over and sat down at one of the tables across from where we were. She pulled her gloves off and tossed them on the table in front of her. "Especially not those of us who are alone and sad on Valentine's Day."

I jumped down off the counter and walked over to sit by her, squeezing her shoulders gently as I passed by. I pulled the chair out and sat down, offering her the goofiest smile I could come up with. She rolled her eyes and looked away, trying to pretend that she didn't think it was funny. I crossed my eyes and pushed the tip of my nose up as I started snorting, making myself look absolutely ridiculous. Suddenly she burst into laughter, leaning back in her chair as she started to relax.

"There, now that's better," I said as I leaned back and smiled.

"Where are the kids today?"

"Oliver is out shopping for his girlfriend and took Megan along with him so she could help. Thomas and Sally are with their dad, trying to help him find the perfect ring so he can propose to his new girlfriend."

"No!" I gasped and covered my mouth. "He's going to *marry* her? They barely know each other…" I knew that they had started to get serious at Christmas but surely they weren't ready to get married six weeks later. My heart ached for Sheila knowing that even though she didn't want to be with Rodney, it still wasn't easy for her to hear about him getting married either. Suddenly I felt my anxiety start to build when I thought about whether to share our news with her today or wait a while. Like a long, long while.

"He says that it's true love and the kids seem to love her, so I guess it is what it is." She shrugged, the sad puppy look returning to her face.

"I'm sorry, honey. I know that this isn't easy for you." I reached over and squeezed her hand. "Do you want something sweet to cheer you up?"

"I figured you guys would be sold out, with everyone being in love and all," she sighed. "Does Ryder have any chocolate covered strawberries left, or are those gone with my hopes and dreams?" She glanced over at him as he stood behind the register and listened.

"Don't worry, girl. I got you," he winked and walked back to the kitchen. I had no idea what he was up to since I knew damn well that there weren't any strawberries left after we used the last of them this morning for a last-minute order.

"How are things going between you guys?" Sheila asked once he was gone.

"It's going good," I sighed and thought about how much to get into with her, and how long before Ryder came back.

"Oh come on, I might be lonely and depressed but that doesn't mean that I don't want all the juicy gossip." She lightly smacked my arm and laughed. I rolled my eyes and shook my head, glancing at the kitchen door to make sure he was still back there.

"Things are good. Ruby has been really helpful with taking care of his mom which has taken a lot of the stress off of him that he was feeling when he first came back. We've been spending so much time together that we kind of decided to live together…" I swallowed hard and looked up at her as I waited for her reaction.

"Oh. My. Gosh!" she squealed excitedly. "Brooke—that's amazing! I'm so happy for you guys!"

"Thanks," I said, relieved that she wasn't upset about it. I knew that Sheila was a sensitive person and I didn't want to add any additional upsetting news to what she had already been given today. "He's been staying at my house and we found that it works better for everyone. Ruby is handling everything there and we still go by and visit a few times a week to check in on his mom. But overall, everyone seems to be adjusting to the changes easily."

"Maybe because it's just meant to be for you guys to be

together. And then you guys can get engaged and start having babies, and live happily ever after."

"I think you're a few steps ahead of us," I joked. Ryder and I had talked a lot about our future recently and both agreed that marriage and kids could wait a while. We weren't in a hurry to rush into anything. For now, we just wanted to enjoy our time with each other.

"Well, all in due time. But at least you guys are doing good working together AND living together. That has to say something about your relationship."

"I am honestly so surprised by how easy it's been working together. We don't get in each other's way and that kitchen is so big that we can do our own thing and not worry about what the other is doing. It's been wonderful. And, I'm really grateful that I don't have to worry about Mr. Rey anymore. Or busting my ass to come up with the extra $500 a month that he wanted. I'm kind of sad that they're already putting something else in over there but it was time to move on."

"Have you guys come up with a name for this one? Or is it just going to be 'the sweet shop' like everyone around town has been calling it?"

"Ugh," I groaned. "That's the one thing that we can't agree on. Neither of us can think of a name that fits both sides. He does a lot of fancy chocolates and I bake a lot of cakes and pastries. There just doesn't seem to be a name that fits both. Or at least not one that we both like."

"Alright, *The Sweet Shop* it is," she laughed.

I laughed with her, straining to listen as I heard Ryder's voice in the kitchen. Once I realized that he was probably

on the phone and not talking to me, I stopped listening and shifted my attention back to Sheila.

"So, have you heard from Parker?" I asked cautiously, hoping that I wasn't bringing up another sore subject.

"No," she sighed heavily and sunk lower in her chair. "Last I heard, he made it back to Nashville but I haven't heard much from him since then. It's my own stupid fault for liking someone who doesn't even live here."

"Maybe you should try to call him? I know things ended awkwardly for you guys but maybe he's feeling too scared to reach out to you?"

"Awkward is an understatement. We had a one night stand on New Year's Eve after we decided that when the ball dropped, so should our pants. It was fun, and it was definitely good—but maybe next time I shouldn't jump the first drunk guy I see."

"I think you're being a little hard on yourself. It's not like you didn't know him and he was some stranger. You guys spent almost every day together from Christmas to New Year's and were texting nonstop when you weren't together. He was just as interested in you as you were him."

"Maybe…" She took a deep breath and slowly let it out. "But it still feels weird. He left shortly after that and we've barely talked since then, other than him letting me know he got there okay. It felt more like he was one of my kids checking in, than a possible boyfriend."

I pulled my lips into a thin line, feeling bad for her that she was having to go through this. I had asked Ryder several times if he knew what was going on with Parker but either he was lying to me or he really hadn't heard from him either.

"I'm sorry honey, I really am. I know how much you liked him."

She nodded as we heard the door to the kitchen swing open and Ryder walked out, carrying a plate of chocolate-covered strawberries. I arched a brow as I looked up at him, wondering where they came from. He held the plate out for Sheila, waiting for her to take one, as he winked playfully at me. Next, he extended the plate to me for me to take one of the last two strawberries. I picked one up and watched as he sat down on the other side and lifted the last strawberry from the plate.

"Happy Valentine's Day, ladies," he said as he lifted his chocolate-covered strawberry in the air to cheers us. "I hope that you feel loved every day of the year and that you feel cherished today."

Sheila took a bite of her strawberry after tapping it against Ryder's, a look of disappointment sitting heavy on her face as she chewed it.

"Don't look so sad, Sheila," Ryder said playfully. My eyes almost bulged out of my head as I kicked him under the table, trying to pull his attention away from her so he didn't make things worse. When he looked at me, I raised both eyebrows and gave him a pointed look.

"What?" he shrugged innocently as he shrugged his shoulders. "Can't I be the optimistic one who thinks her day might just turn around?"

I gave him a puzzled look as I watched the smug smile spread across his face. A few seconds later we heard the door open and the bell chimed. My eyes spotted him first, staring in disbelief at what I was seeing as he walked in and headed for our table.

"Excuse me, miss, I was wondering if you had plans tonight?" His voice was low as he stood behind Sheila, a smile spread across his face as he held a beautiful bouquet of red roses in one hand and a box of chocolates in the other. Slowly, she turned around, her face lighting up as she saw him. She dropped the rest of her strawberry to the table and jumped up, her hands covering her mouth as she stared at him.

"Is that a yes?" he asked playfully before reaching out to offer her the roses. Her hands trembled as she took them, the smile still plastered on her face.

"Yes, Parker, that's a yes," she said happily and wrapped her arms around his neck as she kissed him.

"See," Ryder said, leaning across the table to talk to me. "Sometimes everyone gets a chance to be happy."

I smiled and leaned over to kiss him, knowing that he was right. For once, everyone was happy and things felt like they were going in the right direction.

Chocolate Covered Mistletoe Desserts

I want to thank my wonderful readers who sent me some of their favorite holiday dessert recipes, some of which were used in the book. As a special treat, I'm including a few of them here for everyone to enjoy!

Please note that I am not the person who created these recipes nor am I taking credit for them. Recipes were received from multiple readers who wanted to share their favorite desserts with others. Any likeness to other recipes found in general search results is purely coincidental.

152

White Chocolate Cranberry Fudge

Ingredients:
6 oz dried sweetened cranberries
2 - 12 oz bags of white chocolate chips
1 tsp vanilla extract
14 oz can sweetened condensed milk
Pinch of salt
Sparkling sugar sprinkles (optional)

Directions:

1. Line an 8x8 pan with parchment paper, making sure to cover the sides of the pan.

2. Combine white chocolate chips and sweetened condensed milk in a large microwave safe bowl and cook for one minute, then stir to combine. Continue stirring so the ingredients can melt together, however it may need an additional 30 seconds in the microwave. Continue to stir until it's completely melted together.

3. Once melted, combine the salt, vanilla extract, and dried cranberries. Mix thoroughly before using a spatula to pour into an 8x8 baking pan. After the fudge has been poured into the pan, you can add the sparking sugar sprinkles, making sure to press them into the top of the fudge.

4. Set fudge in the fridge for a few hours to allow it to set up completely before cutting. Be sure to store the fudge in an air tight container, either at room temperature or in the refrigerator.

Peppermint Chocolate Dipped Oreo Balls

Ingredients:

16 ounces of white chocolate (melting wafers or chocolate chips)
1 Package of Oreo cookies
8 oz cream cheese
½ tsp peppermint extract
48 crushed peppermint candies

Directions:

1. Use a food processor to mix the Oreos and cream cheese together until well combined. If you don't have a food processor, you can use a rolling pin to crush the Oreos inside of a Ziplock bag, then combine with the cream cheese. Make sure both are mixed thoroughly.

2. Using a spoon or an ice cream scooper, scoop out small balls of the mixture and roll into 48 balls. Place the balls on a parchment paper lined cookie sheet and freeze for thirty minutes, or until hard.

3. While the balls are freezing, use a rolling pin to crush the peppermint candies into smaller pieces. Spread them out on a piece of parchment paper and set to the side for later.

4. Once the balls are firm, take them from the freezer and set them to the side while melting the chocolate for dipping.

5. In a large, microwave safe bowl, combine the white chocolate and peppermint extract. Start out with melting in 30 second increments, stirring between each one, until fully melted.

6. Using a fork, dip each ball into the chocolate, then roll it in the crushed peppermint candies. Once fully coated, transfer them to a clean piece of parchment paper to allow them to harden.

Be sure to store peppermint chocolate dipped Oreo balls in the fridge (for food safety)

156

Candied Pecans

<u>Ingredients:</u>

2 cups pecans
4 Tbsp salted butter
3 Tbsp brown sugar
1 Tbsp white sugar
1 tsp cinnamon
Pinch of Salt

<u>Directions:</u>

1. Melt butter on medium-high heat.

2. Add in the pecans, making sure to coat each one while constantly stirring.

3. Next, add in the brown sugar, white sugar, cinnamon and salt. Stir constantly until the sugar is completely melted.

4. Spread on parchment paper to cool.

158

Chocolate Truffles

Ingredients:
2- 4 oz Semi-sweet chocolate bars
2/3 cup Heavy cream
1/2 tsp Vanilla extract
Toppings: unsweetened cocoa powder, crushed nuts, or
sprinkles.

Directions:
1. Chop the chocolate into small pieces and set aside in a heat safe bowl.

2. Place the cream in a sauce pan over medium heat and cook for 2-3 minutes or until cream is simmering.

3. Pour the cream over the chopped chocolate and allow the mixture to rest for 3-5 minutes, allowing the cream to melt the chocolate.

4. Add in the vanilla extract and slowly stir until the chocolate has completely melted. Cover the top tightly with a piece of plastic wrap to avoid condensation. Refrigerate for one hour, or until firm.

5. Scoop the mixture into 1 tablespoon-sized mounds, then roll each one into a ball shape. If the chocolate gets too soft and starts to melt, you can chill it until it becomes easier to work with again.

6. Roll each ball into the desired toppings then place them on a parchment paper lined cookie sheet. Return them to the fridge to chill until firm.

7. Store your truffles in an airtight container in the refrigerator. Be sure to take them out at least fifteen minutes before serving to allow them to be enjoyed at room temperature.

Decadent Irish Cream Fudge

<u>Ingredients:</u>

2 cups milk chocolate or semisweet chocolate chips
1/2 cup sweetened condensed milk
1/4 cup Bailey's or other Irish Cream Liqueur
1 teaspoon vanilla extract

<u>Directions:</u>

1. Line a pan with parchment paper and set aside.

2. Add the chocolate chips and sweetened condensed milk to a microwave safe bowl and heat for 30 seconds. Stir with a spoon to make sure the chocolate is mixing with the sweetened condensed milk, microwaving for another 30 seconds if needed. Be careful not to overheat and burn the chocolate.

3. Once the mixture is melted, add in the Bailey's and vanilla extract.

4. Use a spatula to pour the fudge into the pan, smoothing out the top after scraping the sides of the bowl clean.

5. Let set in the refrigerator for a few hours until firm before cutting it.

CANDY COATED PROMISES

Samantha Baca

Cover Design: Richard Baca
Image(s): Canva

One
Sheila

"I look ridiculous," I whined as I tossed my head back and turned away from the mirror. It was easily the tenth outfit I had tried on since I got to Brooke's house.

"You do not look ridiculous," she said sweetly, stepping to the side as she looked me over. "But if you don't like it then we'll keep looking. Tonight is supposed to be fun and I'm not letting you leave here until you feel sexy in whatever you decide to wear."

I pulled in a deep breath and shook my hands, trying to expel some of the nervous energy that was running through me.

"Why am I so nervous about tonight?" I asked dumbly, knowing full well why I was so nervous. It had only been a few hours since Parker had sauntered back into my life, looking delicious with his fitted jeans and a cream-colored turtleneck sweater. I felt like I was in some sort of romance novel where the absurdly good looking guy comes back to save the plain-Jane girl next door while he woos her with red roses and chocolates, making things far too fairy-tale to be real life. But yet, that was what happened. And as far as I knew, I wasn't part of some cheesy romance novel. Was I?

We had agreed to go our separate ways so the girls could get ready while the guys did whatever they were supposed to do. Both of them were gorgeous without having to try which was incredibly unfair as I stared at myself in a sparkly pink dress that my daughter had worn to Homecoming last year.

"I look like Pepto-Bismol." I glanced up and met Brooke's eyes in the mirror as she tried to look away before I saw the lines form on her face while she tried to keep from laughing.

"It's not funny," I joked as I turned around and swatted at her. "I look like something you take when you have the shits!"

"Okay, okay," Brooke laughed, holding her hands up in defense. "No need to get yourself all worked up. We'll find something a little less *pink*."

I rolled my eyes as she laughed her way back to her closet and started rummaging around.

"Did you bring those black skinny jeans?" she called out.

I looked around at the pile of clothes on the floor in front of me and on the chair beside me.

"Yeah, I brought two pairs. These ones that are incredibly comfortable, and these ones that are tighter and have fake leather down the side of them." I held both up for her to see as she walked back into the bedroom. She looked between both of them and then gave me a pointed look at the ones she thought I should wear. I turned my head and eyed them suspiciously as if they had somehow offended me.

"These ones?" I asked nervously, my face pulled up in a grimace. "Really?"

"Yes, really." She put her hand on her hip and tilted her head to the side, her expression softening for a quick second before she shook her head and reconsidered what she was going to say.

"But these fit really good, I already know what will look good with them," I countered, holding up the other pair for her to consider.

"Sheila Jane, those are the same pants that you wear to pull the weeds out front," she scolded.

"And?"

"And no one wants to dive into the garden looking for fresh flowers only to find dirt crusted weeds."

I wrinkled my nose in response and slowly put them down beside me. She walked over and smiled gently at me as she sat down on the bed across from me.

"It's Valentine's Day and Parker just drove all the way down from Nashville to come surprise you with chocolates and roses, while asking to take you out on a romantic date. You deserve to feel sexy and appreciated tonight. So put your weed pulling pants away and go put on the ones that are going to make him want to skip dinner and get straight to the dessert." She winked playfully.

"Is everything always a food analogy with you?" I teased as I got up and walked to the bathroom, pulling the door closed behind me while I changed.

"You know it!" she responded loudly as she laughed from the bedroom.

I pulled the dress up and over my head, sliding it back onto the hanger that was on the floor. I quickly hung it on the shower door before grabbing the pants from the counter. I bent down to step into them, stopping for a moment to look in the mirror, trying to accept that this was what Parker was going to see when he looked at me tonight. While we had already had sex once, that was a drunken one-night stand. Tonight was different. Everything was very deliberate and planned out which had me ready to crawl up the walls as my anxiety started to build.

My hands slowly moved across my stomach, tracing the outline of the stretch-marks that were proof of a body that had carried several kids. While people had always told me how lucky I was that I lost all of the baby weight from each pregnancy, no one knew how self-conscious I was about the way my body didn't actually *bounce back*. The beautiful thing about wearing clothes is that it hides the imperfections that we don't want anyone to see. My mind just couldn't wrap around the idea that if I wanted to be with Parker, then I would have to allow him to see mine.

I stared at my body for a few minutes longer while I traced

the lace that ran along the top of my full breasts, matching the G-string panties that I was wearing. I desperately wanted to feel sexy, the way you're supposed to feel when you're wearing expensive lingerie that lifts and boosts all of your assets. But every time I tried to focus on something good about my body, I just kept thinking about how nervous I was to see how Parker would react.

"How's it going in there?" Brooke called, forcing me out of my trance. I bent down and grabbed the pants, pulling them on before looking around for a shirt to go with them.

"It's fine, but I didn't think about bringing a shirt that would go with these. I guess I have to wear the other ones after all," I sighed, feeling relieved.

Suddenly, the door opened and Brooke stood on the other side, holding out a shirt in her hand. She gave me a smug smile as she pushed her hand closer to me for me to take it. I looked her up and down, noticing that she had changed while I was in the bathroom. Her dark hair had been pulled up into a sleek ponytail that sat high on her head, showcasing a beautiful diamond necklace that hung just above her cleavage. She had on a simple black dress that was fitted in all of the right places, hugging her curves and enhancing the shape of her ass.

"You look incredible," I said with a smile.

"Thank you," she replied sweetly as she pushed the shirt at me again. "Now, get dressed so I can say the same about you."

I rolled my eyes and laughed, taking the shirt from her and

holding it up in the air.

"Brooke, there are no sleeves on this thing!" I said as I turned it for her to see.

"Yeah, I know. But something tells me you'll be plenty warm without them."

I shook my head and pulled the spaghetti strap tank top over my head, pulling the bottom down to quickly hide my stretch marks. I noticed Brooke's gaze as she saw them, looking up to meet my eyes before I could turn away.

"You're beautiful, Sheila. Every single inch of you." Her voice was gentle, easing some of my anxiety. "You look like Ariel," she sighed.

I pulled my brows together and looked at her.

"Megan's friend?"

"What? No," she waved dismissively as if that was the most absurd thought in the world. "From The Little Mermaid." She smiled and walked off, leaving me alone with that piece of insightful information. I laughed and rolled my eyes.

I thought about what she had said when she saw my stretch marks. It wasn't the first time she had seen them, but it was the first time that I had felt that intimate connection with her that she was being honest about what she said. She wasn't saying it just to be nice because she was my friend.

I swallowed to force the tears away and turned to look at myself in the mirror. The shirt was a sheer black fabric that was lightweight and flowy. It actually looked really good with the tight pants that I was adamant about not wanting to wear, though now I couldn't remember why. The outfit looked good and for a moment, I finally felt sexy. I was still taking in the outfit when Brooke came up and stood next to me, looking at my reflection in the mirror. She lifted two necklaces in the air before deciding on one and handing it to me.

It was a long, thin chain that had a single rose gold colored feather charm on it. I slid it over my head and gently laid it on my chest, admiring the way that it fit between my cleavage. I pressed my lips together and took a deep breath knowing that it was getting late and the boys would be on their way to pick us up soon.

We finished getting ready and took turns applying a new coat of lipstick before we heard a knock at the front door. I could feel the butterflies swarming through my stomach as I wrapped one of the curls around my finger anxiously, watching as the red hair twirled around it. I watched as Brooke walked over and opened the door, stepping to the side to let in Ryder and Parker. It felt surreal seeing him there, his jet-black hair glistening in the light as his emerald green eyes darkened when he saw me.

It felt just like a movie, everything completely perfect until the moment I had to move one foot in front of the other. It was too late to think of anything other than the sound I would make as I hit the floor when the four-inch heels I never wear decided to give me a harsh reality check. *Romance novel my ass* I thought on my way down.

Two
Parker

Sheila looked sexy in skin tight black pants that wrapped nicely around her petite frame as she came flying toward me, a sea of red flooding my view before she hit the floor with a loud thud. I had jumped forward, trying to catch her but I was a few seconds too late and too far to be able to stop the fall. There was a loud gasp beside me before the room went eerily quiet while we rushed over to make sure she was okay. I reached her first and dropped down onto my knees, lifting her hair out of her face to get a look at her.

"Sheila, are you okay?" I asked, panicked.

Her eyes slowly looked up at me under her eyelashes, the light blue color pulling me in. She started to laugh as she nodded yes and took my hand when I offered to help her up.

"Yes, I'm okay. Thank you," she giggled. "You'll learn quickly that I have a love-hate relationship with gravity and I tend to spend a lot of time on my back, on the floor."

My eyebrows shot up as I pictured this, knowing that she hadn't realized the sexual innuendo that she had inadvertently laced into her words. I glanced over at Brooke and Ryder who were trying their best to hide their laughter, Brooke nestling her head into his shoulder to shield her face. Sheila looked around suspiciously between us, trying to figure out what everyone was laughing about. Her eyes narrowed at me for a second before turning to Brooke. Before she could look away, they locked eyes and Brooke lost it. Her laughter filled the room as Ryder and I joined in.

"What is so damn funny?" she demanded with her hand on her hip.

Brooke held her hand up to her mouth, trying to stop the laughter but couldn't. I waited to see who was going to be the one to tell her about her little wording snafu but when Ryder and Brooke refused to make eye contact, I knew they weren't giving in any time soon. Sheila looked up at me and gave me the cutest damn smile that made me want to pull her closer to me and kiss her.

"Your words might have gotten the better of you," I explained, waiting for her to put the pieces together on her own. She stood there for a few seconds, hand still on her hip when suddenly it clicked.

"You guys!" she squealed and looked back and forth between us. "You know what I meant," she sighed. "I am on my back on the floor because I fall a lot."

"You sure it has nothing to do with the four kids you have?" Brooke joked, quickly turning to hide her face in Ryder's shoulder before Sheila could look at her.

I let out a chuckle and reached out to hold Sheila's hand. It felt weird not knowing whether or not I should touch her or if she even wanted me to. We hadn't seen each other since the drunken night we shared on New Year's but I hoped that things would fall easily into place and we could enjoy our night together. She had seemed excited to see me earlier when I surprised her at *The Sweet Shop* but suddenly I was getting cold feet and second-guessing myself. She glanced down at my hand and smiled, placing hers in it before I gently squeezed it.

"You look beautiful tonight," I said quietly, pulling her attention to me.

"Thank you, you look quite handsome tonight as well." Her eyes slowly traveled down my body while mine took the opportunity to do the same.

I had been thinking about Sheila for weeks and had spent hours on the phone with Ryder trying to plan the perfect night for us. My goal was to come back to Stone Creek before today but some unexpected news had fallen into my lap at the last minute. This, in turn, derailed the majority of the plans I had made.

We had already missed our dinner reservation and the hotel confirmed that they had given our room away when we also missed check-in. Everything had quickly unraveled and I was left with the last box of chocolates and a bouquet of roses that I had to fight for in the drugstore. In all fairness, I didn't want to fight the little old lady but she didn't give me any other options after she kicked me in the shin and stole my bottle of wine. I had limped to the register with what was left of my dignity, paid for my stuff, and made my way over to surprise Sheila. I was still feeling nervous and anxious, unsure of whether she was going to like what I had planned for us or if she was going to think I was some pathetic loser who didn't know how to plan a proper date.

"Are you guys ready to go?" Ryder asked, breaking me out of my trance.

"Yeah," I said and rocked back on my heels. I looked over at Sheila and panic hit me when I saw her try to take a step and her ankle twisted as she started to fall again. This time I was able to reach out and catch her. She grabbed onto my arm, steadying herself as she looked down to see what happened.

"Stupid heel broke," she muttered, her hand reaching down to slip the shoe off one foot, then the other.

"It's okay, I have another pair you can borrow," Brooke offered and waved for Sheila to go with her. The girls disappeared into Brooke's bedroom while they found a new pair of shoes for her to wear.

"You excited for tonight?" Ryder asked once we were alone.

I rubbed my hands together and shook my head no. I was feeling plenty of things but excited wasn't one of them at the moment.

"Excited wouldn't be the word that I would use right now," I laughed. "Nervous, worried, stressed out—those are all appropriate words for what I'm feeling."

"Don't worry about it, everything will work out," he assured me. I looked at him wearily, not believing him for a second.

"Trust me," he winked as the girls made their way back into the living room. Sheila was pulling on her jacket, tossing her fiery red hair over her shoulder as she shrugged it on. I looked down and felt relieved that she was wearing shoes with a shorter, thicker heel this time. Even with the shorter, less sexy shoes, she still looked incredible and I couldn't take my eyes off of her.

"Okay, let's get going," Ryder said enthusiastically as he clapped his hands together and turned to open the door.

We all followed him outside, shivering in the cold as Brooke locked the door and we scurried to our cars. I walked to the passenger side and opened the door for Sheila, returning her warm smile as she slid inside and buckled her seatbelt. I rushed around to the driver's side, making sure I avoided any patches of ice before I opened the door and climbed inside. I glanced out of the corner of my eye a few times to see if she had noticed that we were following Brooke and Ryder. If she did, she didn't say anything or seem bothered.

A few minutes later I was pulling into the parking spot next to Ryder at the only restaurant that was open in Stone Creek tonight. The line of people waiting inside wound around the hostess station and butted up to the door. I groaned quietly under my breath when I thought about how long the wait was going to be and how our night was going to be wasted in this mess. I looked over when I noticed that Ryder and Brooke hadn't gotten out of the car yet either. He locked eyes with me and shook his head no before nodding for me to follow him.

I smiled nervously at Sheila as I put the car in reverse and followed Ryder out of the parking lot and down the street. I could see the curiosity and confusion on her face as we drove but I didn't bother trying to explain what was going on since I didn't have any idea myself. Soon we were parked outside of a pizza joint that was so empty it almost looked like it was closed. As we got out of the car, I looked at Ryder and pulled my eyebrows together, questioning what the hell he was doing. Another quick wink was all that I got from him before he wrapped his arm around Brooke's waist and led her inside. Sheila and I followed behind.

When we walked in, it looked like we had stepped into some sort of time travel dimension and were frozen in the nineties. The flooring was old and outdated as were the walls that desperately needed a fresh coat of paint. The lighting in the room was minimal and provided by some fluorescent lights that cast an ugly orange glow on everything they touched. Overhead an old Usher song was playing on the outdated speakers that hung in the corner of the lobby by the register. I looked around and saw that the room opened up into a larger room that was filled with booths along the walls and a few game tables in the middle of the room. One wall was reserved for arcade games and by the looks of it, they hadn't been updated since the nineties either.

"This place has the best pizza and is one of Stone Creek's hidden gems that only the real locals know about," Ryder said as he walked over to the counter and waited for someone to come.

"Are you sure they're open?" I asked with a heavy amount of doubt in my voice.

"We're always open, Sugar," a raspy voice said. An older woman who appeared to be in her seventies or eighties walked around the corner and stood behind the counter. Her black and gray speckled hair was pulled into a ponytail that frizzled out around her head. "One booth or two?" She reached down and grabbed a few menus while waiting for our answer.

We all looked at each other, unsure of whether we wanted to sit together or take separate booths. The place was empty aside from us which meant that we were likely to hear each other's conversation either way and part of me thought that it might feel weird to try to have any privacy with Sheila given that it wouldn't be private at all.

"One booth?" Ryder and I asked each other at the same time. Everyone laughed, which helped to ease some of the tension that was starting to build up inside of me. The woman nodded her head as she turned and walked off, leading us to our table. It was the biggest booth in the place and took up the corner which also made it more private, even though we didn't really need privacy at this point. I waited to see whether I should slide into the booth first, or if Sheila and Brooke wanted to sit on the inside. Thankfully I didn't have to ask before they both climbed inside and got situated.

The woman set the menus down on the middle of the table and stalked off, leaving us to look over them. I reached over and grabbed one, feeling silly when I noticed that no one else was bothering to look at it. I looked over at Ryder who was too busy whispering something in Brooke's ear to notice anything else.

"Do you already know what you want?" I asked Sheila.

"I'm not picky, I pretty much eat anything," she replied cheerfully. I loved that she was always so lighthearted and easy-going. Her energy was starting to wear off on me and I felt myself starting to relax more.

"We're sorry that this isn't a romantic dinner out ladies," Ryder said as he pulled away from Brooke's ear, leaving a blush on her face from whatever he had said. "But this place has beer and pizza—and more importantly, no line."

"It sounds great to me," Sheila smiled and reached over to pat my thigh under the table. I reached down and held onto her hand, thankful that she wasn't disappointed. It had been a while since I had been on a date with a woman but the last few had been pretty hard to impress which left me feeling a little desperate for this one to go right.

"You know me, I'm always up for pizza and beer," Brooke said happily.

A young, teenage girl with braces came out a few minutes later and took our order before rushing off to tell the older woman that the table in the back needed beer and she wasn't allowed to touch it. Sheila laughed and joked about how she reminded her of her daughter before looking over at me. I swallowed hard and looked away as I tried to force the anxiety away. There was a lot on my mind but I wasn't ready to unload any of it on Sheila right now. I needed time to process everything that had happened in the last twenty-four hours.

Thirty minutes later, a sizzling hot pepperoni pizza was delivered to our table along with two pitchers of beer. Ryder hadn't been lying, this place had some of the best pizza I had tasted as I chewed my bite that was too hot to be eaten. I forced it down and took a drink of beer, hoping the cold liquid would squelch the burning sensation from the pizza.

I waited a few minutes before taking another bite so it could cool down some. I lifted my beer to my lips and took a slow drink, watching Sheila as she looked around the table with a frown on her face. A few seconds later she lifted herself out of the booth and reached across, moving the napkins out of the way to find the shaker of crushed red peppers. Her eyes went wide with excitement as she sat back down and sprinkled them generously over her slice of pizza.

"You know those are hot, right?" I asked with a raised eyebrow.

"Mmhmm, just the way I like it," she replied, setting the shaker down before picking up her slice and taking a bite. She closed her eyes and let out a heavy sigh as she chewed, the whole thing looking sexier than it should have.

I leaned back against the soft, worn-out leather of the booth and watched her while I slowly drank my beer. She ate her pizza as if no one was watching, wiping her mouth with her fingers in between bites as she moaned and savored each piece. Suddenly, I felt her eyes on me as she noticed me staring at her. I felt a blush creep up my neck, knowing that I had been caught.

"Why aren't you eating your pizza?" she asked quietly, nodding at the untouched slice on my plate.

"It was too hot," I shrugged. "I was letting it cool down."

"It's always better when it's hot," she leaned closer to whisper, "And I'm not just talking about the pizza."

I watched her bring her slice up to her mouth and her lips parted as she slowly licked them before taking a bite. Her blue eyes darkened, sending her not-so-subtle message straight to my dick.

Three
Sheila

"I suck at pool," I joked as I bent down and attempted to line my pool stick up in a position that would hopefully hit a ball. Parker leaned back against a table, one ankle crossed over the other, as he held his pool stick beside him and watched me. Every few seconds I would catch him checking out my rack as I leaned forward, giving him a good view of the girls. I made a quick mental note to thank Brooke for loaning me the shirt.

"Here, let me help you," he offered as he pushed off from the table and set his pool stick down before walking over and standing beside me. I immediately felt the heat from his body as his chest pressed against mine when he leaned forward to help angle my arm in a better position. He slightly scooted forward, his groin lining up perfectly so I could feel the prominent outline of the bulge in his jeans. I held my breath as I waited for him to move again, my body hyper-aware of every touch. One hand reached forward and slid down my arm, wrapping over my hand to help guide the pool stick while the other hand was placed firmly on my lower back, just inches above my ass.

"Try that," he said softly as he slowly pulled away and walked to the side of me. I pulled in a deep breath and held it, forcing myself to focus on the ball and not on the way my body was still humming from his touch. His eyes were locked onto my every movement as I pulled my arm back and pushed the pool cue forward, excited when I saw the ball move across the pool table. I squealed with joy and looked up to find him smiling before he started clapping.

"Great shot." His voice was smooth and sexy, the nervousness I had seen in him earlier now replaced by the relaxed Parker I remembered from Christmas and New Year's. Maybe it was the few beers he had drank or maybe it was just us spending more time together. My nerves had finally calmed down too, thankfully.

"Well, I had a great teacher," I replied with a wink. "I'm sure it was a one-time-only thing."

"Nah, I'm sure you'll sink the next one and kick my ass this round."

It was our third round playing against each other and I hadn't won one yet.

I rolled my eyes playfully and walked around the table, trying to find an easy shot. I scanned the balls, trying to avoid the eight ball while trying to find a solid ball that wasn't stuck in between all of the stripes. I had sunk his balls so many times already, and not in a good way. It was a long shot but I spied a solid ball off to the corner of the pool table and knew that it wasn't the best decision but decided to go for it anyway.

I lined myself up and leaned forward to take the shot, watching as Parker's eyebrows raised in surprise when he saw what I was going to attempt. He turned his head to the side to cough out a laugh he was trying to hide before looking at me and shaking his head in disbelief. I pulled the cue back and pushed it forward, lowering my head as I watched it miss the ball I was aiming for and sink one of his instead. I closed my eyes and waited to look at him, knowing that he was going to give me shit for this.

When I opened my eyes, he was standing next to me, waiting for me to look at him. When I did, he looked from me to the table and back as a giant smile pulled across his face.

"You're not funny," I joked and swatted at his muscular chest. He caught my hand and pulled me close to him, wrapping his arms around me so I couldn't get away. I looked up from under my dark lashes and tried to keep myself from laughing.

"I didn't say anything," he teased playfully before lifting my chin with his finger. Once my head was lifted and I was fully looking at him, his smile grew wider as he said, "you really have a thing for my balls tonight, don't you?"

I felt the heat flush through my body, my cheeks burning from the blush.

"What can I say, you're just so good that women practically throw themselves at you," I joked back. "Not just once, but twice. You must be quite the stud."

He laughed and leaned forward, planting a kiss on my lips.

"How's your ankle by the way?" he asked, his tone shifting from playful to concerned.

"It's fine. As I said, I fall a lot so my body is used to it." I tried to make light of it but it really had been killing me all night. I had tried to take the edge off with a couple of beers but wanted to make sure that I didn't have too many so we didn't end up having a repeat from New Year's Eve. Not that the sex was bad that night, I just wish I had been more sober to remember and enjoy all of it. There were a few parts that were unfortunately a blur. Like, the image of his black hair as it tickled my lower stomach while his face was buried between my legs. That was something I definitely wished I could remember in more detail.

"It's probably a good idea for you to get off of it soon, we can call this our last game if you want?"

"Yeah, that's fine with me." I glanced at the clock on the wall and noticed it was already after nine o'clock and knew it would be closing time soon. Ryder and Brooke were off on the other side of the room playing video games and making bets on what the loser would have to do when they got home later. I was a tiny bit jealous of how easy their relationship seemed to flow and how into each other they seemed to be. Then I reminded myself that Parker and I might be like that someday too but it was still too early in our relationship to have that level of comfort. If you counted the number of days we had physically spent together, it was barely a week and a half of us dating.

"Was there anything you wanted to do after this?" He asked shyly as he moved around the table, clearing the rest of the balls in a few effortless moves. I swallowed hard and froze, realizing that we were at that point where we had to decide if we were going to invite each other back to our place for the night. The kids were with my ex-husband, Rodney, and his girlfriend—possibly fiancé if everything went well—tonight so I had the house to myself. There was also the option to go back to his hotel room with him if he invited me.

"I have the house to myself," I blurted out nervously as I tapped my fingers against the table I was sitting at. "We can go there if you want to. Or not. I don't want you to feel pressured to do it." My face fell as the words came flying out of my mouth uncontrollably. "I don't mean *do it,* I meant if you wanted to come over and—"

"Sheila," he interrupted and pinned me with a look. "I would love to come over and hang out."

I nodded and slowly exhaled, hoping that the next batch of oxygen that I inhaled would at least make it to my brain. Brooke and Ryder finished their game and headed over to the pool table as Parker finished setting it up how we had originally found it.

"They're getting ready to close so we better get going," Ryder said, looking past me to Parker. I took the opportunity to sneak a glance at Brooke who was smiling mischievously at me before she looked me up and down and wiggled her eyebrows. I rolled my eyes and shook my head, feeling somewhat more relaxed now that they had joined us again. It was weird that even though Parker and I had already had sex, I felt like a nervous teenager who was stressing out about doing it for the first time.

"You ready?" Parker asked as we walked back to the booth and grabbed our coats. I nodded and smiled, trying to force any intelligent words to come out but failing in the process. We walked out and thanked the woman at the front before the cold air hit us and the door closed behind us. We said a quick goodbye to each other before we got in our separate cars and drove away. The closer we got to my house, the more nervous I was to invite him in.

<u>Four</u>
Parker

Sheila was quiet the entire car ride back to her place. I started to wonder if it would be better for me to go and let her have the time she needed so she would feel comfortable with having me there. I had spent plenty of time at her house the week between Christmas and New Year's but it was different now that we were a couple. Or at least I thought we were. I pulled into the driveway and looked at her before turning off the car or undoing my seat buckle.

"Are you sure about this? I don't want to make you uncomfortable in any way," I said, reaching across to gently squeeze her hand that was resting on her thigh.

"Yes, I'm sure," she said with a smile. "I'm sorry, I don't know why I feel so nervous tonight." She tried to force a smile but it never got close to reaching her eyes.

"We don't have to do anything that makes you nervous, Sheila. I respect you and we can go as slow as you want to. Okay?"

She nodded her head and smiled again, this time it was more of a smile than before. Once inside, I instantly remembered the time I had spent here with her, including the vague memories I had of New Year's Eve. That was a great night but I really regretted that we were drunk when it happened because I was pretty sure that it was definitely something that I wanted to remember every small detail. Part of me was hoping that we would have a chance to make some new memories tonight.

"Do you want something to drink?" she called from the kitchen while I made myself comfortable on the couch.

"Water is fine, thank you." I didn't want to have any alcohol in my system tonight so I could make sure that anything we did was with a clear head. The few beers I had at dinner were quickly out of my system after an hour or so and I had planned to keep myself in the right mindset tonight.

A few minutes later, Sheila came in with a glass of iced water in one hand and a glass of tea in the other. Her feet were bare after she kicked her shoes off the minute we walked inside. She set the drinks down on the coffee table in front of us and sat down beside me, looking unsure of what to do.

"Here, turn sideways," I said as I reached down and grabbed her feet, pulling them onto my lap as she scooted herself around on the couch. She looked confused until my hands gently started rubbing her foot and working the tender flesh along her arch. I shifted my position and turned slightly toward her so I could watch as her eyes fluttered closed and her head tilted back to rest against the corner of the cushion behind her. My thumbs rubbed along the inside of her foot, gently massaging as she quietly moaned in response.

I went to work on the other foot, kneading each spot and feeling my jeans pulling tighter around the hard-on I was getting from the sounds she was making. My hands slowly traveled up and started massaging her legs as I took the opportunity to check her out in the skin-tight pants while she wasn't looking. Everything about her was so damn sexy, I was already fighting the urge to keep my hands to myself. I had to remind myself that I was a nice guy who was giving her a massage because she deserved it and that I wasn't a dirty pervert who was giving her a massage as an excuse to touch her.

"God, that feels so good," she whimpered, her eyes still closed as her breathing started to change. I watched as her chest started to rise and fall more heavily, her back slightly arched against the couch. Was she getting as turned on by this as I was?

"Good, I'm glad. It's my job to make you feel good," I said lazily as I worked my way back down her leg, to her foot before I got carried away and tried to massage something else. Suddenly my throat was dry so I leaned forward and took a drink of water, hoping it would cool me off some.

"So then what's my job?" she teased playfully and opened her eyes to look at me.

"To sit back and enjoy it."

Our eyes locked and I knew that we both knew the true meaning of my words and that it had nothing to do with the damn foot massage. She licked her lips and before I knew it she was across the couch and straddling me, her hands wound in my hair as her mouth planted on mine. I reached down and grabbed her ass, pulling her closer to me as my dick throbbed against the tightness of my jeans. I groaned as she sank lower, situating herself right on top of me as I imagined being inside of her while she rode me.

My hands roamed all over her body, desperate to touch her as hers pulled my hair before she pulled away from the kiss. We were both breathless as we paused for a second to look at each other before I leaned forward and started kissing her neck. She moaned and the feel of it in her throat against my lips nearly sent me over the edge. I loved that I was the reason she was making these sounds. I ran a hand up and over her breast, pausing for a second to feel the fullness of it before pulling her tank top down enough to free it from her bra. My dick twitched, spurring me on as I leaned forward and pulled her nipple into my mouth, my hands grabbing her ass as she ground her hips against me.

"Let's go to my bedroom," she panted breathlessly before pulling back and climbing off of me. I nodded and stood, thankful for the change in position as I followed her to the room. The lights were still off when she climbed onto the bed, only a trickle of light coming in from the hallway. I wanted to turn on every light there was, just so I could see her body and watch her face as I brought her to climax but something told me that she wanted to come in here for a reason and that reason was because it was dark.

I was unsure of how far things were going so I refrained from undressing, aside from taking off my shoes, before climbing onto the bed next to her. There was a slight disappointment when I saw that she had fixed her shirt and that her breast was no longer out for me to enjoy but I didn't want to overstep by diving back in. I wanted her to make the moves and show me what she wanted and how far she wanted to go.

"You can come closer if you want to," she invited and patted the bed beside her. I smiled even though I wasn't sure she could see it and scooted over. I laid on my side, propping myself up on my elbow so I could look at her.

"You're gorgeous, you know that?" I reached over and gently caressed the side of her face. She was laying on her back, her head turned toward me.

"Thank you," she whispered. "I like the way you touch me, it's gentle but it feels incredible."

I slowly let my fingers slide down the length of her neck before teasing them along her collarbone. I kept my touch light as I ran a finger along the top of her breasts, gently tracing along the top of her bra.

"I like the sounds you make when I touch you," I said as I kept running my fingers along her body, making lazy circles on her stomach before getting to the top of her pants. "These pants are fucking sexy by the way. I honestly have had the hardest time not ripping them off of you all night," I admitted with a chuckle.

"Then maybe I should take them off?" She pulled her lower lip in between her teeth while she reached down and unbuttoned the top button before pulling the zipper down. I pulled my hand back and watched as she lifted her butt and pulled them down, freeing her legs before tossing them to the floor. She laid before me wearing nothing but the sheer black tank top and a black lace G-string. I tried to look up at her, to look her in her eyes, but I couldn't pull my attention away from her perfect body lying beside me, begging for me to touch it.

"Do you want me to put them back on?" she joked nervously when I didn't say anything. My head whipped up to hers and I felt myself blush, thankful that she couldn't see it.

"That is a *hell no*," I chuckled before reaching over and placing the palm of my hand on her flat stomach. "In fact, I was going to suggest that we take this off as well." I lifted the bottom of her shirt and felt the moment her body tensed beneath my hand. I leaned in closer and looked at her, trying to figure out what had caused the sudden shift in her mood.

"Are you okay?" I asked, making sure I hadn't accidentally crossed a line I wasn't aware of.

"Yeah, I just think that maybe I should leave it on. That's all."

I could still feel the tension in her voice and was concerned that something was wrong when she reached up and pulled me down on top of her. She brought her lips to mine and kissed me softly.

"But I do think we need to strip you of some of these clothes," she said playfully, tugging at my sweater as she pulled it up and over my head. I laughed and watched as her hands moved down to my belt, undoing it as her eyes slowly trailed across my stomach. She got so distracted that she hadn't realized that she was still staring at my body while my belt buckle hung loose in her hand.

"Did you want me to finish taking my pants off? You seem a little *distracted*," I teased. She pulled her hands away and I felt her eyes on me as I scooted off of the bed and stripped down to just my boxer briefs. I slowly climbed back onto the bed, hovering over her as she watched me. I lowered myself on top of her, making sure I didn't put my full weight as I adjusted myself.

She closed her eyes as my lips touched the side of her neck, kissing her softly while my hands ran along her sides and up to her breasts. I wanted tonight to be as special as possible and more importantly, I wanted to show her that she could trust me.

"Tonight is all about you, Sheila, just tell me what you want. Say the word and I'll give it to you," I whispered against her ear. Her fingers scratched along my back as her breathing quickened in response to my hand caressing her breast. "Tell me, what do you want, baby?"

"I want you," she whimpered, arching her back beneath me. "I want you inside of me, Parker. Fuck me, please."

I grunted as I reached across the bed to grab the condom I had pulled out of my wallet before tossing my pants to the floor. I quickly tore it open and pulled off my boxers before putting it on. In less than ten seconds I had her stripped of her panties and was sliding inside of her while she moaned my name and dug her nails into my back.

The sex was fucking fantastic and I wish I could have lasted for hours because that's how good it was. Her body melded perfectly into mine as we climaxed together. Everything about it was perfect until I looked down and saw that she was crying.

Five
Sheila

I tried to quickly wipe the tears away with the back of my hand before Parker could see them. I coughed to try to hide the sniffle when I felt his hand reach up and gently caress my cheek as he laid his face next to mine on the pillow.

"I'm so sorry, Sheila. I don't know what happened but I'm sorry that I've upset you," he whispered and pulled his hand away.

"You didn't do anything wrong. I'm just a mess today and didn't expect to have such an emotional response to us having sex. I'm the one who should be sorry. That was mind-blowing and by far, the best sex I've ever had, and I'm over here crying like a baby. Please don't think that I didn't enjoy it because I promise you that I did."

I felt my body start to shiver, the intensity of the emotions taking over. Parker reached down and grabbed the extra blanket that was laying at the foot of the bed and brought it up to cover me. I kept waiting for the moment when he would decide that this was too much emotional baggage and say goodbye before bolting out the door, never looking back. I wouldn't blame him, there was always a lot on my plate between my kids and my ex-husband. Not many people wanted to get involved in something that sometimes got down-right messy.

"You don't ever have to apologize to me for being emotional. I'm here if you need to talk but I understand if you don't want to. Just let me know how I can be there for you and what you need."

I felt his hand reach down and squeeze mine, a comforting reminder of what a sweet person he was.

"Thank you," I sighed and took a slow breath in, trying to clear my mind. "My ex-husband was supposed to propose to his girlfriend today and for whatever reason, it's getting to me."

I waited for a few minutes to see what his reaction to this news was before continuing. He nodded his head sympathetically and stayed silent.

"I don't have feelings for him and I haven't in a very long time. But something about him moving on with his life and asking her to marry him just gets under my skin. Maybe it's because she's barely older than our kids or maybe it's because they've barely been dating for six months. Either way, it just really bothers me that he is so ready to settle down with someone he barely knows when he wasn't willing to do that for his own family. He met her in Nashville and thanks to their new relationship, he hasn't been around as much to see the kids and to take them on his weekends. It's a lot to unload on you, I know. I'm sorry, I just needed a minute to get it all off of my chest and thought it might be better for you to know what was happening."

"I get it, I'm kind of in a similar boat. My daughter has been seeing an older man for a couple of months now and won't listen to me or her mother about taking it slow and making sure that this is what she wants before she settles down. She's barely twenty-two years old, her life hasn't even started yet."

I turned my head to look at him as I propped myself up on my elbow.

"You have a daughter?" I was completely surprised by this information given he had never mentioned a daughter or family before this.

"Yeah, I had her when I was eighteen. Her mom and I dated when we were in high school and she got pregnant right before graduation. Her dad's work relocated him to Arkansas, so she went with her parents so they could help her with the baby while I went to college. We hadn't been dating long so the pregnancy was hard for both of us because neither of us knew each other well enough to have a child together. We stayed friends and I went to see her as often as I could but as Genevieve got older it got a lot harder for her to understand why I didn't live there with them. When her mom started dating Sean, it was even harder for her to understand the new family dynamics. I walked away to let him have the family life they needed for Genevieve's sake but I've regretted it every day for the last fifteen years."

"Wow, I had no idea," I said quietly, processing everything.

"I don't talk about it with a lot of people. Ryder doesn't even know about my family life and has no idea that I have a daughter. We hadn't talked until she showed up in Nashville a month ago and tracked me down. I've been trying to figure things out since then."

"And here I thought I was the one with a lot on my plate," I joked, hoping to lighten the mood between us.

"You definitely have a lot on your plate. I couldn't imagine what you're going through knowing that your ex-husband is ready to move on with someone so young. I don't think I would be okay with it if it was me."

"Rodney is a piece of work. Always has been. He's never been the one to do the right thing. Rather he chases down whatever the shiny new toy is that catches his eye. After he left, I had to figure out quickly how to pull myself together and be strong for my kids, and I've been doing that ever since. It's not unusual for him to spring crazy shit on me but even this is uncharacteristic for him. The man who couldn't commit to anything is all of a sudden desperate to commit to a woman he barely knows."

I chuckled and rolled my eyes, knowing it was too dark for him to see me. I felt bad bringing down the playful, fun vibe we had going early and wanted to find a way to create it again. For the first time in who knows how long, I had the night free to myself and didn't have to worry about the kids showing up unexpectedly.

"Do you want to go watch a movie or play a game?" I offered, hoping he would say yes.

"I would love to but it's getting late and I have to head back to Nashville in the morning. Can I take a rain check?"

I tried to keep the disappointment out of my voice when I told him not to worry about it. We got up and dressed quickly in the dark before I walked him to the door. A gust of wind blew in as I opened the door and brought an icy chill along with it. I shivered as I leaned up on my tiptoes to kiss him before he rushed off to his car and drove away. I closed the door and locked it before allowing myself to sink to the floor in a pathetic, miserable puddle of salty tears and crushed emotions.

<u>Six</u>
Parker

The line at the coffee shop was long and wrapped around the building. I leaned forward and peered around the steering wheel to see how many cars were in front of me before deciding whether or not to say screw it and skip the coffee. The drive back to Nashville was long enough that I needed the coffee given that I hadn't been able to sleep well last night after I left Sheila's.

I hadn't planned to tell her about Genevieve but there was something about her that made me want to confide in her and talk to her about my problems. Maybe it was because we connected so well, or maybe it was because she had her fair share of things to deal with that I assumed she would be able to relate to what I was going through. I had planned to talk to Ryder about everything that had happened but it had been such a whirlwind that there hadn't been time.

Things had been busier than normal with trying to wrap everything up with the shop in Nashville before I could officially turn everything off and sell the building. Ryder had been great with helping me tie up loose ends but there was still a lot of work that I had to finish up. Things were going great and I was making a lot of progress until the day the doors opened and a young girl with jet-black hair and almond-shaped green eyes walked in, looking exactly like a female version of myself. My heart had skipped a beat as I stood there, speechless, staring at my daughter that I had only seen in pictures over the last fifteen years.

I had no warning from her mom, Amy, that she was coming to Nashville to look for me. Last I knew, she was still in Arkansas with her mom and Sean, along with her younger siblings. After sitting down and talking with Genevieve for a few hours, I learned that she had moved to Nashville a few years ago to go to college and was finishing up her degree when she found out that I lived there. Desperate to meet her real father, she tracked me down and we've kept in touch ever since.

The past month had been a complete blur with everything happening around me so fast. I had wanted to work on getting to know Sheila, even if it was a long-distance relationship to start with while wrapping things up in Nashville and getting things situated in Stone Creek. After Ryder moved, it didn't make sense for me to stick around in Nashville anymore. My family and I weren't close. I didn't have anyone to stay for. Until now. I had no idea how long Genevieve was planning to stay in Nashville but I found it getting harder and harder to want to leave, knowing that she would be there and might think that I was walking away from her again.

I was lost in thought as I pulled forward to the drive-thru window and the woman slid it open to give me my total. I passed her my credit card and took the coffee from her hand while she processed the payment. I forced a smile as she handed me back my card, along with the paper bag that had my freshly toasted bagel. The car slowly rolled forward to allow the car behind me to scoot up to the window while I worked on setting the coffee down in the cup holder next to me before driving off to get on the freeway.

It was still early in the morning, the sun barely peeking over the mountains as it made its grand entrance. I pulled the bagel out of the bag after I merged onto the freeway and set the cruise control. After I finished the last bite, I wiped my mouth and tossed the napkin into the empty cup holder beside me. I picked up the coffee and took a sip when my phone rang, immediately connecting it to the Bluetooth in the car. I glanced at the screen and saw Ryder's name, knowing that he was already on his way to work by now.

"It's true, the wicked never rests," I teased when I answered the call. I heard him chuckle on the other end.

"Yeah, not when you have a day filled with custom orders of *I'm sorry for missing Valentine's Day* chocolates and truffles. My phone was ringing off the hook last night with desperate men who needed a favor."

"It's a good thing Brooke knows what you do for a living or that could have gotten awkward…" I laughed.

"No kidding. But you know, for the right amount of money, I'm a pretty accommodating kind of guy."

"I'm just thankful that Brooke is stuck dealing with your nasty ass now and not me." I glanced over my shoulder, making sure the lane next to me was clear before switching lanes.

"So, how did it go last night with Sheila?" Ryder asked as I heard loud noises in the background.

"It was good, I enjoyed our time together."

I kept my answer short and vague, not ready to dive into the details of my own personal drama and definitely not one to gossip about anything she had told me. I figured if she wanted him to know, she would tell Brooke who would inevitably tell Ryder.

"Such a classy answer," he joked before cursing under his breath as another loud noise echoed in the background.

"Well, I am a classy gentleman. Unlike some people I know."

"Yeah, it's a good thing we balance this friendship out with your angelic ways and my deviant tendencies." I could imagine him winking as he said it, a total Ryder thing to say.

"Anyways, I just wanted to check in and see if there's anything that you need me to do on my end to help wrap up the deal in Nashville."

"Things should be all set this week and as far as I know, there's nothing on your end that I should need."

"Awesome. So when are you planning to tell Sheila that you're moving here? Brooke was just telling me that her neighbor is moving at the end of the month and plans to turn her house into a rental. Do you want me to get you some information on it?"

"Not yet," I muttered, trying to stall before having to come clean to him about why I couldn't just pack up and move out there yet.

"Not yet that you haven't told Sheila? Or not yet that you don't want me to get you the information?"

"Both." I blew out a breath and gripped the steering wheel tighter, thankful that there was very little traffic this early in the morning.

"Why? What's going on?" His tone was short and I could tell that he knew something was going on.

"It's nothing, I just need a little more time."

"Time for what? Just a few weeks ago you were practically ready to sell your soul to wrap up that deal so you could sell your house and move down here. What's changed since then?"

I waited a few minutes before responding, tapping my fingers against the leather on the steering wheel. This was it. The moment I would have to come clean and tell him about the secret that I had kept from him for the past ten years.

"My daughter."

Seven
Sheila

I woke up the next morning feeling like a damn train had run me over, rather disappointed that I was still here to feel the aftermath. My head was pounding, a combination of too much beer and not enough water, as well as dehydration from an excessive amount of crying. After Parker left, I had thought it was a good idea to stay up late and watch home videos of when the kids were little and Rodney and I were still together.

I spent the night thinking about our life together and all of the sacrifices that I had made over the years to make sure that the kids were happy and that I stayed on Rodney's good side. He was never abusive but immature beyond belief and had threatened to stop paying child support anytime he didn't get his way. It was constantly this balancing act of the kid's needs and Rodney's needs, never my own. I never worried about whether I was happy.

As I watched the videos, I got more and more depressed as I recognized how much I had changed each year. When the camera was on me and I knew that I was being videoed, I was always smiling and being the best mother that I could be. I hardly recognized the woman I was when the camera wasn't focused on me and I saw how tired and unhappy I really looked.

My body protested as I rolled over and climbed out of bed, the soreness from falling last night a quick reminder of how the evening started. I laughed out loud to myself, imagining what a klutz I looked like to Parker when I practically went flying into his arms. His face was etched with concern when he tried to catch me but couldn't and for a moment, I felt like someone other than Brooke and my kids cared about me. I felt seen and was no longer the invisible woman who worked her magic to make everyone else happy.

I wandered to the kitchen and started a pot of coffee knowing that I was going to need more than just one cup to get through the day. Sundays were supposed to be my hectic days of getting things ready for the next week and usually, I could delegate chores to the kids to lighten the load but they were still at their dad's. I was told that I could go get them this evening after they had supper, which meant that I had the day to myself.

While I desperately wanted to curl up on the couch and hide from the world and my problems, I knew that I was better off if I kept myself busy and got stuff down around the house. I always felt better when my to-do list was short and things were done so I didn't have to stress about them. After I cleaned out the fridge, tossed the leftovers that no one had bothered to eat, started a load of laundry, took the trash out, and vacuumed the house, I finally sat down and took a quick break.

It was after eleven and I imagined that Parker would be back in Nashville soon, though I had no idea what time he left. I had the urge to check in and make sure he was okay but decided to text Brooke instead and wait for Parker to reach out to me when he was ready. Things weren't necessarily awkward between us but they weren't the warm-fuzzy Hallmark feelings you see on TV either. We both unloaded a lot of personal issues onto each other before he left and went back to his hotel, texting to let me know he was there and thanking me for a wonderful evening. Regardless of where we might stand in our relationship, at least he was still a gentleman about it.

Brooke text back a few minutes later to confirm that she and Ryder had an incredible night together and were up until three this morning making love. I rolled my eyes and set my phone down, trying to push the jealous thoughts aside before responding to her. It wasn't her fault that she was happily in love while I was miserable and hopeless. I went to the laundry room and moved the wet clothes to the dryer before starting another load. As I walked back into the living room, I heard my phone ringing on the coffee table, excitement rushing through me that it was Parker calling me. My face scrunched in disappointment when I saw Brooke's name instead.

"Hey," I mumbled before plopping myself down onto the couch.

"Wow, who peed in your Cheerios this morning?"

"No one. I'm just cranky this morning." I looked down and

picked at a loose thread hanging off of one of the throw pillows next to me.

"Why are you cranky? Did you guys not have a good time last night?"

"We did," I sighed and extended my legs out across the couch. "I'm just feeling cranky about stuff with Rodney and his new fiancé."

"Have you heard from the kids? Did he end up going through with it and asking her?"

"I have no idea. I haven't talked to them and I'm supposed to get them this evening. You know Rodney, if I mess up his day there will be hell to pay and I don't need that right now."

"He's such a dick," Brooke sighed. "I'm sorry that you're having a hard time with it. I know that you don't care about him or what he does but I imagine that it's hard to wrap your head around him proposing to a girl that's barely older than your kids."

"Yeah, and it's great that he's finally found *the one* but it's like a punch in the gut that we were never good enough for him to make that same kind of commitment. I guess I just expect too much from people."

"You always want to see the best in them and there's nothing wrong with that," she tried to reassure me. "How did things go with Parker? Did he have any *special news* to tell you?"

I froze for a minute and thought about what she just said. What did she mean by special news? He had told me about his secret daughter but had also said that Ryder didn't know about her. Had he talked to Ryder since last night and told him? It wasn't that unlikely that Ryder wouldn't tell Brooke something he had heard so I guess it made sense that she might know about it.

"Yeah, he told me last night," I said cautiously.

"What do you think? Isn't it great?" Her excitement radiated through the phone and tried to penetrate the thick layers of moodiness that were still surrounding me.

"I guess. I mean, I don't see how it impacts me."

Now I was really confused as to what Brooke was talking about.

"I would think that YOU of all people would be ecstatic about this. And it *absolutely* impacts you."

"Why? Because I have four kids? It's not like there's some special club that people with kids are part of."

"What are you talking about?" she asked, confused.

"Parker's *special news*," I said sarcastically.

"Sheila, what news are you talking about?" Her tone changed and I could tell that I was about to find out that there was more to Parker than I thought I knew.

"That depends, what are you talking about?" I wasn't ready to share his news about having a daughter with Brooke if he hadn't already told Ryder, but I had no idea what other news she could be talking about.

"Parker is wrapping up things in Nashville with the business he used to run with Ryder and once everything is finalized, he's selling his house and moving to Stone Creek."

I leaned forward and straightened on the couch, trying to process what she just said.

"What?"

"Parker is moving to Stone Creek to be with you and to help Ryder run the business side of things for us. Didn't he tell you?"

"No, I guess we never got that far in our conversation."

My mind was racing with other thoughts as Brooke went on about how her neighbor was moving soon and would be renting her house. Ryder was supposed to talk to Parker about getting information on it in case he wanted to jump on it right away as soon as it was available. She kept talking for a few minutes while I tried to force the bile down that was threatening to come up. For the life of me, I couldn't figure out why he wouldn't tell me himself that he was planning to move to Stone Creek. The only thing that I could think of was that maybe something had happened and he changed his mind. Something like a daughter that came back into his life out of nowhere.

Eight
Parker

"I already told you, I won't have the final offers until Monday morning so there's no use in drawing up the paperwork until the deal is closed and I decide which offer I'm going to take," I snapped into the phone at my realtor who had been pressing me all week long to accept one of the handfuls of offers that had come in after the recent open house. The week had been mind-numbingly dull as I tried to focus on the things that needed my attention. Instead, my mind kept wandering back to Sheila and the fact that I had barely talked to her since I left last weekend. I had debated packing a quick overnight bag and driving down to Stone Creek to see her but I wasn't sure whether she would want to see me after Ryder told me that Brooke had *accidentally* shared my little secret about moving there.

I assumed this was the reason she had been avoiding me and honestly, it was the reason I had also avoided reaching out to her. I knew that she deserved to hear about it from me instead of Brooke but there was nothing that I could do about that at this point. I had planned to tell Sheila that I was getting ready to move there soon but then my world was turned upside down so quickly that it made it hard to know what my next step was. The open house only added salt to the wound when Genevieve showed up unexpectedly and ran off before I could explain to her what was happening. It felt like every decision I made was the wrong one, and no matter how hard I tried, someone was bound to get hurt.

I finished the phone call and set my phone down on the kitchen island before opening the fridge and pulling out a bottle of water. I slid the barstool out and sat down, forcing myself to clear my mind and figure out my next step. There were only a handful of items left to finish wrapping up the sale of the business which was a relief. I reached over and picked up the pile of papers that I had printed earlier with each of the offers that I had received on the house. Each one was well above the asking price and a few were cash offers with the request to have the deal closed within thirty days. I looked around the house that was still spotless from the open house and tried to feel any sort of connection to it but couldn't.

Everything about the house was very clean, sleek, and modern. It had been a model home at one point and after I purchased it I didn't see the need to change much from how they had already decorated it. There was never the desire to change anything to make it feel cozier. I didn't hang any pictures on the wall or set any out on the fireplace mantle. I had been in this house for fifteen years though it still looked like no one had ever lived here.

I thought back to Sheila's house and the walls covered with

pictures of the kids as they grew up. A handful of pictures were strategically placed around the house of other family members, but the majority of them were the kids. There was something about her house that made me feel like it was home but I couldn't figure out what it was. It wasn't the clutter and chaos of having four teenage kids with their stuff strewn about or the dishes piled up in the sink as they waited for their turn in the dishwasher. It wasn't the warm colors on the walls or the way you could sink into the couch from the wear and tear of a family that spent plenty of time on it. It was more than that and something that I had never known myself. Family.

Sadness crept over me as I thought back to my childhood and the house I grew up in. It wasn't much different than the one that I lived in now. Cold. Sterile. No pictures on the wall and no clutter around the house. The couch had been kept in almost perfect condition, only used when people would come by and my parents would attempt to entertain. Other than that my time was spent in my room studying, after making sure all of my chores had been completed properly. My free time consisted of guitar practice during specific hours and reading books that were selected by my parents. Neither of which were things that I personally enjoyed.

My phone vibrated on the table, pulling me out of the unhappy walk down memory lane. I picked up and saw a text message from Ryder, asking if I was planning to come down this weekend. I sucked in a deep breath and slowly exhaled before I responded no. I was frustrated with myself and knew that the best thing for me would be to go to Stone Creek and try to make things right with Sheila but I had no idea what to say to her until I knew what I was doing. Was I selling my house in Nashville and moving to Stone Creek or was I going to try to track down my daughter and stay in Nashville so I could make that relationship work?

After deciding that I wasn't going anywhere, I got up and grabbed a cold beer from the fridge. It had been a long week and I was thankful that it was finally Friday. Maybe being by myself this weekend would help clear my head and allow me to make the decisions that I didn't want to. I sat down on the couch and kicked my feet up on the coffee table while I flipped through the channels on the TV, looking for something to watch. I felt my phone vibrate against my thigh and grumbled, knowing that it would be Ryder giving me shit about not coming down to talk to Sheila. I found an old action movie and set the remote down before digging into my pocket to pull out my phone. I was pleasantly surprised when I saw that I had a text message from Sheila and not Ryder.

Sheila: Are you still alive?

I felt myself grinning like an idiot as my fingers quickly rushed to respond.

Me: Yes, I'm alive and well. How are you?

I waited impatiently, watching the dots move across the screen as she typed.

Sheila: I'm okay. I went by Rodney's to pick up the kids this afternoon and met his fiancé. I knew that she was young but I didn't expect her to be gorgeous. It hit me harder than I thought it would but I've been trying to keep myself distracted so the kids don't ask me what's wrong.

My stomach knotted as I read her text message. The thought

that she was comparing herself to her ex-husband's new fiancé really ate at me. Instead of texting back, I shifted my position on the couch and held my phone up to my ear, waiting for her to answer.

"Hey," she said quietly. I glanced over at the clock and the wall, making sure it wasn't too late to be calling her. I couldn't imagine that the kids were going to bed at nine o'clock on a Friday night but what the hell did I know? It wasn't like I knew anything about raising kids or what time they were expected to go to bed at that age.

"Hi," I replied, a little too quickly. "Did I call too late? Or am I interrupting something?" I was suddenly nervous and second-guessing my rash decision.

"No, you're fine. I'm just feeling a little tired so I was resting in my room while the kids play video games in the living room."

"Are you okay?"

"Yeah, I'm good. Just a long day with an emotionally draining afternoon that carried over to a taxing night after I got into it with Oliver."

I had spent plenty of time with her four teenagers while I was there during their Christmas break and knew that Oliver tended to give her a harder time than any of the other kids. Maybe he thought it was his place as the oldest child? Or maybe it was just because that's what sixteen-year-old kids did?

"I'm sorry, that sounds rough." I didn't know what else to say and wasn't sure whether I should pry about what happened with Oliver.

"It is…" she sighed heavily. "So how did the open house go? Brooke said that Ryder told her that you had a handful of offers that were expected to come in from it."

I could hear the hesitation as she asked it, unsure of whether she should. Now was the time to man up and talk to her about what had happened, I owed her that.

"It went well, there have been several offers that have come in that were well over the asking price so now I'm just waiting for the rest to come by Monday morning, then I can try to make a decision."

"Try?"

I waited a minute before answering, hoping that I would be able to find the right way to tell her the real reason why I was reluctant to sell my house and move to Stone Creek.

"I'm not sure that I'm going through with selling it. Some things recently happened and I need to step back and figure out what's best for everyone at this point."

"Your daughter?"

I had expected to hear anger or resentment from her but instead, she sounded calm, like she understood what I was going through.

"Yeah," I paused and waited for the right words to come to me.

"I don't want to risk ruining my relationship with her by leaving. I hadn't had a chance to talk to her about it before she showed up when they were doing the open house. She was pretty upset about it and I haven't talked to her since. I've tried calling a couple of times but I get sent straight to voicemail."

"I'm sorry, that has to be hard. I don't blame you for taking the time to think through everything so you can be sure you made the right decision. As a parent, our children should always come first. Even if that means that you stay in Nashville."

"I'm the one who should be sorry," I apologized. "You should have heard about the move from me, not Brooke. I didn't want to tell you until I knew for sure that I was moving. After Genevieve showed up and told me that she was living in Nashville, it changed everything. After twenty-two years she came looking for me and I didn't want to let her down. I know what it feels like to have parents who are never there and I didn't want her to have that. When I walked away, her mom and I agreed that it was best for Genevieve to have a stable family life, even if that meant that I wasn't part of it."

"While I do wish you would have told me yourself, I'm not upset about what's happening. I get it, I really do."

I let out the breath I had been holding and allowed myself to relax on the couch. I felt silly about being so worried about how she would react to everything and regretted not talking to her about this sooner.

"You're an incredible woman, Sheila."

"I don't know about that but thank you."

"Trust me, you are," I assured her, knowing that she was still feeling down about meeting her ex's new fiancé. "And your ex is an idiot for ever letting you go."

"He has a new fiancé who is young and beautiful, I'm not sure that he would even care at this point."

"Trust me, it's his loss."

She was quiet on the other end for a few minutes and I had to pull my phone away to look at it to make sure we hadn't been disconnected.

"Is there anything that I can do to cheer you up?"

"I think I'm just going to make myself a cup of tea and head to bed. It's getting late anyway."

"Well, I hope you get some rest and maybe we can talk tomorrow?"

"Sure, that sounds nice. I have to drop the kids off at my mom's in the morning and then I'm free the rest of the day."

"Perfect, we shall talk tomorrow."

"Goodnight, Parker," she whispered sweetly.

"Goodnight, beautiful."

I hung up then grabbed my laptop from the other end of the coffee table and opened it to make a reservation at the hotel for tomorrow with an early check-in. After making sure it was booked I shut down the computer and made my way to bed.

Tomorrow was going to be an early day and I didn't plan to waste one minute of it.

Nine
Sheila

"I don't know where your other shoe is, Sally, you need to go check in your room. Lord knows it's a disaster in there." I threw my hands up in the air in defeat before watching my youngest stalk away to go look for the shoe that was no doubt, wedged under something in her room. She was twelve going on eighteen with an attitude worse than that of her fifteen-year-old sister, Megan. Sometimes I wondered if the toddler years were better or worse than the teenage years. At least by this point they could all feed and bathe themselves so that had to count for something. Right?

I cringed as I heard the sound of things being tossed around in her room and knew that the temperamental teenager was about to reappear. I glanced behind me at the kitchen table, content to see that the other three kids were calm and eating their breakfast. My phone vibrated in my pocket, alerting me to a new text from Parker. It was short and asked me to meet him at the hotel in an hour. I glanced at the time and knew that it would be tight but I could make it after I dropped the kids off with my parents if they ever got around to finishing getting ready. I felt a mixture of nervousness and excitement to see him and found myself rereading the message to make sure I wasn't mistaken. It seemed too good to be true that he was here!

"I still can't find my shoe," Sally muttered as she slammed the one in her hand down on the kitchen table. I pulled my brows together and looked at her. A quick eye roll then the shoe was promptly removed from the table, along with a dramatic, heavy sigh.

"Why can't you wear one of the other pairs of shoes that you have?" I put my hand on my hip and waited, knowing that it was going to be a fight regardless of what I said. Unless I could magically make the shoe appear, nothing was going to make her happy.

"Because I told Jenny that I would wear these ones. She has some just like it and said she would wear hers and take me shopping today," she whined and looked down at the table.

I felt my stomach clench, hearing her talk about Rodney's new fiancé.

"Her name is *Jen,* not Jenny," Thomas corrected as he pushed the last of his cereal around in his bowl with his spoon.

"She said that I can call her Jenny if I want to." Sally jutted her chin out and pouted. Out of all of the kids, she and Thomas fought the most. They were three years apart and while he was a great big brother to her, he also gave her the hardest time for being the baby of the family.

"Okay, enough," I said, interrupting them. "Do you remember the last time you wore them?" I turned my attention to her, hoping to speed up this process before we ran out of time. She looked up at the ceiling as she tried to recall when it was. Megan sighed and pushed her bowl away before she got up and offered a sympathetic smile at me.

"Come on, I'll go help you look for them," she offered and walked down the hall to their bedroom.

Twenty minutes later and the kids were ready and piling in the car. I checked my purse to make sure I had my phone with me, just in case Parker called for any reason before I headed over to meet him at the hotel. After I dropped the kids off I took a few minutes to touch up my makeup in the car and apply a fresh coat of lipstick before making my way to go see him. Once I parked and got out, I pulled out my phone and checked the text message to confirm the room number before getting in the elevator. My fingers trembled as I slid them down the front of my pants, hoping to wipe away the sweat from my palms before I was back in Parker's arms. I couldn't remember the last time that I had butterflies and giggled at the thought.

My purse hung across my shoulder as I waited for the elevator. It was quiet this morning which wasn't unusual given we didn't have many out-of-town guests unless it was a holiday. The bell dinged and I waited for the doors to open before I stepped inside and pressed the button for the third floor. The elevator was older than the hotel itself after it was recently renovated, squeaking as it struggled to make its way up the first two floors.

Once it reached the third floor the bell chimed again before the doors creaked open, allowing me to exit into the newly carpeted hallway.

I walked down the hall, checking the room numbers on the wall until I got close to his. As I approached the room he was supposed to be in, I could hear voices floating out through the door that wasn't shut all the way. I stopped and double-checked my phone, confirming that I was looking for room number 324. As I was looking up to see the number on the wall, I heard a woman's voice from inside the room. A shiver ran through me as I listened from the other side.

"I'm sorry that you had to find out that way. I wanted to be the one to tell you." Parker's voice echoed clearly through the door.

"You really hurt me by not telling me yourself. I thought this was something special for you too. If I would have known that it wasn't then I wouldn't have bothered coming all this way to talk to you about it."

The woman's voice pierced straight through to my heart and part of me wanted to run and run away while the other part needed to know who she was and what was happening. Was he seeing someone else and hadn't told me about it? We weren't official so it wasn't like he couldn't date other women if he wanted to, though he didn't seem like he was that type. But then again I had to find out from Brooke about his plans to move to Stone Creek so maybe I couldn't trust him to be fully open and honest with me or to tell me if he was seeing someone else.

I leaned closer to the door, desperate to hear more. I stood as close to the wall as possible, allowing it to support me while I balanced on my tiptoes. I was hoping that all of my yoga classes would pay off and that I would for once be graceful and not fall on my face.

"I know that I hurt you and I'm sorry. That was never my intention. I want this to work between us and I need your help to make that happen. Do you think you can give me another chance to make this right?"

My heart felt like it was shattering inside of my chest. What was happening? I felt my phone vibrating in my pocket, pulling my attention away from Parker and this mystery woman. I pulled it out and silently cursed Brooke when I saw her name flashing across the caller ID. The voices on the other side continued their conversation, however, it was now more muffled since I wasn't leaning against the door anymore. Just as I was about to resume my position, I lost my balance and stumbled against the door, forcing it to fly open.

Standing in front of me was Parker with a surprised look on his face. The woman had her back to me, nothing to tell me who she was other than long, black hair that came down to her ass. Her body was curvy and toned in jeans that looked like they were painted onto her. Everything after that felt like it happened in slow motion as she turned around to see what had happened, her hair flying over her shoulder dramatically like she was in a commercial for hair care products. The moment her green eyes landed on mine I felt my world crumble around me.

"Jen?" I asked in disbelief, looking between her and Parker. "What are you doing here? Does Rodney know that you're here? Are you guys *sleeping* together?" My questions came out in rapid succession, not allowing either of them time to answer before I shook my head, turned, and stormed down the hallway. I was waiting impatiently at the elevator when I heard footsteps thumping down the hallway. I didn't have to look up to know that it was Parker.

My blood was boiling as my foot tapped angrily on the carpet. This fucking elevator was taking forever and I didn't have the time or patience to wait for it. Parker was only a few feet away from me and the elevator showed it was still on the seventh floor. I huffed out a heavy breath and walked over to the stairs, flinging the door open at the same time Parker caught up to me and grabbed the door.

"Sheila, wait," he said as he reached for my arm to stop me. I flung around and glared at him, the anger from a few minutes ago ready to boil over.

"Out of all the women in the world that you could be dating, you just had to go and find the one who is also fucking my ex-husband?" I knew that my words were harsh and my tone even harsher. I didn't care about that right now because this hurt deeper than anything else I had been through before, including when Rodney left us. Maybe this was different because I actually found myself falling for Parker and after all of these years I finally realized that I had never really loved Rodney. It didn't matter either way given that both of them were apparently in love with the same woman and that woman wasn't me.

"Please trust me when I say that there is absolutely NO WAY in the world that I am sleeping with her." He let go of my arm and held his hands up in front of him.

I folded my arms across my chest and tilted my head, daring him to explain what was happening if he wasn't sleeping with her.

"Okay, then why is my ex's new fiancé in your hotel room?"

"Because that's my daughter, Genevieve," he said softly, stepping back and holding the door open for me to come back into the hallway.

I slowly walked forward, unsure that I had heard him correctly.

"What?" I practically whispered. My brain was struggling to process this information when I saw her walk up behind Parker and smile nervously at me.

"I thought your name was Jen?" I asked, looking past Parker to see her.

"Legally my name is Genevieve but my dad is the only one who calls me that. I've been going by Gen since middle school."

This was unbelievable. I stood there for the longest time just looking at them, unable to take my eyes off of the twins standing before me. I had no idea what her mom looked like but Genevieve was the spitting image of her father. They both shared the same jet-black hair and emerald green eyes, hers more prominent with the colors of makeup she was wearing. The jealousy that I had felt the moment I saw her at Rodney's house was somewhat gone now that I was associating her as the daughter of the man I possibly loved instead of the fiancé of the man that I once thought I loved.

"This is too much, I need to sit down," I mumbled to myself, looking around as if there would be a chair in the middle of the empty hallway.

"Why don't we go back to my room and we can all talk?" Parker suggested as he led me down the hallway by placing his hand on my lower back and guided me.

Once we were inside I chose a chair by the window and looked outside, watching the snow fall peacefully while waiting for someone else to start talking.

"I didn't mean for you to meet Genevieve this way, or for it to look like something else. When I texted you to meet me here, I had no idea that Genevieve was in Stone Creek. She had finally answered my call and when I told her that I was here for the weekend, she agreed to come meet me here," Parker explained, looking between us as Genevieve sat on the edge of the bed and folded her hands in her lap. "I didn't know that she was Rodney's fiancé until a few minutes before you got here. I had no idea why she would be in Stone Creek until she told me that she came down to spend the weekend with him and his kids."

I glanced over at her and took a few minutes to take her in. She was young and honestly not much older than my kids, granted she was twenty-two and my oldest was only sixteen. But there was something about her that screamed that she was still a teenager, not a woman ready to marry a man who was approaching forty and had four kids that she would be their stepmom.

"Does Rodney know that you're here?" I asked cautiously, knowing that he likely didn't. He had always been controlling when we were married and I doubted that he had changed much since then. Especially when his wife-to-be was a very beautiful young woman who could easily get any man she wanted. What the hell was she doing with him anyway? Suddenly, I wanted better for her and didn't even know her.

"No, he doesn't know that I'm here. I've been wanting to tell my dad that we're engaged and have him meet Rodney but he's been reluctant to come back to Nashville with me. I came down here to try to talk him into going back with me this weekend since the kids are with your parents. I figured if I pushed him hard enough, he would go. And he wouldn't have any excuses not to. But when I was on my way into town I had another call from my dad and knew that I needed to answer it before he started to worry about me. I asked if we could get together and talk this weekend, thinking he would still be in Nashville when I drug Rodney back with me, only he surprised me when he said he wasn't free because he was coming to Stone Creek."

"Wow," I sighed. "I still can't believe all of this. My ex-husband's fiancé is really my boyfriend's daughter." I shook my head in disbelief, feeling the flush on my cheeks when I realized that I had just called Parker my boyfriend for the first time. His eyes went wide at the same time Genevieve's did.

"I'm sorry—I don't know why I said that," I rushed the words out as quickly as I could. "We haven't decided what we are. Or what we aren't. I mean, we haven't officially labeled ourselves as anything—"

"I'm your boyfriend, Sheila," he said with a smile, walking over to where I was sitting. "That is unless you've changed your mind? I know this is a lot to take in."

I saw a smile spread across Genevieve's face as she watched us. I reached out and took his hand that he was offering and stood up. Wrapping my hands around his neck, I pulled him close and whispered, "I would love nothing more than to be your official girlfriend."

He pulled his head back and looked deep into my eyes before planting the sweetest kiss on my lips. Genevieve playfully cleared her throat to get our attention before the kiss turned into something more.

An hour later we were laughing and joking in Parker's hotel room and I realized just how amazing his daughter was. She was incredibly bright and full of fun, random facts. When she laughed, her eyes lit up the same way Parker's did and the lines at her eyes crinkled as well. She was a perfect combination of sweet and sassy with a touch of sarcasm that I'm sure her dad was thankful he had missed out on during her teen years. Lucky bastard.

Ten
Parker

When I woke up this morning I had planned to drive to Stone Creek and spend the weekend with Sheila, cheering her up from being down after meeting her ex's new fiancé. Little did I know that I would get a surprise visit from my daughter at my hotel room because she happened to be in Stone Creek herself, to talk to her new FIANCÉ. Who happened to be one of my least favorite people after getting to know Sheila. I also never saw it coming that Sheila would walk in on our conversation and immediately assume that I was sleeping with her ex's new fiancé. We were both blindsided when we made the connection that my daughter was marrying her ex-husband. If I didn't approve of her getting married before, I was definitely not approving of it now that I knew who the guy was. I was exhausted—mentally, physically, and somewhat emotionally after this morning and all of the information that had been unloaded in a short period of time.

I was thankful that Genevieve stuck around long enough for me to talk to her and Sheila at the same time. I needed to discuss the possibility of moving from Nashville to Stone Creek and the reasons why I couldn't make a decision yet. I had worried that it would be awkward and uncomfortable talking to both of them given that each of them was a reason for my inability to make a decision. I wanted to stay in Nashville for Genevieve and I wanted to move to Stone Creek for Sheila. Talking it out as a group was surprisingly easy and both of them understood the opposite side. Sheila wanted me to do what was right for my daughter and Genevieve wanted me to make the move to be with my girlfriend.

After a lengthy conversation about Genevieve and Rodney, I found out that she was debating whether to stay in Nashville or move back home to Arkansas with her mom, though she was having a hard time deciding because she didn't want to leave me. Her mom's health was declining and she wanted to be there for her. The problem was that Genevieve loved it in Tennessee and had no desire to move back home. She didn't want to put the burden of caring for an ailing parent on her younger siblings and Sean was working extra shifts to try to make ends meet since Amy couldn't work anymore.

When we asked her how Rodney felt about moving to Arkansas she confessed that she hadn't told him about her plans yet. She admitted that everything had happened so quickly and she had been caught up in the excitement of a new relationship that she didn't really think it through when she said yes to marrying him. I had watched Sheila's reaction to see if she would speak up and say something about it, knowing that things would also change for her and the kids if Rodney decided to move to Arkansas with Genevieve. She didn't say anything and her expressions were pretty neutral so it was hard to tell what she thought about all of it. I knew that she had mentioned that she constantly had to stay on his good side so he didn't stop making his child support payments, but aside from that, I wondered if she would care if he left. She had confessed how hard he made things on her with the kids and that he had already started spending less time with them after he started dating Genevieve because he was constantly in Nashville with her.

I rolled over on the bed, careful not to wake Sheila up, and grabbed my phone from the nightstand. It was after ten o'clock and we hadn't left the room since she got here. We ordered room service for lunch after Genevieve left and spent the rest of the afternoon making love and talking. It felt good to be with her and suddenly I knew the answer to the question I had been stressing about for weeks. I was moving to Stone Creek to be with the woman I loved. I sent a quick text message to my realtor confirming that I would look over the final offers this weekend and have a decision for him by Monday morning. It felt good to know that things were finally moving in the right direction. Or so I thought.

Eleven
Sheila

I woke up to Parker's hand wrapped snugly around my waist, his breath warm against my shoulder while he slept snuggled against my back. Yesterday was a whirlwind of information to process but somehow I was feeling better about things today than I had been yesterday when I first got to the hotel. This nervousness had been eating away at me ever since Parker left after Valentine's Day last weekend and I couldn't help but wonder what it meant for our relationship. Or if we were even in one.

After spending the day with him and talking things out, everything felt like it was falling into place. We had said the slightly terrifying words out loud, that we were boyfriend and girlfriend. After Genevieve left, he told me that he was going to accept one of the offers on his house when he got back to town on Monday. From there he would work on getting everything moved to Stone Creek. His excitement about it quickly transferred to me and we spent the night making plans for all of the things we wanted to do when he got settled in. Of course, he still had to find a place in Stone Creek but that didn't stop us from daydreaming about our future together.

I had played around with the idea of having him move in with me since I knew there weren't a ton of places available in Stone Creek and Brooke's neighbor had already rented out their place. There were too many variables that I needed to consider before I dove off the deep end and opened my big mouth. First and foremost, how the kids would feel about it. They had gotten to know Parker over Christmas when he spent the holidays with us but they didn't know that we were seeing each other or that I had been keeping in touch with him since then. I felt guilty not telling them about it but I also didn't want to get their hopes up that something would happen with us and then let them down if things went south.

The sun crept through the sheer curtains, casting a warm glow in the room. I had no idea what time it was but I guessed that it was still early. My body desperately wanted to stretch and move around but I didn't want to wake Parker up since he sounded like he was sleeping so well. I closed my eyes and tried to fall back asleep, knowing that I wouldn't be able to. I was one of those people who once you're up, you're up. My phone vibrated on the nightstand beside me but it was just out of reach to where I couldn't get it without pulling away from him. While he might be able to stay sleeping if I did, I wasn't ready to not be in his arms. It felt safe and cozy and for the first time, I felt loved and wanted. I could stand holding onto this feeling a little while longer.

A few minutes went by before my phone vibrated again. Then again. I groaned silently, debating whether or not to leave my warm happy place. I glanced over and looked at it, willing it to stop.

"Just answer your phone," Parker mumbled against my shoulder, the stubble on his jaw tickling my skin as he slowly pulled away and rolled onto his back, locking his hands together above his head. The sheets shifted when I sat up and grabbed my phone, leaving his bare chest uncovered. My eyes wandered his body, taking in the smooth olive-toned skin that I wanted to run my tongue along. Even just laying there, his muscles were so well defined that he looked like he should be on the cover of a magazine promoting some sort of fitness routine. My phone started vibrating again but I made no effort to answer it as I stayed gazing at his perfect body, lost in thought.

"Sheila, you can eye-fuck me all day if you want to but that phone isn't going to stop ringing until you answer it." He opened one eye and looked at me with a raised eyebrow. I could feel the heat flush through my body as I blushed and looked away, forcing myself to redirect my attention to my phone. I looked at the caller ID and closed my eyes.

"It's Oliver, I need to take this real quick," I explained as I climbed out of bed and pulled the sheet around me, leaving him the blanket. He smiled smugly as he caught my eye, the blanket barely covering his dick that was already nice and hard, bulging under the covers. I subconsciously licked my lips and shook my head as I made my way to the bathroom and closed the door behind me. It was odd that Oliver was calling, especially this early in the morning, and I started to get a terrible feeling that something was wrong.

"Hey, Ollie, what's wrong?"

"Is it true?" His tone was sharp and I knew he was pissed off. He sounded just like his father when he was angry.

"Is what true? What's going on?" I racked my brain trying to figure out what was going on and what could possibly have him this upset first thing in the morning. He was fine when I dropped them off at my parent's house yesterday and when I checked in with the kids last night before bed.

"I heard dad on the phone this morning," he snapped out. "He said that you were dating Parker and that he's moving in with us. Is that true?"

I sat down on the edge of the bathtub and closed my eyes, allowing myself a minute to gather myself before speaking. Of course, Rodney would hear about my relationship with Parker from Genevieve but I didn't think he would be so quick to spin lies about it to the kids before I could talk to them.

"Honey, there's a lot that we're going to talk about later when we get home but I don't want you worrying about that right now. Okay?"

The other end was complete silence and I wondered if he hung up on me.

"Oliver?"

"Yeah," he sighed sarcastically.

"Just making sure you were still there," I said gently, trying not to piss him off any more than he already was.

"I'm still here. Unlike some people, I don't run off to meet my secret boyfriend and stay the night at their hotel."

"Excuse me?" I snapped, feeling my anger escalate quicker than I could try to control it. "You better take a minute and THINK before you say another word to me." I shook my head, catching my reflection in the mirror. Once I had better control, I started speaking again. "You do not talk to me like that ever again, do you understand me?"

"Yes ma'am," he muttered into the phone.

"Oliver," I warned.

"Yes. Ma'am." His voice was louder as he dramatically enunciated each word.

"You need to remember that you are *sixteen* years old. You're not an adult yet and you have absolutely no business putting your nose into my business. I will discuss my relationship with you when *I* am ready. Not the other way around. Do I make myself clear?"

"Yes, ma'am."

"Good. Then that's the end of this discussion until I decide that we will talk about it. Understood?"

"Understood."

I pushed the air out of my lungs that I had been holding in an attempt to not completely lose my cool with him. After I slowly exhaled I could feel myself getting calmer.

"Why was your dad there anyway?" I asked, suddenly confused about why Oliver was with Rodney when he was supposed to be with my parents.

"Dad came and got us last night from grandma's house. He said that it was supposed to be his week last week and that if you wanted the child support payment then you needed to let him have his time with us."

In an instant, my blood was boiling as my jaw clenched. He had some fucking nerve.

"Well, that was nice of him to call me and let me know," I replied sarcastically even though my frustration wasn't with Oliver. "Sorry, I didn't mean to take my frustration out on you."

"It's okay," he said quietly.

"Does your brother and sisters know about me and Parker?"

"I don't think so. They were still asleep. I had a headache so I had been up for a while but he didn't know that I was up. I had gotten out of bed and was going to get a glass of water when I heard him on the phone and stopped. He doesn't know that I heard him on the phone talking about it."

"What exactly did he say?" My curiosity got the best of me and I found that I needed to know what was said, even if it meant that I was asking my child to rat out their father.

"He said that Gen wanted him to move to Arkansas with her

after they got married but she knew that he wouldn't be able to leave us kids. Then he said, 'she's moving her new boyfriend in with her at the end of the month and doesn't care about how it will affect the kids, so I can just move the kids with me to Arkansas and she won't be able to say anything about it.' I stopped listening after that and went back to my room."

My chest tightened at the thought of Rodney trying to move and take the kids with him to Arkansas. There was no way that I would let him move away with my kids but I also knew that he would immediately stop his child support payments if he didn't get his way. This had been a constant threat from him over the years and now I was kicking myself for not sitting down with a lawyer sooner to find out what the legal ramifications would be if he tried. I could take him to court and fight it but Oliver would be eighteen in a few years and I would stop getting his payment anyway. There was also the option of finding a second job to replace the missing child support or the option that I dreaded the most. Sell the house and move back home with my parents.

"Mom?" Oliver's voice jolted me and snapped me out of the depressing thoughts that were quickly multiplying.

"Yeah son?"

"I don't want to move to Arkansas. I want to stay here. With you."

"I know Ollie," I sighed. "Try not to worry about that right now, okay? We'll get everything situated soon but I guarantee that your dad isn't taking you kids anywhere without one hell of a fight from me. Okay?"

"Okay," he mumbled sadly, all of the anger that was there at the beginning of the call now gone.

"It'll be alright, I promise. Think about what you guys want for dinner tonight and we'll pick something up on our way home. Then we'll all sit down and talk about everything tonight as a family. Sound good?"

"Yeah, that sounds good."

"Alright, I'll see you tonight. And Ollie, please don't tell your siblings about any of this. It's best if we can all sit down and talk through things together. I don't want them to be stressed out or freaking out that they're moving before I have a chance to talk to your dad."

"I think it's too late for that. Dad just called all of us into the living room for a family meeting."

"I'll be there soon, just hold tight."

I sighed and hung up the phone. Today was not going the way I had thought it was an hour ago. I got dressed and walked out of the bathroom to find Parker sitting in bed, the blanket still barely covering him, while his fingers moved quickly across his phone. His eyes lit up when he saw me then changed when he noticed that I was dressed.

"Everything okay?"

"Um, no, not really." I thought about how to explain everything without getting into too much detail. "Apparently Rodney knows about our relationship and is telling the kids that you're moving in with us by the end of the month. That is, if he doesn't take them with him when he moves to Arkansas with

Genevieve."

I watched as the different emotions flashed across his face, starting with shock and ending with anger.

"Are you fucking serious?"

"Yup. That's Rodney for you." I walked over to the table where I had left my purse and picked it up. "I need to get going. I'm going to head over to Rodney's house and try to talk to him and the kids before things get too crazy."

"I thought the kids were with your parents?" He pulled his brows together.

"Yeah, me too. Turns out that he went by to get them last night because he decided he wanted his time with them after standing them up last week when he was supposed to have them."

"And your parents just let him take them?"

"I haven't talked to them yet but if I know him, he probably told them everything they needed to hear about how I knew he was picking them up and that I said it was okay. He's the best manipulator, as you can see."

"Why don't I come with you? Maybe I can help somehow?" He pulled the blankets off and climbed out of bed, bending over to pull on his boxers that were still laying on the floor.

"Thank you but I think it's best if I handle this by myself."

He stopped and turned around, a hurt look on his face.

"If you're sure that's what you want."

"It's never about what I want. It's about working around the landmine that is Rodney and keeping it from exploding. I've been working at keeping the peace for so long that anything new can set him off before I have a chance at calming him down."

"So how exactly do I fit into this picture? I'm your boyfriend but I'm not allowed to support you and stand up for you against your ex-husband who is going to be my future son-in-law?"

"I haven't had time to think through any of that yet," I explained desperately, feeling like I was on a downward slope with him now too. "I want you to be involved in things with the kids and me but I don't think this is the time to start. We barely just started seeing each other and now there are all of these other variables getting in the way. It's just too much right now."

He looked away and ran a hand down the scruff on his face.

"Okay," he blew out and looked down at the floor, his hands on his hips.

"Parker, I'm sorry. I didn't mean to hurt your feelings."

"You didn't. I just don't get why it's so hard for you to let someone else help you or try to be there for you. Rodney already knows about us and if he's going to be a dick to you and threaten to move to Arkansas with your kids, I should be able to stand up for you and help however I can. I get that our relationship is new but he's going to be part of my family anyway once he marries my daughter. Whether you like it or not, I'm still involved with this guy. I just wish you would trust me enough to let me try to help you."

"You don't know what kind of person he is, Parker. No one can help me," I said sadly. "I appreciate that you so desperately want to protect me and my kids but I haven't come this far and worked this hard to risk everything if things don't work out. It's all candy-coated promises."

"Candy-coated promises?" he repeated with a frown.

"They sound sweet but they're too good to be true."

"So what are you saying, Sheila?"

"Maybe we're rushing into things too fast. Maybe it's best if we slow down and take a break."

"A break?"

"From each other…," I whispered, not wanting to say the words even though I knew that I needed to. Parker didn't need to get caught up in my family drama and if I had any leverage against Rodney trying to pack up the kids and move them to Arkansas, I was going to have to walk away from the one person who had finally worked his way into my heart. I swallowed hard to try to keep the tears away that were threatening to spill over at any moment. With my purse on my shoulder and my head held high, I turned around and walked out, leaving a broken-hearted man to deal with the mess I had just created.

Twelve
Sheila

"There is NO WAY IN HELL that I am letting you move to Arkansas with my kids," I said assertively, leaning forward across the table as I pointed a finger in Rodney's direction. The kids were off in their rooms, likely listening to music and playing video games instead of doing their homework. Or eavesdropping through the walls if I knew them.

Genevieve sat quietly beside Rodney, unable to look at me. I had been there for over an hour and we had been screaming at each other for the last forty-five minutes. I didn't believe in yelling or screaming to get what I wanted but when I got here my blood was already boiling, and I was on an emotional rollercoaster after everything that had happened in the last twenty-four hours.

"So, you can have some man you barely know move into your

house while my kids live there, but I can't have them live in my house with my WIFE?" Rodney shouted back, slamming his fist down on the table, rattling the empty beer cans in the middle.

"I never said that Parker was moving in with me. Parker and I never even talked about it as an option so I have no idea where you got that information from but it's completely wrong. Parker and I *were* dating and he *was* planning to move here, but we never discussed him moving in with me."

"What do you mean you guys *were* dating? What happened?" Genevieve asked, finally jumping into the conversation.

"I mean that we broke up this morning when I realized that my life was filled with endless drama and that he deserved better than that," I snapped at her, barely taking my eyes off of Rodney to cast a glance at her. Her face fell as she lowered her head and folded her hands together in front of her on the table. I instantly felt bad for lashing out at her. This wasn't her fault and my frustration was getting the better of me.

"Well whether you're with pretty boy or not—doesn't make any difference. I bring in the money so that means that I get to decide where I live and whether to take the kids with me or not." He leaned back, the buttons of his flannel shirt pulling tight across his newly formed beer belly. He let out a loud belch and chuckled, not bothering to apologize for it. I turned my attention to Genevieve and tilted my head as if to ask her *really?* It seemed that he didn't care about his appearance now that he had found a young, beautiful woman who was willing to settle down with him.

"I appreciate the child support money that you pay for the kids but I assure you that I will find another way to replace that income. You will NOT threaten me again with child support. Those days are over."

He snorted and wiped at his nose with his finger before turning to look at Genevieve who looked like she would rather be anywhere other than here.

"I am not playing, Rodney. Threaten to take my kids from me one more time and it will be the last thing you do." I pinned him with a look and for the first time in my life, the anger in my eyes seemed to penetrate this thick skull. For a brief second, I saw a flash of realization that he knew that I wasn't playing by his rules anymore.

I don't know what came over me but I was finally feeling confident enough to stand up to him. Maybe it was my conversation with Parker this morning or the fact that I had felt like shit after I walked out and left him when he was only trying to help. When I thought about it, I had been a complete ass to completely disregard what he was saying and to refuse his help. I tried to picture how Rodney would have reacted when I walked in with my incredibly sexy, well-groomed boyfriend who looked like he could be a model. Compared to Rodney with his sandy-blonde hair that desperately needed to be cut and his clothes that were wrinkled and probably on day 4 of wearing, there was no doubt who the better man would have been in this room.

"Well, we'll just have to wait and see what the kids want to do. It's not up to you and never has been, you should know that by now." He pushed away from the table and walked over to the fridge, bringing another beer with him without offering anything to Genevieve or myself. I watched as she squirmed uncomfortably in her seat and I wished that I could pull her aside and have a talk with her to try to knock some sense into her before she went through with marrying him. I loved my children dearly and I would always be thankful that he gave them to me, however, I didn't want her to follow in my path. She had her whole future ahead of her and she shouldn't throw that away for someone like Rodney who would just let her.

"I really doubt that the kids are going to want to pack up and move in the middle of the school year and leave their friends. They've known the kids in town their whole life, Rodney, you know that. Oliver is starting his junior year in the fall and is already thinking about asking his girlfriend to prom. Megan made it on the junior varsity volleyball team as a sophomore— you can't just take that away from her. Thomas is finally adjusting to high school, it would be like starting over as a freshman in another school. Sally is graduating from eighth grade. These are all things that they're not going to want to miss and they shouldn't have to."

"Yeah, well, life ain't fair darlin'. Sometimes you just have to roll with the punches and go where the good Lord puts you. It ain't up to you or—"

"I don't want to marry you," Genevieve blurted out, interrupting him. Her eyes filled with panic as she looked up at him.

I felt my eyes bulge out of my head, turning to look at her at the same time Rodney's head whipped in her direction.

"What are you talking about?"

"I can't marry you, Rodney. I'm sorry. I just don't think that this is going to work for me and I wish I would have seen it sooner before I said yes. But I didn't and I'm sorry but I can't marry you." She rushed through her words, afraid to look at him when she finished.

I breathed out a breath of relief, thankful that she was a smart girl after all and that she wasn't making the same poor decisions that I had made all of my life. Rodney was a sweet talker which was probably the only reason she had ever started dating him. He could charm a used car salesman into giving him a car for free while thinking it was their idea.

"Gen, please don't do this," he begged as he turned in his seat to look at her. He reached across the table to hold her hands before she pulled away, out of his reach.

"You did this to her, didn't you?" he snapped at me as he swung back around to face me. "You filled her head with lies so she would leave me and you could get your way!"

I stared at him in disbelief and shook my head.

"I didn't say a damn thing to her about you. Maybe she just came to her senses and decided to walk away before she got caught up in all of your drama."

Gen stood up and took a deep breath before speaking.

"I grew up thinking that my biological dad didn't want anything to do with me because my mom never bothered to tell me anything different. When I would ask about him, she would blow me off or change the subject. After she started dating my stepdad, I would get in trouble if I asked about my real dad. I remembered him coming to visit a handful of times but never knew why he stopped. It wasn't until I found him a month ago and we had the chance to sit down and talk, that I realized why he hadn't been around. It was because he thought he was doing the right thing and giving me a better family life that wasn't complicated."

She paused for a minute and smiled at me, her hands trembling at her side. My heart hurt for her, hearing her speak about the childhood that she wished for with Parker.

"When we first started dating, things were fun and exciting. We went to concerts together and you took the time to ask me about school. Things were going really good and I didn't care about the age difference between us at first. Then I found out that you had an ex-wife and four kids that you hadn't told me about in the beginning. I should have known then that this wasn't the right relationship for me but I tried to ignore those feelings because I liked you so much. But now that I see how you treat Sheila, the mother of your children, I can't look away from that. Nor can I look away from the fact that you care more about your own happiness than you do about what would make your kids happy."

Rodney's face fell and for a moment I wondered if she had actually gotten through to him.

"So, you're saying that if I treat Sheila better and *try* to do what makes my kids happy, you'll give me another chance?"

I looked down and pretended to be busy with my phone to avoid the awkward silence that was now lingering in the room.

"No, Rodney. It means that I've already seen the real side

of you and I want to be with someone who wants to put his children first without it being a condition of the relationship. I have my own issues with an absent father in my life, I will not be involved in a relationship that creates those issues for anyone else."

I felt my chest well up with pride, amazed by how wonderful of a person she was. I could feel her gaze on me and smiled back at her.

"Well, then I guess it's settled that the kids and I aren't moving to Arkansas. You get your way, like always," Rodney muttered, looking down at the table as he spun the empty beer can in his hand.

"Like I've told you before, it's never about getting my way. It's about doing what's best for our children, Rodney. This isn't a game to see who they like better between the two of us, it's about making sure we work together to be a solid team that puts their best interests above everything else."

"Whatever you say," he sighed before he pushed his chair back and walked away.

"I'm sorry you had to be here for that, I can imagine it was uncomfortable for you," Gen apologized once we were alone.

"You don't ever need to apologize for speaking up for what you want," I assured her. "I'm proud of you. Not many people can stand up for themselves and know what they want out of life."

She grinned nervously, rubbing her hands together.

"I was so scared, I've never done anything like that before in my life." Her eyes lit up with excitement. "I felt in control and for once, I didn't feel like anyone was treating me like a child. It's such an amazing feeling, like I feel totally unstoppable right now. I should call my dad and sit down to have the talk he's been wanting to have."

"Sounds like a good idea." I stood up and pushed my chair under the table. She was already calling Parker when I walked down the hall and knocked on the kids' doors, letting them know it was time to go. When I turned the corner to go into the living room, I ran right into Genevieve.

"Sorry," I laughed and stepped out of the way. "I'm like a magnet for running into people."

"Same here, I can easily trip over air," she joked.

"Were you able to get in touch with your dad?" I asked, desperate for any information on Parker since I hadn't talked to him after I broke things off between us.

"He didn't answer. I left a voicemail but I'm guessing he's already on the road back to Nashville."

I offered a half-smile, unable to force my mouth to commit to a real one.

"I'm sorry that you guys broke up. I hope all of this wasn't the reason for it." She gestured to the air around us and I knew that she was talking about her relationship with Rodney.

I sucked in a shaky breath, unsure of whether I wanted to get into the details of my relationship with Parker with his daughter. I was already growing pretty fond of her in such a short time but needed to remember that there might need to be some boundaries between us if things did end up working between her dad and me.

"It's just the usual relationship stuff," I said dismissively as I heard the kids coming down the hall. "We're going to grab a pizza and head back to my house, do you want to join us?"

Sally's face lit up when she heard the invite and started bouncing up and down excitedly while begging Gen to say yes.

"Sure, I would love to." Gen smiled and took Sally's hand as they walked out to the car. I knew that sooner or later we would need to sit down and tell the kids that Rodney and Gen had broken up but for now, everyone was happy and that was how I planned to leave it.

262

Thirteen
Parker

Growing up in a house with parents who were never there, physically or emotionally- left a longing inside of me that I had tried to ignore for years. I pushed myself through life, always chasing after the next goal, feeling success with every achievement. It wasn't until I met Sheila and I had a glimpse into her family life that I realized that the one thing I had been longing for and was never able to fulfill was the feeling of love and acceptance from my family. My parents told me they were proud of me a handful of times in my life, but I couldn't remember the last time that they said they loved me. When I was a teenager, I sat down one day after school and asked them why we didn't say we loved each other. It seemed so odd because all of my friends did it with their families so why didn't we do it? Their answer was that only petty people who had nothing else in life felt the need to validate their feelings with words.

I decided to head back to Nashville after Sheila left. My mind was still trying to process everything, which explained why my knuckles were white as my fingers clutched the steering wheel angrily, the car accelerating past one hundred. I knew that I should slow down and focus on the road instead of obsessing over every tiny detail about our fight before she decided we needed to take a break. I guess you couldn't really call it a fight. I asked her to let me in and wanted to support her and she shut me out before she broke up with me.

The sky was alarmingly white with the threat of a major snowstorm, just like the weatherman had promised on the radio when I got into the car. I hoped that I would be able to pass through before it started. I leaned forward against the steering wheel and glanced up, confirming that I was about to drive through the thick of it. The snow started to come down in heavy sheets of thick, white flakes, and within a few minutes, I could barely see a few feet in front of me. I slowly released my foot from the gas, knowing better than to try braking and risk losing control of the car. The outside temperature on the dashboard showed twenty-four degrees which guaranteed there was a layer of ice already on the road given how much precipitation was in the air.

I continued to grip the steering wheel with both hands, keeping my eyes on the road while focusing my attention on my surroundings. There were a few other cars that were in front of me before we got into the storm but I had no idea how far ahead they were now. I imagined they had slowed down long before I thought to. The chill from outside was forcing its way in, sending a shiver through me despite the heavy jacket I was wearing. I reached down to turn the heater on full blast. All of a sudden, a blast of cold air shot out of the vents, startling me. I looked down to make sure the knob was turned to heat instead of cold, knowing that I couldn't afford to take my eyes off the road for even a second in this storm.

After I adjusted the knob, which must have accidentally been bumped recently, I looked up and held on tight to the steering wheel as the back end of a semi-truck came swinging right into the front end of my car. The last thing I heard was the sound of metal crunching and glass shattering around me.

Fourteen
Sheila

Three large pepperoni pizzas and four two-liters of soda later, the kids and I were stretched out in the living room. The movie we had been watching had ended, but we were all too full to bother with getting up to get the remote to change it from the six o'clock news. A red bar ran along the bottom of the screen with a series of weather-related warnings for the snowstorm that was supposed to be hitting Stone Creek this evening. I thought back to what Gen had said earlier and hoped that Parker hadn't tried to make it back to Nashville in this storm. Maybe he was in the shower or out with Ryder? Anything would be better than him attempting to drive a deserted stretch of highway in a storm that was predicted to be one of the deadliest storms in over a decade.

The screen changed and a man wearing a blazer that was two sizes too small started moving around in front of the green screen that was laid out with updates on where the storm had already dropped a few feet of snow and where it was headed next. I leaned forward, trying to see what the orange-colored box meant that stretched over Stone Creek, all the way to Nashville. Fifteen feet of snow was expected to fall before midnight which meant that no one was getting in or out of Stone Creek for a while. It also meant that if anyone was already trying to drive through this, they were likely stuck and stranded for a while.

The newscast switched back over to the regular anchor who was now giving travel safety tips for those who had to go anywhere within the city. While they discouraged anyone from driving in this, they also had due diligence to educate the viewers on making sure they had the essentials in their car, just in case. As they went down the list of blankets, bottles of water, flashlights, and batteries, I picked up my phone, hoping Parker would have reached out to me to let me know where he was. I knew that he didn't owe it to me and that it was beyond unlikely that I would hear from him, but I was desperate to know that he was safe.

"Have you heard from your dad?" I asked Gen as a commercial for teeth whitening came on. I didn't want to miss the news, just in case there was any useful information that she could pass along once she talked to him.

She shook her head no, picking her phone up to try again.

"It rings and goes to voicemail. He hasn't answered any of my text messages either."

I nodded, not wanting to alarm the kids by talking about how worried I was that he might have gotten caught in the snowstorm.

We didn't know where he was or why he wasn't answering his phone, but the last thing I wanted to do was worry the kids that something bad had happened. I sent a couple of silent prayers up before I got up and walked into the kitchen, pacing back and forth while I waited for him to pick up.

The sound of the beep was annoyingly loud in my ear as if it was a direct sign of him rejecting me by refusing my call. I knew it was silly to assume that he had seen me calling and chose to ignore it because he was still mad at me, especially since he hadn't answered any of Gen's calls and he wasn't mad at her. A feeling of dread ate away at me as I started to consider that something might actually be wrong and that I wasn't just imagining it.

I waited a few minutes before sending a quick text, letting him know that I was just checking in to make sure he was okay because of the storm that was supposed to hit before he got back to Nashville. My fingers trembled as I pushed send, the anxiety starting to build inside. I chewed my nail while I watched the confirmation pop up that the message was delivered and waited a few more minutes for it to show read. Suddenly, my phone started to vibrate in my hand, the excitement quickly replaced with disappointment when I saw Brooke's name on the screen and not Parker's.

"Hey," I tried to sound as cheery as possible.

"Well don't you sound as happy as a clam? What's wrong?"

"Nothing," I lied. I wasn't ready to get into the details of my day with her just yet. Between breaking up with Parker and dealing with Rodney who was also just dumped by Gen, it was a lot to go over and required more energy than I had. "I just had a long day and had to deal with Rodney."

"Oh, that explains the bad mood," she said sympathetically, knowing my past with him well enough to not have to ask for more information.

"What's up?" I asked as I cleaned up the kid's mess from the kitchen table so I didn't have to do it later.

"I was wondering if Parker was there with you? Ryder has been trying to reach him but he's not answering his calls or texts."

My stomach dropped along with the pile of empty pizza boxes that were in my hand before I could take them out to the trash in the garage. Something was definitely wrong if none of us were able to reach him.

"Sheila? Did you hear me?" Brooke's voice was louder on the other end, forcing me to focus instead of going down the rabbit hole of tragic what-ifs.

"Yeah, I heard you. No, he's not here and I haven't heard from him either."

"Is everything okay? Did you guys have a fight?"

"I don't want to get into it now but we broke up this morning," I sighed heavily as I bent down to pick up the boxes.

"Sheila, why didn't you call me?" Her voice was surprisingly empathetic, void of any judgment.

"Because the day has been long and I haven't had a chance."

"Okay, I get it. I won't pry. But if you hear from him, will you please let me know so Ryder will stop worrying?"

"Yeah, I'll let you know. I'm sure Gen will hear from him before I will so I'll keep you posted. So far he hasn't answered her calls or texts either."

"Who's Gen?"

Suddenly it occurred to me that Brooke and Ryder didn't know about Parker's daughter because he had been planning to tell them this weekend before everything got so crazy. We had talked about meeting them for lunch today, but that was before I broke his heart and left before breakfast. It was still hard to believe that I had barely found out about Genevieve a week ago and that it had barely been twenty-four hours since I found out that she was also the same person as Rodney's, now former, fiancé. There was a lot to unpack and I felt uncomfortable telling Brooke all of Parker's secrets over the phone when we should have been more concerned with where he was.

I took a slow, steady breath in and tried to think as quickly as I could. I was a terrible liar but this was a time when I needed to come up with something and fast.

"Sheila—who is Gen?" Brooke asked again, more aggressively this time.

"She's his daughter," I breathed out.

"What?!"

The phone was silent for a few minutes before she came back on the line.

"How does Parker have a daughter that no one knew about? Including his best friend?"

"It's a long story and honestly, it's not mine to tell. Parker was planning to talk to Ryder today, I don't know what happened or where he is."

"But his daughter is there with you? Why? How old is she? Did he just abandon a child and left town and no one has heard from him? This is all too crazy and wild, I just can't believe that he would—"

"Brooke!" I said sharply, forcing her to stop before she got herself too worked up and out of control.

"Sorry, this is just a lot to take in."

"That's why I didn't want to tell you over the phone. Gen is Genevieve, his daughter, who is twenty-two years old. She's here with me because she was at Rodney's house while I was there fighting with him about the kids."

"Why was she at Rodney's?"

"Because Genevieve is – was—Gen, his fiancé."

"No. Way."

"Way."

"Okay, you're right. That's a lot to process."

"I told you," I chided.

"Well if you, or *his daughter,* hear from him, please let us know. We're really worried about him with this storm. If he tried to make it to Nashville—"

"I know," I whispered. Neither of us had to finish that sentence. We knew what it meant if he was on the road in the middle of this storm.

"I'll talk to you soon," I assured her before hanging up the phone and walking back into the living room. It was eerily quiet as the kids all stared in horror at the tv screen, no one noticing that I had walked in. I quickly turned my attention to the tv and listened as the screen changed and a live view was broadcasted from the helicopter that was trying to get close enough to the scene of the accident. A semi-truck was laying on its side, several feet down the side of the hill, and beside it was the car it had plowed into, crushing the front to the point where you couldn't recognize what kind of car it was. As the helicopter moved around and changed angles, it gave a quick glimpse of the backside of the car.

Gen's head turned and whipped up to look at me, fear in her eyes when we both recognized the black BMW with the custom license plate. The car had plowed headfirst into an embankment of snow that had already accumulated but according to the news anchor, the driver could not be located. Law enforcement was working on getting a search and rescue team out there as quickly as possible, however, the storm would make it nearly impossible until it passed through. My heart felt like it was about to explode in my chest as I thought about losing the one person who I had finally allowed myself to love.

Fifteen
Parker

I blinked slowly, trying to force myself to wake up. Everything around me was blanketed in white as the icy chill of the snow stung my skin. I knew that I needed to get up and find help, but my body refused to move. It was hard to tell if there was an injury that was preventing me from moving or if I was in some sort of nightmare that I couldn't wake up from. You know the kind that feels so real that you believe you're in it, then you desperately try to escape from whatever demon is trying to kill you before it's too late. As a cold gust of wind whipped past me, I closed my eyes and prayed that the demon was on its way.

Off in the distance, I could swear that I heard the faint sound of people yelling and sirens that were muffled by the snow that was piling up around me. I didn't have to open my eyes to know that the snow was only a few inches away from covering my face and completely burying me. Regardless of how many voices I thought I had heard, no one would reach me in time. It was too late. I let out a shallow breath and allowed myself to succumb to the numbness that had enveloped me.

Sixteen
Sheila

"It's been over twelve hours," I exclaimed as I paced back and forth in front of the kitchen table while Brooke and Ryder watched helplessly. They came right over after we saw Parker's car on the news and the rest of the night had been an emotional blur since then. Gen stuck around and helped me get the kids to bed when they all refused to sleep until they knew that he was safe. After some gentle persuading from Gen and a promise from Brooke that we would wake them up as soon as we heard anything, they all shuffled off down the hall and made their way to bed. Whether or not they were sleeping was a different question that I didn't bother to ask right now.

"They'll find him, Sheila, they have a huge team of people looking for him," Brooke assured me before getting up and pulling the kettle from the stove and serving us all a cup of hot tea. I leaned my head back and ran my hands down my face, saying another prayer that they would find him before it was too late.

I had started to research what was considered 'too late' earlier and was finding plenty of articles that outlined in gory detail what would happen to a body that was left in the snow after x number of hours. I was fully engrossed in an article when Ryder took my phone and refused to give it back two hours ago. My anxiety was at an all-time high as I contemplated every possible scenario and their outcomes. Maybe it wasn't his car, maybe someone else has a car exactly like his with the same custom license plate that was also heading to Nashville. Or maybe he wasn't ejected from the car and thrown into the middle of nowhere on the side of the road in a freaking blizzard that decreased visibility which made it nearly impossible for anyone to find him. Maybe someone was close by when it happened and had already found him and were working on keeping him safe until help could find them. Or maybe he was gone and I was the reason for all of this.

Out of all of the maybes that I had come up with, that last one was the hardest to accept. If I hadn't broken up with Parker this morning then he wouldn't have left in the middle of a deadly snowstorm. I had already beat myself up with all of the *would've, could've, should've* and was driving everyone around me crazy with how obsessive I was getting about it. The problem was that aside from the kids, I've never had anyone in my life who I've loved so much that it killed me to think of living a life that didn't include them. Sure, I loved my parents, as well as Brooke and Ryder, but this was a different kind of love. This was the kind of love that forced its way through an ironclad heart and made a permanent scar to make sure it could never be erased. The kind of love that shattered your soul when you thought about life without ever feeling it again.

Brooke set the cup of tea in front of me on the table and

nodded at it. She snuggled up against Ryder and wrapped her arms around his neck while sitting on his lap with his arms around her waist. I knew that they were only trying to comfort each other while we waited for news on Parker but a shot of jealousy coursed through me at what they had.

"Sit down and have some tea," Gen coaxed from the other side of the table, holding her cup in between her hands. I felt my heart skip a beat when she smiled at me, looking just like her dad. With a heavy sigh, I pulled the chair out and sat down. The energy that was flowing through me needed an outlet which resulted in me tapping my foot anxiously underneath the table. Not knowing where he was or if he was safe was worse than anything I had ever gone through with my kids, and they had put me through a lot over the years, especially as they became teenagers.

It was after ten o'clock when we all moved into the living room and sat down to watch the news. The air was thick and filled with desperation as our eyes stayed glued to the tv. Luckily, this snowstorm was unlike anything Stone Creek had seen in over a decade which meant that it took priority and they cut straight to updates on the storm instead of the usual boring stories. I watched as the same weatherman from earlier appeared on the screen, giving updated snowfall totals for each county. My heart started to race when they switched back to the news anchor, hopeful that they would have an update on the accident. I leaned forward and waited.

A few minutes later it went to a commercial and I felt the disappointment start to consume me. Surely, if he had been found, it would have been a top news story. That could only mean one thing… he hadn't been found.

Seventeen
Parker

"Can you open your eyes?"

"Sir, what's your name?"

"Can you hear me?"

"We need you to stay with us, don't you give up on us now."

"Shit, we're losing him!"

"Don't you do this buddy, you've come this far… hold on a little bit longer."

"Starting compressions!"

"Someone get me an update on where his family is. Now!"

"One. Two. Three. Four. Five. Six. Seven. Eight. Nine. Ten.

Eleven. Twelve. Thirteen. Fourteen. Fifteen."

"We need some help over here!"

"Son of a bitch!"

Eighteen
Sheila

"Mommy, can I have pizza for breakfast?"

I opened my eyes to Sally standing in front of me, holding up a slice of cold pizza.

"Sure, just make sure to heat it first. Thirty seconds in the microwave," I mumbled, forcing myself to sit upright in the chair I had fallen asleep in. She walked into the kitchen and tossed it in the microwave without a plate, clearly following the only directions I had given her. I rolled my eyes as I thought about how much simpler it would have been to let her eat the pizza cold but part of me felt like I needed to be a good mom and have her warm it up. Eating cold pizza felt like something you did when you no longer cared about anything and I didn't need my children to know that was how I felt.

By midnight, Ryder and Brooke had decided to go home and

promised to call if they heard anything. Gen fell asleep on the couch shortly after they left. The house was quiet and calm which was unusual given all of the kids were home and needed to get ready for school. I was about to get up and head down the hallway to wake them up when I realized that school had to be canceled from the storm. The storm that had kept us up all night worrying about Parker. The storm that possibly took the only man I have ever loved.

Sally waited patiently at the microwave, standing on her tiptoes to watch as the slice of pizza spun around in circles. Once I heard it beep, I quickly yelled to remind her to use a spatula to get it out of the microwave so she didn't burn herself. She laughed and peeked around the wall, waving it in her hand at me. I smiled and leaned back in my chair, feeling my spirits lifted with her sweet personality.

I picked up the remote and turned the volume up enough to hear the news while Gen and the other kids slept. Nothing new had been reported about the storm other than a handful of accidents that had happened in town. The list of school and business closings ran across the bottom of the screen before it switched to a story about a local charity that was hosting a bake sale next week to raise money for the local church. I could feel the tension radiating across the back of my neck and shoulders. My body ached from sleeping in the chair and desperately needed to be up and moving to get some of the blood flowing through it again.

I stood up and reached above me, feeling the glorious relief as I pushed harder and stretched as long as I could. The tension started to alleviate a little as I rubbed my hand along my neck and rolled it. I was bending over, reaching for my toes to stretch my legs when I heard a phone vibrating on the coffee table. I shot straight up and grabbed it, noticing it was Gen's at the same time that her eyes fluttered open. Without saying a word I pushed it toward her, holding my breath as she took it and answered it.

"Yes, this is Genevieve," she paused and waited, nervously chewing her fingernail. "Yes, I'll be right there. Thank you so much for calling."

She hung up the phone then jumped up and smiled at me.

"They found him! He's at the Cedar Bay Hospital. The officer couldn't give me any details on how he's doing but at least now we know where to find him."

"Oh my God, that's incredible," I said breathlessly. My fingers trembled as they hovered over my trembling lips as I tried to keep myself from crying.

"Do you think someone can come watch the kids while you go with me to the hospital?"

I pulled my head back in surprise and looked at her.

"You want me to go with you? What if he doesn't want to see me?"

She reached out and grabbed my hands, holding onto them as she spoke.

"Of course I want you to go with me. I couldn't imagine going with anyone other than the woman who is head over heels in love with my dad. You need to be there. And more importantly,

I need you to be there with me… Will you come?"

"Yes!" I squealed and squeezed her hands. I quickly called my mom and asked her to come watch the kids before calling Brooke and Ryder with the update. Ten minutes later, I was putting on my shoes while saying goodbye to the kids and my mom before rushing out the door to jump in Ryder's new truck. Cedar Bay was only an hour away but the snow and ice hadn't been cleared in that area yet which meant that it might slow us down getting there. Ryder had offered to drive us so we didn't have to take two vehicles and since he had recently bought a new truck that he wanted to test out in the bad weather.

The drive to the hospital was quiet. Either we were all too nervous to talk, or we were too tired to bother. I was thankful and relieved that Gen wanted me to be there and prayed that Parker felt the same way when he saw me. There was a lot that I needed to explain to him but that would happen later. For now, I just needed to know that he was alive and okay. Until then, nothing else mattered.

Nineteen
Parker

"Can you tell me your name?"

"Parker Hudson," I croaked, my throat dry and sore after having the tube pulled out of it. The older man with white hair nodded and jotted something down on the clipboard he was holding in his hand.

"Do you know what day it is?" He pulled his brows together doubtfully and waited.

"I don't have any idea. Sunday? Tuesday?" I shrugged my shoulders before remembering that I was wearing a brace around my arm and that the doctor had confirmed that I had fractured my clavicle, amongst other things.

"That was a hard one, sorry," he mumbled and made an additional note before setting the clipboard down on the counter behind him and setting the pen on top. He turned to look at me, his hands folded in his lap as if he was bracing himself for delivering bad news.

"Do you remember what happened? Why you're in the hospital?"

"I was heading back to Nashville and got caught in a snowstorm. I looked down for half a second to turn the heater up and when I looked up, a semi had lost control and plowed right into me. The car spun off the road but I don't remember much after that. Only that I woke up in the hospital."

He nodded and pulled a piece of loose paper from underneath the clipboard.

"According to the police, the impact of the collision with the semi was enough to eject you from the vehicle minutes before the car hit a tree. Luckily, the car hit the tree with enough force that it knocked it over and into the powerlines which was how the rescue crews were able to find you. It took them a little bit of time to get to you because of the storm but the tree led them right to you. I would say that you had quite a bit of luck on your side or a guardian angel looking after you because not many people survive being in the bitter cold that long. We're going to keep you for a few days for monitoring but if everything looks good by Wednesday, we'll go ahead and release you."

"Sounds good, thanks, Doc."

He smiled and patted the table beside me before grabbing his clipboard and walking out the door. I had already seen a handful of nurses and doctors since I had "woken up" and each of them gushed about how lucky I was to still be alive. How I must be some sort of living angel, put here for a divine purpose. I couldn't wrap my head around the details of what happened because everything kept going back to one thing— Sheila.

290

Twenty
Sheila

The walk through the hospital felt like it took forever and everyone we stopped to ask for help was completely useless. Unfortunately, Gen didn't get anything from the police officer other than that Parker had been taken to Cedar Bay Hospital. We didn't know if he was in the emergency room, the ICU, or somewhere else. It was almost like the officer didn't care about whether she needed that information and I imagined that he was given an update at some point before he called her, yet he treated it as something on his to-do list. Call the family of the man who miraculously survived in the freezing cold for over twelve hours—check.

We walked quickly, trying to find our way around the hospital to the welcome desk. They would be able to look him up in their system and send us on our way. Ryder had parked on the east side of the hospital which shouldn't have been a problem, other than it planted us square in the middle of their radiology and imaging departments. It felt like a ghost town as we wandered the hallways, feeling like we were in some sort of blinding white corn maze. My stomach growled at the smell of the cafeteria food and I knew we were getting closer.

As the hallway came to an end, forming a T, we stopped to look at each other to see which way we should go. It was odd that there weren't any signs up to point us in the right direction but then again there was a fresh coat of paint on the walls which would explain the headache I was starting to get. I moved my head back and forth, trying to find the smell of food. It was stronger to my left so I nodded in that direction and took off walking in search of help.

The hallway continued a few feet before it opened up into a circle with a welcome desk in the middle. I felt my shoulders relax, thankful that we could finally stop this wild goose chase. I made my way over and smiled as I waited for the woman to finish her phone call. She was an attractive woman, probably close to my age but I doubted that she had four children given how perky her boobs were in the tight low-cut sweater she was wearing. Self-consciously, I glanced down at mine and realized that I hadn't bothered to change out of the Pink Floyd t-shirt I had thrown on last night before I fell asleep on the couch. Though my boobs were big, they weren't perky like hers, and this t-shirt did nothing to scream sex-appeal if anyone was looking.

I started panicking, wondering if I should have cleaned up better before we came so that I looked good for Parker when she hung up the phone and smiled at us. Now wasn't the time to worry about how I looked. I knew better than that and felt silly for even thinking about it in the first place. I was nervous to see Parker given how things had ended between us, but I seriously doubted that he would use my current appearance as a basis on whether to talk to me about what had happened.

"How can I help you?" she asked, her voice smooth and sexy like she should be answering a phone-sex line instead of working at the hospital. I bet she would make good money with her voice without having to try. Maybe she does it on the side and she was finishing a call when we walked up. She had blushed and looked away, pulling the mouthpiece of her headset closer to her body as she tucked her chin to her shoulder.

"We're here to see Parker Hudson," Gen explained while I was lost in thought. "The Stone Creek police department said that he was brought here after they found him in the woods."

"Oh! Yes! The Clark Kent looking guy," she gushed excitedly. "Let me see where he is, last I knew they had rushed him to the emergency room." She lowered her head and began typing quickly on the keyboard in front of her. Her freshly manicured nail tapped impatiently on the top of the mouse while she waited for the screen to load the results. "It looks like he's been moved to the tenth floor, room 1028."

"Thank you, we appreciate your help," Ryder said and knocked on the top of the desk a few times before turning around and leading Brooke to the elevators.

"No problem. The nurses and I look forward to giving him our well wishes soon now that I know he's been moved from the ER," she purred and locked eyes with me. I pulled my head back in surprise, my fist balled at my side when I felt Gen link her arm in mine and pull me away.

"She's not worth it," she whispered as we trailed behind Ryder and Brooke. "I know that I haven't *known* my dad for long, but I feel like I can honestly say that he would *NEVER* go for a woman like that."

I felt the anger and jealousy still pushing through me as I toyed with the idea of going back and punching her perfectly inflated boob to see if I could deflate it. It would delay me seeing Parker by a few minutes, but it would be worth it to knock Malibu Barbie down a peg or two.

"I've known Parker for over ten years and while I *didn't* know that he had a daughter, I can confirm that he would run away from a woman like that. Pretty much every man I know would."

He turned and winked at me over his shoulder as the elevator dinged and the doors slid open. We piled in, and I tried to fight the laughter that was tickling the back of my throat. I lifted my hand to my mouth and stared at the numbers on the wall, the tickle getting stronger. My eyes shifted to the numbers above the door and I watched as each one lit up with each floor we passed. We were almost to the tenth floor and I could feel the urge to burst into laughter getting stronger. I couldn't tell if it was a nervous reaction or simply a coping mechanism for everything that I had recently been through but suddenly the walls of the damn broke and everything came flooding out.

My body shook as I laughed hysterically, reaching over to grab the rail on the side of the wall as I snorted with each breath I tried to take in. Tears were rolling down my face while everyone stared at me in confusion.

"I'm sorry," I gasped, waving my hand in the air to try to dismiss what was happening. "Just ignore me, I'm fine," I snorted and started laughing again. Soon the laughter was contagious and everyone was wiping tears from their eyes as the doors opened to the tenth floor. We scooted off the elevator and popped into the family waiting area so I could try to get myself together. I was starting to get control again, forcing myself to take deep breaths as my sides hurt from laughing so hard. I couldn't remember the last time that I had *really* laughed at something.

"Are you sure you're okay?" Brooke asked, running a hand under her eye to wipe away the eyeliner that had started to smear.

"Yeah, I'm fine," I laughed. "I was so caught up in being angry at that woman that I had seriously thought about running back and punching her in the boob." I lowered my head and started laughing again, the replay of the image I had conjured up replaying in my mind.

"I wouldn't say that she didn't have it coming," Gen joked and leaned against the wall, her hands planted behind her butt.

"I don't even know where that idea came from. I've never had the urge to punch someone in the boob just because they were being flirty about a guy I liked."

"Well, love will do that to you," Brooke sighed and glanced up at Ryder.

"So you're telling me that love leads to having terrible ideas?" I put my hands on my hips and narrowed my eyes at her. I was playing but also stalling now that I knew we would be seeing Parker in a few minutes and I would have to face what happened between us and that I was the reason he was here to begin with.

"I wouldn't worry too much about it." She pursed her lips and shook her head.

"Why's that?" I frowned.

"Because you already have terrible ideas," she laughed, followed by Ryder. He offered a sympathetic smile as I glared at him with daggers in my eyes.

"I DO NOT have terrible ideas. When was the last time I had a terrible idea?" I asked, hands still on my hips. Brooke smiled coyly at me before she grabbed Ryder's hand and started walking down the hallway, forcing me to follow.

"When you wanted to skip and drink wine," she said over her shoulder as I felt Gen walking beside me. "And your worst one is thinking you can stall in the waiting room to keep from having to go in and talk to Parker."

I stayed quiet, not bothering to answer since anything I would have said would be a lie. Brooke knew me better than I knew myself so I should have seen that one coming. We walked down the hallway, ignoring the nurses that were busy at the station off to the right. I slowed my pace when I saw the room numbers getting closer, my heart skipping a beat as we got to his.

"Are you ready?" Ryder asked Gen and me as we stood pale as a ghost in front of the door, holding hands. I sucked in a deep breath and waited as Ryder opened the door.

Twenty One
Parker

"I meant it when I said the last person I wanted to see was you," I mumbled as I rolled onto my side, ignoring the person who had opened the door. I closed my eyes and tried to force myself to sleep, the inability to feel warm keeping me awake. No matter how hard I tried I couldn't escape the icy chill that seemed to still linger inside my body. It was as if my veins had been frozen and the blood inside was slowly trickling along, too cold to get where it needed to go.

"Well aren't you a peach?" Ryder joked.

I whipped my head around and looked, excited to see Ryder standing there with Brooke, Genevieve, and Sheila. My heart started beating wildly in my chest, my hands anxious to reach out and touch Sheila. To make sure she was real and that I wasn't dreaming of her or having another hallucination like I had when I was in the snow.

"I thought you were someone else," I mumbled, trying to explain myself. My eyes stayed glued to Sheila as I watched how she nervously shied away and tried to hide behind everyone else. She kept her head down and studied the ugly tile on the floor to keep from looking at me while she pulled at a loose string on the Pink Floyd t-shirt she sleeps in. I found myself smiling at the memory of her waking up in that same t-shirt on New Year's morning after we had spent the night together. She apologized for her faded, worn-out t-shirt but I loved her in it. It was perfectly Sheila. No-fuss and no high maintenance to make her look beautiful. She could wear a garbage bag and still look sexy.

"How are you feeling?" Ryder asked as he stepped closer, Brooke right behind him. I tried to catch Sheila's eye, but she continued to avoid me. I glanced over at Genevieve and while she didn't avoid looking at me, she was staring out the window with tears in her eyes.

"I'm alive, so I'll take that," I joked, instantly regretting it when I saw the reactions on their faces. "Sorry, that was a bad attempt at lightening the mood." I shook my head and ran a hand through my hair. "I feel like shit but at least there's nothing serious that they're worried about. Right now I'm resting and drinking plenty of warm fluids while they run an IV through me. I was lucky that I landed in an area that had a lot of leaves piled up which added some insulation. Thankfully, I was dressed in plenty of layers that helped save me."

"I still can't believe it," Ryder shook his head and stood next to me. "I'm so thankful that you're okay."

I could hear his voice crack and knew that this was hard for him. I reached up and gently patted his arm with the little strength that I had. His hand found mine and patted it in return before I let it fall beside me, the energy to keep it up there too much for me to handle. I wanted to reach out and pull Genevieve and Sheila over to me to make sure that they were okay, but I was scared as shit to even talk to them. Everything was new and I had no idea how to tread these new waters with a daughter who I just recently reconnected with and a woman who I was head-over-heels in love with. I wasn't the kind of guy who did love so I had NO IDEA how to handle this.

"Gen, did you want to come see your dad?" Brooke asked softly, doing all of the work for me as if she knew I was struggling with what to do.

She turned and looked at me, tears staining her cheeks as she nodded yes. I held my arms open for her, hoping she would accept the invitation. She rushed over and bent down, wrapping her arms gently around me as we hugged. I couldn't remember the last time I hugged her but something told me that it was when I said goodbye to her fifteen years ago. She trembled in my arms, her tears dripping onto my shoulder. I hugged her as tight as I could with what strength I had left. A few minutes later, she pulled away and wiped her face with the back of her hand.

"Are you really okay?" she asked before sitting on the edge of the bed after Brooke and Ryder had taken the two seats off to the side by the window.

"Yes, sweetheart, I'm really okay."

"I was so scared that I was going to lose you," she whispered, fighting back more tears.

"You will never lose me again, I promise you that. I will always be here for you and I'll use my superhuman powers to escape death as many times as I need," I teased before adding, "but I really hope that there won't be any more near-death experiences in my future. I barely dodged this bullet, I can't imagine that I would be that lucky a second time around."

Everyone chuckled except for Sheila. I hadn't forgotten that she was there. I intended to give her time, allow her to feel comfortable before I tried to talk to her. I knew things were bad with how we left them this morning, but I prayed that she would be open to talking it out and seeing if we could work through everything together. I didn't care anymore about whether she let me be a part of her life with Rodney in the way that I thought I needed. I was convinced that she was delicate and fragile, that she needed protecting. But I was completely wrong about that. She was fierce and strong, the kind of woman who didn't need a knight in shining armor to come save the day. This was probably a good thing since I couldn't remember where I had stored my shining armor…

The room grew quiet and an awkward silence prevailed. I wasn't the only one who had noticed that Sheila was still hiding in the corner of the room as Brooke kept leaning to the side, trying to get her attention before not-so-subtly nodding in my direction for her to come talk to me. I was about to say something funny to draw her attention over to me but before I could think of what to say, the door opened and the one woman I *didn't* want to see walked in.

She stood in the doorway, surprise on her face as she looked around, her face recently touched up with a new layer of powder and a fresh coat of red lipstick. Her black hair was neatly tucked behind her ear, each strand perfectly in place.

"Well, hello darlings," she purred as she squared her shoulders and ran her hands down the front of her dry-clean-only navy blue blazer that matched the pinstripe satin shirt underneath. "It looks like we have company, dear," she said crisply as her eyes narrowed at me in disapproval.

302

Twenty Two
Sheila

If I wanted to crawl in a corner and hide when I thought about seeing Parker, this woman made me want to crawl under a bed and pull the blankets down over me so she would never find me. Everything about her demanded attention from her salon colored hair to her overly priced heels that probably cost more than my monthly mortgage payment. Her smile appeared forced, even through the layers of Botox that was already pulling her skin tight across her thin, angular face. We all stared on, in confusion, as Parker worked his jaw back and forth, glaring at her. I stepped to the side, moving out of the way as the door opened again and a man walked in.

He looked like he was ready to go play golf at some ritzy country club with his pristine white sweater wrapped around his broad shoulders. His navy blue pants paired perfectly with the white polo that was neatly tucked in and adorned by a thin black belt. He stood next to the woman and attempted to wrap an arm around her shoulder before her side-eyed glare made him rethink it. He lowered his arm by his side and stood up straight, more rigid than I had ever seen anyone. As I looked at the power couple before me, I couldn't help but wonder if their outfits were strategically matched with navy and white, or if it was purely coincidental.

"I see you have company," the man commented, barely moving his head as he glanced around the room.

"Nothing gets by you, Dad," Parker mumbled and shifted in the bed. Genevieve was standing beside him, fiddling with her fingers while avoiding the penetrating stare the woman was giving her.

"That's no way to speak to your parents," the woman attempted to lecture, only to get an eye-roll in return.

"Everyone, these are my parents. Willa and Bradly Hudson." He nodded in their direction.

"*Doctor* Willa Hudson," she corrected.

"My *mother* is a retired Oncologist who used to work at this hospital. Now she serves on the board of directors which is how she was informed that I was here, after I was brought in." He looked from Ryder to me, an apologetic look on his face.

"Well, it's not like you would have bothered to call and tell us yourself. Unlike your *friends*. I guess we see where we rate these days." Her tone was harsh.

"Gee, I'm sorry mom. I guess I didn't think to call and tell you that I was laying in the snow after being ejected from my car when a semi came crashing into me. I was barely alive when someone found me, and they rushed me to the hospital. But how careless and selfish of me not to call you the minute that I woke up." He worked his jaw back and forth again, the tension in his shoulders visible from across the room. I wanted to walk over and hold him, protect him from this woman, and promise to never leave him again.

"And just for the record, I didn't call my friends to tell them I was here. I'm glad that they're here, but I don't know how they found out that I had been in an accident or that I was at Cedar Bay."

"An officer called me with the update. I had called them asking for information after we saw the accident on the news, and I recognized your car. Sheila and I had been calling them throughout the night, asking for an update, but they didn't have one. I got a call this morning, and we rushed right over," Genevieve explained calmly.

"And you are…" Willa's eyes narrowed in at her as if she was trying to figure out why she looked familiar.

"I'm Genevieve." She looked nervously at Parker, unsure of whether she should say more. It was obvious that Willa and Bradly had no idea who she was. Willa's eyes popped open in surprise when she heard the name, quickly looking at Parker for an answer to a question that she hadn't asked.

"She's my daughter," he said proudly. He reached up and squeezed her hand, never taking his eyes off of his mother.

"Her name is Genevieve?" Willa questioned quietly, her

attitude from a few minutes ago already starting to dissipate.

"Yes. Amy and I named her Genevieve after—"

"I know who she was named after," Willa bit out, cutting him off. "I guess I shouldn't be surprised that you would name your child after her given that you didn't bother to tell me that you *had a child*. How old are you my dear?" She laced the fake pleasantries on thick enough to smother the entire room.

"I'm twenty-two."

Willa and Bradly exchanged a glance as they calculated the math in their heads then looked back at Parker.

"You had a child when you were eighteen and didn't bother to tell us? You were still living under our roof, under our control—" Willa's voice started to rise.

"Keyword—control. I moved out the second that I turned eighteen and didn't bother looking back. Which also meant that I didn't bother with telling you that I had gotten Amy pregnant or that she was moving to Arkansas to be with her family so they could help her raise the baby. You were already packed and ready to walk out the door on my eighteenth birthday to come start your new life in Cedar Bay so what difference would it have made?" Parker's voice was filled with anger as it rose to the same volume as Willa's. She pulled her shoulders back and tilted her side to look at him, an almost hurt look on her face.

"I can't believe you honestly think that we would have walked away and not wanted to be there for our grandchild. For you. To help you raise it. Is that why you let Amy take her away to

Arkansas?"

"Oh please, Mother. You were barely there for me as a child, why on earth would I think that you would have stuck around and been there to help me raise your grandchild? Amy took her because we both agreed that it was the best thing for the baby. I had no idea what it took to be a good father because I didn't have a good example of parenting while I was growing up."

"That's a terrible thing to say. We gave you everything you could have ever wanted. Plenty of private tutors, summers away at camp—what more could you have wanted?"

The room was silent as we all watched the drama that was unfolding in front of us. Now I understood what Parker meant when we first walked in and he made the comment about being the last person he wanted to see. My heart had dropped out of my chest, and I hung paralyzed in the corner of the room, worried that I had made a terrible mistake by coming. I wasn't completely sure that I hadn't made a mistake or that he did want to see me, but I was pretty confident that the comment was meant for his parents and not any of us.

I studied his dad for a moment and wondered why this entire time he had stayed quiet. He hadn't tried to jump into the conversation at all and if I had to guess, I would say that Willa was controlling with him as well. Hell, she probably picked the outfit he was wearing just so he would have to match her. She didn't seem like the type of woman who easily relinquished control in any aspect of her life.

Parker had been looking down at the floor while his mom spoke, refusing to meet the cold stare that she was giving him.

Slowly, he looked up and locked eyes with her.

"Love. Compassion. Empathy. Understanding. Guidance. Parents that actually gave a damn about me as a person and not what I looked like on paper."

My heart shattered for him. We hadn't talked about his past much. He was always tight-lipped about it and now I knew why. I couldn't imagine growing up in a house where I didn't feel loved or wanted by my parents and I made sure that my children never felt that either.

"I think we've had enough excitement for the day, honey. Why don't we let Parker catch up with his friends, and we'll check on him later?" Bradly reached over and gently touched Willa's elbow, turning her away and walking out the door. She stayed silent and held her head high as she left with a smug look on her face.

After the door closed behind them, the tension in the air seemed to evaporate, and everyone let out the breath that they had been holding. It had been uncomfortable, to say the least, but I was more concerned with how Parker was doing than anything else. I looked up at him at the same time that his eyes found me again, and everything in the room felt like it froze in place. No one else was there but the two of us, as we silently said all the things we needed to say to each other. I felt tears prickle my eyes, a sting in my throat as I tried to keep myself from crying.

"You know, I could really use something to drink. Do you ladies want to go with me to see if we can find a vending machine and give these two a moment to talk?" Ryder asked, grabbing Brooke's hand as they stood up and walked toward the door. Gen's smile spread tightly across her face as she looked at me and gave me a quick hug before leaving. I waited for the sound of the door closing behind them while I thought about what to say. Once we were alone, I took a few steps toward him and stood at the end of the bed, trying to work up the courage to speak.

"Parker, I'm so sorry," I choked out, still fighting the tears back so I could talk. "I never should have ended things with you, and this is all my fault." My head dropped forward in shame as a tear slid down my cheek.

"Sheila, come here," he coaxed and extended his hand to me.

Refusing to lift my head and look at him, I reached out and took his hand. I could feel the tingle I got every time my body touched his, as the butterflies spread right through me. He pulled me closer until I was standing right beside him.

"Sit down next to me, please," he said as he scooted over and made room for me. I glanced down to make sure that his IV was out of the way before I sat on the very edge, only a sliver of my butt cheek actually touching the bed. I could feel his gaze on me, waiting for me to look up at him. When I continued to refuse, he gently reached over and tipped my chin up with his finger.

"You're not the one who needs to apologize, Sheila. I should be apologizing to *you*. I should have never been so aggressive with forcing myself into your life with Rodney, and I'm sorry for putting you in that position to begin with. Our relationship was so new, and I didn't wait for us to define the boundaries before I stepped right over them. I'm so sorry that I pushed you, and I promise that I won't do that again. You have my word."

I saw the emotion in his eyes as his voice cracked toward the end. There was pure honesty and sincerity in every word, something that I had never experienced before. Rodney was the only serious relationship that I had, and I married him knowing that most of what he said was simply what he thought I wanted to hear. It felt weird to hear someone say something that they actually meant.

"You didn't overstep. I should have stopped and thought things through before I rushed out of your hotel room. You were only trying to be helpful and I completely disregarded you and treated you like you were Rodney. I didn't give you the chance to show me that you could be there for me before treating you as if you had somehow already let me down."

I felt like a huge weight had been lifted as we talked things out and cleared the air between us. He rested his arm on my thigh and laced his fingers in between mine.

"Well, if you'll still have me as your boyfriend, I promise to talk to you about things beforehand and to let you guide me on what you want and need. I don't want a relationship like my parents have where my mom orders my dad around. I want us to be equal in everything and for us to support each other. But above everything else, I just want to wake up next to you every morning and see you in this Pink Floyd t-shirt that you love so much," he teased as he reached over and tugged at it.

"This t-shirt has seen me through some tough times… I'm not

giving it up any time soon," I warned playfully.

"Good," he said with a laugh. "Because I'm getting quite fond of it. It's almost thin enough that I can get a sneak peek of the goodies if you know what I mean…" He wiggled his eyebrows. I felt my cheeks flush with heat as I quickly dropped his hand and pulled the shirt out to see if it was as see-through as he said. He leaned back and rested his arm above his head, chuckling while he watched me freak out. I reached over and playfully swatted at him before laughing and shaking my head.

"You jerk, you had me worried that I was running around in a slutty shirt," I scolded and narrowed my eyes at him.

"It was worth it to see you get riled up. I missed my feisty little woman."

"Well, the lady at the Welcome Desk downstairs sure took a liking to you—or should I say *Clark Kent*. It doesn't look like you would have any trouble finding another woman if you needed to."

"Clark Kent, huh? Well, I can tell you right now that this superhero only has eyes for you. You're my only Kryptonite."

"Oh my god, that was the cheesiest line I've ever heard." I rolled my eyes and laughed. "And I *married* Rodney!" I laughed harder as his bottom lip jutted out in a fake attempt at pouting.

"I still have to get used to the idea that my girlfriend used to be married to my future son-in-law. I don't think I ever want to know any details from you or from Genevieve about that man. It just creeps me out." He shivered and made a disgusted face.

"I don't think you have to worry about that anymore," I said before realizing that I should let Gen tell him about her and Rodney. My face turned red which he noticed immediately.

"Why not? What happened?"

"It's not for me to tell. Gen can explain it when she gets back," I said passively, hoping that he wouldn't press the issue.

"Am I going to have to go kick his ass? Did he do something to her?"

I looked over my shoulder as the door creaked open and felt relieved when I saw Ryder, Brooke, and Gen coming back in.

"Just in time," I muttered under my breath as I stood up and turned to face them. Parker reached up and pulled me down next to him again, this time facing the same direction. I tried to make sure I wasn't sitting on his IV or any other medical equipment before I allowed myself to snuggle up next to him.

"Do I need to go kick Rodney's ass?" he asked Gen as she sat down on the stool that was under the cabinet by the wall. Her expression changed from panic to confusion before she looked at me for clarification. She shrugged and waited for him to go on.

"Why would you need to kick Rodney's ass?" she replied with her brows pulled together. She twisted the top on her bottle of water and took a drink. Brooke and Ryder sat down in the seats beside the bed after Brooke handed me a bottle of lemon-flavored iced tea. I mouthed a quick *thank you* to her before returning my attention to Parker and Gen.

"I was talking to Sheila about how weird it was that my girlfriend used to be married to my daughter's current fiancé and she said that I didn't have to worry about that anymore. What happened? Did he do something to you that I need to go kick his ass for?"

Gen giggled and wiped her mouth with the back of her hand after she almost spit out her mouthful of water.

"No, you don't need to go kick his ass because we're no longer together. I decided to break it off with him."

"You broke up with him?"

"Yes," she confirmed with a soft chuckle.

"But not because he was being an asshole to you?"

"Right," she nodded. "Because he was being an asshole to Sheila and I didn't want to be with someone like that."

"He was an asshole to you?" he asked, turning his head to look down at me as I stayed tucked in under his arm.

"He's always an asshole, what's new?" I shrugged.

"I'm gonna—" his voice trailed off, filled with anger.

"Kick his ass?" Ryder offered sarcastically.

"Yeah, right after I get done with you," he pushed back with a smug smile that had all of us laughing.

"Maybe when you're not hooked up to life-saving machines in a hospital, old man." Ryder's eyes lit up with amusement as he continued to poke at him.

"Hey, you're not that far behind me." He raised his eyebrows, looking just like his mom for a second, though I would never tell him that.

"I've still got a few years before I hit the big FOUR. ZERO."

"I'm like a fine wine my friend, I only get better with age." He gently squeezed my shoulders and placed a kiss on top of my head. "I like having you next to me, you warm me up better than any of their so-called *life-saving* treatments," he whispered in my ear. I felt the pride swell inside of me as I pushed myself closer to him, ready to warm him up the best I could.

"So, are we having a big party for the big day? I can make the cake…" Brooke offered excitedly. If there was one thing Brooke loved more than Ryder, it was baking cakes and throwing parties.

"I don't see any reason to," Parker said with a scowl. "It's just another day."

"You just survived a near-death experience after being ejected from a car and left in the freezing cold for hours. That's something to celebrate so, yes, we are having a party, and yes, I will help you plan it, Brooke." Gen gave Parker a pointed look before folding her arms over her chest.

"Fine, whatever makes you guys happy. Just one request though…"

We all waited silently for him to tell us what it was. Finally, an ornery smile pulled across his face as he said, "Don't you dare invite my parents."

The room was filled with laughter as we all agreed that we wouldn't invite them.

"Can I ask you a question?" Gen asked once the laughter had settled down.

"Sure," Parker said softly.

"Who am I named after?"

It had been on my mind from the moment Willa reacted to the name and I was curious who they had named her after as well. Parker closed his eyes and lowered his head, taking a moment before letting out a gentle breath.

"You're named after your great-grandma. Genevieve was my mother's mom and she practically raised me when my parents weren't around. My mom had a terrible relationship with her mother and she hated that I was so close to her. They were constantly at odds with each other and my mother hated everything about how easy-going and carefree my grandma was. She was the only person that I had growing up that had ever taken the time to show me how to love someone."

He paused for a moment and I could see the emotion on his face as his eyes filled with tears. He quickly tried to blink them away before they spilled over and down his face.

"I had told her about you when your mom and I first found out that she was pregnant. She understood my decision to let Amy take you to Arkansas and she supported us. After you were born, she and I drove down to meet you and she fell madly in love with you. You looked up at her with these big, beautiful eyes and wrapped your fingers around hers, and you bonded quicker than anything I had ever seen. We decided to honor her by giving you her name."

"Honor her?" Gen asked in a whisper.

"She was very sick and passed shortly after you were born. Stage four colon cancer."

My head felt dizzy as I pulled all of the pieces together.

"But your mom…" I said, letting my thoughts trail off into thin air.

"Is an Oncologist?" he offered, finishing my sentence. I nodded sadly, knowing where this was going.

"She was one of the best but unfortunately, even the best couldn't save my grandma."

"I'm so sorry," I choked out, the emotional toll of the day finally catching up with me. Everyone else murmured their condolences as well.

"Thank you. I miss her every single day and I constantly feel the void of not having her here when I have exciting news that I want to share or when I'm having a bad day and need someone to talk to. But I know that she's always there in one way or another, and yesterday, I sat and talked to her for a while as I waited in the snow for them to rescue me."

We all stayed quiet, unsure of what to say.

"I know that everyone thinks that I'm crazy, and the doctors have all explained that I was likely having hallucinations in my altered mental state as my body tried to compensate for the extreme hypothermia. But I remember her very clearly and whether it was me on the brink of death, getting to visit with an angel, or simply a hallucination to keep me calm during a terrifying moment in my life—it doesn't matter to me. I'm just thankful that I had her with me to get me through it. Her strength is the reason that I'm here. It's always been what has pushed me forward and guided me in life."

"It's such an honor to share her name and I hope that I can live a life that would have made her proud," Gen said as the tears rolled down her face.

"You've already done that," Parker assured her. "You make all of us proud and I see so much of her in you."

I closed my eyes and laid my head on his chest, listening to the beautiful sound of his heart beating. For once in my life, I finally felt like I had everything I could possibly want.

Epilogue - Fourth of July
Sheila

"Be careful with that sparkler, Thomas," I warned. "If you catch your sister's hair on fire again, you won't get any allowance for the rest of the year."

"Come on mom, it was just the one time and it all grew back," he whined and held his sparkler an inch too close to his sister's hair. Sally had just turned thirteen and was determined to look more grown-up than she needed to which meant we were in the stage of her trying every hair and beauty product that she could get her hands on. This week it was hairspray.

"Try me and see what happens." I tilted my head and placed my hand on my hip, my warning look penetrating past him to Rodney as he walked around the corner carrying a plate covered in foil and a blonde woman practically on his hip.

"I would do as you're told, son, your mama doesn't look like she's playing," Rodney called over his shoulder to Thomas who rolled his eyes and took off to chase the other neighborhood boys who were now running in circles with their sparklers. I don't know if it was the long holiday weekend or the amount of sugar that they had already consumed from the other houses during the street party, but these kids were out of control today.

"You know my look well," I teased with wide eyes, reaching for the plate that he extended to me.

"I've seen it a time or two," he said playfully, lowering his head and tilting it to the side where the blonde was still standing. I took a moment to take her in, relieved that she at least appeared to be closer to our age than Gen was. Her blonde hair looked dry and brittle, a good sign that she wasn't young and blessed with naturally healthy hair. Nor did she seem like a high-maintenance girl that was going to blow all of his money on deep conditioning treatments.

Brooke had given me a gift card to the local salon for my birthday, and I spent the day doing just that—getting my hair cut and colored, as well as the deep conditioning that everyone swore by. By the time I left, I felt like a new woman, and I considered which child I might give up to free up some funds each month so I could keep going back for that luxury treatment. Parker was so impressed by it that we had the hottest sex that night, followed by another round of intense love making the next morning. I was lost in thought, thinking about the night of seven orgasms, when the woman quietly tried to clear her throat to get Rodney's attention. I snapped out of my trance and smiled at her.

"Hi, I'm Sheila," I said as I extended my hand to her. She

shook it with an impressive grip—not too hard and not flimsy like most people when they saw my petite frame.

"I'm Lizzie, Rodney's girlfriend," she said shyly. They looked at each other and shrugged, reminiscent of two teenagers going on their first date together.

"It's nice to meet you."

We made small talk for a few minutes before they made their way over to the area where the kids were playing with the sparklers. I glanced over to make sure that Thomas hadn't caught anything on fire before checking on the other kids. Oliver was sitting on the front lawn talking with Ryder and Brooke while Megan was cozied up next to her boyfriend on the tailgate of his truck as they watched the kids play. Sally was now the one chasing Thomas, which wasn't unusual in the least.

I set the plate down that Rodney and Lizzie had brought, pulling off the foil to the plate of red, white, and blue Rice Krispy treats. They were arranged in different sizes and laid out on the plate in the shape of a flag. I smiled when I thought about how much Rodney had changed in the last six months and how far we had come since the day Gen broke up with him. While he made a few attempts to get her to take him back, he didn't obsess about it like he usually would have. Instead, he stopped drinking and started coming around more to spend time with the kids.

Parker had warmed up to him after they were forced to spend more time together once he officially moved in with me. At first, I was stressed and worried that I would have to walk on eggshells to keep the peace in the house between the two, but thankfully Parker was a mature adult who handled himself around Rodney without sinking to his level of immaturity. The next thing I knew, I came home one day from picking up a pizza and found both of them sitting on the couch watching football while Rodney waited for the kids to get their things ready to go to his house.

Six months had changed a lot, and I felt the void of having Gen in Arkansas with her mom. I knew that Amy was sick and that Gen wanted to be there to help take care of her, but I also worried that she was giving up so much of her own life to do so. I also worried about Parker and how he would take it watching his daughter take care of her dying mother after having been the one to take care of his dying grandmother, who was like a mother to him. Things were hard and stressful, but Gen stayed in touch with us. We looked forward to our weekly phone calls with her.

I looked down and checked the time, making sure that we didn't miss tonight's call. I wanted her to come to town for the holiday weekend since it was the annual Fourth of July street party tonight and Parker's birthday party tomorrow night. Unfortunately, she couldn't get away at the last minute, and her stepdad needed her help while he worked a double shift. I felt strong arms wrap around my waist and grinned as I laid my head against Parker's chest while he held me from behind.

Everyone was distracted by the fireworks that were starting now that the sun had set and the sky was dark. His hands slowly worked their way up from my stomach and squeezed my breasts before rubbing them with the palms of his hands.

"You better be careful, someone might catch us," I warned, not giving a damn whether anyone caught us or not. His hands were magical and my body craved his touch.

"Well, I just happen to know a place we can go," he offered seductively, nipping at my ear before pulling away and leading me away from the crowd. There was just enough light between the houses for us to safely sneak back behind the old wood shed that sat in the corner of the backyard. I could see everyone clearly but felt excited to know that no one could see us. Unless they were right in front of us, no one would know we were back here.

Parker leaned against the shed and pulled me against him, covering my mouth with his as his hands wrapped around the back of my neck. I ran my hands up his chest, digging my nails into his skin just enough to get the reaction I wanted out of him as he growled under his breath. He pulled away and nudged my head to the side as he started working its way down my neck, kissing the spots that he knew turned me on. My breathing got heavier as the ache between my thighs started to throb.

"Tell me what you want," he whispered, his hand roaming over my breast before dropping down to my shorts and cupping my pussy. I hissed in response, my back arching instinctively.

"I want you to fuck me," I panted breathlessly.

"Where?"

"Here."

"Here?"

"Now."

He growled low in my ear before spinning me around wrapping his arm around my waist. I reached down and unbuttoned my denim jeans, pulling them down to my thighs as quickly as I could as I heard him unzip his pants. He gently pushed me forward so I was bent slightly at the waist as he slid himself inside of me, my pussy already wet and ready for him. I spread my legs apart as far as I could, letting my shorts slide down a little, as he thrust inside of me. My hand grabbed onto the side of the shed to hold myself up while I bit back the urge to scream his name and draw attention to us. He continued to slam into me from behind, while I watched our neighbors stuff their faces with hotdogs and corn on the cob.

I could feel myself getting closer as I reached down and rubbed my clit roughly, trying to bring myself to climax at the same time he had his release. He chuckled and placed his hand over mine, working his fingers in the same rhythm as I clenched my pussy around his thick cock and drained the orgasm out of both of us. His hand held me in place as my body went limp, completely satisfied, and relaxed.

"You gotta be quiet, I'm pretty sure Mrs. Woodcock heard you moaning at one point. She turned to look for the noise before a firework grabbed her attention again," he teased as he pulled out and slid himself back inside of his shorts. I giggled as I pulled mine up and buttoned them before adjusting my shirt to make sure I didn't have anything showing that shouldn't be. The last thing my kids or anyone else needed to see was their mom coming from the dark backyard with a nipple hanging out.

We finished up and snuck into the back door of the house, ready to go clean up and pretend like we had been inside all along. When we walked inside, I didn't expect to see anyone in the house so I jumped and screamed before realizing that it was Gen.

"Gen! What are you doing here?!" I rushed over to hug her before Parker could beat me to it.

"Sean's parents came into town this weekend and they offered to look after my mom while I came down to celebrate dad's birthday," she explained excitedly between hugs.

"That's so great! Why didn't you tell me earlier that you were coming?" I asked as I reached up and tucked a stray hair behind my ear. There was something thin and hard beneath my fingers and I started to freak out that it was a bug when I pulled it out and saw that it was just a twig from the tree that hung over the shed. I quickly tossed it behind me into the sink, hoping she hadn't noticed.

"I wanted to surprise you guys," she said with a sly smile. "And it looks like I did just that…"

"We were just watching the fireworks before coming inside to get more chips," I lied as quickly as I could.

"Sure you were," she teased.

"It's good to see you," Parker said as he wrapped an arm around her shoulder and walked with her to the front door. He turned to give me a sexy smile. I could hear him asking about her new job before the door closed behind them. I turned and held onto the sink, shaking my head at how Parker and I almost got caught worse than Gen just assuming she knew what we were doing. I looked down at the twig and giggled, never feeling so young and free before in my life.

PUMPKIN SPICED POSSIBILITIES
Samantha Baca

Cover Design: Richard Baca
Image(s): Canva

<u>One</u>

Gen

"Shh, don't talk, mama," I whispered as the tear escaped and slid down my cheek. I squeezed her hand gently, afraid to hurt her.

"Just listen to me," she said, her voice quiet and raspy as she struggled to get the words out. "I love you more than you'll ever know. Don't be afraid to live life and be happy."

I sucked in a deep breath and forced myself to hold it. Now wasn't the time to break down and cry. She needed me to be strong for her, even in her last minutes. The doctor had confirmed that she would pass soon, and I was holding onto every second that I had with her.

"Live your life," she whispered again, squeezing my hand with the little strength that she had left. "I just want you to be happy."

"Okay, mama," I agreed, the tears flowing freely as she closed her eyes and relaxed against the pillow. With one last breath, she was gone.

I heard people moving around me as my step-dad, Sean, talked to the doctor on the phone, confirming that she had passed. I debated whether to go find my siblings and make sure they were okay. Instead, I felt numb as I sat there, staring at her.

She was beautiful. Every tiny detail about her that I had taken for granted all of these years was now staring me in the face, as I tried to freeze them in my memory so I would never forget her. Like the small scar just above her eyebrow from where she had pierced it as an act of rebellion against her parents when she was sixteen, or the way her lips turned up in the corners whenever she was trying to be serious but found something to be funny and couldn't keep a straight face.

I held onto her hand, afraid to let go for the last time. I allowed myself to fall into the grief that was ready to consume me, as I thought about her last words to me.

Don't be afraid to live life and be happy.

<u>Two</u>

Gen- 2 Months Later

I drove with the radio blaring, drowning out the silence, as I made my way to Stone Creek, Tennessee. I hadn't been back here since my mom had taken a turn for the worst in September. She had been sick for a while, then all of a sudden, something changed, and she went from okay to terminal within a week. I'd spent all of my time by her side, desperate for any time with her.

After losing my mom, everything around me started to spiral out of control. So many things had changed that I was left with nothing that felt normal anymore. Sean decided to move to Alabama with the kids to be closer to his family and offered for me to come with them. While I wasn't opposed to moving and starting over, there pwas something inside of me that said that Alabama wasn't the place for me.

I had talked to my dad, Parker, several times over the past few months, and despite his numerous attempts to convince me to *move* back to Tennessee, I gave in and agreed to come *visit* for Thanksgiving. Not that I had much to feel thankful about these days. I had spiraled into a depression so dark that even Darth Vader looked like a bright ray of sunshine.

The last time I was in Stone Creek, I had spent so much time with his girlfriend, Sheila and her kids, that it actually felt like being with family, which was what I needed right now. It wasn't that I didn't love Sean, my step-dad and siblings, I just didn't feel like going to Alabama and dealing with people asking us how we were doing and talking about my mom when they barely even knew her. Sheila and Parker were the perfect combination of being around family without having the loss of my mom shoved in my face at every turn. And if all else failed, I could always count on Brooke, Sheila's best friend, to bring wine and help me forget whatever I needed to.

The speed limit decreased, as I took the exit I needed and headed to their house. It still felt weird to say that I was going to my dad's house for the holidays, yet here I was.

I parked and got out, grabbing my duffle bag from the seat next to me. I slung it over my shoulder and tucked my phone into my pocket, as I looked at the house. I pulled in a deep breath and reminded myself that I could do this. There was no reason to break down and cry. I was strong, and today was supposed to be a fun day.

"Gen!" Sally yelled, flinging the door open as she ran out to meet me at my car.

"Hey," I laughed, wrapping my arms around her. "Did you get taller?" I asked, looking down to see her face.

"My mama says that I'm growing like a weed," she laughed. "But I'm sure that I'll slow down some, now that I'm thirteen."

I laughed with her, as we walked up to the house. I felt terrible that I had missed her birthday this summer and made sure to bring a gift with me to make up for it. She opened the door, and the smell of turkey and fresh-baked bread floated out, making my stomach growl.

We went inside and closed the door behind us. I set my bag down on the floor beside the couch so it was out of the way.

"Hey," Parker said as he walked out of the kitchen and saw me. "You made it!"

"Hi, Dad," I replied against his chest as he hugged me tightly.

I expected him to say something about losing my mom, but I was thankful that he didn't. Sheila had called me right after it happened when she couldn't come to the funeral with Parker. They had both been incredibly supportive, and I couldn't thank them enough for everything they had done for us. From the beautiful flower arrangement they had at her service, to the trays of desserts that Brooke and Ryder sent with my dad, they all went above and beyond.

"I hope you're hungry," he teased, pulling back to look at me. "Sheila and Brooke have been cooking up a storm in there. We should be ready to eat soon."

I looked around, remembering the time that I had spent here with Sheila last year. No one could find my dad, and we didn't know that he had been in a terrible car accident.

I said quick hellos to the kids, smiling when I saw the scowling look on Parker's face as Megan introduced me to her new boyfriend. Oliver had his longtime girlfriend there too, but it didn't seem to bother Parker as much as it did that his *daughter* had a boyfriend. For a moment, I was thankful that he got to miss out on that part of my life. Lord knew that I sure gave my momma a load of trouble with the guys that I brought home, and ninety percent of Sean's grey hair was from my teenage years.

"Something smells delicious in here," I said happily as I walked into the kitchen and wrapped my arm around Sheila's shoulders.

"Hey, sweetie!" She turned her head and planted a quick kiss on my cheek, before turning her attention back to the pot of gravy that she was thickening.

"Hi, Brooke," I said, giving her a quick hug in between her transferring dishes from the oven to the table. "Can I help with anything?"

"You have perfect timing," Brooke joked, tossing me a set of oven mitts. "Can you grab the green bean casserole from the oven for me?"

She rearranged a few things on the table that was already packed with food and smiled, pleased with herself.

"It's great to see you, I'm glad you came down to have Thanksgiving with us." She waited for me to set the casserole down on the trivet that she left for me before giving me a real hug.

Sheila finished with the gravy, scooping it into a white gravy boat and setting it on the table before wiping her hands on the apron she was wearing.

"I think we have everything," she sighed. "Am I forgetting anything?"

I looked at the table, unable to think of a single that could be missing.

"It looks complete to me," I laughed, my stomach growling with anticipation as my mouth started to water.

"Well then, let's eat!" She patted my back and pointed to the turkey-shaped name tags that were arranged on the table. I found my name and smiled, knowing that Sally was responsible for this when I found myself sitting between her and Parker.

I washed my hands and took my seat as everyone started piling in. The noise in the small room got loud quickly, but at that moment, I felt like things were normal again for the first time in a long time.

Three

Gen

"Can you pass the mashed potatoes?" Thomas asked over the noise of everyone else talking. I reached over and grabbed the bowl, passing it his way.

There was more food than I knew what to do with, but I piled it on my plate, ready to eat my feelings away. I kept my head down, pushing my food around with my fork, as I tried to make room while Parker opened a bottle of wine.

Once everyone was settled, Sheila said a quick prayer before we started eating. I tucked a strand of hair behind my ear, making sure it didn't get in the way when I realized how hungry I was.

"Wine?" Parker asked, lifting the bottle over an empty glass for me.

"Sure," I smiled, taking the glass when he was finished.

"Sheila?" he offered, nodding to her empty glass.

"No, thank you," she said quietly, keeping her head down as she poked at her turkey with her fork.

"Since when do you not want wine?" Brooke teased, lifting her glass to take a sip. "The only time I've ever known you to say no to a glass of wine during the holidays was when you were—"

I watched as Sheila's face went pale before it quickly turned as red as her fiery locks that framed her face.

"Oh my God!" Brooke gasped, covering her mouth as she set her glass down in front of her. "Are you?"

I glanced over at Parker, who looked like he was in shock, his mouth hanging slightly open as he held the bottle of wine in the air.

"I don't know," she snapped, glaring at Brooke. "Not that it's anyone's business, but yes, I'm late."

"Sheila—" Parker stuttered, not sure what to say.

"Please don't start freaking out," she begged, turning to him. "This is why I haven't said anything yet. I was planning to take a test first, I just haven't had time to go get one."

"There's some in the bathroom, mommy," Sally said happily beside me.

Sheila looked at her with her brows pulled together in confusion.

"I think you might be mistaken, honey," Sheila said sweetly. Sally was her youngest child, but being thirteen, there was a chance she knew what she was talking about. "You must be talking about something else."

"No, it's a pregnancy test."

"How do you know what they look like?" Oliver asked, a look of bewilderment on his face. He was the oldest and I had quickly learned that he was overly protective of his mother and siblings in the short time that I had known him.

"Because there's a picture of them on the box that was in the cabinet under the sink. And then there was a test in the trashcan, with the two pink lines and everything," Sally informed him.

I looked around and waited as the tension mounted in the room.

"Brooke? Are you pregnant?" Sheila asked, turning her attention back to her best friend.

Ryder's face turned beet red as he choked on the piece of bread roll that he had popped into his mouth a few seconds before. He coughed and thumped his chest with his fist to try to dislodge it.

"Calm down, Ryder," Brooke said, reaching over to pat his back. "I'm not pregnant. *You* don't have to freak out."

"Well, then why is there a positive pregnancy test in the—"

Sheila's voice fell when we all heard a sniffle from the other end of the table.

"I'm so sorry, mama. We didn't mean for it to happen," Megan whispered, tears rushing down her face. Her boyfriend, Zach, sat next to her, his head bowed to avoid looking at everyone.

I dropped my fork to my plate, too caught up in the drama that was unfolding in front of me to be able to eat.

Everyone sat there in silence for a few minutes, unsure of what to say.

"I'm going to go get another bottle of wine," Ryder said, excusing himself from the table.

"Where are you going?" Brooke asked as he rushed out of the kitchen, grabbed his jacket, and bolted out the front door.

"Remind me not to miss my birth control," she muttered under her breath as she leaned back against her chair and took a long sip of wine.

"Well," Sheila said, clearing her throat. Both hands were planted firmly beside her plate as if she was struggling to control herself. "This is certainly a surprising turn of events. Nonetheless, today is a day to count our blessings, so let's focus on what we have and enjoy the company of those who have joined us."

She relaxed in her seat for a moment before adding, "Megan, Zack—we'll discuss this after dinner."

Everyone began eating quietly, the only sound in the room was the scraping of forks against the empty plates. I wasn't sure if everyone was so hungry that they devoured every last bite of food, or if they were desperate to occupy their mouths so they didn't have to talk to fill the awkward silence that was lingering in the room.

Ten minutes later, I was helping Sheila clean up while Parker and Brooke sat with the kids in the living room.

"So," she said heavily, dropping a handful of forks into the sink filled with hot, soapy water. "How are you doing?"

"That's a loaded question," I laughed, knowing that either way, whatever conversation we had was going to be a heavy one. "I'm trying to keep myself busy and figure out what to do next."

"I'm really sorry about your mom," she said softly, gently squeezing my shoulder as she turned to grab a stack of plates from the table.

"You can set them there, and I'll wash them," I offered, my hands busy washing the silver wear at the bottom of the sink.

"Na, we'll just rinse them off real quick and toss them in the dishwasher. I only wash the forks because we don't have enough for dinner and dessert, and we can't be missing out on dessert!"

"That would be a sin," I teased, laughing along with her.

"Whew, don't even get me started on that topic," she muttered, adding another stack of dishes and setting them on the counter by the dishwasher.

At that moment, Ryder came back and set two bags down on the counter.

"What's that?" she asked, nodding to them.

"Wine." He shrugged.

She raised a brow and rested her hand on her hip.

"And chocolate. And maybe a few boxes of pregnancy tests. I didn't know who all needed them, so I just bought everything they had."

She walked over and opened the bags, gasping when she looked inside. She pulled two bottles of wine out of one bag, along with two giant bags of assorted mini candy bars. I held back my laughter as I watched her pick up the other bag and dump it on the table, filled with boxes and boxes of pregnancy tests.

"Ryder!" she scolded. "There's at least two hundred dollars worth of pregnancy tests in here!"

"I just wanted everyone to be sure," he said sheepishly, raising his hands in the air. "I think the lady felt bad for me, so she gave me her employee discount, so technically, a handful of those were free."

I turned my head and burst into laughter, no longer able to contain it. Sheila joined in with me as I tried to hide my face with a soap bubble-covered hand.

"I'm just gonna take this in there," he said, grabbing his food from the counter. "Make sure to take the test soon, and maybe have Brooke take a few too?"

"Oh my God," she laughed. "You're worse than a kid."

"Just one or two—you know, make sure my super sperm haven't made their way in yet. It seems to be in the air."

"Pregnancy isn't contagious," Brooke whined, walking in and joining us in the kitchen. She stopped dead in her tracks. Her long, chestnut-colored hair was pulled back into a ponytail, showing the icy blues of her eyes as she caught sight of the table. "Did you buy the whole damn store?" she asked, folding her arms over her chest as she turned to look at him.

"Yes," he nodded quickly. "There are a few boxes in there for you."

He ducked out of her way in time to miss her smacking him, before he darted into the living room with his food.

We all stood there, staring at the table of sin: wine, chocolate, and a year's supply of pregnancy tests.

"Well, what are you waiting for?" Brooke asked, jerking her head toward the table. "Have the kids finish cleaning up, and we'll go take a few and see what they say."

I turned around to give them some privacy, suddenly feeling out of place being there. Being twenty-two, I didn't feel like I fit in with anyone. I was much older than any of the kids and more than ten years younger than them. I turned the water on and started rinsing the forks.

"What are you doing?" Sheila asked, walking over to stand beside me. I turned and looked between her and Brooke. They were both watching me and waiting.

"Rinsing the soap off of the forks?" I replied stupidly.

"Leave them. The kids will do it. I'm sure Megan would *love* to come do some chores," Sheila said sarcastically. "Come on, you're coming with us."

"Grab a bag of chocolate and a bottle of wine," Brooke instructed before walking down the hallway with her arms full. Sheila grabbed the bag from the table and tossed all of the tests back inside before yelling for the kids to finish the dishes.

We went into her bedroom and closed the door. Brooke sat down on the bed and nodded for me to join her as she twisted the cap off of the bottle of wine.

"Ryder knows that I get too impatient to deal with opening the bottle, so he gets me the sweet ones that have a twist-off top," she exerted as she twisted it open.

Sheila was standing in the middle of the room, staring into the bag in her hands.

"Just grab one and go," Brooke suggested, taking a drink directly from the bottle.

"How did I even get here?" Sheila muttered, still looking at the tests. "I'm a mother of *four* teenagers. I'm too old to have another."

"You don't know for sure that you're pregnant. So go take the test, then we can either freak out about it or laugh about it while drinking wine and eating chocolate."

"Fine," she sighed, taking the bag with her into the bathroom.

Brooke opened one of the bags of chocolate and set it on the bed between us. I reached in and grabbed a few, making myself busy while we waited. I don't know who was more anxious about it—her or me.

Five minutes passed without any word from Sheila, and I started to get worried.

"Son of a bitch!" she exclaimed loudly on the other side.

Brooke and I looked at each other and then burst into laughter.

The door flew open, and a bewildered Sheila emerged. She held two pregnancy tests, one in each hand, with her brows shooting clear up to her forehead.

"How did this happen?!" she asked, walking over and holding them out for us to see. Both had a very solid, very definitive positive line on each test.

"Well, I think we all know how this happened," Brooke teased, earning a dirty look from Sheila.

"It's not funny—I'm old enough to be a grandma."

She gasped the moment she said it.

"Oh my God! I *am* going to be a grandma! A *pregnant grandma*!" She plopped down on the bed between us, letting her head fall as she cried.

"Hey, it's going to be okay," I said softly, squeezing her shoulder gently, as she had done for me earlier. "You'll see."

"She's right," Brooke assured her. "It'll all be alright. You've got all of us to help you and Megan through this. That's what family is for."

I felt an odd flutter in my stomach when Brooke said it, but she was right—we were family. From the moment I walked into the house this afternoon, I felt like I was home, like I belonged. And that was a feeling that I was desperate to hold onto for as long as I could.

Four

Gen

"Thanks for coming with us," Sheila said as we got out of the car and headed toward the clinic. I had initially planned to head back home after the holiday but then realized that there was nothing to rush back for. I hadn't been working while my mom was sick and couldn't bring myself to find a job after she died. I knew that I would have to find something sooner rather than later, but my grief assured me that there was plenty of time.

"No problem," I replied, smiling over at Megan, who looked terrified to be here. Sheila had scheduled appointments for them first thing Friday morning and was lucky to get back-to-back spots Monday morning. I guess it was just part of being in a small town where people weren't flocking to the gynecologist's office first thing after Thanksgiving.

"I'm kinda glad that Parker had to work this morning and couldn't make it," Sheila admitted with a laugh as she held the door open for Megan and me. "He's been more freaked out about it than Ryder was, but only because he's worried about whether the baby is okay. I need to see the doctor first, *without* having to babysit him right now."

She laughed, and I knew that she was kidding but that there was also plenty of truth to it. I had seen how shocked he was by the news, followed by the instant fear that she should be sitting down and resting, offering her water every twenty minutes to make sure the baby had enough liquid to swim around in. He and Ryder were peculiar little creatures when it came to pregnancy, but both for different reasons. While Parker was excited to be having a baby, Ryder was still checking in every few minutes to see if Brooke should take a test—just in case she caught it.

We sat down in the lobby and waited. I couldn't imagine that it would be long, given no one else was here and the parking lot was nearly empty when we parked. Ten minutes later, an older nurse with wiry grey hair escorted us back to the exam room and showed them the gowns they needed to put on after they decided who was going first.

I turned to give them privacy as Sheila helped Megan get situated. A few minutes later, there was a knock on the door before it opened, and the most gorgeous-looking specimen of man walked into the room.

I must have swallowed loud enough for everyone to hear me, because he turned and looked, his brow raised in concern. Suddenly, my mouth was as dry as cotton, and I wished that I was invisible, as his charcoal grey eyes studied me.

It felt like minutes had passed with us staring at each other before he turned his attention to Megan and Sheila.

"Hello, ladies," he said, extending his hand to shake theirs before turning back to reach for mine. "I'm Doctor Hayes. I see in your file that you're both here for an ultrasound to date your pregnancy—is that correct?"

"Yes," Sheila confirmed, looking at Megan with a tight smile. "My daughter, Megan, will be going first."

"Sounds good," he said, setting the folder down on the counter behind him. I turned away, giving them privacy as he started the ultrasound.

"Okay, everything looks good so far," he replied quietly, more to himself than anything. "Right here is your baby, and here is its heartbeat."

I turned to the screen in time to see the tiny tadpole-looking fetus he was pointing to before he reached over and turned the speaker up. The quick sound of a heartbeat echoed through the room, bringing tears to Sheila's eyes as she reached down and held Megan's hand. They both started crying, and I felt myself getting emotional, knowing that I would never have this experience with my mom.

I tried to push the pain of jealousy aside and focus on the moment.

"It looks like you're around eight weeks, and based on the date of your last known period, I would say that you're due around July 10th."

"Oh my God," Sheila whispered, leaning down to kiss Megan's

forehead. "I'm really going to be a grandma."

"Congratulations," he said, printing the ultrasound pictures after putting the wand away. He reached over and handed them to Megan.

"I'll let you get changed, and then I'll be back to do the next one." He looked directly at me as if he assumed that I was his next patient.

"Oh no, I'm not pregnant," I rushed out, holding my hands up in front of me.

"It's me," Sheila laughed. "I'm apparently a pregnant grandma—which is something that I would have never imagined I would ever say in my life."

"Sorry," he apologized, his eyes quickly traveling the length of my body before looking back at Sheila. "I'll let you get changed, and I'll be back in a few minutes."

He walked out and closed the door behind him. I let out the breath that I hadn't realized I was holding. *What in the world was that?* I felt so jolted by him that I hadn't heard Sheila talking to me.

"Gen? Are you okay?" she asked.

"Me? Yeah, why?" I turned to find her and Megan watching me, curiosity plastered across their faces.

"No reason," Megan replied with a giggle as she finished getting dressed.

"He's cute," Sheila noted with a nod toward the door as she stood beside the table. Before I could answer, there was another knock on the door as he came in to get the exam table ready for Sheila.

I was thankful for the distraction, so I didn't have to answer her. But she was right, he was cute.

Twenty minutes later, we headed out of the clinic with two hormonal pregnant women who now shared the same due date. They laughed, then cried, then laughed some more about the irony of it all. But as we left, all I could think about was the cute doctor who had gotten me so flustered that suddenly I found myself wanting to stick around in Stone Creek for a little while longer.

356

Five

Gen

"You're *eight* weeks pregnant?!" Brooke exclaimed as we sat down at the high-top table by the window. "How did you not know you were pregnant before then?"

"I don't know," Sheila sighed. "I guess I just assumed that since I was on birth control and thirty-five years old, that it was more likely to be menopause than anything else."

"You just turned thirty-six," Megan countered, picking at the paper straw wrapper in front of her.

"That's enough out of you," Sheila warned, narrowing her eyes. Even I had been in the family long enough to read the playful tone of it. Sheila vehemently denied that she had turned a year older after celebrating my dad's fortieth birthday this summer.

"How are you feeling, Megan?" Brooke asked, turning our attention to her.

"Um, fine, I guess."

"Did you know that you were pregnant before your mom found out that she was?"

Her face went pale quickly as she continued to pluck at the wrapper.

"Megan, you know that I would have gotten you on birth control if you had told me that you were going to start having sex," Sheila said with a stern but loving tone.

"It's not like it works anyway," she muttered.

"What's that supposed to mean?" Sheila narrowed her eyes again, but this time there wasn't a hint of humor. "Because *I* got pregnant?"

"No," Megan sighed heavily, pushing the paper away from her. She looked up at Sheila and shook her head. "I tried taking them. They didn't work."

I leaned back in my seat and eyed Brooke cautiously, wondering if we should step aside and give them some privacy to discuss this. Instead, she leaned forward and rested her elbows on the table as she waited for them to go on.

"Where did you get birth control?" Sheila asked, her voice rising a full octave.

"I borrowed some."

"You *borrowed* someone's birth control?" Sheila shook her head and rubbed her temples with her fingers. "Megan, you can't just borrow peoples' medicine that you don't know. That's not how it works, and it could be really dangerous."

"It wasn't just *anyone,* mom. I'm not *that* stupid." She huffed and folded her arms over her chest.

"Okay, then whose did you take?"

"Yours."

Brooke and I let out a small gasp at the same time. I covered my mouth and felt my jaw drop as I stared at Sheila, waiting for the smoke to start puffing out of the top of her head.

"Megan Renee Roberts!" Sheila's voice boomed through the small bakery. Thankfully, no one else was in here, but Ryder came rushing out to see what the fuss was all about. Brooke lifted her hand and waved him back into the kitchen as we sat and watched the rest of the drama unfold. I was surprised that Parker hadn't heard the commotion from his office in the back, but maybe it was better that he wasn't there for this.

"You took my birth control?"

"Not the full pack," she said defensively.

"How many did you take?"

"I don't know. A few?"

"What the hell were you thinking?"

"I was trying *not* to get pregnant. Duh."

I bit down on my bottom lip, fighting the urge to say

something. Sheila closed her eyes and leaned back against the chair. I wanted to be helpful without overstepping, but by the looks of it, Sheila needed all of the help she could get right now.

"That's um, not really how birth control works," I said lightly, pulling Megan's attention to me. "You have to take the pills daily for them to prevent pregnancy. If you miss one—or a few—it can make them ineffective that month, meaning that you would need to use another form of birth control."

She stared blankly at me as if I had just told her some ridiculous math riddle that I needed her to solve.

"By taking your mom's pills, it made her birth control ineffective that month, which is how she got pregnant."

Her eyes widened with shock as she turned to look at Sheila.

"It's *my* fault that you got pregnant?" she whispered, covering her mouth.

"Yes and no," she shrugged. "Yes, because you took my birth control which screwed up the month, but no because I should have been paying attention to notice that some were missing. But honestly, Megan, how did you not know how they worked? Why didn't you come ask me?"

I felt the tug in my heart as I thought back to the awkward conversation that I had with my mom after I had sex for the first time. I can't say that I knew much more than Megan did, but I was also younger and didn't feel like I could ask the questions that I needed the answers to before I made such a life-changing decision.

"I was afraid that you would be mad at me," she admitted.

"For asking about birth control?"

"For wanting to have sex."

The front door chimed as it opened. Brooke got up and walked behind the counter to greet the customer.

"Honey, you're sixteen years old. I'm not surprised that this is something that you would start thinking about. Honestly, I wish that you would have waited, or at least come talk to me first, but I'm not mad at you."

"I love you, mama," Megan said, leaning over to hug her.

"I love you too. Now go check in with Ryder and see if he needs any help around here. If you're gonna have a baby, you're gonna start learning how to take care of yourself, and that means getting a job."

"Mama," Megan whined with a frown.

"Now." She pointed to the kitchen and waited while Megan got up and left to find Ryder.

After a few minutes, she let out a heavy sigh and closed her eyes.

"What in the world am I going to do with *two* babies at the same time?" she asked, looking at me with a desperation in her eyes that I had only seen once before when Parker was missing.

"It'll be alright," I assured her even though I had no idea whether it would be or not. "You guys will figure it out. You always do."

"She's still just a baby herself, and here she is, having one. I know that I'm going to have to help her raise it, and I just don't know that I have it in me to even start over again with my own. That makes me a terrible person, doesn't it?"

I thought about my answer for a moment before I responded.

"No," I shook my head. "It doesn't make you a terrible person. It makes you an honest one who is genuinely concerned for these babies and making sure that they have the best lives possible. *That* makes you a wonderful person."

She smiled softly and pulled her shoulders back as she inhaled slowly. The customer left, and Brooke went to the back with Megan and Ryder as Parker headed up front.

"Hey," he said happily, walking over to where we were sitting. He leaned down and kissed Sheila. "I heard Megan talking to Ryder. I didn't know you guys were here. How'd your appointments go?"

He pulled out the barstool beside her and cupped his hands over hers. I got up to leave and give them some privacy but her eyes immediately locked onto mine.

"You can stay Gen, we don't need privacy," she assured me.

"The appointments went well," Sheila said, giving Parker her full attention. "Megan and I are both due on July 10th."

"You're both due on the same day?" he asked in disbelief, as a crooked smile spread across his face. "What's the chances of that happening?"

Sheila and I looked at each other and burst into laughter.

"Pretty good, actually," she said with a chuckle. "It turns out that Megan thought that she only needed to take a birth control pill when she had sex, so she was *borrowing* mine. I hadn't noticed that any were missing, therefore, I got pregnant, and she didn't know that she needed the entire months' worth, so she got pregnant too."

Parker's eyes widened as his hands fell from Sheila's and landed on the table with a thud.

"Woah."

"Yeah," she agreed lightly. "So, there you have it. We're both pregnant and due at the same time because she decided that we should share a pack of birth control."

"That's so crazy. But everything is alright with the baby? Both babies?"

She let out a laugh, patting his hand gently.

"Yes, my love. Both babies are perfectly fine and growing how they should be right now. We're both around eight weeks, and we'll go back for another ultrasound in four weeks."

"Okay, I'll make sure that I can be there for that one. I'm sorry that I couldn't make it this morning."

I sat there watching them, happy that my dad had finally found someone he loved so wholeheartedly.

"Thank you for going with them this morning, Gen. That really meant a lot to me," he said, turning to me.

"No problem, I enjoyed being there. It was an honor to see the babies and hear their heartbeats."

"You got to hear the heartbeat?" Parker asked excitedly, turning to Sheila.

She nodded happily as I reached into my pocket and pulled out my phone.

"I hope you don't mind, but I recorded it for you," I said, sliding my phone over to them. "Just push the play button."

Parker did as instructed and covered his mouth as his eyes teared up when he saw the ultrasound image on the screen and heard the baby's heartbeat. I hadn't *intended* to get a good shot of the cute doctor as well but found myself grinning when I saw his side profile in the corner of the video.

"I'll send it to you guys so you have a copy,' I offered as he passed my phone back to me.

"I can't believe that we're having a baby," he whispered, looking down at her stomach. "This is so *unreal*."

"I'm really happy for you guys," I said, feeling myself get choked up. It was true, I was happy for them. It was a fresh start with a new life, and I found myself a little jealous of it. Not that I wanted to have a baby right now, but just the excitement that was in the air around us from the new life that was coming.

"Hey, Gen, I wanted to talk to you," Parker said, clearing his throat. He shifted awkwardly, and I could tell that he was uncomfortable with whatever he was about to say. "I know that I wasn't there for you much when you were growing up, and I'm really sorry about that. I wish that I could go back and change things, but I can't. But I hope that you know that I would go to the ends of the earth to make you happy and that I'm so glad you're back in my life. I know that it doesn't change your childhood, and I'm sorry about that."

He was starting to ramble, and suddenly, I got what he was trying to say.

"Dad," I said calmly, loving the look on his face when I called him that instead of Parker. "I'm okay, you don't have to apologize for my childhood. I had a great one, and I understand why things happened the way that they did. You do *not* need to feel guilty about having another child and being there from the beginning with this one, so please don't."

His face was etched with worry, and I felt bad that he was so torn up about this.

"Really—I promise. I'm fine, and I'm super excited to be a big sister again. It'll be fun having new babies in the family."

"Does that mean that you're going to stick around for a while?" Sheila asked with a smile. I could see the hope on both of their faces as they waited for me to say yes.

The answer was right there on the tip of my tongue, but yet I couldn't get it out.

"I'm not sure how long I'll be in town," I said, feeling the knot in my stomach.

<u>Six</u>

Tanner

"Are there any more patients on the schedule for today?" I called up to Dottie at the front desk as I finished my notes in the file I had been working on.

"No, Doctor Hayes, your schedule is free for the rest of the day."

"Please, call me Tanner," I said, as I walked up to her desk and set the file down.

I looked around at the empty waiting room, surprised that no one else was waiting.

"So that's it? No one else?"

"Nope, not until…." She pushed her glasses up her face and leaned closer to the computer screen. "Tomorrow at eleven am. Ms. Dodson will be in for her annual exam."

"Wow, okay then." I shrugged, unsure of what to do with my downtime.

"How was your first day?" she asked, leaning away from the computer and turning to face me.

"It was fine, a lot slower than I had expected," I admitted, leaning against the wall behind me. "I'm used to seeing more than three patients in a day. Doctor Long didn't give me too many details on what to expect when I took the job," I laughed, wondering if she was worried that I would change my mind when I heard how slow it would be.

"She usually only sees three or four a day when she's here, though it's split up more to fill out the whole day. You got a doozy with yours all lined up, back to back." She laughed and shook her head as if we had been through some major rush.

"Well, the first one was a two for one special," I joked, remembering the three women who waited for me in the exam room this morning. I hadn't known what to expect, but I was a little blindsided by the trio—but in a good way.

I had taken the time when I was writing my notes down to look through the files and found that the two I had seen were related, mother and daughter. It made sense given that they looked alike with their pale skin and light blue eyes—and the fiery red hair. But the other girl that was with them was the complete opposite. She had long, dark hair that offset the emerald green eyes that widened the moment she saw me. The fair skin that blushed the perfect shade of red as she tried to avoid my heated gaze. I had seen plenty of beautiful women before, but there was something about her that immediately grabbed my attention and made me want to keep it there.

"It's such a shame," Dottie said, interrupting my thoughts as I imagined her plump pink lips against my mouth.

"What is?" I asked, furrowing my brow in confusion.

"That little Megan Roberts is *pregnant,*" she whispered as if anyone was around to hear us. "Her mama is a good woman, but Lord knows, she's had her hands full with four kids. After her husband up and left her, she had to raise them all on her own. No wonder her daughter is in the same position she was."

"Well, I don't know how Doctor Long likes to do things here, however, where I come from, it's in poor taste to gossip about the patients we see or discuss the reason for their visit. Please let me know if you'd like for me to pull up a copy of the privacy disclosure that I recently signed with my new hire paperwork, I'd be happy to loan it to you as a refresher."

She snapped her mouth shut and glared at me. I knew this wasn't the best way to make friends in a new—and incredibly *small* town, but I was never one to gossip about people. I sure as hell wasn't about to start now.

Seven

Gen

"Ugh, are they making *you* work here too?" Megan groaned as she came out from the kitchen of The Sweet Shop. I was leaning against the counter behind the register, waiting for Brooke to get back. She had asked if I could help out for a few minutes while she ran to the store to grab some more sugar after scolding Ryder for forgetting to put it on their order this week.

"No, I'm just helping out for a few minutes while Brooke is gone," I said.

"Well, be thankful that they're not making you work here. It's such a drag and *soo* boring."

"I'm sure there are worse jobs out there," I laughed, thinking back to the summer that I worked as a mascot for the baseball team. Wearing a giant, furry bumblebee costume was hard enough, but add in the heat and humidity, and it was downright miserable.

"I don't know why I have to have one. My mom thinks that she can just boss me around and force me to do whatever she says, but I'm gonna be a mom soon, and all of that is going to stop."

I scrunched my face and shook my head. If only she knew just how hard it was without your mom, then maybe she wouldn't be complaining about hers.

"She means well," I said lightly, not wanting to get into an argument this early in the day.

"I just know that she's going to try to tell me what to do and how to do things. She never waits to see if I can figure it out on my own. Instead, she just pushes until she gets her way. You're so lucky that you don't have to go through that," she scoffed.

I sucked in a breath and forced myself to hold it to keep from saying something that I shouldn't.

Her face reddened when she realized what she had said.

"Oh my God, Gen! I'm so sorry. I didn't mean—"

"It's okay," I said quickly, putting my hand up to stop her. "But I see a car outside, so I'd get back to work before Brooke comes in."

I didn't know if it was her car for sure, but I was desperate to shift the conversation to *anything* other than my mom. Megan nodded and grabbed the basket of cleaning supplies she had brought out with her, and started wiping down the tables. I let out the breath that I had been holding and tried to get my nerves to calm down again. The bell chimed as the door opened, the bright morning sun reflecting off of the glass and almost blinding me. I held up my hand to shield my eyes, assuming that it was Brooke.

"Did you bring me something sweet?" I teased, trying to make a joke out of the bags of sugar I knew she was bringing back. I lowered my hand and felt my heart skip a beat when I saw that it wasn't Brooke after all. Instead, it was the hot doctor from the clinic.

The sun filtered into the room, casting a warm glow on his short, blonde hair that looked effortlessly tousled on his head. He walked across the room with the confidence of someone who knew that every woman would stop in their tracks for a good look at him. As he got closer, I felt my stomach tighten, unsure of what to say.

"I thought *you* were supposed to have something sweet for *me*," he teased, pointing to the sign above me that read: The Sweet Shop.

"Oh, um," I laughed nervously, twirling a strand of hair around my finger as his charcoal grey eyes watched me. "Sure. We have everything. What can I get you?"

He took the last few steps to the counter and kept his eyes on me for a few seconds before lowering to look inside the pastry case that Brooke had stocked this morning before she left. I took the opportunity to check him out, noticing how fit his body looked in the snug t-shirt and jeans compared to the scrubs he was wearing the other day at the clinic.

"Everything looks delicious," he said softly, continuing to admire the selection. "What do you recommend?"

I felt the heat from his gaze as it traveled over my body as he stood up and locked eyes on me.

"I don't know," I stammered. "What do you like?"

"I like everything."

"Well… then… um…," I panicked for a moment, trying to figure out what to say. It was like he was sucking all of the brain power out of me with some weird Jedi mind tricks.

"What's your favorite?" he asked, the corners of his lips turning up into a smile as he took a few steps to the side, and I moved behind the case.

"My favorite?" I repeated, my voice suddenly squeaky.

"Mmhmm."

"I guess it would be the cream cheese danish especially if it's warmed up. The cream in the middle gets nice and warm—it's like an explosion on your tongue."

I felt the heat prickle my skin as the blush quickly spread over me, completely mortified by the words I had just spoken. *What the hell? An explosion on your tongue?*

I tried to shake it off and pretend that it hadn't happened, but when he pulled his lower lip in between his teeth to keep from laughing, I knew that he had read into it the same way that I had.

Before I could say anything more, I heard the bell chime as the door opened. I prayed that it was Brooke, because I definitely couldn't be trusted to watch her store while she was gone. I heard their laughter as she and Sheila headed our way.

"How's it going?" Brooke asked, looking between us with a curious smile on her face. She set the bags of sugar down on the counter and stood next to me. I glanced over at Sheila, as she set her bags down with the others. She was oblivious to the fact that her doctor was standing in front of me and responsible for the crimson blush on my face.

"I was just telling—I don't think I got your name," he paused, staring deep into my eyes as he pinned me in place.

"Gen," I whispered.

"Right—Gen, that I was looking for something sweet to satisfy this new craving that I have, and she kindly recommended the cream cheese danish." He continued to hold my gaze as he spoke to Brooke.

"Well, let me get those packed up for you," Brooke said with a touch of uncertainty in her voice. "How many would you like?"

"Two, please. And warmed up, if you don't mind."

"Sure, I'll have these ready for you in a few minutes."

Brooke quietly worked beside me, reaching in to grab the pastries while I tried to look anywhere but at him.

"What's the name for the order?" Brooke asked casually, pulling out a pen to write on the pastry bag.

He looked around the shop, noticing that there were no other customers. I knew what she was doing and tried to hide the nervous laughter that was threatening to boil over inside of me. This was all too much, and I was a flustered mess.

"Rushes come in out of nowhere," Brooke lied with a smile. "I would hate to give someone else your perfectly warmed-up cream cheese danishes that Gen was so kind to recommend."

I watched the dimples in his cheeks deepen as he grinned and looked over at Brooke.

"Tanner."

She smiled and jotted the name down before heading to the kitchen, linking arms with Sheila as she dragged her in with her.

"So, how long have you worked here?" he asked, sitting on the edge of the table behind him.

"I don't, I was just helping out while she ran to the store."

"I see," he chuckled.

"What's that supposed to mean?" I asked a tad defensively. I was already feeling self-conscious and overly exposed from being this close to him. It was like he could read every single insecurity that I had.

"Nothing," he laughed harder and held his hands up in front of him. "I just didn't expect your level of expertise with the pastries this morning. That's all."

"Hey—you asked what I liked, and I told you," I teased, his

laughter calming me. He wasn't a scary man, just so incredibly good-looking that I felt myself freezing around him and tripping over my own words.

"Well, it's nice to see a woman who knows what she likes."

The look on his face didn't go unnoticed by me, but before I could come up with a witty comeback, Brooke and Sheila came out with his order.

"Here you go, Tanner," Brooke said, handing him the bag with his name on it.

"Thank you, how much do I owe you?"

"It's on the house," she replied easily, coming to stand behind the counter with me.

"Thank you for the generous offer, but please, I insist on paying."

"Well, technically, Gen was helping you, so you guys can work out the payment details together."

I could hear the not-so-hidden innuendos laced in her words and tried to scowl at her as she looked away.

"Hey, Sheila, can you help me put these away?" Brooke said awkwardly, pointing to the bags of sugar and nodding her head so hard that I was afraid she was going to need a chiropractor to adjust it back to its normal position.

Once they were gone, he leaned closer to the counter and locked eyes with me. I felt the heat prickle my skin again as my body temperature rose a degree or two.

"I would love to take you to dinner sometime," he offered with a smile that felt like it would melt my panties off right then and there. "You know, for payment," he added, raising his bag in the air and sending the heavenly aroma through the space between us. Without thinking about it, I closed my eyes and took in a deep breath, my mouth salivating when I remembered how delicious they tasted.

When I opened them, I found him staring intently at me, his Adam's apple bobbing as he swallowed hard.

"You don't have to take me to dinner, really," I said quickly, suddenly nervous with the way he was looking at me. My heart started racing, making my palms sweaty. I pulled the sleeves of my sweater down a tad to try to dry my hands.

"Nothing would give me more pleasure," he insisted, his voice flirtier than before.

"I'm not sure when I would be free," I lied. "I'm supposed to head home soon."

"Where's home?"

"Arkansas."

A flash of disappointment crossed his face before he subtly shook it away and smiled again.

"Well then, how about tonight?"

"I, um…" I was struggling to come up with an excuse, when I

heard Sheila pipe up from the kitchen.

"She's free tonight," she hollered loudly before giggling with Brooke.

I felt my body stiffen in response. There was no way that I could go to dinner with him. I would make a complete fool of myself. I had already done so a handful of times in the short amount of time he had been there this morning.

"Perfect," he said with a shit-eating grin. "Here's my card. My cell is at the bottom. And since I'm worried you're gonna pull a Cinderella move on me later, why don't I pick you up here?"

I heard more giggling and turned to glare at the door. I sighed heavily, folding my arms over my chest, as I turned back to him.

"I don't know," I countered again. "I don't even know you."

"Well, I have heard that most people do that over dinner—you know, get to know the other person while sharing a meal?"

I pulled my lips together and rubbed them back and forth. Why was I so nervous about this? It's not like he was asking me to go to some seedy dark alley with him in the middle of the night. It was just dinner in Stone Creek. Everyone here would be talking about it anyway, so I was probably safer than I'd ever been on a date before. Once word got out that I was going on a date, I could bet that Parker would find a reason to be in the area, just in case I needed him. He was funny like that.

"Alright," I said softly, my resolve starting to wear off.

"Great," he rushed out, probably afraid that I would change my mind if given a chance. "I'll be here at seven."

"Okay," I mumbled, feeling a mix of butterflies and nausea at the same time.

"Have a nice day, ladies," he called out by the kitchen door where they were hiding, waving two fingers in the air as he left. "I'll see you tonight, Gen." He looked over his shoulder and shot me another panty-dropping smile.

The door opened, and a gust of cold air whipped in, slapping me in the face. What in the world had I just gotten myself into?

Eight

Gen

"What did you guys just do?" I hissed, pushing through the kitchen doors and swatting at Brooke and Sheila who were crouched on the floor, giggling.

"What?! He was cute and *totally* into you," Brooke squealed.

"He is *not* into me," I objected. "I just made a complete ass out of myself in front of him, and now, he probably thinks that I'm some bimbo who will be an easy lay."

"Why on earth would he think that? What happened before we got here?" Sheila asked, pulling back the liner on the cupcake that Brooke had given her.

"Nothing," I sighed. "He was asking for recommendations, and I got overly detailed about the danishes and may or may not have said something along the lines of how the warm cream explodes on your tongue."

Their eyes bulged out as they covered their mouths with their hands, trying to hide their laughter.

"I know, I know," I whined. "It's terrible! I didn't realize that I had said it until it was too late."

I looked down at my boot and rubbed the toe of it along the black mark on the tile.

"It's pretty funny," Sheila admitted, taking a bite out of her dessert. "I don't think it was that bad."

"Oh, I'm sure he's just waiting to take me out tonight so he can *show me* how cream explodes on your tongue," I said dryly.

"I don't know if it's just because I'm pregnant, but that sounded way dirtier than it should have been."

"That's because I meant it to be dirty," I laughed. "Because *he's* going to think of it in a dirty way. He's probably sitting in his office, eating his damn pastries, and envisioning some gross picture from some overrated porn site."

"I think you're being overly dramatic," Brooke said, coming to stand beside me. She patted my back and then handed me a cupcake. "I know that it's not a cream cheese danish, but trust me—the double fudge frosting is even better. I don't need the dirty details of it—just eat it and save those for your date," she teased.

"It's not a date," I objected. "It's just dinner so he can pay what he owes for the damn pastries. Which I have to admit—you guys have a weird way of doing business down here." I shook my head and licked the frosting, pulling a dollop onto my tongue and letting the rich flavors sit there for a few seconds before I swallowed.

"It *IS* a date and a cute one at that. He seems totally into you, Gen. Why don't you want to go?" Sheila asked softly.

"I just don't want to give him the wrong idea—which I already have. Besides, he's gorgeous—he can literally get any woman he wants—why would he want to go on a date with me?"

I took another bite, letting my worries go with the sugar-induced high that I was on.

"I don't know him," Sheila said around a mouthful of cake. "But he seems nice. Besides, it's just one date. You don't have to see him again after that, if you don't want to."

I pushed the last bite into my mouth and thought about what she said.

"What do you mean you don't know him?" I asked, swallowing hard to force the thickness of the frosting down.

"He's new in town, nobody knows him," Brooke answered. "But from what I've been hearing, Doctor Long said that they're suddenly seeing a boost in patients with everyone wanting to come in for annual checkups. Apparently, the women here are willing to drop their panties for Doctor Hayes."

She wiggled her eyebrows suggestively, and I rolled my eyes, knowing that I was easily one of those women. Hell, I was ready to take them off and throw them at him just from the look he gave me while we talked about orgasmic pastries.

"Does it bother you that I would be going on a date with your doctor?" I asked Sheila.

"Why would it?"

"Well, because… you know. He'll have seen you down there already, and then if we…." I let my thoughts trail off, unable to force them out of my throat.

"You mean you're worried that if *you* have sex with Tanner, it might be weird for Sheila because he's also seen her vagina, and she's dating your dad?" Brooke offered, looking between us.

"Well… Yeah." My cheeks burned from the flush of heat spreading over them, as I talked to them about this.

"Trust me, Gen, it doesn't bother me at all. What he does is completely professional—for both of us. But, if it makes you uncomfortable, I can ask Doctor Long to take over once she's back. I don't have to go back for a few weeks anyway."

I pushed myself up onto the counter against the wall and thought about it. I didn't want to make her switch doctors, especially if she really wanted to see Tanner. But at the same time, I couldn't help but wonder if it would be weird that he had seen her down there. I had to keep reminding myself that it was just one date, and I would be leaving soon, so it shouldn't matter either way.

Nine

Tanner

"Who's next on the schedule?" I asked Dottie from across the office. Today was supposed to be slow, that's why I took my time to stop for breakfast before I came in. It was just an added bonus that I ran into Gen at The Sweet Shop. I couldn't get her out of my mind after I left and found myself thinking about how flustered she was. I pictured her flushed cheeks while eating the danishes in my office this morning—behind a closed door. I felt like I was fifteen again, getting an erection at just the thought of something sexual with a beautiful girl.

"You have Joleen Palmer at one o'clock, Doris Jaden at one fifteen, Loretta Jones at one-thirty, and then Janie Lewis at two o'clock."

I glanced at my watch. It was already 12:55, which meant that I had five minutes before the next patient.

"I thought you said that today was a light day?" I asked with a hint of annoyance.

"It was. Most of these were scheduled this morning."

I ran a hand down the scruff on my face and sighed. I was going to regret asking this.

"Do I even want to know why?"

"You can't go jogging at the park, shirtless, and not get the women around here talking," she laughed, walking into my office with the stack of files for the patients that I needed to see.

"Apparently not," I mumbled under my breath.

"Ms. Palmer is in room one, she's already changed into her gown. Ms. Jaden is also checked into her room. I'll work on getting the other two situated once you're ready."

I looked down at the files and fought the chuckle, when I noticed what they were all here for today: annual checkups and pap smears.

Today was going to be a long day, but at least I had a date with a beautiful girl to look forward to.

After a long day of convincing women that I did not need to be between their legs longer than necessary, I was having a hard time clearing my head. I was thankful to have a nurse with me in the rooms for each exam, but that didn't stop the women from making side comments and asking if I was single. Small town life was completely different than the big city, and I was starting to wonder what I had gotten myself into.

By four o'clock, I was done and leaving the office to get ready. I had plenty of time to kill, so I stopped by the store and stocked up on groceries and a few bottles of wine—just in case I needed them this weekend. We didn't get much snow in Los Angeles, so I didn't know what to expect when the news reported a heavy winter storm this weekend. Better safe than sorry was my motto.

I took a shower and got ready, anxious to go pick Gen up at seven. I wasn't sure if the shop even stayed open that late, but I didn't want to give her the chance to say no. Maybe it was overly selfish of me, but there was something about her that pulled me in and made me want to spend more time with her— even if it was limited.

I hated the idea of her leaving and had no idea how long she would be in Stone Creek before she had to go back to Arkansas. I was hoping to find out more information tonight, if I could get it out of her. She was young and beautiful—I just didn't know *how* young she was.

By 6:45, I was heading over to The Sweet Shop. My nerves were a wild mess of excitement along with some first date jitters. I pulled into a parking spot by the front door and got out, not stopping to take one last quick look in the mirror. While I wanted to make sure I looked okay, I didn't want anyone to see that I doubted myself. If I knew one thing about women—it was how much they loved a confident man, and that's what I was aiming for tonight.

I opened the door and walked inside. I was surprised that they were still open and had a handful of customers scattered around the room at the different tables. The other woman that was there this morning looked up from behind the register and smiled, giving me a quick wave.

I headed that way when I didn't see Gen.

"She's in the back, she'll be out soon."

I smiled and felt the rush of panic disappear as quickly as it came on.

"I'm Brooke, by the way," she said, extending her hand over the counter to me. "I didn't realize that I hadn't introduced myself this morning until after you left. Sorry about that."

"No worries," I assured her, letting go of her hand when I heard the kitchen door open. I turned to look and felt my heart skip a beat when I saw Gen standing there, looking more amazing than ever.

Her long dark hair was pulled up, exposing her slender neck that begged to be kissed. Red lipstick brought my attention to her lips as she nervously licked them, instantly making my dick hard. I looked up to find her green eyes studying me, the smoky makeup intensifying the sexiness that was radiating off of her.

I swallowed hard, trying to find the words to say as she walked over to me. Her slender figure was on full display in the tight jeans she was wearing with knee-high black boots that had a super thin heel that made them even sexier. The cream-colored sweater was the only thing that pulled the outfit in some and didn't scream *sex* to me, even though it was wrapped snuggly around her full breasts.

"You look amazing," I whispered, letting my eyes leisurely

travel the length of her body again. She shyly tucked her chin and looked away.

"Thank you," she said quietly.

"Are you ready to go?"

I was suddenly eager to get out of here and be alone with her. Maybe it was because I was excited to spend time with her, or maybe it was just because I didn't need the folks of Stone Creek talking about the new doctor with the boner in the middle of the bakery on a Friday night.

She nodded and smiled, though I could see her nerves were just as bad as mine right now. I hoped that it was more excitement than anything else, but I wasn't sure.

"It was nice seeing you again," I said to Brooke before walking away.

"You too," she smiled and looked at Gen like a mother would. "Where are you guys going tonight?"

I cleared my throat, suddenly feeling a little nervous like I would if I were meeting her parents for the first time.

"I made a reservation at Genaro's."

"In Clarksville?" Brooke asked, her eyebrows shooting up in disbelief.

"Yeah… why?" I eyed her suspiciously.

"I hate to break it to you, but I don't think you're going to make it. The storm has already started moving in, and I heard that they might shut down the highway out there soon because of decreased visibility."

Son of a bitch!

"I hadn't heard," I groaned through clenched teeth. I had spent the morning looking up the nicest restaurants around Stone Creek and finally decided that it might be a good idea to go somewhere in another town to keep the gossip mill to a minimum.

"You might be able to find something in town, but a lot of places will be closing early tonight. The storm is supposed to be a bad one."

I looked at Gen with despair in my eyes, hating that my plans had already fallen through.

"I'm sorry, Gen. I had no idea. We don't get much snow where I'm from, so I didn't know what to expect with this storm they've been talking about."

"It's okay," she said quickly, and I knew that she was taking this opportunity to cancel the date. "We can go somewhere else if you want?"

I pulled my head back in surprise. She wasn't canceling?

"I don't know where to go," I replied slowly, trying to think as I spoke. "The only place I can offer is my house, but I don't want you to think that I'm—"

"It's fine," she assured me, resting her hand on my arm. "If you want to stop and grab some groceries, I can cook something for us. Or we can always grab a pizza and take it back to your place?"

"Actually, I just picked up groceries this morning, so I can cook for you if you'd like?"

"That sounds amazing."

I smiled and felt on top of the world as we said goodbye to Brooke and got into my car. It was a quick drive to my place, but the anticipation of spending time with Gen without any interruptions made it feel like it was taking forever.

392

Ten

Gen

"That smells amazing," I said, as I leaned over the island and watched him stir the sauce he was making.

"Thank you, it's one of my favorites. It's a creamy garlic penne dish that I like to make when I'm craving something savory."

I didn't comment on the *creamy* part but felt my mouth watering at the thought. I watched as he moved around the kitchen effortlessly with his sleeves rolled up, showing off the definition in his arms. I felt a tingle between my thighs as I watched his hands, noticing the gentle way he worked the knife as he cut the cooked chicken breasts into thin slices before tossing them in the pan with the sauce and noodles.

I was practically drooling into my wine glass, and it didn't have anything to do with the heavenly aroma floating around me. I took another sip and looked up to find his eyes on me, watching my mouth as my lips parted to take a drink. My breathing grew heavy as he licked his lips and let his eyes roam down my body. I swallowed the sip of wine and felt the tingles shooting through every nerve in my body.

He reached over and grabbed the bottle of pinot noir and raised his eyebrows to ask before refilling my glass. I nodded and extended it toward him, feeling the electricity between us as his fingers grazed mine in the process. I pulled my glass back and took another sip, fighting the urge to jump over the counter and kiss him.

I didn't know what had gotten into me. Maybe it was the idea that I could have whatever fun I wanted to now because I would be leaving soon, so there was no risk of commitment or having to deal with any awkwardness later. Or perhaps it was the glass of wine that I had with Brooke while she and Sheila helped me get ready for the date and talked me into living in the moment, enjoying whatever tonight turned out to be.

He refilled his glass and took a quick sip, his lips glistening before he licked them and set the glass down.

"Alright, dinner is ready," he said, walking over to the stove and turning off the burner. He filled both plates and carried them over to the table before pulling my seat out for me.

I smiled and sat down, setting my wine in front of me while I waited for him to join me. A few minutes later, he came over and set a basket of bread on the table between us and sat down.

My stomach growled, and I felt the need to put something in my body other than wine. Not that food was exactly what I wanted inside of me at the moment, but it was a good start to soak up some of the alcohol that was swimming around, making my insides feel slushy.

"This looks and smells amazing, thank you," I said as I pierced a noodle with my fork and took a bite. The flavor was so intense that I closed my eyes and let out a soft moan as I chewed. "Oh my God," I moaned quietly.

I heard a low chuckle, and my eyes fluttered open to look at him. He was leaning back in his chair with his arms folded loosely over his chest as he watched me.

"Sorry," I muttered, embarrassed as I tried to look away.

"For what?" he said seductively. "It's hot as hell when you make that sound—don't ever apologize for it."

I rubbed my lips together nervously, unsure of what to say. We stayed there, staring at each other for a few minutes before he spoke again.

"I guess you have a thing for warm, creamy things?" He arched a brow as his dimples deepened with his grin.

I hid my face in my hands and laughed. It was so embarrassing, but when he joined in, it lightened the mood.

"I still can't believe I said that," I admitted, peeking at him through my fingers. "But, yeah, I guess we can say that it's true." I looked down at the plate of delicious food in front of me, remembering the taste that teased my tongue a few minutes ago and sent me into this state of bliss that I didn't want to come out of.

"You know what you like, there's nothing shameful about

that," he said, his voice still lower than before.

"What do you like?" I asked, suddenly feeling bold. I took another bite, making sure I didn't moan loudly with this one.

"I feel like that's a loaded question," he said, his charcoal eyes darkening.

"Fair enough," I laughed after finishing my bite. "Okay, what do you like to eat?"

There was so much sexual tension in the air that I could practically hear it sizzle and crackle between us.

"There aren't many things that I won't eat. I have a pretty diverse palate."

I nodded and took another bite. I noticed how tight his jaw was as he took a bite and chewed, his eyes fully focused on every move I made.

"What brought you to Stone Creek?" I asked, trying to fill the silence and get out from his penetrating stare. If he didn't stop, we would both be naked and going at it on his living room floor in a matter of minutes. I could see it in his eyes—he was feeling the same thing that I was.

"Work," he said before taking another bite.

I could tell that he didn't want to say more than that, so I let it be. We ate in silence for a few minutes before he turned the questions back around on me.

"What about you?" he asked.

"My dad lives here. I came to visit for the holiday."

"The rest of your family is in Arkansas?"

I bit my lip, trying to keep it from trembling.

"They used to be."

He lowered his fork to the plate and folded his hands in front of him, giving me his full attention.

"Used to be?"

I swallowed hard, trying to force the emotions down that were threatening to bubble up.

"My mom passed away a few months ago. My step-dad and siblings are moving to Alabama in a few weeks to be closer to his family."

He gave me a sad smile as I lifted my glass and took a sip.

"I'm very sorry for your loss."

"Thank you," I whispered, pushing my noodles around the plate with my fork.

"If you don't mind me asking, what's in Arkansas?"

I set my fork down and sighed heavily before looking up at him.

"Honestly? I don't know. Nothing, I guess." I shrugged and

shook my head as I looked away to keep him from seeing the tears that were dotting the corners of my eyes. "I haven't figured out where I'm supposed to be, so I just assumed that I would go back there. It's where I grew up, but I don't have anyone left there."

"Why don't you stay in Stone Creek? You said your dad is here, right?"

There was an odd pleading tone in how he said it, almost as if *he* wanted me to stay.

"I don't know," I answered honestly. "He has his hands full already, and now he has a baby on the way. I don't want to get in the way."

"I doubt anyone could ever think that about you."

I felt the corners of my lips tug upward into a smile.

We talked through the rest of dinner, sticking to lighter topics like the weather in LA and how funny small-town people are when someone new shows up. It was nice to feel so connected to him on so many different levels. By the time we were done, I got up to take my dishes to the sink when he stopped me.

"I'll take it," he said, his hand lightly touching mine before I could pick up the plate. We stood inches apart, and the heat radiated between us.

"I can help, I don't mind," I said quietly, looking up into the liquid pools of desire.

"It's okay. Why don't you go make yourself comfortable on the couch, and I'll be there in a minute?"

I nodded and pulled my hand back, my heart racing in my chest and a slow ache starting to build between my legs.

I waited for him to grab the plate and head to the kitchen before I sucked in a clean breath of air that wasn't laced with his intoxicating scent and went to the living room. The snow was falling outside, covering everything in a beautiful blanket of white. I was leaning against the wall, watching the peacefulness of the snow, when I heard his soft footsteps behind me.

"I should walk away and give you space," he whispered in my ear as his hands rested lightly on my hips. "But you're like a drug that I can't stay away from. You're so addicting that I find myself wanting more the closer I get to you. So if you want me to, I can take you home before anything happens. Because I can't promise you that I'll be able to keep my distance from you if you stay."

I could feel his heart beating wildly in his chest as it pressed against my back, the hard bulge in his jeans a clear indicator of how bad he wanted this as it rubbed against my ass when he moved.

"Do you want me to take you home, Gen?"

I closed my eyes and sucked in a long, slow breath. My mom's last words to me constantly played over and over in my head— *don't be afraid to live life and be happy.*

I turned to look at him, our bodies pushed against each other.

"No," I whispered.

He pinched his eyes shut as I ran my hands up his chest, feeling the hard, rigid muscles underneath.

"Gen," he hissed in warning. "If you do that, I might not be able to stop myself."

"I don't want you to stop," I said eagerly. "I don't want either of us to stop tonight. I just want to live in the moment, Tanner."

"Are you sure?" he asked through clenched teeth. "I need you to be real clear on what you want, Gen. Tell me."

I looked into his hooded eyes and wrapped my arms around his neck.

"I want you to fuck me until I can't see straight."

I heard a low growl from his throat before he reached down and picked me up, tossing me over his shoulder as he carried me to bed.

<u>Eleven</u>

Tanner

The first thing that I was going to do after tonight was buy Gen a new pair of shoes that came off in one quick pull. I loved how sexy her boots were—and I was tempted to fuck her with them on, but given that I desperately wanted to see her completely naked, I had to take the time to get them off.

She giggled as I tugged and pulled and struggled to free her of the fashionable death contraptions before she reached down and unzipped them. Apparently, any brain cells that I had were functioning in the *wrong* head since I hadn't noticed that easy trick. Within seconds, her boots were off, and I was pulling her jeans down her long legs and throwing them to the floor.

I couldn't keep my eyes off of her as she laid on my bed, her eyes filled with desire that radiated out of her. I wanted to savor every inch of her and take my time making love to her, but at this rate, I was going to be lucky to last three seconds. She was so fucking gorgeous that I could barely keep it together long enough to get us undressed.

Once her clothes were off, I pulled my shirt over my head and tossed it to the floor. Her eyes widened as she licked her lips as she checked me out. I quickly stepped out of my jeans and hooked my thumbs into the waistband of my boxer briefs before sliding them down and letting my erection spring free. Her jaw dropped open, and I couldn't wait to see my cock inside of that beautiful mouth of hers.

I walked over to the bed and climbed on top of her, propping myself up on my elbow as I gently stroked her cheek before kissing her. The kiss started soft but quickly got more heated as our bodies eagerly waited to explore each other. I trailed kisses down her neck and along her collarbone before working my way down her chest. My tongue ran circles around her pebbled nipple as my hand dipped down between her legs.

She gasped as my finger glided across her slit and then went inside of her. Her pussy was so wet that my finger easily slipped in, followed by another. I continued to lick and tease her nipples, taking my time to suck them with just enough pressure to get the moan out of her that I wanted. She clenched her thighs in response, and I felt her get wetter.

I grinned as I enjoyed the way her body was reacting to me. Slowly, I worked my way down and parted her thighs with my head before pulling my fingers out. Once she was fully opened, I licked her slit, sucking up the trail of wetness before plunging my tongue inside of her. She gasped again, this time, reaching down to hold my head in place as she ground her hips to get the friction that she needed.

I moved up, focusing my mouth on her clit as I sucked, teasing it in circular motions with my tongue. I could feel her body tightening around me and knew that she was on the verge. I kept going, sucking hard as she pulled my hair and let out a moan that was much louder—and sexier than I had heard before with the food. I felt her pussy spasm around my fingers, taking satisfaction knowing that I was responsible for that orgasm.

"Tanner," she panted heavily. "Tanner, I need you inside of me."

"I'm coming, baby," I whispered, moving up her body before reaching over to the nightstand to grab a condom. "Roll over," I commanded, as I slid the sheath over my dick.

She did as asked and got on her hands and knees with her ass facing me. Everything about her was perfect, from the perfectly round globes of her ass to the tight pussy that was waiting for me. I reached down and held onto her hip, keeping her in place as I slid myself inside of her.

"Fuck," she moaned and instantly started moving her hips against me.

"You got that right," I growled, holding her hips as I drove into her from behind. I wasn't sure how she wanted it, or what she was into, but I knew that this position had the opportunity for another orgasm, and I wanted to feel her come on my cock.

"Harder," she begged, pushing her ass into me. "Please, give it to me harder!"

I felt like I was going to explode as I pounded into her in a way that made her moan and cry out every time I did.

"It's—oh my God. Oh my God!" she cried and spread her legs further. "It's too much pressure, I'm gonna come again!"

"Come for me, Gen," I coaxed. "I want to feel your pussy clench around my cock, draining it. Come on, baby, give me that orgasm."

"I—I—I can't!" she cried, and then I felt her body give in as she spasmed around me. "Oh my God! Tanner! Tanner! Tanner!" she screamed breathlessly.

I kept thrusting, my orgasm close behind hers. I pumped harder and faster, ropes of cum shooting into the condom as I tried to catch my breath. Once I was done, I paused for a moment to catch my breath, gently rubbing my hands up and down her back soothingly.

I pulled out slowly and made sure the condom stayed on. Once I was fully out, she collapsed onto the bed and rolled over. While I was cleaning up my mess, I heard her gasp as she looked down at the wet spot on the bed.

"Did the condom break?" she whispered, her hand covering her mouth in shock.

"No, baby, it didn't break," I assured her, laying down next to her and pulling her over, so she didn't have to be in it.

"Then what happened? What is that?"

I studied her for a quick moment, wondering how old and

experienced she really was.

"That's just proof that you had a good orgasm."

"What do you mean?" She pulled her brows in together, confused. "I did that?"

I nodded and leaned down to kiss her forehead.

"I'm so sorry—I don't know how that happened. I'm so embarrassed!"

She pulled her hands up to cover her face.

"Why would you be embarrassed?" I asked, reaching up to pry her hands from her face. "It's sexy to see how turned on you were."

She didn't say anything, just looked at me with uncertainty in her eyes.

"Gen, have you ever had an orgasm like that before?"

She shook her head.

"Not all women are lucky enough to have them, but you seem to react well to having your g-spot stimulated, and that's the orgasm that did that." I nodded to the wet spot without going into any more detail. She laid her head against my chest and rested without saying anything else. My body felt completely spent and relaxed, but my head was flooded with concerns over what I had just done. I knew that we both wanted this tonight, but I couldn't shake the thought that she was more innocent than I had imagined.

406

Twelve

Gen

What in the world had come over me? I wasn't the kind of girl who just jumped into bed with a man she barely knew, but there was something about Tanner that made me feel oddly comfortable with it. Maybe it was the insane chemistry between us, or perhaps it was the tender way that he was running his fingers up and down the length of my arm as I curled into his side. Either way, I wasn't feeling the pain of regret that I thought for sure would follow my impulsive decision.

"Are you okay?" he asked softly, his lips feathering across my ear and sending shivers through my body.

"I am, thank you. You?"

He let out a deep breath, and my head moved with the rise and fall of his chest. It was such a relaxed movement that I worried we would end up falling asleep soon if we didn't move out of this position. *Was that really such a bad thing?*

"I'm more than good," he confirmed. "I have a beautiful woman lying in my arms after having mind-blowing sex with her. I might even be wonderful at this point," he laughed.

He thought that it was mind-blowing? I knew that *I* thought it was pretty incredible, but I didn't expect him to be so impressed by it. I wasn't a virgin, but I also hadn't been with that many guys, and most of my sexual experience was pretty vanilla, to say the least. To hear that he thought that *I* was mind-blowing was, in fact—blowing my mind.

"I enjoyed it too," I giggled when his hand reached down and grabbed my ass. The feel of his hands on my body again sent a jolt straight to my core, and I started to feel the dull throb between my legs again.

"You might just be the death of me," he teased, letting his hand slip further to where his fingers lined up at my entrance. "But what a way to go."

I closed my eyes and gasped as he parted my legs and slid a finger inside. My body was on fire, and I found that I couldn't get enough of this man. He brought out some wild sex beast that I didn't know was inside of me, and it was ready to get its fill of him.

An hour later, we were both sweaty and tired, sprawled out naked on his bed. The snow had already gotten worse outside, with the storm moving in quickly. I glanced at my phone and cringed when I realized that it was already after ten o'clock, and I didn't want to have to ask Parker or Sheila to come pick me up this late, especially in this weather.

"You can stay the night," he offered as if reading my thoughts.

I clutched my phone to my chest and considered it.

"I don't want to inconvenience you. I can call and ask someone to come pick me up." I felt stupid for not insisting that I drive myself over, but it didn't matter at this point—I was already here without my car, so I had to make a decision.

"It's not an inconvenience at all. I wouldn't have offered if I didn't mean it. I may be from LA, but that doesn't mean that I can't drive in this storm," he laughed. "If you'd rather go home, I'm more than happy to take you, but like I said, you're welcome to stay here if you'd like. No pressure either way."

"Are you sure?" I asked, biting my bottom lip.

He didn't say anything, just arched a brow at me and smirked as if he already knew that I wanted to stay.

"I'm just going to call Sheila real quick, so she doesn't worry," I said nervously, still holding my phone against me.

"Take your time. I'll give you some space," he replied, getting up from the bed and tugging on his boxer briefs. "I'll be in the living room."

I nodded and waited until he left before I sat on the edge of the bed and called Sheila. I chewed my nail while I waited for her to answer, wondering if it was too late and I was waking her up.

On the fifth ring, she answered, sounding out of breath and winded.

"Hey, everything okay?" I asked, hoping that she didn't sound that way because she was doing what I had spent most of my night doing.

"Yeah," she huffed. "I'm fine. Sally's hamster got loose, and I was chasing it through the living room. That little fucker is fast."

I covered my mouth to try to keep from laughing.

"How's your night going?" she asked, ignoring my chuckle on the other line.

"It's good," I said slowly, deciding how much to tell her. "*Really* good."

"Does that mean what I think it means?"

"It does," I giggled. "I don't know what's gotten into me!"

"I would say *who*," she teased. "But we already know the answer to that one."

I laughed and laid back on the bed, memories of his body on top of mine playing in my head as goosebumps spread across my skin. I had thrown on a t-shirt that he gave me, but aside from that, I was still completely naked.

"So, how was it?" Sheila asked.

"Great. Wonderful. Fantastic." I paused and let out a heavy sigh. "I can't even begin to describe it."

"It sounds like you're having a good time, especially given

how late it is," she teased.

"About that," I said, feeling nervous all of a sudden. "I was calling to let you know that I won't be back tonight. I didn't want you guys—mainly Parker—to worry."

"You're staying the night?!"

I could hear the excitement in her voice, and it sent another rush of giddiness through me.

"Yeah, he asked if I wanted to."

"I'm really happy for you, Gen. Call me if you need anything, and be sure to use protection. You know what happens if you don't," she joked.

"Don't worry, I've learned a few tricks from Megan. I'll be taking mine *and* yours, just to be on the safe side."

She laughed, the sound pulling a smile across my face.

"Well, Lord knows that I don't need them anymore. Go have fun, and I'll talk to you tomorrow."

"Okay, good night. And please don't tell my dad that I'm spending the night at some guy's house that I don't know."
I winced at the thought of having to see him tomorrow and having him know why I didn't come home tonight.

"What am I supposed to tell him?"

"I don't know?" I paused for a moment. "That I'm sleeping over at a friend's house?"

"Do you really think he's going to believe that?"

I groaned, knowing that he wouldn't. I hadn't spent nearly enough time in Stone Creek to make any friends, and I purposely kept it that way because I knew that I wouldn't be staying.

"No, but it sure beats the—your daughter was whoring it up last night with some sexy stranger that she barely knew before she climbed into bed with him."

There was silence on the other end, and I had to pull my phone away from my ear to make sure she hadn't hung up on me.

"Okay, you're right. I'll think of a lie of some sort. Maybe I'll be lucky, and he'll already be asleep."

"Or you could just distract him so he doesn't realize that I'm not home, and I'll sneak back in the morning?"

"I'm going to pretend that I didn't hear you just say that," she pretended to scold.

"What? It's not like it wouldn't work? Plus, you would get something out of it too," I joked, hinting at the possibility of her having some alone time with him.

"No, I'm going to pretend that I didn't hear you because I'm a terrible liar, and your dad will know something is off if I try. So go, have fun, and try to be back before he gets up in the morning."

"Deal," I laughed.

It felt nice talking to Sheila about things, even if it reminded me of my conversations with my mom when she was still alive.

I put my phone down on the dresser and made my way into the living room, where I found Tanner sitting on the couch, watching the sports channel.

"Hey," he said when he noticed me walk in. "Everything okay?"

"Yeah, I just let Sheila know that I wouldn't be back tonight, so they didn't worry or try to come look for me in this storm."

"That was very considerate of you. I'm sure she appreciates it."

I smiled, unsure of what to say or do. Part of me wanted to go curl up next to him again, but then I worried that I would be overstepping. We weren't dating, just two people on a date that were having A LOT of sex.

"Since you're staying over, did you want another glass of wine?" he asked, turning off the tv and standing up.

"Sure, that sounds nice. Thank you."

I followed him into the kitchen and sat down on the padded stool at the island, watching as he grabbed two clean glasses from the cabinet before reaching into the fridge for the bottle of wine. The muscles in his back tightened and flexed as he moved around without a shirt to obscure my view. My fingers itched to reach over and touch him, to trace circles along every inch of his beautifully toned body.

It was pretty unfair that he was this gorgeous, nice, *and* a doctor on top of everything else. He was like this perfect package of sexiness that I couldn't wait to unwrap.

He uncorked the wine, the soft pop sounding more erotic than it should have been. Just being near him was enough to make every nerve stand on end and had my body begging for his touch. He filled both glasses and handed me one, a sexy smirk painted on his gorgeous face as if he knew what I had been thinking.

"Do you want dessert?" he asked, raising his eyebrows.

"Is that a trick question?" I replied, wondering if he was hinting at another round in the bedroom. In that case—yes, I definitely wanted dessert, and my appetite was getting bigger by the second.

He chuckled and opened the freezer, pulling out a carton of ice cream and setting it on the island beside me. Next, he grabbed a can of whipped cream and some hot fudge and added them to the pile he had started. He opened the hot fudge and scooped some into a bowl before popping it into the microwave. A few seconds later, he took it out, testing the warmth with his finger as he stirred it around.

"Do you like hot fudge?" he asked, his voice low and gravely again.

I nodded, watching him as he crossed the room and stood in front of me. He set the bowl down next to me and turned me on the stool, so I was facing him.

"Take off your shirt," he commanded, the growing bulge in his boxers hinting at his arousal.

I didn't take my eyes off of him as I reached down and grabbed the bottom, pulling it over my head and tossing it to the floor beside me. I shivered as I sat naked in front of him, his eyes roaming over every inch of my body.

He pulled his lower lip in between his teeth, his eyes locking onto mine. He reached over and dipped his finger into the hot fudge, then slowly rubbed it across my nipple. I gasped at the sensation from the heat on my skin to the feeling of his wet tongue as he leaned forward and licked it off. My fingers wrapped in his hair, holding him closer as he sucked harder.

My eyes were closed as he added more to the other nipple before continuing with his deliciously brutal torture. My back arched, and my legs spread as I made room for him between my legs while he sucked the thick fudge from my breasts. It was pure ecstasy, and I already felt like I needed him again. I was panting, clawing at his back as he chuckled against my neck.

"I thought you asked if *I* wanted dessert," I teased, grabbing his head and holding it in front of mine. "You don't share very well, now do you?"

"What did you have in mind?" he asked, his grey eyes darkening.

I licked my lips, suddenly feeling braver and more confident than before. I gently pushed him away and got up from the barstool, reaching for the can of whipped cream.

"Drop them," I demanded, nodding to his underwear that was barely containing the massive hard-on.

He smiled a crooked smile and raised an eyebrow as he hooked his fingers in the waistband and did as I asked. I watched wide-eyed as his cock sprung free, ready for me to have my way with it.

I shook the can and kept my eyes locked on his as I kneeled before him. With a quick flick, the cap was off, and I was spraying a line of whipped cream along the length of his dick, watching as his body reacted to the cold sensation. I set the can beside me and leaned forward, slowly licking it off.

I swirled my tongue lazily around his length, satisfied with the change in his breathing as he got more aroused. Once the whipped cream was off, I looked up and smiled as he watched me take him into my mouth. I relaxed my jaw and leaned forward, taking as much of his cock in as I could. He gasped as his hand grabbed the back of my head, working me to the rhythm that he liked as my head bobbed back and forth quickly. I reached down and gently caressed his balls with one hand while the other hand stroked him where my mouth didn't reach.

"Fuck, Gen," he panted, his body stiffening around me.

I flattened my tongue and sucked harder, getting wetter as I felt his body react to me. I was about to get off from making him come, which only spurred me on even more. I let go and used both hands to grab his ass, forcing him to fuck my face as I sucked harder. I could tell by his breathing that it wasn't going to be long before he came.

"I'm gonna come," he warned, giving me time to pull away. Instead, I wrapped my mouth tighter around him and kept going until I felt the salty liquid hit the back of my throat in rapid bursts. Once he was finished, I pulled away and wiped my mouth with my fingers before taking his hand as he helped me up.

"That was fucking incredible," he murmured as he wrapped his arms around my waist and pulled me close to him. "I don't think I'm going to be able to stop fucking you tonight."

"Good, because I don't want you to."

He let out a low growl in my ear before lifting me over his shoulder and grabbing my ass cheeks before leading me back to the bedroom.

"Wait! We forgot the ice cream," I yelped, giggling when his hand slapped my ass.

"I'll buy more," he said sexily. "Right now, I want you again."

Thirteen

Tanner

I was exhausted. Absolutely, completely exhausted to the point that I couldn't find the energy to lift my arm and turn off the tv after Gen fell asleep in my arms. I wasn't eighteen anymore—that was for damn sure. But I was still pleased that I had the stamina to keep me going after our insane night of constant fucking.

No matter how hard I tried, I couldn't keep my hands off of her. But the best part about it—she couldn't resist me either. There was this strong pull between us that neither of us were willing to fight. Maybe it was because it felt so damn good to just give in and enjoy each other.

It was after two in the morning by the time we gave in and went to sleep. When I woke up in the morning, I was surprised to find the bed empty with only a note beside me. I groaned and ran a hand over my face before reading it, already knowing what it was going to say.

I picked it up and let out a sigh before reading it.

Tanner, after depriving me of ice cream last night, I felt it was only fair to make you pay. I have commandeered your bathtub and do not plan to give it back until my skin is more wrinkled than a raisin.

I felt my cheeks split, as the laugh bellowed out of me. I tossed the note on the bed and jumped up, hoping to catch her before she got out. I made a quick pit stop in the guest bathroom before knocking on the door to the master bath.

"I'm not a raisin yet," she teased from the other side. "I refuse to get out before then."

I laughed and opened the door, leaning against the frame as I took in the beautiful sight before me.

The large soaking tub was filled to the top with bubbles while Gen relaxed beneath them, her hair pulled up into a messy bun. I could barely see the top of her breasts under all of the bubbles and found myself yearning for more.

"I won't kick you out," I said, licking my lips. "But that doesn't mean that I won't come join you."

A flash of desire streaked across her face as she scooted forward and smiled. I pulled off my briefs and kicked them to the side, wondering how much more my dick could take. I hadn't had this much sex since I was a teenager, and I was already in my thirties. A lot had changed over the years, but apparently, Gen was the secret to keeping my dick young.

I climbed in behind her, laughing when some of the water sloshed over the side from the movement as the water raised around us. Once I was situated, I wrapped my arm around her waist and pulled her back against my chest.

It was still early in the morning, barely after seven, but I didn't know what time she was planning to leave. It was an odd feeling, but deep down, I hoped that it wasn't any time soon. It wasn't just the constant physical interaction between us, but I really did enjoy her company and found that I wanted to spend more time getting to know her.

"Do you have any plans today?" I asked, hoping to sound as carefree as possible.

"You mean other than forcing myself into your tub and refusing to leave until I'm a raisin?" she joked, tilting her head to look at me. "That was all that I had planned."

"Good," I whispered. "Because I was hoping that maybe we could spend more time together. Get to know each other better."

She giggled as I ran my hand up her thigh and kissed her neck. Thirty minutes later, we were both full raisin status, and the water was cold. I offered her a pair of my sweats and a t-shirt, so she didn't have to wear the same clothes as last night, but I had to admit that it made my dick hard thinking about her not wearing any panties.

I was just about to ask what she wanted to do today when her phone rang. Her eyes widened, and she chewed her nail as she debated whether to answer.

"It's Sheila," she said, looking up at me. "I probably need to take this since I told her that I would be home this morning."

I nodded and turned my back, trying to give her privacy as I got dressed.

"Hey," she answered.

I bent down and pulled my shoes on when I heard the change in her tone.

"Sheila, what's wrong? Are you okay?" She hesitated for a moment, then looked at me with panic in her eyes. "Yeah, he's right here."

She held the phone to her chest and spoke in a hushed tone.

"Something's wrong with the baby."

I pinched my brows together and took the phone as she handed it to me.

"Hey, Sheila, what's going on?"

"I'm so sorry to bother you," she said, crying. "I think something is wrong. I woke up bleeding."

"It's okay, you're not bothering at all. How much blood?"

"Not a lot. It was on the sheets, I didn't notice it until I came back from using the restroom. It was still dark, so I didn't notice if there was any blood when I peed." She hesitated for a moment. "I'm really scared that something is wrong. I'm not through the first trimester yet, and I know that—"

"Hey, let's not think the worst right now, okay?" I rushed to assure her. "Can you meet me at the clinic in fifteen minutes?"

"Yes."

"Okay, I'm heading there now. Do you have someone that can take you, or do you need me to stop and pick you up?"

"I'll have Parker drive. We'll be there soon."

I let out a deep breath and handed Gen back her phone after Sheila hung up.

"Is she okay?" she asked nervously.

"I won't know much until I can examine her at the clinic. I'll do an ultrasound, and we should have some answers then."

I grabbed my phone and keys from the nightstand and tried to calm my own nerves.

"Are you ready?"

She nodded, and we rushed out the door. The snow was still falling as we drove to the clinic. It was hard not to speed because I felt the urgency talking to Sheila, but I also didn't want to risk us getting in an accident on the way because of the weather.

By the time we got there, there was another car waiting in the parking lot. We got out, and I rushed over to open Gen's door, feeling the penetrating glare from the man with Sheila.

"How are you feeling?" I asked Sheila over my shoulder as

I unlocked the door. I pushed it open and stepped to the side, letting them through before I pulled it closed and locked it.

"I'm okay, just a little sore and have some mild cramping."

I tried to keep the frown off my face as I walked us down the hallway to the first exam room. I turned on the light and opened the drawer where the gowns were kept.

"Go ahead and get undressed from the waist down, and I'll be back in a minute to check you," I said, handing her the gown.

I walked out and closed the door behind us as Gen stepped out with me.

"I'm so worried," she admitted shyly, wrapping her arms around herself. She looked so small in my clothes as they hung loosely around her body.

"It'll be okay," I assured her, pulling her in for a hug. It felt nice to hold her against me, and I wanted to stay in that moment forever.

Suddenly, the door opened, and I was greeted with a frown as Parker's dark green eyes studied us.

"She's ready."

I sucked in a deep breath and followed Gen inside.

"Do you want me to wait outside?" Gen asked her, standing by the bed.

"No, you're fine to stay," Sheila said, squeezing her hand.

"This is Parker, by the way," she added, nodding to him as I sat down on the stool in front of the bed and pulled on a pair of latex gloves. "He's my boyfriend, and he's also Gen's dad."

I tried to keep the shock off of my face as the news hit me like a ton of bricks. No wonder this guy was shooting daggers at me every chance he got. It had nothing to do with Sheila but everything to do with him seeing me embrace his daughter in the hallway *after* showing up with her in my car.

"It's a pleasure to meet you," I said calmly, offering him the most professional smile that I could muster. When he didn't say anything in return, I decided to go about my business. He stood there scowling, arms folded over his chest as if he didn't trust me. In all fairness, I couldn't say that I blamed him, given how we were meeting for the first time.

I did a quick exam before pulling off the gloves and turning on the computer to do the ultrasound.

"Everything looks fine," I said as I typed in my password. "Your cervix is fully closed, and I didn't see any signs of bleeding. We'll get a better look with the ultrasound," I continued as I handed her the wand to insert inside of herself. Once it was situated, I took it from her and gently moved it around until I got the image I was trying to find.

I leaned forward and studied the screen, making sure I wasn't missing anything.

"The baby looks great," I confirmed, smiling over my shoulder at her before returning my attention to the screen. "I don't see anything that concerns me."

"That's great news," Gen said, relieved.

"Thank you, Doctor Hayes. I appreciate you taking the time to come down here and check me."

"It's not a problem at all," I replied, leaning forward to turn the audio on. "Here's the baby's heartbeat. Nice and strong."

I held the wand in place and turned around, watching as Parker's stone-cold expression changed the second he heard it. His eyes grew bigger, and his arms dropped as he stepped closer to Sheila and looked back and forth between the screen and her stomach.

"That's our baby?" he whispered. She nodded as a tear slid down her cheek.

"That's our baby."

I didn't want to interrupt this moment, so I held the wand for a few more minutes, allowing them this opportunity to bond over this blessing. I glanced up at Gen, who had tears of her own dotting the corners of her eyes.

I looked away, giving them their privacy before turning off the sound and pulling the wand out. Once she was situated, I turned my attention back to her.

"Everything looks fine," I repeated. "The bleeding could have been from a number of things— cervical changes, intercourse—" I was about to go on when I noticed the blush creep up her face as she looked away.

I cleared my throat before continuing.

"Sex during pregnancy is safe and can cause bleeding during the first trimester. Since the bleeding has stopped, I would recommend drinking plenty of water and resting if it helps put your mind at ease."

"Thanks, Doctor Hayes," Sheila said sheepishly.

"See, I told you we shouldn't have done that," Parker whispered, not realizing that it was loud enough to hear.

A phone started ringing, and Parker reached into his pocket to get it.

"It's Ryder," he said to Sheila before going to the hallway to answer it.

Once the door clicked shut, I focused on entering my notes in the system from the unexpected visit.

"Sheila!" Gen blurted out quietly.

"What? You told me to distract him, so I did."

I coughed to hide the chuckle that was trying to force its way out.

"Why didn't you just put on Titanic? You know that movie always puts him to sleep."

"Because he was getting all antsy, asking where you were. Ryder had texted him about you being on a date with the hot new doctor in town, and he started to get all worked up. It was either that or have him come looking for you in the middle of the night during this crazy storm. Plus, it was a nice distraction if I do say so myself," Sheila teased.

"Eww. Yuck."

"Don't be such a prude," Sheila joked.

If she only knew how sexual Gen was, she wouldn't think she was a prude at all.

"It's my dad," she whined. "It's always going to be gross."

I decided that was my cue to interrupt and stop the conversation from getting any worse. I tore the ultrasound pictures off the printer and handed them to Sheila.

"You're all set to go, I'll step out so you can get dressed."

"Thank you, and again, I'm really sorry for dragging you down here. Can I make it up to you by having you over for dinner? I make a killer meatloaf…."

I glanced at Gen, trying to gauge her reaction but couldn't read it.

"Please, I just feel terrible."

"I'm not sure that Parker would love the idea, but thank you so much for the offer. Really, you don't owe me anything. I was just doing my job."

"Parker will be fine with it," Sheila said happily as the door opened and he walked in, another frown on his face.

"I'll be fine with what?"

"Doctor Hayes is joining us for dinner tonight," Sheila announced matter-of-factly.

I raised my eyebrows at Gen, desperate for her to say something if she didn't want me to come over. Instead, she just smiled then turned to look at her dad with a worried look on her face.

And just like that, I was meeting her family and going over for dinner.

Fourteen

Gen

"Are you sure this is a good idea?" I asked Sheila as she pulled the meatloaf out of the oven and set it on the stove.

I had spent the day at home, trying to get a feel for how Parker was handling the news that I was dating the man who was also his girlfriend's gynecologist. I really wanted to spend it with Tanner, but things felt awkward when we got ready to leave the clinic, so I went ahead and grabbed a ride back with Sheila and ensured Tanner that he didn't have to come to dinner.

We had texted a few times throughout the day, and he promised that he would *discreetly* bring my clothes back from last night and that he was looking forward to dinner tonight. Sheila had also *conveniently* arranged for the kids to stay the night with her parents tonight, so it was just the four of us for dinner.

"Too late to back out now," she laughed as the doorbell rang. "Can you go grab that?"

I sucked in a deep breath and adjusted my sweater that suddenly felt too tight as I headed toward the door. Thankfully, Parker was in the bathroom, which gave me a few minutes to talk to Tanner without him hovering or overhearing our conversation.

"Hey," I said, opening the door and stepping to the side. "How are you?"

"I'm good, how are you?" he asked, sliding his hand around my waist to my back as he gave me a quick kiss.

"Nervous," I admitted, feeling my emotions getting the better of me.

"Me too," he laughed, handing me the bottle of wine that he brought. "Liquid courage," he shrugged and raised his eyebrows.

I shook my head and smiled, suddenly feeling more relaxed. I could still feel the heat from his fingers and missed his touch.

"Come on inside," I invited, leading him through the living room to the kitchen.

"Tanner brought wine," I announced, handing it to Sheila as she turned around. Her face was beaming with a smile that hurt my face from how tight it stretched across hers.

"Thank you so much, that was very sweet of you. Dinner will be ready in a few minutes, go ahead and have a seat."

We sat on one side of the table, the uneasiness steadily starting to creep back in. A few minutes later, Parker came in and forced a smile as he saw Tanner sitting beside me.

"Doctor Hayes," he said as he extended his hand to shake. Tanner stood up and took it, smiling the same tight smile that I had seen earlier.

"Please, call me Tanner," he insisted, sitting down.

Parker nodded but didn't say anything as he walked over and wrapped his arms around Sheila's waist, whispering something in her ear. She giggled and swatted at him.

"Make yourself useful and take the mashed potatoes to the table, please," she said with a teasing tone.

"Yes, ma'am," he joked, reaching around her to grab the bowl.

She joined us a few minutes later after bringing over the meatloaf, some freshly baked rolls, and the tub of butter. Once she was sure that we had everything we needed, she took her seat beside Parker.

"Everything smells delicious," Tanner said, giving her the smile that made my knees weak. "Thank you again for the invite."

"It's our pleasure. Now let's eat before it gets cold." Sheila smiled and gently nudged Parker in the side.

"Would you like a beer, Tanner?" he asked, his voice hoarse as if it pained him to ask.

"Sure, thank you."

"Gen?" He gave me a look I had seen him use plenty of times with the kids and had to fight back the laugh. I was twenty-two years old and had drunk with them plenty of times over the past year.

"No, thank you," I said with a light laugh. "I think I'll have some of the wine that Tanner brought since Sheila can't partake."

We got our drinks and got settled again, silence falling around us as we ate. Sheila didn't lie—her meatloaf was amazing, and I found myself wanting to eat seconds because it was so good. My stomach was already tight from being overly full.

I helped clean up the dishes and kicked Sheila out to go rest while Tanner helped me. It was nice having a few minutes by ourselves.

"It's not as bad as you thought it would be, is it?" he asked quietly, standing next to me as he dried the dishes that I handed him. We had already loaded most of them into the dishwasher except for the few that were too big and needed to be hand washed.

"Honestly, I didn't know what to expect. Parker wasn't around much when I was growing up, so I didn't have those experiences with him when I started dating. We're still trying to figure out our relationship, but I think it's hard for him to see me with you."

"Because I'm so much older?"

"I don't know," I answered honestly. "Maybe that, or possibly because you're his wife's doctor and you're sleeping with his daughter. It could be a combination of things."

He didn't respond right away, he just furrowed his brow as he thought about something.

"Does it bother you that I'm older than you?"

I turned the water off and shifted to look at him.

"No. Does it bother you?"

He shook his head, but it wasn't a clear enough answer for me.

"It doesn't bother me, but I worry that you're so young and innocent, and here I am, corrupting you."

I let out a laugh, unable to control myself.

"Trust me, I don't think you're corrupting me. I haven't done anything that I didn't want to."

Which was true. Everything that we'd done were things that I wanted, and even though I wasn't as experienced, I didn't regret doing them. It was like he was liberating a side of me that I didn't know was locked up.

"You're still innocent, aren't you?"

"Are you asking if I was a virgin before we had sex?" I asked, confused.

He waited, struggling with what to say.

"No, Tanner. I wasn't a virgin. I had been with a few guys before you, I just didn't experiment much when I was with them. Sex isn't new to me, just the other stuff that we did. Which I happened to like a lot, by the way."

"I never want to take advantage," he replied quietly.

"You're not," I assured him, rubbing my hand soothingly up and down his arm.

"I don't think everyone feels the same way," he muttered, glancing into the living room before going back to drying the dishes.

I looked past him and found Parker sitting on the couch with Sheila's legs draped over him, scowling at us.

Fifteen

Tanner

Dinner wasn't as awkward as I thought it would be, and by the end, I was hopeful that I had started to win Parker over some with our shared love for the Tennessee Titans. I'd never been much of a sports fan, but I found that moving to a small town meant that I needed to pick a team— and quickly. Stone Creek just happened to love football, even though I never really understood why people loved the sport so much.

I helped Gen clean after we were all done and took my cue to leave before Sheila insisted that I stay and hang out a bit. I could tell by the way Parker was working his jaw back and forth that he wasn't fond of having me there. The tension in the room grew thick when we didn't have much to talk about.

"So, Tanner," Sheila said, redirecting the conversation for what felt like the fiftieth time in an hour. "What made you decide to come to Stone Creek?"

I hated this question and usually sidestepped around it with some vague response, but for whatever reason, I decided to open up to them.

"My mom," I said, looking down at the beer bottle in my hands as I rested my elbows on my knees.

"Is she from here?"

I looked at Gen then turned my attention to Sheila, pulling my shoulders back as I sat taller.

"No, we have no connections to Tennessee whatsoever. She grew up in a small town and lived there her entire life. Once I graduated high school, I couldn't wait to get the hell out of there and move to a big city. I got a full-ride scholarship to Stanford and then put myself through medical school. I did my residency in Los Angeles and decided that I wanted to make more of a difference, so I ventured down the small town path and ended up here."

Okay, so it wasn't the full details that I could have shared, but I didn't want to depress everyone with my sob story.

"What made you decide to go small town?" Sheila prodded.

I leaned back against the couch and felt Gen's hand brush against mine. She smiled softly as she waited to hear the rest of my story.

"My mom got sick and didn't tell me until it was too late. Since she lived in a small town, she didn't have the same resources available to her that she would have if she were in a big city. By the time I found out, it was too late. There wasn't anything that I could do to help her. The cancer had already spread through her body at that point.”

“I’m so sorry,” Gen whispered quietly beside me.

“What kind of cancer?” Parker asked, surprising me.

“It started as cervical cancer. It showed on early scans when she started to feel sick, but her doctor didn’t catch it. She could have had a complete hysterectomy and would likely have survived it, but by the time they caught it, it had already metastasized through her body.”

I felt Gen’s body trembling beside me and looked to find her crying. I wrapped my arm around her and held her, rubbing her back softly.

“Gen lost her mom a few months ago,” Sheila explained quietly. “I’m sorry for your loss, Tanner.”

“Thank you,” I sighed heavily, still comforting Gen. “After she passed, I decided that I didn’t care about the money or working for some prestigious hospital. I switched my specialty and decided to find a small town and do something good with my knowledge and skills. Give them the resources that I wish my mom had.”

“It’s a touching story,” Parker said, the gruff in his voice finally subsiding. “We’re lucky to have you as Sheila’s doctor.”

“I’m happy to do what I can while I’m here.”

Gen wiped the tears from her face and pulled away, looking at me through the tears that were still flooding her eyes.

"Are you not staying in Stone Creek for long?" she asked, sniffling.

"It's a temporary job, six months at most. From there, we'll see what town I end up in next."

"So you're not staying here?"

I felt the tension in the room thicken again.

"No, that was never the plan," I said softly, noticing the hurt in her eyes.

"Well, it's getting late, so I'm going to head to bed," Parker said, breaking the silence that had fallen over the room. He stood up and stretched before extending a hand to help Sheila off the couch next to him.

"Yeah, me too," she said, playing along with his excuse to give us some privacy. "Goodnight, you guys. Thanks again for your help this morning, Tanner."

"No problem," I said, giving them a quick wave as they headed toward the hallway. "Thank you for dinner, it was delicious."

Sheila tossed a *you're welcome* over her shoulder as Parker led her to their room.

Once we were alone, I turned to look at Gen. She was still crying, her face red and splotchy as she blew her nose into a tissue.

"Are you okay?" I asked, gently rubbing my hand on her knee.

"I'm fine," she lied, sucking in a jagged breath. "It's not like this was anything serious. I was planning to leave soon anyway, so why does it matter that you are too?"

I felt the pain in my stomach as I realized what she was really upset about. And just like that, we had crossed a line we hadn't even seen until now.

Sixteen

Gen

"Good morning," Parker said from the kitchen table, reading the newspaper as I passed him to get to the coffee.

"Morning," I mumbled, watching the dark liquid fill my cup, reminiscent of how dark my life felt these days. "I'm going out for some fresh air."

I didn't wait for him to say anything or to try to talk me out of it. I knew that it was cold outside and that I would freeze my butt off, but I didn't care. Maybe the cold would match the numbness that I had woken up to.

I opened the backdoor and was surprised to find Sheila sitting at the patio table, wrapped up in a blanket with a coffee cup in her hand.

"It's hot chocolate," she said, lifting her cup. "The doctors say that you can have one cup of coffee a day while you're pregnant, but since we all know that I need a minimum of *four*,

I've been sticking with hot chocolate."

"Fair enough," I said, taking the empty seat beside her.

We sat in the cold for a few minutes, sipping our drinks as our teeth chattered from the cold.

"How are you feeling this morning?" she asked, breaking the ice.

I took another drink, trying to figure that out myself.

"I have no idea. I feel stupid for how I acted last night and woke up to a handful of text messages from Tanner, asking if we can talk."

"Why do you feel stupid?"

"Because," I sighed. "I was so upset over hearing that Tanner wasn't staying long—yet, I'm not either. It's crazy, I really don't know what came over me."

Sheila lifted her mug and took another sip.

"Maybe it's because you like him so much?" she offered, holding her cup in front of her face with both hands.

"I barely even know him," I groaned, realizing how childish it sounded. "We had one date and then spent time together yesterday, and I'm acting like he's the love of my life and abandoning me."

"Well, he could be."

"Okay—now you're the one who's being crazy," I laughed, feeling the way my stomach twisted at the idea that I could be in love with someone I hardly knew.

"Maybe. But I knew right away with Parker and look at us now. Sometimes you just feel it and know that you're meant to be with that person. It's hard to describe, but things just fall so easily into place, and everything feels natural that you don't have to struggle to make it work. It just does on its own."

I thought about what she was saying. It was similar to how I felt with Tanner. Everything about him felt easy, and we didn't seem to argue or disagree on much—not that I could really say that given we had spent less than seventy-two hours together. But deep down, I felt like I knew him and that he understood me. It was like we had this connection—both mentally and physically—that I had never experienced with someone else before. The pull between us was so strong, and I couldn't imagine that it was all in my head.

"What if I'm just that desperate to find somewhere to belong that I latch on to the first guy who pays attention to me? So much has changed in the last few months that maybe I'm really just in love with the *idea* of falling in love. Maybe it's just grief mixed in with hormones, and this is all skewing my judgment?"

Sheila set her cup down on the table and turned to look at me, pinning me in place to make sure she had my full attention.

"I know that you've lost so much already, but I hope you know that you will *always* belong here with us. We love and adore you, Gen. You're our family, and I hope you think of us as yours too."

I watched the tears well in her eyes as my throat prickled while I tried to keep mine away.

"I know," I choked out. "I love you guys too. I just don't know where I *belong*. My mom kept telling me to go live my life and be happy, but I don't know what that's supposed to mean. Did she have stuff that she wanted to do and never got around to it? Did she regret having me so young because it kept her from living her life? I feel like there was some sort of a hidden meaning behind her words, and now I'll never know what it was. Maybe I was just clinging to Tanner because he felt fun, and I didn't have to worry about anything else."

"I was eighteen when I had Oliver," she sighed. "Now I look at Megan, pregnant at sixteen and still a baby herself. But when I think back to when I had him, I didn't feel like a child. I felt like an adult, and I knew that I had responsibilities to take care of. My life has been spent raising four kids and making sure that I teach them how to be the best people they can be before releasing them into the world. I don't regret a single day of it, and I can promise you that even if your mom had stuff she wanted to do, there weren't any regrets about having you at a young age and spending her life raising you. It's what we do as parents—it's both a sacrifice and a reward at the same time."

"How am I supposed to know what I want to do with my life? Or what will make me happy?"

"Nobody can answer that but you. But I think you're taking the right steps to try to figure it out. Nothing has to be decided right now, but if you see an opportunity and you want to take it—then go for it. You have plenty of time to decide what you want in life. Right now is about figuring out what makes you happy."

My stomach sank when an image of Tanner flashed through my mind. I hadn't felt this happy in a long time, and I knew it was because of him. It was the little things, like how he would flirt with me and make me blush or when he would say something funny to make me laugh. I hadn't stopped smiling since I first agreed to go on a date with him, and now I felt like I couldn't get that happiness back.

"Being an adult sucks," I muttered, lifting my coffee to take a drink. The cold was starting to settle in my bones, making me shiver.

"It'll get better, just wait and see." She smiled and took another sip of her hot chocolate. We sat there for a few minutes before Parker came out, threatening to carry our stubborn asses in if we didn't get inside where it was warm soon.

I helped Sheila make breakfast, thankful for the quiet while the kids were still at their grandparent's house. I needed time to think and found frying bacon to be oddly satisfying. Once the food was ready, we sat down and joined Parker at the table.

"Everything smells delicious," he said, pulling a napkin out from the holder on the table. "Thank you, ladies, for breakfast."

"You're welcome," Sheila replied, leaning in to give him a quick kiss.

I bit off a piece of bacon, looking down when my phone vibrated on the table. It was a text message from Tanner, wishing me a good morning. I needed to talk to him about last night, but my head was still a mess. Until I could sort things out on my own, I didn't want to make things more convoluted with him.

"Tanner?" Sheila asked, nodding to my phone. She took a bite of eggs while Parker stayed quiet, his jaw tightening as he took a bite of the sausage link.

"Yeah, he wants to talk."

"That's a good sign," she assured.

"We'll see," I sighed, taking a bite out of my toast.

"Why do you think it's not a good sign?" Parker asked, his tone overly protective. I already knew that he was hoping for this to mean that we were over.

"I didn't say that it's *not* a good sign," I muttered, still feeling irritable with him from yesterday. "I just don't know if there's anything for us to talk about. He's not staying here that long, so why does it matter how we feel about things?"

"In all fairness, you're not planning to stay either," Sheila reminded me.

"I know, I know. It's just already so messy, and things just barely started. I wish I could go back to the other night where we were blissfully unaware of the impending deadline."

The scowl creased harder on Parker's face when I mentioned being with Tanner the other night.

"I'm going to ask you something, and I want you to be completely honest. Give me the first answer that pops into your head." Sheila raised her eyebrows and waited for me to agree.

"Alright, fine."

"*If* Tanner wasn't leaving in a few months, would you stay in Stone Creek to be with him?"

"Yes."

I felt my cheeks flush as my pulse started racing when I realized how easy it was to answer that question without thinking about it.

"Well then, I think you've got the answer that you were looking for."

"What answer? What was the question?" Parker asked, looking between us.

"What makes her happy," Sheila said quietly, giving me a soft smile that told me she knew what I was feeling inside.

The rest of breakfast was uneventful, with Sheila distracting Parker with questions about what he wanted to do for Christmas. His parents had been asking to come in to see them, but he was adamant about keeping them as far away as possible. I ignored the conversation and thought about what I would say to Tanner when I saw him. Once we were finished, I sent him a quick text, asking when we could meet up, and then jumped in the shower.

I got ready quickly, thankful that I didn't have to share the bathroom with anyone else or rush for whoever needed it next. The snow was still coming down heavily, so we agreed to talk at his place. I offered to drive there, so that I didn't have to worry about finding a ride home later, again, but he quickly declined and confirmed he would pick me up in thirty minutes.

My hair was down with loose waves covering the black turtle neck that I needed to hide the few hickies he had accidentally left me. It was soft and comfortable, which was all that mattered at this point. I threw on a pair of comfy, worn-in jeans and did my makeup. It wasn't much, but at least it hid the fact that I cried myself to sleep last night.

I checked my phone, finding a message that he was on his way. I grabbed my stuff and rushed to the front door when Parker stopped me.

"Gen—can we talk for a minute?"

"I'm sorry, Tanner will be here any minute to pick me up."

He ran a hand down his face and sighed.

"I know that I haven't been in your life long enough to have much of a say as your dad, but I don't think you should date him."

I folded my arms over my chest and stared at him.

"Why not?"

"Because," he exhaled. "He's practically ten years older than you for starters, and two, he doesn't even plan to stay here more than a few months."

"Is that really what's bothering you?" I asked, holding his stare and not backing down.

"Yes, he's too old for you."

"You didn't say anything when I was dating Rodney, and he was even older."

"I didn't know you well enough back then to say something," he gritted out.

"You don't know me well enough now, either."

I could see his temper flaring as my blood ran just as hot.

"That's not fair, Gen. I'm trying and have been since you gave me the opportunity."

"It's not fair of you to tell me who I can and cannot date. He's a good man."

"You don't know that."

"Well, Sheila thinks he's good enough to care for her and the babies," I bit out.

"That's not the same, and you know it."

I heard a car door close and knew he was there.

"It doesn't matter either way. He's here, so I'm leaving. Don't bother waiting up for me tonight."

I didn't wait for his answer as I opened the door and stepped outside.

Tanner was smiling as he walked over, fully decked out in a heavy coat and gloves with a beanie that sat low on his head. He looked like the kind of guy you would see on the cover of an outdoor sports magazine.

"Hey, how are you?" he asked, pulling me in for a hug once we reached each other.

"I've been better," I said, feeling the weight of the fight with my dad sitting on my shoulders.

He pulled back slightly and studied my face, making sure I was okay.

"I'm fine," I rushed out. The last thing that I needed was for him to feel the need to go talk to Parker and get him even more riled up. "Let's get inside the car before we freeze."

Once we got back to Tanner's house, my blood pressure had returned to normal, and I felt terrible for how I had left things at home. I was so mad at my dad that I hadn't even said goodbye to Sheila before I left.

He was busy in the kitchen as I sat on the couch, curled up under a blanket and watching the snow fall outside. It felt calm and peaceful here, and I hated how easy it was to feel at home in his place. A few minutes later, he came and sat beside me on the couch, handing me a cup of hot chocolate with a giant marshmallow floating on top and a thick peppermint stick to stir it with.

"You're the cutest," I said as my cheeks split into a smile. I stirred the hot liquid carefully, feeling like a kid again.

"I'll do whatever it takes to get that smile out of you."

Bonus points.

"Well, I definitely needed one," I admitted.

"Do you want to talk about it?" he asked, setting his cup down on the coffee table to give me his full attention.

I took a deep breath and slowly let it out.

"I got into a fight with my dad right before I left."

"About me?"

I nodded.

"He doesn't want you to see me."

He didn't ask it as a question. It was a statement that I didn't bother to deny.

"I'm sorry," he apologized.

"For what?" I lowered my cup to the table, turning to face him.

"For being the source of conflict between you guys. I know how important family is, and I never want to come between one."

My stomach tightened. I wondered if he was going to use this as his excuse to break things off with me before he left, since things were too complicated.

"My dad is a brilliant man. He's built several businesses from the ground up and has done very well for himself over the years. However, he wasn't around much when I was growing up, so he didn't have a say in what I did or the guys that I dated. Just because we've gotten closer recently doesn't mean that he gets to have one now. I decide what I want and make my own decisions."

He leaned back against the couch and stared at the wall across from us.

"What do you want?"

My palms started sweating when I thought about it.

"You."

His eyes grew wider as he turned to look at me. I could see the questions flashing across his face that he didn't dare speak.

"I know that we haven't known each other very long, and maybe I'm feeling something that you're not," I blurted out quickly, hoping that I hadn't scared him with my confession.

He held his hand up to stop me as he grinned the cheeky smile that I loved.

"I want you too, Gen."

Seventeen

Tanner

It felt good to have Gen laying in my arms again. After not getting a response back from my texts last night, I was worried that I had ruined things between us before they had a chance to start. I had spent most of my night staring at my phone, willing it to ring, and was exhausted this morning.

"So," she said quietly, her cheek pressed against my chest. "We've done well with avoiding the elephant in the room, but I need to know—how long are you here for?"

I knew that we would have to talk about it sooner rather than later, but I had been trying to postpone it as long as possible after her reaction to it last night.

"Doctor Long and I have an agreement to discuss my position after New Year's. We'll sit down and see whether this is a good fit for her practice, and whether this is something that I want to make a longer commitment to."

"How do you feel about it so far?"

"Honestly," I sighed. "I don't know. It's only been a week, but I'm already starting to remember why I left small-town life to begin with," I laughed.

"Is it really that bad?" she asked quietly.

I paused and thought about it.

"Not bad, just different. I'm used to doing what I want without having to worry about other people talking about it. Here, everyone knows my business whether I want them to or not."

"I get that. I lived in Nashville when I was going to school, and it's definitely different than the small town I grew up in."

"So, what about you? How long are you planning to stay in Stone Creek?"

She squirmed in my arms, and I felt the way her body stiffened.

"I'm not sure. I haven't really given it much thought yet."

"Do you think you'll end up staying here after all?"

"It's a possibility."

She shrugged and laced her fingers between mine as she laid against my chest. I couldn't see her face from this angle, so I had no idea if she was upset. She was quiet and didn't offer much other than that, so I decided to change the subject.

"Are you going to be in town for the big carnival thing?" I asked, not remembering what it was called. All that I knew was that it was a big event in Stone Creek, and several of the locals had already asked if I was going.

"The Winter Fair?" she asked, turning her head to look at me.

"Yeah, that's it," I laughed. "I couldn't remember the name of it, which is surprising given how much everyone has talked about it."

"I plan to be here for it. I promised Sally that she could take me and show me around since it'll be my first one."

"Sally is your sister?" I asked, trying to remember the siblings' names she had told me about the other night.

"I consider her my sister, but she's Sheila's daughter with her ex-husband, Rodney."

"The guy you were engaged to?" I pulled my brows together, remembering the jealousy that had washed over me when I had heard about that from Dottie a few days after I had told her to stop gossiping about people.

"How did you hear about that?" she asked, shocked that I knew.

"Small towns," I chuckled. "Nothing stays a secret for long."

"Ain't that the truth," she grumbled. "But yes, Rodney was my fiancé. I met him while I lived in Nashville, but I didn't know the crazy little love triangle that was going to unfold. I had just gotten in touch with my dad again while he lived in Nashville and had no idea that he was dating Sheila or that she was Rodney's ex-wife."

"What made you guys decide not to get married?"

"Once I met Sheila and saw what a wonderful person she is, it shifted the way that I saw Rodney. I didn't want to get in the middle of it, and I found myself taking her side when it came to the kids. Then, I realized that he wasn't what I wanted after all. He was way too old for me, and we were just at different points in our lives."

"How do you feel about our age difference?" I asked cautiously, rubbing my finger lightly up and down her arm.

"Honestly, I don't have a problem with it. You're not that much older than I am, and I feel like we're more on the same page than I ever was with Rodney."

"I'm thirty-two, Gen. You're barely twenty—" I left off the rest of the sentence, realizing that I didn't know how old she is. I had only guessed that she was in her early twenties.

"Twenty-two," she finished for me. "But I'm turning twenty-three in January."

"Still, there's a ten-year age difference between us. That doesn't bother you?"

"Should it?" She sat up and turned to face me, crossing her legs into a pretzel as she sat on the other side of the bed.

"No," I sighed. "I just wanted to make sure that you knew how old I was."

"Well, now that we've got the important things settled, why don't we stop talking and do something that we both want?"

I watched her crawl across the bed, her dark eyes clouded with desire as she climbed on top of me and pinned my back to the bed.

"And what's that?" I asked, knowing full well what she had in mind as my dick hardened beneath her.

"I'll give you a hint," she whispered, pulling my t-shirt that I loaned her up and over her head before tossing it behind her. She leaned down and kissed me, her naked breasts warm on my chest as her nipples puckered from the cold.

She slid down my body, still straddling me, and pulled off my sweats and boxer shorts, letting my erection spring free. Her hand gripped it firmly, stroking it up and down as she locked eyes with me and licked her lips. Slowly, she lowered her head and took my length in her mouth, opening her jaw to accommodate as much as she could. She started slow, her tongue swirling in circles around the head while her hand tightened around me as she pumped faster.

I closed my eyes and relished in the sensations running through me as her beautiful mouth sucked me hard and fast. I was on the verge of climax, but the only thing that was running through my mind was that I needed to slow things down between us before one of us got hurt.

Eighteen

Gen

The last few weeks had flown by faster than I had realized. Sean had called to let me know that they were officially moving to Alabama to be with his family in March and asked if I had changed my mind about coming with them. When I declined, he made sure to let me know that I had some time to get my stuff from the house and to go through my mom's things before he packed any of it up. It was another piece of the puzzle that I wasn't ready for, but I knew that I had to get that closure at some point.

Tanner and I had been seeing each other almost every day, and I stayed at his house most nights—much to the irritation of Parker. I had hoped that by being in Stone Creek, our relationship would get stronger, but it seemed that my choice in men only made it harder. I loved my dad, but I hated that he wouldn't give Tanner a chance to show him what a good man he was and how much he cared about me. We had been technically dating for three weeks, and while that didn't seem like a long time, it felt like one of the best relationships I had ever been in. For once, I was happy again.

"So, are you excited about the Winter Fair?" Brooke asked as I wiped down the counter by the register. I had agreed to help out while Autumn—the girl who has worked for Brooke for years and helps run the place when she's gone—was on vacation in Delaware. Since I was staying in town for a little while, I figured I might as well make some money and fill my time while Tanner was at work.

"I'm looking forward to checking it out. Sally insists that I've never seen anything like it and that I'll be in complete awe the moment I see it."

"Well, she's right. I can assure you that you've never seen anything like it," she laughed. "Whether or not you're in awe, I couldn't say. But, at least it's fun!"

"Are you and Ryder going together?"

"We'll both be working the booth there, but we'll take some time and go walk around like we always do. That's the nice thing about small-town life—I can ask someone to watch our stuff, and I know that nothing bad will happen."

She had been on the *Keep Gen In Stone Creek* bandwagon for a few weeks and constantly tried to sell me on staying. I don't think anyone was worried that I was going to go back home to Arkansas now that Sean and the kids were leaving. Instead, I think they were concerned that I would move with Tanner and fall in love with life in a big city.

"Well, I'll have to be sure to stop by the booth so I can watch it for you. But don't blame me if a pastry or two is missing—you can't trust me around sweets, and you already know that."

"Don't worry," she laughed. "There won't be any cream cheese danishes at the fair. I've learned to keep those *far* away from you while others are around."

My cheeks tingled when I thought about how many times Tanner and I had enjoyed the danishes recently, and I giggled when I thought of the places that they had been. Tanner was all for experimenting with food, and it turns out that other creams explode on tongues as well.

I kept my head down to hide the blush that was covering my face from the dirty thoughts I had gotten lost in.

"Are you going to see Tanner for lunch?" Brooke asked, walking behind the counter to the register.

"I'm not sure. Why?"

"He placed a lunch order, and I was going to see if you would deliver it for me?"

"Sure," I said, feeling the excitement at the thought of seeing him again.

"Cool, I'll go see if Ryder has it ready."

A few minutes later, she came out empty-handed and walked to the coffee bar on the counter behind the display case of pastries.

"It's not ready yet, but I'll get the drinks going," Brooke confirmed.

"Drinks?"

"Yeah, he ordered two pumpkin spiced lattes."

"What is it with him and those drinks?" I groaned, rolling my eyes. "It's like he lives for them."

Brooke laughed as she pressed buttons then stepped back when it started brewing.

"Hey, don't pick on him for his love of pumpkin," she teased. "Pumpkin makes people happy and more optimistic."

"Is that a scientific fact, or are you just making stuff up because you're also a pumpkin obsessed weirdo?"

"Hey—it's not just pumpkin," she corrected. "It's pumpkin *spiced*. There's a difference. And I like to think of it as pumpkin spiced possibilities because it makes you feel so happy inside that you can do anything!"

"Wow," I said sarcastically, shaking my head. Before I had time to say anything more, the door flung open, and Sheila rushed in, looking frazzled.

"Howdy, howdy, who's ready to get rowdy?" Brooke asked, using the phrase that Sheila always used.

"No—there's no time to get rowdy," Sheila said, still flustered as she tossed her purse onto the counter and looked at us. "Christmas is less than a week away, and I haven't finished my shopping."

"What's new?" Brooke laughed, earning a glare from Sheila.

She pulled her lips together to keep from laughing, sensing that Sheila wouldn't find it funny.

"What's new is that I have to buy a gift for Rodney's girlfriend, and I don't know what to get her." She lifted her hands in the air in front of her and raised her brows while waiting for us to say something.

"Why do you have to get her something?" Brooke asked, frowning.

"They've been dating for over six months," she sighed heavily. "The kids love her, and honestly, I really like her too. She's been great and keeps Rodney in line, which has been really helpful these days."

I hadn't seen Rodney mad or upset that many times while we were dating, but I was there when Megan told him that she was pregnant and saw a completely different side of him. He didn't get angry or yell at her, but I swear that he looked like one of those old cartoons where he had smoke coming out of his ears and was a few seconds away from having his head pop off.

"What about a sweater or a pretty scarf?" I offered, not knowing her well enough to suggest anything more personal.

"I don't know her size, and she has sensitive skin, so I worry about getting her something that will make her itchy."

"You could always get her a nice bath set," Brooke suggested. "Maybe some candles and those little balls that you put in the tub, and they fizzle around you?"

"They don't have a tub at Rodney's house."

"Jewelry?" I threw out, knowing that it was a terrible idea. Sheila scrunched her face and shook her head no.

"Can you just come shopping and help me?" Sheila asked Brooke, batting her eyes as she pressed her hands together and begged.

Brooke eyed her suspiciously, folding her arms over her chest.

"I won't make you lock arms with me, while we skip and drink wine," Sheila muttered with a smirk. "Lucky for you, I can't have wine, so you're getting off easy with this one."

"Fine," Brooke sighed. "But I can't go until Gen gets back since Autumn is out of town, and Ryder has that meeting this afternoon with Parker and the supplier that we've been talking to."

"I'll go check on the food," I said, taking the dirty rag with me to put in the hamper in the back office.

I grabbed the order from Ryder right as he was heading out of the kitchen to bring it to Brooke.

"I added an extra sandwich," he said with a smile, handing me the brown paper bag. "I thought that you might be joining him for lunch."

"Thank you, that was very nice of you."

I felt better talking about my relationship with Ryder than I did Parker since he was more open-minded and didn't lecture me on what a big mistake I was making by dating an older man who would be leaving soon.

I grabbed the tray with the coffees from Brooke and jumped into my car, excited to see Tanner.

Once I got there, I handed Dottie the coffee that he had ordered for her. Black—no cream or sugar. Tanner joked that she liked it dark because it fed her soul, but I didn't doubt it wasn't true. She gave me the go-ahead to go to his office since I had his food order.

I was about to knock on the door when I noticed it was open a crack and he was on the phone. Just as I was about to turn and walk away, I heard something that caught my attention. I balanced the tray in my hand while gripping the bag between my fingers as I leaned closer to the door.

"Sure," he said excitedly. "I can be there January fifth."

I felt a lump in my throat as my heart fluttered at the thought of him leaving. Maybe I was wrong and had assumed that I knew what the phone call was about?

"I can't wait," he added. "It'll be nice to be back in the big city again."

I set the tray of coffee down on the floor outside of his door next to the bag of food and left. Just as I was walking out the door, I heard him calling my name behind me. I got in my car and didn't look back as I sped out of the parking lot, the tears rushing down my cheeks.

Nineteen

Tanner

I was out of breath from trying to chase after Gen's car after she flew out of the parking lot and almost got hit by a car in oncoming traffic. My heart beat wildly inside of my chest, and I wondered how much of my conversation she had heard.

I walked back inside, giving Dottie a dirty look as I stormed past her to my office. I grabbed the food and lattes from the floor and set them on my desk, running a hand through my hair in frustration. This wasn't supposed to be the way this happened. I had purposely instructed Dottie not to come back to my office while I was on the phone and assumed she understood that no one else was allowed back either.

Sitting down in the plush leather chair, I pulled out my cell phone and tried calling Gen. It went straight to voicemail again. I sent her another text message, asking her to call me. I needed to explain what happened before things got too out of control.

The stress of the day had my stomach in knots and made lunch sound unappealing. I tossed the food into the fridge, thankful that the sandwich would still be good tomorrow, so I didn't waste it. I finished the latte in record time and got started on the second one right before the next patient came in. I was already on edge and jittery, why not make it more fun with an extra caffeine boost?

By four o'clock, I still hadn't heard from Gen and knew that I wouldn't. I packed up my stuff, ready to get the hell out of there for the day. It was less than a week away from Christmas, and I was feeling the same stress that I felt every year around this time.

I took a chance and stopped by The Sweet Shop on my way home, hoping that Gen was still at work. When I walked inside, I was disappointed to see that she wasn't there as Parker and Ryder hung out behind the counter.

"Hey, Tanner," Ryder said pleasantly. "What can I help you with?"

"I was actually looking for Gen," I replied softly, feeling the heat of Parker's glare. "Have you seen her?"

"She went home early. Said she wasn't *feeling well*," Parker bit out. He hadn't bothered to move as he stared at me with his arms crossed firmly across his chest.

I nodded and turned to walk out.

"The funny thing is that she was fine this morning before she came to work," he added smugly. "Then, after she delivered your lunch, she came back feeling sick. So either Ryder poisoned her with the sandwich he sent over for her, or you did something to upset her." He sucked in a deep breath and tilted his head slightly to the side.

"I'm sorry for bothering you guys," I said and walked toward the door. "When you see Gen, please tell her that I'm looking for her and want to talk to her."

Within seconds, Parker was across the room and closing in on me. I heard Ryder's heavy footsteps as he trailed behind him. I felt a strong hand grab my shoulder and spin me around. Parker's face was etched with anger as his nostrils flared.

"If you know what's best for you, you'll leave my daughter the fuck alone," he growled, inches away from my face as his fingers firmly dug into my skin.

"I can't do that," I admitted, looking down at the floor.

"Why not? Do you think you can just break her heart and play with her emotions? She deserves better than that, and I'll go to my grave making sure she has it."

"You don't think that I know that?!" I shouted, forcing him to let go and take a step back. Ryder's eyes widened as he waited to see what was going to happen between us.

"I know that she deserves better than me, Parker. I tell her that all the time. She doesn't listen."

"So make her."

"Have you tried to tell Gen to do something she doesn't want to?" I asked with my eyebrow raised.

A slight smirk tried to force its way onto his face as the corners of his mouth tipped up slightly.

"No matter how hard I try, I can't walk away from her. She's like a magnet that has this hold on me that I can't break free of." I shook my head and looked away. "I tried not to fall for her, but I'm in love with her, and nothing is going to stop it."

Parker's face softened slightly when he heard me declare my love for his daughter. That didn't mean that he approved of our relationship, but maybe he understood it better now.

"Have you told her how you feel?" he asked.

I shook my head no.

"Are you going to?"

I refused to answer, knowing that I didn't have the right answer.

"Are. You. Going. To?" he asked again, enunciating each word clearly.

"No," I sighed, shoving my hands into my pockets to keep from punching something.

"Why not?"

"Because it's better for her that she doesn't know. If I tell her that I'm in love with her, then she'll feel obligated to put her life on hold to be with me, and I don't want that. I want her to be happy and to do the things that she wants to do while she's still young. Her life is just starting, and I don't want to be the reason that she puts it on hold."

Parker closed his eyes and blew out a hard breath.

"You know, you're making it really hard not to like you, Doctor Hayes," he said.

"You can call me Tanner," I teased, feeling the shift between us as the tension thinned out.

"We'll see about that."

He clapped a hand on my shoulder and winked.

474

Twenty

Gen- 5 Days Until Christmas

"I'll be back before the Winter Fair, I promise," I said loudly, hoping that the speaker in my phone wasn't cutting out again as I started to wind through the forest. The cell reception was poor, and I knew that the call was going to get dropped soon.

"I've gotta go, Sally. I'll call you tonight, okay?"

Before she could confirm, the line went dead. I tapped my fingers on the steering wheel and tried to think of anything other than Tanner while I watched the road for wildlife. The snow was thick on the ground around me, with a few icy patches on the road, but overall, the trip wasn't bad so far. It was a last-minute decision to head back to Arkansas, but I knew that I needed to do it.

I had called Sean this morning and let him know that I was headed back for a few days. The kids were excited to see me, and I had been missing them terribly. It was also the first

Christmas that I hadn't celebrated at home, which was even more reason to get back before the twenty-fifth, even if I didn't stay for the actual day. I had left at five o'clock this morning, surprised by my ability to get up that early. It was a seven-hour drive which meant that I would be home mid-day and not have to do the last stretch in the dark.

Sheila and Parker were sad to see me go, but they understood where I was coming from. The holidays felt hard this year without my mom, and I was desperate to find something to fill the ache that I had in my heart from spending my first Christmas without her. I hadn't bothered to talk to Tanner before I left and figured that this was the easiest way for us to split and go our separate ways since he was leaving in a few weeks anyway.

Once I got through the thickest part of the mountain, I had better service and turned on the radio. Music was the best therapy, and I needed as much as I could get. By three o'clock, I was relieved to be pulling up to the house and back home. I felt a mix of sadness and excitement all rolled into one as I grabbed my duffle bag and got out.

I took a deep breath in and slowly let it out as I tried to prepare myself to go inside. The door flew open, and my sisters came running out to greet me. I smiled as I reached down and hugged them, knowing that I was home again. We went inside, and the smell of chili immediately made my stomach growl. Sean knew that it was my favorite comfort meal, and there was no doubt that he had made it especially for me, knowing how hard this was going to be for me.

I set my bag down in the mudroom and pulled my coat off

before hanging it on the rack on the wall. The cold was still biting at my skin as I rubbed my hands together to warm up and walked into the living room.

My heart sank when I noticed that the tree wasn't up and there were no decorations anywhere in the house. It was five days until Christmas, and they still hadn't decorated? I tried to remind myself that they were grieving too and that this was just as hard for them as it was for me. Or at least half as hard.

Sean came out of the kitchen with a hand towel hung over his shoulder and a spatula in his hand.

"Hey, Gen, welcome home," he said as he wrapped an arm around to hug me.

"Thanks," I muttered, feeling completely lost. "Where's the tree and the decorations?" I asked.

"The kids didn't want to put one up this year because it reminded them too much of Amy," he said with a shrug.

"You mean their mom?" I felt the cold, icy tone slip right out of my mouth.

"Sorry, I'm used to calling her Amy."

I arched my brow, calling him on his bullshit excuse.

"She would have wanted you guys to decorate. She loved Christmas," I whispered, my throat tight as I fought to get the words out. "The tree was her favorite part."

"I know, it's just so much work, and the kids didn't seem to be that interested in it."

"Then you do it for them," I balked, surprised by how little he seemed to care.

"I haven't had the time," he sighed. "I've been busy packing stuff for the move and donating the stuff that we're not going to take."

"Donating?" My eyes widened. He had promised that I would get to go through my mom's stuff before he got rid of anything, yet everything already looked and felt different.

"Just random stuff around the house," he assured me, heading back to the kitchen. "I've left some boxes in your room with stuff for you to go through when you're up to it. Whatever you don't want, I'll add to the next donation drop-off."

I stayed in the living room, listening to the sound of the kids upstairs as music floated down and the sound of fighting came out of one of the rooms. Aside from the girls rushing out to say hi, no one seemed to care that I was home. They were busy doing whatever it was they were doing before I got here.

I tried to calm myself down, but the more I thought about everything, the angrier I got. I stormed into the kitchen and stared at Sean with my hands on my hips.

"We need to put a tree up," I insisted. "It's Christmas. The kids deserve to have a normal holiday the first year without our mom. So, we're putting the tree up."

Sean sighed and placed his hands on the counter as he hung his head.

"We can't put the tree up," he said quietly.

"Why not?"

"Because I donated it."

"You what?!" I felt like my head was going to spin off and fly into another dimension.

"I donated it after the kids said that they didn't want to put it up this year."

I covered my mouth and tried to keep the sob from escaping as my eyes filled with tears.

"We've had that tree since I was five years old. We put it up every single Christmas and decorated it as a family."

"I'm sorry, Gen. I just didn't want more to pack up and move to Alabama. I promised the kids we would get a new tree next year when we're in our new house. They were excited about it."

"This isn't about them!" I shouted, feeling myself losing control. "This is about me! I wanted that tree. It was important to me!"

I took a shaky breath, clenching and unclenching my fists at my sides.

"Where are the decorations?" I asked, my teeth gritted.

He winced as he said, "I donated those too."

I turned on my heel and stormed out of the kitchen and up the stairs to what used to be my bedroom. I slammed the door and locked it before sliding down the back of it and crying on the floor.

Twenty One

Tanner- 4 Days Until Christmas

"Another pumpkin spiced latte?" Megan asked with little enthusiasm in her tone. The only reason that I knew her name was from the first time I met her at the ultrasound, not because she had been especially friendly with me at the second appointment or any of the other times I had run into her since then.

"Actually, I was hoping to see Gen," I said, looking around, trying to find her.

"Gen's not here. Won't be back anytime soon either," she replied snidely.

"What does that mean? Did she quit?"

"No, but she went back to Arkansas. I can't say that I blame her. I would get the hell out of here the second I could if it weren't—"

"Aren't you supposed to be cleaning tables?" Parker interrupted, coming out from the kitchen. He was dressed in his usual jeans and a dark-colored fitted sweater. It matched his mood—dark and lacking color on the outside. He scowled as she rolled her eyes at him and muttered something under her breath as she walked away.

"Kids," he joked, taking her place behind the counter. "Did she get your order?"

"I actually came to see Gen," I explained again. "I really need to talk to her and haven't been able to reach her since yesterday when she came to deliver my food at the office."

"Sorry, I can't help you there. She's not talking to me either."

"Did she really go back to Arkansas?" I asked, hoping that Megan was making it up.

He nodded his head.

The bell above the door chimed, and I turned to see Brooke and Sheila walking in.

"Hey, Doc, I thought I was supposed to see you this afternoon?" Sheila asked, looking between Parker and me.

"Yeah, I just stopped by for a few minutes to talk to Gen."

"She's not here," Brooke answered, shrugging out of her coat and tossing her purse onto the table next to her before pulling off her gloves.

"So I've heard," I muttered, running a hand down my face.

"She was having a hard time with it being a few days before Christmas," Sheila explained, coming behind the counter to give Parker a quick peck on the cheek. "It was her mom's favorite time of year, and she thought that going home to where she's always celebrated the holidays would make it easier for her."

I swallowed hard, knowing that feeling all too well.

"Well, I'm glad that she's somewhere that's bringing her comfort during this hard time," I said, meaning every word. I hated that I wasn't going to get to spend Christmas with her and that I didn't know whether or not she was coming back, but I understood what she was looking for.

"That's the unfortunate part of it—she's not. When she got home yesterday, only a few of her siblings came down to greet her. The house wasn't decorated, and they didn't put the tree up. She asked her stepdad about it, and he said that he had donated it, along with the ornaments that she and her mom had collected since she was a little girl."

It felt like my heart was being shredded into a million pieces.

"You've got to be kidding me," I balked. "Who would do such a thing?"

"He insists that he didn't know that it would mean anything to her and that it was an honest mistake. She's been miserable and called me last night crying."

"Why doesn't she come home?" Parker asked, gently pushing a strand of hair out of Sheila's face.

"She's feeling lost right now. She doesn't know where she belongs and is desperately trying to find something that feels normal in this new world that she's been forced to live in. Her mom was the only constant that she's ever had in her life, and now she's gone. Gen just needs some time to heal and take that first step forward. It'll be hard, but we'll be there for her every step of the way."

"Sheila, I'm sorry, but I need to cancel our appointment today," I blurted out suddenly. There were a million thoughts running through my head, and I had a lot that I needed to get done in a short period.

"Oh, okay," she replied, taken aback. "Is everything okay?"

"No, but it will be. There's something that I need to do."

"Is there anything that we can do to help?"

"Yeah, can you point me in the right direction to Arkansas?"

Twenty Two

Gen- Four Days Until Christmas

"I know that I promised, Sally," I said softly, hating that she was crying on the other line. "I'm still going to try to make it back for the Winter Fair if I can."

"But it's in *two days*. Mom said that you might spend Christmas in Arkansas with your other family."

"I haven't figured out what I'm doing yet. Things are really hard for me right now."

"I know, I'm sorry," she sighed, and I was glad that she didn't have any idea what I was going through, even though she was trying to relate to me.

"If I don't make it back," I sucked in a deep breath and tried to force the words out, knowing that I had already broken my promise to her and that I wouldn't be back in time. "I will make it up to you. Okay?"

"Alright."

"Can I talk to your mom?"

I knew that I needed to fill Sheila in on our conversation so she would understand why Sally was in such a bad mood—other than she was a hormonal teenager who hated the world most days lately.

"She's not here."

I pulled my head back, surprised. It was Friday afternoon, and Sheila was always off from her job early. On top of that, they usually gave her the days leading up to Christmas off to spend time with her family. The holiday fell on a Monday this year, so I imagined that she would have been off today.

"Where is she?"

"I don't know. She and Parker left earlier for some secret something or another. All that I know is that Megan and Oliver are in charge until my dad and Lizzie come to pick us up."

"Oh, well, maybe they're just out running errands and finishing up their shopping," I suggested, remembering how stressed Sheila was yesterday about not being done yet.

"Who knows," Sally muttered, not having the same amount of interest in it as I did.

"Well, if you need anything, just call me."

"I'll be fine," she sighed, the teenager in her coming out again. "I'm not a kid, and I'll be stuck at my dad's house anyway."

"Alright, well, I'll talk to you soon."

I ended the call and laid down on the bed. Deep down, I was more hurt with Sean than I was angry, but since no one seemed bothered that I didn't come out of my room to spend time with them, I hadn't made much of an effort.

Instead of going through my mom's stuff and letting Sean donate what I didn't want, I had loaded up the trunk of my car and packed it so full that it barely closed. I'd decided that I wasn't going to get rid of anything until I decided that I was ready, even if it meant that I had to find someplace to store it until then.

I had taken the time while he was out with the kids earlier and walked through the house, hoping to feel her in it still. I closed my eyes and sat on the couch where she used to braid my hair as a teenager before I would spend hours at the creek with my friends. I remembered the way her fingers felt as she maneuvered my hair effortlessly into a fishtail braid or whatever crazy concoction that I had wanted that day. She never complained about it, just sat on the couch and listened to me talk about whatever teenage drama I had going on at the time while she did my hair.

Being alone in the house was helpful, and I found that I could still feel her stronger in certain parts than others. Most of what I had left was from the memories that I had been cherishing inside my head and not from the few things that were left that hadn't been packed up yet. I browsed the photos on the mantle above the fireplace and took the ones that were my favorite, leaving Sean the ones that had him or the kids in them. I doubted that he would even notice the others were missing—

like the one of my mom and dad, holding me a few days after I was born. It was the only picture that I had of the three of us, and I was damned if I wasn't going to be the one to keep it.

The day was getting late, and I knew that soon the house would be full again and that I wouldn't have any more time to myself. I took what I could and made peace knowing that this would never be home again, and that was okay. When I thought about home, I started to picture Stone Creek and the family that I had gotten closer to there.

I was still lying on my bed when I heard car doors close. I pulled the pillow over my head and grumbled, not ready to see or deal with anyone yet. My heart was still in a fragile state, and I couldn't bear any more sadness or disappointment tonight. I got up and made an effort to go downstairs to greet them, knowing that I needed to spend some time with them before I left to go back to Stone Creek, and they moved to Alabama. It felt weird how easy it was now to decide that I was going *home*.

As I got to the last stair, there was a knock on the door. I walked over and rolled my eyes as I pulled it open.

"Did you forget your keys again?" I teased, knowing that Sean and the kids were lazy enough to knock instead of bothering to unlock the door themselves. Only, it wasn't Sean or the kids.

I recognized the spicy fragrance of his cologne before I saw him, the pull of my body to his as strong as it always was. My mouth suddenly went dry, and I couldn't get any words out.

"Can I come in?" he asked, shivering in the cold even though he was bundled up.

"Um, yeah," I said slowly, still unable to believe that he was there. I stepped back and held the door open for him to come inside.

"Us too?" Sheila asked as she and Parker came around the giant bush that lined the sidewalk to the door.

My eyes almost popped out of my head as I watched them walk through the door behind Tanner.

"What are you guys doing here?" I closed the door quickly, shutting out the cold before it could come in and ruin this perfect daydream that I was having.

"Tanner had something that he needed to say to you," Parker said smoothly, sitting down on the couch.

"You can't just make yourself at home," Sheila scolded, standing next to him.

"No one's here," I interjected, glancing from Tanner, who was standing in front of me, to them. "Besides, it would be fine if they were."

I turned my attention back to Tanner and noticed his Adam's apple bob as he swallowed down his nerves.

"Gen, I'm sorry to just barge in here without asking, but I have something to say to you that couldn't wait."

"Okay," I whispered, still trying to wrap my head around the fact that he was here—in my house—well, technically my *old* house.

"I am head over heels in love with you, Gen. I can't stop thinking about you, and when you're not around, I feel like my days are dark and dull. You're the light that brightens the room when you walk in, and you're the only person that I've ever felt so comfortable opening up to. I know that you're trying to find the next path in your life, but I needed you to know that I need you in mine. So, whatever decision you make, I hope you'll consider making one that allows me to stay in your life."

He paused for a moment and glanced over his shoulder at Parker. Something had definitely changed between them, besides that Parker was being nice and not shooting daggers at him with his eyes. My dad nodded, and Tanner turned back to me and continued.

"If you want to live in Arkansas, I'll find a clinic to work at out here. If you want to go to Alabama, I'll follow you there. There are endless options for work, Gen, but only one true love, and that's you."

The tears slid down my cheeks faster than I could stop them. My throat burned, and my eyes blurred as I struggled to find the words to say.

"Tanner, I know about you taking the other job."

I bit my tongue to try to keep the tears back as my lower lip trembled.

"What other job?"

"The one that you start in the *big city* on January fifth. I heard you on the phone and heard all about it."

"Gen, that wasn't what you thought it was."

I wrapped my arms around my middle protectively. How could he sit there and tell me that I was wrong when I knew what I had heard?

"I was standing right there. You said it yourself."

He took a step toward me, a mischievous smile on his face.

"I know what I said."

I was starting to feel frustrated and hated not knowing what was going on. Sheila and Parker sat there quietly, not bothering to jump in and help.

"Okay, then what exactly is going on?" I demanded, angrier than I had expected.

"I was planning a trip," he said vaguely.

"A trip?"

He nodded.

"I take one every year right after New Year's, so I can be gone on January seventh."

"Why?"

My anger was slowly starting to fade as my curiosity piqued.

"Because," he breathed heavily, reaching out to hold both of my hands. "I lost my mother on January seventh."

His words plunged through my heart, twisting inside the wound that was already open and oozing.

"I have a little sister, Emily, that I take with me. She's fifteen now but still loves when we take trips together. She doesn't know why we go in January, and I hope that she never remembers."

"Was she young when your mom died?"

"It happened a few years ago, but she has Down's Syndrome and doesn't remember *when* it happened. It's hard enough that she knows that my mom is gone, but I always feel this responsibility to distract her—us, on the anniversary of when it happened. Just in case she starts to remember. I don't want her to feel that pain and my theory has always been that she can't feel the pain if we're out having fun."

I didn't bother wiping the tears away as he shared this intimate story of his life with me. We were so similar in so many ways that I now understood why he got me better than anyone I'd ever met.

"When you heard me on the phone, I was talking to my other sister and planning a trip for all of us at Disneyland."

I lowered my eyes in embarrassment.

"I'm so sorry," I apologized. "I just heard you talking about a date and the big city and assumed that you were taking a new job after we had talked about your contract ending at the end of this month."

"It's okay," he smiled, reaching for my hands again now that I was done wiping tears away. "I've been trying to find you so I could explain, but you've been a little hard to track down."

"I know, I'm sorry that I didn't give anyone much notice before I left. I thought that coming back would help me find what I was looking for and help me through the holidays without my mom, but it just left me feeling emptier and more alone."

"I think we have something that can fix that," Tanner said, his cheeks splitting as the smile stretched across his face and showed off his perfect white teeth. "Come with me," he insisted, pulling me toward the door. Sheila and Parker got up and followed us outside.

Parked in the street, in front of the house, was Sheila's SUV. I heard the click as it was unlocked before Tanner opened the back door.

I gasped and covered my mouth as I stared inside.

"You found it?!" I asked emotionally, my voice cracking at the end.

"We went by several shops in town until we found the one that Sean had donated it to," Parker explained. "We would have been here sooner, but Sheila saw a few things that she just *had to have*," he teased.

"Hey, I was finishing my Christmas shopping," she insisted. "We are four days away, and you're still not done, mister." She wagged her finger at him playfully.

"I can't believe that you went and bought my old tree. That's the sweetest thing that anyone has ever done for me, you guys."

"We knew how much it meant to you," Sheila said softly, rubbing her hand across my back.

"It was Tanner's idea," Parker added. "He was coming here to get it, with or without us."

"That means so much to me, thank you," I cried, my face raw from the saltiness of my tears.

"There's more," Tanner said, gently leading me to the back of the SUV. He pressed the button to open the trunk, and I looked inside. My eyes widened, and I turned to look at him.

"You bought all of the ornaments too?"

"Actually, no," he said softly. "When I explained what had happened, the guy just gave them to me. It turns out that he knew your mother and used to teach her piano when she was a little girl."

"Mr. King," I smiled, knowing exactly who he was talking about. "He's one of the nicest people that I've ever met."

"He said the same about you. In addition to giving us the tree and the ornaments, he also added a new one for you to add to your collection."

Tanner reached inside and pulled out a small brown paper bag. My fingers trembled as I took it and carefully pulled out the box inside. He took the bag from me and smiled while I opened it.

Inside was a beautiful white ceramic angel with wings that were paper thin and sheer. Her hands were pulled close to her chest as she held a small red heart inside them.

"Look at the bottom," Tanner suggested.

I gently tipped her over, making sure that my grip on her was tight enough to keep me from dropping it while soft enough not to break anything.

On the bottom, in a fine ink, were the words: home is always where the heart is.

I turned my head and tried to keep the sob from escaping my throat as Tanner wrapped me in his arms and held me.

"I know that you've felt lost and like you haven't found your way," he whispered. "But we're here for you, Gen. Just tell us what you need, and we'll take care of you."

"I can't believe you guys came all the way down here and did all of this for me," I whimpered.

"You're our family," Sheila reminded me. "We will always be wherever you need us. Nothing will ever change that."

The past few days, I had felt so down and alone, and not even fifteen minutes with them, I felt like I belonged. I was happy and felt wanted.

"It's getting too cold for my liking," Parker complained, rubbing his hands together. "Just tell us where you want the tree, and we'll help you put it up and decorate it."

"I want to take it home," I said proudly, looking up at the house behind us.

"Okay, I'll start unpacking the ornaments first," Parker confirmed, moving toward us.

"No," I breathed, finally feeling like I could take a deep breath. "I want to go home. To Stone Creek, where I belong."

<u>Twenty Three</u>

Tanner- 3 Days Until Christmas

"Where do you want to put it?" I asked Gen once we finished unpacking the tree and decorations from the SUV. Parker and I were exhausted from driving to Arkansas and then back with little rest in between. We were able to tow Gen's Corolla back with Sheila's Tahoe, which allowed us to all ride back together after we moved the tree to Gen's car to make more room. We rested while the girls took turns driving back to Stone Creek and talking, but I still felt like I needed another ten hours of sleep to feel back to normal.

"Can we put it over there, by the window?" she asked nervously, pointing while chewing a nail on her other hand.

"It can go anywhere you want it," I smiled, leaning in to kiss her on the cheek.

It felt wonderful to have Gen back at my house, and the stack of boxes in the corner of the living room didn't bother me either. It was all of the stuff that she had packed up and brought back with her from Arkansas that she was trying to store in her car until she figured out where she was going to live.

Parker and Sheila had the room for now, but when the new babies came, they would need to spread out, which meant that Megan would need her own room again. I offered Gen to stay with me as long as she wanted and had to convince her to move her stuff out of her car. Before Gen left for Arkansas, I had felt torn on whether or not I wanted to continue my contract in Stone Creek or move somewhere else. But now that I knew what it felt like to be without her, I didn't want to let her go ever again.

"Thank you," she whispered, the tears swelling in her eyes again as she stared at the tree in front of the window where the snow was falling outside.

"You don't have to thank me." I wiped the tear from her cheek with my thumb and wrapped a hand around her waist. She leaned into me and rested her head against my chest.

"It means so much to me that you went through all of this effort for me. I know that it's silly because it's just a tree, but—"

"Gen, it's not silly. It's special, and that makes it important. Don't ever apologize for how you're feeling. I'm glad that we were able to help get the tree and decorations back for you."

"Me too. It's not the same as spending Christmas with her, but I feel like she's still here with me," she choked out.

"She is," I whispered, feeling the tightness in my throat.

We spent the afternoon decorating the tree and drinking wine, laughing at my failed attempt to get the star on the tree at the perfect angle and ended the night wrapped in each other's arms. If I ever wondered whether or not small-town life was for me, I found my answer every time I looked into her beautiful, green eyes. I would go to the ends of the earth to be with her.

Twenty Four

Gen- 2 Days Until Christmas

"Over there is where they have the face painting booth, and then around the corner is where Mr. Gianni has the *best* caramel apples!" Sally shrieked, pulling me by one hand while Tanner held the other.

I don't know what she was more excited about—the Winter Fair itself or being able to show me around. Well, technically, *us* since Tanner had never been to one either.

"This is amazing," I said happily, taking in the sights around me. There were booths set up along both sides of Main Street, which had been blocked off hours ago as they started setting up for the fair. Each booth was decked out in beautiful white Christmas lights, creating the illusion of houses stacked along the street. The trees on the sidewalk had been lit up as well, but the real sight to see was the forty-five foot Christmas tree in the middle of the street where the carolers were gathered, singing Silent Night.

"You definitely don't see anything like this in the big city," Tanner mumbled, looking around in awe. "Or at least, I never have. They have big events that I've been to, but they don't have *this* vibe."

I nodded, knowing what he was talking about. I felt it too and found it hard to describe because I hadn't felt anything like this before either.

"I'm gonna go find my mom and Parker. I'll catch up with you later," Sally said before she ran off.

"Will she be okay on her own?" Tanner asked, looking over his shoulder to watch where she went.

"Yeah, I see Parker over there." I nodded to where he was standing by Brooke and Ryder's booth, his eyes fixated on Sally as she wandered around on her way to them.

We walked around, holding hands, and enjoying the festivities together. After a bit, we sat down for dinner and enjoyed a warm bowl of soup with freshly baked bread that was to die for. Even though I wasn't in Arkansas and didn't have my mom with me, I was starting to feel the Christmas spirit around me.

After a while, we met up with Sheila, Parker, and the kids, which was a hard enough feat, getting everyone in one place at one time. I knew that it wasn't a coincidence, but when the kids were grinning from ear to ear, I knew that something was up.

"What's going on?" I asked, looking between everyone, waiting for an answer.

"You'll find out in just a few minutes," Sheila said lightly, her eyes sparkling with happiness.

A few minutes later, Brooke and Ryder came rushing over, pulling their coats tighter against them.

"Alright, we're here!" Brooke exclaimed, her smile matching the others. Ryder gave me a quick hug and kissed the top of my head, making me even more suspicious.

"Okay, let's get going then," Parker said, clapping his hands. He started walking toward the massive Christmas tree with everyone following behind him.

"What's happening?" I whispered to Brooke, who was walking beside me.

"You'll see," she laughed, knowing better than to tell me what was going on.

I started to feel the excitement build up inside of me and wondered if Tanner was in on whatever this was as well. He didn't look at me as I glanced up at him, just squeezed my hand and kept walking.

A few minutes later, we were lined up to see Santa, and I felt the laughter starting to bubble over.

"You brought me to see Santa?" I asked, giggling.

"Yes and no," Parker laughed. "I mean, it's up to you if you want to tell him what you want for Christmas. I won't stop you."

We took a few steps forward until the girl dressed as an elf called us over and told us where to stand around Santa. There was a large backdrop behind us that had been built to look like the north pole. A jolly-looking man sat in the oversized plush white chair, waiting for us to get situated. The elves sat the kids in front of Santa while the adults stood beside him, Ryder and Brooke on one side and Sheila and Parker on the other.

I wasn't sure where to go, so I just stood there, feeling like I didn't have a place that I belonged. I wasn't one of the kids, so it felt weird to sit in front with them, but I also didn't fit in with the other adults. I swallowed hard, fighting down the panic that I started to feel from being the odd one out.

"Okay, follow me this way, miss," the older elf said. I took their lead and accepted their hand as they helped me up to where Santa was sitting without stepping on any of the kids along the way.

"You can sit on the arm of the chair," the other elf noted, pointing to the wide space with plenty of room for me to sit.

I noticed that Tanner was still standing off to the side and hated that he wasn't included. I was about to get down and go over to him when Parker spoke up.

"We have one more person," he said, pointing to Tanner. "My future son-in-law needs to be in our first family picture."

I whipped my head back and looked at him, unsure that I had heard him correctly.

When I turned around again, Tanner was standing beside me, kneeling on one knee with a ring box in his hand. I covered my mouth, trying to force the tears away.

"Tanner!" I exclaimed.

"Gen, I know that you and I haven't been dating very long, but I've gotten a glimpse at what my life would be like without you, and I don't ever want to feel that way again. You're the sunshine that brightens my darkest days. You're the beauty that colors the world around you and makes it a better place to be. And most of all, you're the sweetest, most genuine person that I've ever met, and I would be so honored to spend the rest of my life trying to be the man that you deserve. Will you marry me?"

I heard the gasps and oohs whispered around me as the tears flowed down my face. I jumped up off of the chair and knelt in front of Tanner, holding his face in my hands as I kissed him.

"Yes, Tanner, I'll marry you!"

We stood up, and he slipped the most beautiful antique ring on my finger. I stared at it for so long that I forgot anyone else was around us.

"It's beautiful," I whispered.

"It was my mom's. I promised her that I would give it to the woman I would spend forever with."

"I love you so much, Tanner."

He pulled me in closer for a kiss that took my breath away.

"Um, I hate to interrupt this sweet moment, but can we do the family photo?" Parker asked playfully.

"Yes, yes!" I laughed, taking Tanner's hand as he helped me back up to the side of the chair. He took his place on the other arm, and soon, we were all saying cheese and taking our first official family photo.

I thought that I lost my family when my mother died, but little did I know that I had another one waiting to love me as much as she had.

<u>Epilogue</u>

Gen- Six Months Later

"Happy Father's Day," I said as I hugged Parker.

"Thank you for making me a father," he whispered, hugging me tighter.

Our relationship had changed so much over the past six months that I lived in Stone Creek. It helped that we had dinner together as a family a few times a week and that Sheila and I talked every day. I never imagined that I would have another woman that I was as close to as I was with my mom, but somehow I was lucky enough to have that with Sheila.

"Can I help with anything?" I asked, walking into the kitchen where Sheila was standing at the stove, boiling corn on the cob. Her hair was piled up on her head into a giant ball of red frizzy hair, the heat and humidity adding to the curliness.

"Ugh," she groaned, looking over her shoulder. "I am too pregnant to be standing at this hot stove. I've got an oven inside of me, I don't need anything else to make me hotter."

"Here, why don't I take over that for you?" I offered, gently grabbing her shoulders and turning her away as I took the tongs from her hand.

"You're a doll, thank you."

I gave her belly a quick rub to say hello to the baby and began turning the rest of the corn in the pot. I wasn't sure how long they needed to boil, but I was desperate for something to keep my mind busy. I had practiced what I was going to say all day, but yet I still couldn't find the courage to spit it out.

Tanner was outside at the grill with Parker while the kids helped set the table under the tree in the shade. Sheila had also instructed them to put as many fans outside as possible to help cool it off some.

"How much longer does it need to boil?" I asked, turning to find Sheila bent over, her fingers clutching the table as she sat on the edge of the chair.

"Sheila? Are you okay?" I quickly turned off the stove and moved the pot to the back burner when I saw the puddle beneath her. She was breathing heavily, her eyes squinted closed in pain. "Oh my God, you're not due for three more weeks!"

"I know," she gritted out.

I turned and opened the backdoor, looking for Tanner, hoping he was still close by. I groaned when I didn't see him, knowing that I would have to leave Sheila for a minute to find him. I let the door close behind me as I ran outside, finding him by the shed in the back.

"Tanner! Tanner!" I called, the panic in my voice enough to get his attention. Parker's face fell, and they both took off running toward me.

"What happened?" Tanner asked when he was close enough for me to hear him.

"Sheila is in labor," I breathed, running back with them. Why was their backyard so freaking big?

We all rushed back in and found Sheila standing at the table, holding onto the back of the chair as she cried out in pain. She had on a loose, flowy summer dress that was now stained from where she had been sitting when her water broke.

"Are you having contractions?" Tanner asked, rushing to get to Sheila. He quickly assessed her before yelling over his shoulder to Parker. "Grab me some towels and a blanket! Gen, rush out to the car and grab my bag!"

Parker took off down the hallway while I rushed out to get what he needed.

A few minutes later, I was back inside, setting the bag down beside him. He wasted no time opening it and grabbing a clean pair of gloves. He slid them on and lifted Sheila's dress out of the way.

"Okay, Sheila. You are completely dilated, and I can see the baby's head. On your next contraction, I want you to push as hard as you can. Okay?"

She nodded, panting as Parker stood behind her and helped to hold her. I stood off to the side, out of the way. I didn't know whether I should leave and give her some privacy, but then I also didn't want to go far in case Tanner needed something.

Sheila started grunting again as another contraction started.

"Push," Tanner said as Parker held her dress out of the way. She cried out as she pushed harder, her legs shaking beneath her. "Don't let her fall. These next few pushes are going to be intense as she pushes the baby out."

Parker nodded and kept his grip around her waist, planting a kiss on the top of her head.

"Okay, Sheila, you're doing great. I need you to push even harder with the next contraction, okay?"

She cried harder as her scream echoed through the kitchen.

"Perfect! Her head is out, but you need to keep pushing for me. On three, I want you to push again. Ready? One. Two. Three. Push!"

I covered my mouth as I watched the baby's tiny body come out as Tanner masterfully delivered it and wrapped it in one of the clean towels that Parker had brought out.

"Okay, let her sit down," Tanner said to Parker. Slowly, he eased her onto the chair after I rushed over and put a towel down for her to sit on. It wasn't much, but I imagined it would be softer than the chair.

"Here's your beautiful baby girl," Tanner whispered, carefully handing the baby to Sheila. Parker hugged her from behind and bent down to see his daughter. I wiped the tears from my eyes and smiled. It was one of the most beautiful things that I had ever seen.

I stepped out to give them some privacy while Tanner finished up. The kids would be excited to meet their new sibling but definitely didn't need to see any of that right now. Besides, I imagined that Sheila would want some privacy before her kids came in and saw her fully exposed.

Thirty minutes later, I was sitting at the back table while Thomas and Oliver took over grilling the food that Parker and Tanner had started before Sheila went into labor. Brooke and Ryder pulled up out front and made their way out to the back before going inside. I had texted her to let her know that Sheila was in labor and that I would update her as I knew more.

"Did she have the baby?" Brooke asked as she rushed over to where I was sitting.

"She did," I sighed, remembering the moment that she was born. "I haven't seen them since then, though."

"I'm sure they're just getting her situated and cleaning stuff up," Brooke said quietly. I chuckled, knowing how much Ryder had been nervous about all of the new babies coming soon.

"There was a lot to clean up," I laughed, remembering the mess that was still there before I came outside.

"Does it make you think twice about having kids?" she asked with a smile.

"Na, I think I'll be just fine."

I felt my cheeks burn after I said it, wondering if anyone else had heard my slip.

Just then, the back door opened, and Tanner came out. He was grinning from ear to ear.

"Hey, guys," he said as he came over to hug Ryder and Brooke.

"How's Sheila and the baby?" Ryder asked.

"They're both doing great," he said, sitting down beside me and wrapping an arm around me. "They'll be out in a few minutes."

"We can go inside if it's too much for her. I don't want to stress her with moving around too much," I said nervously.

"She'll be okay, trust me. I could barely keep her in the chair long enough to deliver the placenta," he joked.

Ryder's face paled, and he looked away.

The back door opened again, and Sheila walked out, holding the baby wrapped tightly in a clean receiving blanket. Parker was right behind her, one hand on her waist as he helped her down the two stairs outside.

"Hey, everyone," Sheila said, sounding tired.

Ryder whistled and got the attention of Megan and Sally, who were off sitting at the other table across the yard. They got up and came over to join us as Thomas and Oliver closed the lid on the grill and stood beside Ryder.

"We would like you guys to meet Layla Mae Hudson," Sheila announced, gently rubbing the baby's cheek with her finger.

"She's beautiful," I whispered as she held her out for me to see, making her way around to everyone.

I felt Tanner's hand tighten around my waist as he hugged me, knowing the secret that I was still keeping from my family.

After Sheila had taken the baby around to meet everyone, she sat down in the plush chair that Parker insisted on bringing outside and nursed the baby. The guys plated the meat while Brooke and I got the food from inside prepared and brought it out to the table. As everyone was sitting down to eat, Parker stood at the end of the table by Sheila and watched her with his baby.

It melted my heart to see how much he loved them. And now that I had Tanner, I understood what that love was like. It was different than anything I had ever felt before. As Parker sat down, I stood up, suddenly feeling like my legs were going to give out. Tanner stood up beside me, squeezing my hand encouragingly.

"Before we get started, I have something that I would like to say," I announced nervously.

Everyone stopped what they were doing—except for the baby, she was going to town and didn't look like she would stop any time soon—and gave me their attention. I cleared my throat and pulled in a deep breath.

"This time last year, I was struggling with my mom's illness and didn't know then how much my life would change within a year. After she died, I felt lost and couldn't find my way. The last words that my mom said to me were that she wanted me to live life and be happy. For the longest time, I thought that there was some hidden meaning in that. Maybe she wanted me to travel the world and have all of these crazy adventures. Or perhaps she just wanted me to be happy. Either way, I keep those words close to my heart every single day. I make sure that whatever I'm doing, it brings me happiness.

"In a few months, I will marry the love of my life, and I can't wait to start that chapter with him. I have a family that I love and adore, and I don't know what I would do without you guys. Each one of you is so incredibly special to me, and I will never be able to tell you how much you mean to me."

I paused and took a deep breath, my fingers shaking at my sides.

"Family is important to me, and that's why Tanner and I are happy to announce that we're growing our family."

He pulled me into his side and whispered in my ear, "I love you."

"You're pregnant?!" Sheila asked excitedly, startling the baby.

"Yes," I laughed. "I'm due November twenty-third."

"Aww, a little pumpkin spiced baby!" Brooke exclaimed, clapping her hands.

"Like you said, pumpkin-spiced possibilities," I laughed, feeling my heart grow bigger with how excited my family was for our new baby.

I looked up at Tanner, the man who came into my life when I

didn't know how much I needed him. My life felt like it was spinning out of control, but he ended up being the rock that helped ground me. We both knew the pain of losing a parent and carried that grief with us daily, but when we worked as a team, that grief was bearable, and our love outshined our darkest days.

Other Books By Samantha Baca

The Haven Brook Series

(small-town romantic suspense):

'Til Death Do Us Part (Haven Brook Book 1)

https://books2read.com/u/m2RJNR

The Cradle Will Fall (Haven Brook Book 2)

https://books2read.com/u/b6O0QE

The Ties That Bind (Haven Brook Book 3)

https://books2read.com/u/mqgoz8

A Very Haven Christmas (Haven Brook Book 4- Novella)

https://books2read.com/u/mvqGjj

Three Strikes, You're Gone (Haven Brook Book 5)

https://books2read.com/u/mvqL2z

The Dark Shadows Trilogy

(romantic suspense)

Five Steps Ahead (Dark Shadows Book 1)

https://books2read.com/u/38Q0gO

Ten Seconds Too Late (Dark Shadows Book 2)

https://books2read.com/u/3JRgVB

Against The Clock (Dark Shadows Book 3)

https://books2read.com/u/m2YwoR

The Stone Creek Series

(small-town- novellas)

Chocolate Covered Mistletoe (Stone Creek Book 1)

https://books2read.com/u/3LRk9N

Candy Coated Promises (Stone Creek Book 2)

https://books2read.com/u/mldP5Y

Pumpkin Spiced Possibilities (Stone Creek Book 3)

https://books2read.com/u/bojdwV

Beaumont Creek Series

(small town)

Just One Time (Beaumont Creek Book 1)

https://books2read.com/u/3G52zK

Second Chances (Beaumont Creek Book 2)

https://books2read.com/u/4Aj6Z0

Third Time's The Charm (Beaumont Creek Book 3)

https://books2read.com/u/b5lEyG

Four-ever Single (Beaumont Creek Book 4)

https://books2read.com/u/4j5jMX

Fifth Wheel (Beaumont Creek Book 5)

https://books2read.com/u/4XwKwa

Whiskey Mountain Series

(small-town- novellas)

Something To Talk About

https://books2read.com/u/4X62ag

Something To Think About

https://books2read.com/u/3GWAan

Something To Believe In

https://books2read.com/u/3yVzgB

Something To Live For

https://books2read.com/u/mllEOP

<u>Sugarplum Falls Series</u>

<u>(Holiday Novellas- can be read as standalone)</u>

Blame It On The Mistletoe

https://books2read.com/u/bw1rqe

Blame It On The Eggnog

https://books2read.com/u/38PPY6

Blame It On The Candy Canes

https://books2read.com/u/31DNo7

Blame It On The Blizzard

https://books2read.com/u/b6z6XE

Standalone Books

One Last Wish

https://books2read.com/u/mqg7D9

Finding Love In Apartment 2C (novella)

https://books2read.com/u/bze9aZ

Cocky Counsel: A Hero Club Novel

https://books2read.com/u/31Kzkn

All Is Fair In Food And War (novella)

https://books2read.com/u/bp8qjX

Holiday Books

(novellas)

Snow Place To Go

https://books2read.com/u/4A560N

A Christmas Wish

https://books2read.com/u/4EKXpE

Holiday Hijinks

https://books2read.com/u/4DP6Ze

About the Author

Samantha lives in the southwest with her husband and two small children after abandoning her childhood dream of living in a cabin in Colorado when she found that she couldn't afford to live there and was deathly allergic to the woods. When she's not writing, she's usually spouting off sarcastic remarks while drinking wine out of a coffee mug to look like a functional adult while chasing down her toddlers. She enjoys spending time with her family, watching reruns of Friends, and the 24/7 flow of coffee that can be found in her veins. Be sure to follow her on social media for updates on what she's working on.

You can find her here:

Facebook: https://www.facebook.com/AuthorSamanthaBaca

Instagram: https://instagram.com/author_samantha_baca

Goodreads: http://www.goodreads.com/authorsamanthabaca

Facebook Reader Group:
https://www.facebook.com/groups/2945710968775398/

Webpage: https://authorsamanthabaca.wordpress.com

Newsletter: http://eepurl.com/g0NcSj